The Rise of Spero

Julianne Kelsch

Salt Lake City, Utah

Julianne Kelsch
Utah
www.juliannekelsch.com
julie@phoenixrosebooks.com
Publisher's Note: This is a work of fiction. Names, characters, places, and incidents are a product of the author's imagination. Locales and public names are sometimes used for atmospheric purposes. Any resemblance to actual people, living or dead, or to businesses, companies, events, institutions, or locales is completely coincidental.

Book Layout ©2013 BookDesignTemplates.com

The Rise of Spero/Julianne Kelsch. -- 1st ed.

This book is dedicated to those who have felt the heavy weight of depression, grief, or any struggle that has had you feel as if you were plunged into darkness. It is my sincere hope that you remember the light that shines within, that you rediscover your access to it, and that you let it boldly shine!

A special dedication goes out to my mom, whose encouragement is largely the reason this book was written. There were many times I questioned whether I was the one to tell this story, whether I could do it justice. On those days when I wanted to give up, her support helped me choose to keep going.

CHAPTER 1

*R*eality is but a mirror of the world one's experienced, a mirror often distorted; in dreams one may find the truth of reality, for it is in dreams that we discover who we really are.

These words, whispered on a gentle wind, seemed to flow from the trees as they surrounded Kyra and embedded themselves in her heart.

Reality. What was her reality?

She lay with eyes closed, mouth clenched against the pain that pulsed through her body. But though her abdomen felt as though fingers of flame laced through it, her mind was the opposite, alight with pure joy.

She was free! Free of the torment of the Malic'Uiel, free of their lies and deception, free from the poisonous chains they'd forged around her heart. She couldn't help but bask in that knowledge. The physical pain in her body spoke to her humanity, to her weaknesses and failings, but it also spoke to her strengths. She'd beaten them. She'd done something no other man or woman before her had done.

Hope flared in her breast.

If she had reclaimed her mind, could her father as well?

The memory of his capture was as potent now as it had ever been, as if it had happened yesterday; she almost wished it had. Many months had passed since he'd been taken. She remembered the night vividly – the Phantom tearing him away, her father's sacrifice, and her own screams as she tried to reach him before it was too late. But she'd failed, and he'd paid the price.

She relived that memory and her experience of it as an onlooker, studying it but separating herself from it. Em was strong, a fighter. If she found her way back, so could he.

Reality. She needed to come back to it. Yes, she was free, but certainly not safe.

She forced her eyes open and scanned the surrounding area. She lay in a clearing surrounded by deep forest. Birds hopped between branches and their song filled the air.

Birds! She hadn't seen a bird in so long. The sight filled her heart with gratitude. Beneath her, thick foliage acted as bedding for her battered body. She tried to sit up but hissed as pain shot through her. She almost laughed. Gilrich had stabbed her! What sweet justice for him, since she'd helped the Malic'Uiel enslave his mind.

Labored breathing drew her attention to two men in the clearing with her – well, one man and one monster, a Cadaver. She glanced over at the Cadaver – Gilrich – unconscious, there in the clearing. His breaths were quick and seemed to catch in his lungs, but he lived.

Gilrich's mind had been taken by the Malic'uiel – his deformed body spoke to that. Her own body, once deformed as well, was now perfect. She nearly cried as she held her hand out in front of her, a hand that was wonderfully, beautifully human. As the Malic'Uiel had taken her mind, so they'd also taken her body. But, she now knew, when she ripped their chains from her mind, her body had also become free. She'd fought for her mind, for her soul, and won. Could Gilrich's mine be freed as well?

Possibly.

As she pondered Gilrich's fate, pieces of her last moments with the Malic'uiel fell into place, tiny bits at first, but quickly turning into an onslaught.

She'd been in the Citadel with her Master, Lord Passus, the Malic'Uiel she had been required to answer to while imprisoned by them. Though he was her master, he was not *the* Master. There was another Malic'Uiel who all the other answered to. From her time with them, she understood that the 'lesser' Malic'uiel controlled the cities, and took the names of those cities, while the true Master, the leader of the Malic'Uiel, oversaw them all, ensuring success and compliance in her land, the land of Spero.

Gilrich was once her friend. He was once human. But Lord Passus had tortured his mind and twisted his body until he was a Cadaver, a slave who existed only to do their bidding. He'd been tasked with taking her 'to the brink' as Lord Passus had called it. The Malic'Uiel needed her alive, but nearly dead was fine. Gilrich had done exactly that. She pressed her hand against her stomach; blood soaked the tunic and dripped through her fingers. Yes, he had done his job well. She flinched at the memory of his blade stabbing into her stomach.

Shortly after the attack, she'd begun to lose consciousness. But there was a light...it had come from her and protected her from Lord Passus. She drew her hand up, peering at the flesh as if she could see the light once more. She did not know what it was or how she'd gained its power, but that light had stopped them from harming her further.

Well, the light and Caden. He'd come, appearing out of nowhere, and taken her away from them. That memory was weak, as she'd been in and out of consciousness, but she could almost feel the strength of his arms around her now and the way her soul had longed for him.

Those final moments with the Malic'Uiel seemed surreal now, as if they had happened in another life.

But the three of them were here, in this clearing, alive and free. Caden lay next to her. His eyes were closed, but from the rise and fall of his chest, she knew he was alive.

She realized he was awake when his hand found hers and squeezed. "We have to get out of here." The words were barely more than a shaky whisper, but he pushed himself to his knees; his whole body trembled with the effort. Face pale, he forced himself to stand, wheezing with every breath.

Gilrich was as ferocious as any Cadaver, and he'd attacked Caden, stabbing him repeatedly. Kyra watched his struggle, knowing she should be worried about his injuries, but she couldn't seem to feel anything more than a sense of calm. And admiration. Caden had stepped into the lair of the enemy to take her from their grasp. He'd saved her life.

For now.

Blood still dripped through her fingers from the wounds in her stomach. It seeped from the wound, staining the grass beneath her. She held up her hand and watched as it slid down her wrist. A new reality took shape and more memories of her final moments in captivity flooded her mind.

The light. *Her* light. It had taken Lord Passus, enveloping him with swirls of color and chaos. She'd felt his terror as it happened, but then the light obliterated him. He'd vanished and all the souls he'd trapped in his being exploded from him, finally free of his dark grip.

A rising sense of panic washed over her.

She'd destroyed him. She'd destroyed her master. She'd sworn to serve him, but then had done the opposite!

Guilt threatened to snare her, guilt and fear riding on the tide of panic. The Malic'Uiel offered no forgiveness. They'd told her many, many times. She shoved the fear down. Lord Passus deserved his fate. She would not harbor guilt for him.

Glancing at Gilrich once more, her stomach clenched in a different kind of anxiety, threatened by something much closer than the Malic'Uiel. Gilrich had used her dagger against her. Would he do it again? It lay near him, covered in her blood.

Gripping the plants to her right, she forced herself to roll over, coming to her knees in the same moment. Warmth bloomed on her stomach as blood pulsed from the wound. Caden was right. They had to get somewhere safe. They both needed help.

She struggled to her feet, stumbling near Gilrich to reclaim her dagger. He would not be using it against her again.

"Where do we go?" she asked Caden, wiping the blood from her weapon. Her voice, clear and calm, sounded strange to her. As a slave to the Malic'Uiel, she'd lost her voice; it had been guttural and harsh, grating in her own ears, as deformed as her body had been.

"We're going to Tutis. That's where the army is."

Kyra clutched her stomach, her body hunched over. "They took a city, then?" The voice didn't matter. Her abdomen was on fire, and she felt like throwing up. Gilrich's attack had left its mark.

"They did. And they freed the slaves beneath. Those men and women are the reason we won."

Kyra swallowed hard, remembering a young child she'd encountered as prisoner to the Malic'Uiel, a child also named Caden. It had been her job to guard him and his mother. Following the demands of Lord Passus, she had nearly sacrificed the child to them. But she couldn't do it. His mother had been instrumental in helping her find hope in the middle of her own personal hell; she couldn't let them have her child.

"Let's hope we can save them all," she murmured, hoping for a better life for young Caden and the others enslaved with him.

"We will," Caden said, his jaw clenched in determination. "Give me your dagger." He held out his hand, waiting for the weapon.

She nearly turned it over to him, but stopped. "What are you going to do with it?" she asked, wary.

He gestured to Gilrich. "We can't leave him alive."

She immediately pulled back, holding the weapon behind her. "You're not killing him," she said. "He's coming with us."

"Are you mad?" Caden demanded. "He's a Cadaver. He only follows their orders. He nearly killed you!"

She shook her head, lips pressed in a tight line. "The *Cadaver* nearly killed me. Gilrich did nothing."

Caden glared at her, frustration evident. "You've lost your mind."

She chuckled. "Those words are far more true than you realize. But I found something, too. I believe I can save him."

Caden's jaw dropped. In all their experience with Cadavers, none had shown that they could be saved. Once a human was enslaved by the Malic'Uiel, their mind became the target and their humanity whittled away until there was nothing left but a monster. The humanity died long before the body ever did. At least, that's what Caden and the others believed. Kyra's own experience – once a Cadaver and slave, now a human again – told her they were wrong.

Kyra straightened, trying to breathe through the pain. "I was a Cadaver too, Caden. You didn't see me, but I was as bad as any of them. Deformed, horrifying, longing for the will of the Malic'Uiel. I brought Gilrich to this fate." She glanced at Gilrich's body again, a single tear escaping. "I will not see him die because of me."

Caden's gaze skipped between Kyra and Gilrich. His fist clenched and unclenched and his jaw was tight. For a moment, Kyra wondered if he'd wrestle the dagger from her and kill Gilrich before she could stop him.

She stepped closer to him, resting her hand on his arm. "Caden, Gilrich is your best friend. You can't just leave him to this, to life as a Cadaver, and you can't kill him; I will stop you."

He met her eyes with his, holding them. "He nearly killed you. You may still die," he whispered, his hand reaching to touch her bleeding abdomen. "The Gilrich I knew no longer exists."

She smiled softly, gesturing to Gilrich's body. "You have the power to see into his mind. Why don't you find out for yourself if he's still there?"

Caden's unique power, transferred unintentionally from a Phantom desperately trying to live, gave him the ability into the minds of others, among other things. He'd helped her more than once by using that skill.

"You want me to...connect...with that?"

"Yes," she said, her voice losing its power. The blood flowed faster through her fingers now, and the trees spun. She sank to her knees, holding herself up with the hand that held her dagger. "Tell me he's still there," she whispered.

"Fine." He stepped to Gilrich, resting his hand on his old friend's head. Kyra watched while he closed his eyes, focusing his thoughts on whatever magic enabled him to read the minds of others.

It had been so long since she'd seen him. She let herself appreciate his humanness now. His thick brown hair had grown in the months since they'd been separated; it hung haphazardly across his forehead. He was taller than Gilrich by a hand-span or so, and his body was solid, with strong shoulders and wiry muscles. If he were looking at her, his eyes would be gray; they would convey more than his words ever did. She couldn't help but note the contrast between him and his once best friend.

Gilrich, still unconscious, did not look like a man. There was a time when he'd been her best friend as well. Then, he was slight of build with light brown hair, an easy smile, and the ability to be happy no matter what. He always seemed to find the sun. But she'd lost that man to the Cadaver he'd become. Now, his spine curved and twisted, with his neck jutting out in front of him creating a brutal hunch. His elongated fingers hung like claws from his arms, hard and grasping, always reaching for their next victim; they were no longer the hands of a man. Even the bones in his legs and arms had slowly deformed as he'd embraced the Malic'Uiel. He wore a cloak, but she knew beneath the thick fabric his limbs would be twisted and knobby.

The worst part to look upon was his face. His kind blue eyes were gone. Instead, cloudy, colorless eyes bulged out of a face that looked as if it had been flattened against a wall and never recovered. Enough remained for him to be recognizable, but the Gilrich she'd loved was gone. Slowly, she let her head drop, breathing to keep herself conscious.

She would just have to bring him back.

Kyra.

There was the voice again, the one carried through the trees. She realized after a moment that the voice was in her mind.

Yes? She asked.

Go to Caden.

She nodded, struggling to her feet to do the voice's bidding. When she was next to him, she slumped back to her knees.

He jumped at her presence next to him, dropping his hand from Gilrich's head. "He's still there," he murmured, not meeting her gaze.

"You've connected with a Cadaver before. Is he as far gone as that man was?"

"No."

When he didn't elaborate, she pushed further. "Why does that bother you?"

"It doesn't," he said, "but it scares me. I don't dare hope, Kyra. You believe the impossible."

The silence stretched on between them, an invisible ribbon of his anxiety. Kyra finally spoke. "I came back, Caden. I was him. And I came back."

Caden was quiet for a few moments, but then he took her hand and squeezed it tight. "You came back," he whispered.

"And so will he."

Finally, his eyes met hers and she saw the depths of their pain. "He may, but at what cost? How long do we force him to suffer this monstrous existence on...on what? Hope?"

"If he can be saved, so can the others."

Caden hesitated, grappling with himself. She understood his conflict. To end the life of the man they both loved was a cruelty to all of them. But to leave him alive, to leave his soul trapped as a Cadaver, was a different kind of cruelty.

"Just give me time," she said. "I don't ask for forever. I just ask for time. Let's see if he shows improvement. If I am wrong, we will not leave him in this state."

"He will suffer, Kyra. He won't be given freedom in Tutis."

She glanced at the Cadaver – Gilrich – and her chest tightened. "I know," she said. "But I don't know any other way." She swayed as a wave of dizziness washed over her. Pressing her hand against her stomach, she clenched her jaw as pain followed the dizziness.

Caden tried to hide his fear as he slumped against him. "Okay," he agreed hastily. "I'll talk to General Prait. Just don't die on me!"

"I won't die," she mumbled.

The expletive that followed barely registered in her mind. The dizziness wanted to take her.

"Get us to Tutis, Caden," she said, the words slurred. She knew he could do it. He'd gotten them here, to this clearing, away from the Malic'Uiel. With his power, it would be easy for him to teleport them.

THE RISE OF SPERO

"I can't," he said, eyes wild and desperate. "I'm weak. My energy is depleted."

Only now did she see the full extent of his injuries. Gilrich had been thorough when he'd attacked Caden. Multiple stab wounds in his left arm and near his shoulder bled into his tunic. The most vital parts of Caden's body had been missed, but his skin was ashen and she knew he'd lost a lot of blood – too much blood. That loss coupled with the strength he'd used to get them here...he was right. He wouldn't have what he needed to transport them to Tutis.

You must give him your strength. The voice returned, giving counsel now.

Kyra nodded, responding to the voice though it only lived in her head. She flattened her hand against his palm. "Take what you need from me. I know you can do it."

He shook his head, his voice hard. "I'm not a Phantom."

"No, you're not. But you have their power. Take my strength to get us there."

"If I take from you, you may not make it."

"If you don't, none of us will make it."

Caden ran his fingers along her palm, his jaw tight in indecision. "I could kill you," he whispered.

"You won't."

Slowly, resolve hardened his features as he fought with himself. If they stayed, they would all die. If he trusted her and did as she requested...maybe. Maybe they could live. He reached to touch Gilrich's still shoulder. "You sure about this?" he asked.

"Yes."

He inhaled deeply, then let the breath out in a burst, his eyes locked on hers. His grip tightened around her palm while his power flowed into her. She forced her body to relax, forced her mind to open. His fire raced through her body, pulling what it needed from hers to fuel his. As it spread, she weakened, but she didn't take her eyes from his, trusting that he could do this. Her previous sense of peace returned, and she knew, somehow, that they'd be okay.

The world faded around them; the trees shimmered and then disappeared entirely. In the same moment, the walls of Tutis began to take shape, first a blur but then the blur sharpened, the city coming into focus. The closer they got, the weaker Kyra felt. Tutis faded in and out of her vision. Finally, the city gates shimmered into existence.

Gilrich remained unconscious while Kyra collapsed, fighting the darkness threatening to consume her.

"Kyra!" Caden said, shaking her shoulders roughly. "You promised I wouldn't kill you. Don't you dare let go!"

Kyra gripped his hand while blackness fluttered at the edge of her vision. The world swirled around her. She shivered as cold washed over her.

Protect the city. The voice spoke with authority. *Do it now or none of you will make it.*

"I can't," Kyra whispered.

You have to.

Kyra glanced at the city walls. Then she found Caden's panic-stricken gaze.

"I can't," she whispered before the blackness engulfed her.

CHAPTER 2

C aden gripped Kyra's body, desperate to keep her alive. He'd done what she asked and stolen her vitality – now she was paying for it.

"Don't you leave me!" he screamed, shaking her roughly. For a moment she held his gaze then her eyes glossed over, and she stared past him, unseeing. "Don't you leave me!"

Slowly, her eyes closed, and she let out a long sigh.

"Kyra," Caden sobbed, pressing his hand to her chest. Her heart fluttered beneath his fingers. He bent his head, using his magic to push what little life he could into her fading organ. Her heart quickened, thumping harder, and she pulled in a ragged breath, but her eyes did not open. Her body lay before him, slack and lifeless.

The gate behind him creaked open and he felt a hand on his shoulder. "Let's get her inside, Caden."

The voice belonged to General Prait. "It's not safe out here."

Caden surrendered her body to General Prait, who lifted her easily. Two soldiers followed, binding Gilrich's hands before dragging him into the city behind the General. Caden followed last, his body trembling, heart aching, feet just managing to shuffle across the threshold.

When the doors to the gates closed, Kyra began convulsing in General Prait's arms. He fought to hold her but lost his grip and she tumbled to the ground.

"What happened? Caden cried, rushing to kneel next to her. When he touched her arm, the convulsing stopped. Her eyes fluttered open, and though she looked straight at him she seemed to stare through him, as if she were in a trance. Slowly she pushed herself up. Fresh blood dripped from her stomach, but she paid it no mind.

"No," Caden said, gripping her arm to keep her from standing. "You need to rest."

She shrugged him off, ignoring him and bypassing the General who stepped toward her, confusion etched on his features. She moved as if she was aware of nothing and no one around her. Slowly she climbed the steps to the parapet, where she paused to gaze across the land and the forest beyond. Caden didn't believe she saw any of it.

"What is she doing?" General Prait asked.

No answer followed the query. None of them knew.

Kyra reached up and removed a pendant from around her neck, holding it to the sky. Caden knew the necklace held a symbol – a small rectangle encasing three small balls. The first ball was balanced in the center and touched on both sides by a triangle that encased the remaining two balls. After he'd saved her from the Malic'Uiel, Kyra had told him she knew what the symbol meant, and that somehow it was important, but she hadn't told him why it was important. Before her imprisonment, the two of them had searched together to discover its meaning. But they'd failed, and she'd become a slave to the Malic'Uiel.

Kyra seemed to study the symbol for a moment, then she replaced the necklace and closed her eyes. Her body went still. At first, her arms dangled at her sides, but then she turned her hands and opened her palms to face the forest beyond.

The air became heavy. Like a dangerous calm before the storm, the world slipped into silence. No creature – man or animal – dared breathe. Tutis, a small city housing the largest remaining pocket of humanity, became silent. Those that were within sight of Kyra turned to her without knowing why. The other residents – soldiers, men, and women who'd been kept for breeding the Malic'Uiel army, and the children of those unions – all stopped. None were aware that they'd done so. Outside Tutis, the birds quieted their song, and the breeze faded as if the very world held its breath.

Then, a single bolt of lightning raced across the otherwise blue sky. It arced into Kyra, burying itself in the necklace she wore, creating a ball of electric light that grew as the lightning pulsed into her body. She absorbed the energy, her body acting as conduit, as the grounding source for it. She took one small step back to steady herself then lifted her hands higher, opening her chest and allowing the energy to flow into it. Suddenly, the lightning burst out of her, exploding in a dome that encompassed the entire city before racing to the tree line beyond. When the dome broke, the electricity arced downward, burying itself in the ground. As it disappeared, the heaviness faded. Humanity felt it could breathe again; breeze and birdsong returned. Kyra, unmoving until that point, turned and stumbled to the top of the stairs, where she collapsed.

Caden dragged himself up the stairs, his body screaming with every step, until he knelt next to her. She didn't move. Her eyes were open and glazed over, her lips tinted blue and her face a deathly white. When Caden touched her hand, he recoiled.

The flesh was cold.

Gently, he laid his ear on her chest. The faint beat of her heart gave him a moment's relief. She was alive, for now.

"She needs a doctor," he said to the General, who had come up the stairs behind him. "We have to save her life."

"What the hell did she just do, Caden?"

"I don't know."

"How did she do it?"

Jaw clenched, Caden glanced at the General. "I don't know that, either."

General Prait hesitated above her still form with his hand poised above his dagger. Caden guessed his thoughts. Unconscious, she was not a threat. But should she wake...

"She's not going to harm us," Caden said, hovering over her body, protecting her from him. "I don't know what she did, but I know she will not hurt us."

General Prait's lips were a thin line and his hand twitched above the blade. "Where did you find her, Caden? She was their captive. Did they send her back to trap us?"

"They didn't send her back. I freed her from them. They were going to kill her." Caden swayed and caught himself on the wall. "General, I need rest. She and I both need medical care. I pushed my body too far today. I promise, I'll explain everything I know and get the answers you need. But for now, I ask that you please trust me."

General Prait gave himself a moment to study Kyra. Unconscious, she was as innocent as a child. Her face had a faint glow, and though her body was battered, peace lay on her features. He finally nodded, but he looked wary as he picked her up. "Bring the Cadaver," he commanded his soldiers as he carried Kyra past them. "Lock him up. We'll deal with him later."

The soldiers dragged Gilrich to his prison while General Prait carried Kyra to the infirmary. Caden shuffled next to him, watching her with concern.

Inside the infirmary, Dr. Bron, an older woman who'd been with the army since its conception, greeted them. Her gray eyes widened when she saw Kyra. "I never thought I'd see this one again."

General Prait grunted. "I want her separate from the rest. Where can I lay her?"

"Follow me."

They walked through a small building filled with cots. Most of the cots were full of men and women who'd been wounded in the battle for Tutis just days before. There was a small common area behind the building. Here, more wounded recovered. These people were no longer bedridden, but neither were they up to full strength. The area had been created for them to get fresh air and sunshine while they recovered.

"This will work for her," Dr. Bron said, gesturing to a cot near the back of the building. She brushed a strand of damp gray hair, which was peppered here and there with black, from her thin face. Then she gave her attention to Caden. "You look like you should be here with her, Caden," she said.

Caden sighed. "I don't argue with that."

General Prait placed Kyra gently on the cot. She barely seemed to breathe. When he turned to Caden, his lips were tight and his eyes drawn in the kind of weariness that doesn't come from lack of sleep. "I need answers, Caden, and I needed them before you brought her here."

"I know, General. I'm sorry. There wasn't time."

"We'll discuss this tomorrow." General Prait's voice was curt. He looked like he wanted to say more, but he just hesitated once more before glancing at Kyra and tenderly pushing a tendril of hair away from her face. "I do hope you're right, Caden." His softened features were that of a father gazing at a long-lost child. He straightened then and gestured to Caden. "Patch him up, Dr. Bron. He needs help as much as anybody."

Just before General Prait left the infirmary Caden called, "General?"

He stopped, not looking at him.

"The Cadaver, it's Gilrich. Don't kill him. Kyra thinks she can save him."

The only response was the tightening of the General's fists. After a minute he blew his breath out in a huff. "A Cadaver in the middle of our city, and light bolting out of the heavens. Let's hope she didn't just damn us all."

After the general left Caden, he called his captains and council together. They met outside the city gates so he could get an accurate assessment of the city's defense and lay the plan to bolster them.

The army had only been in Tutis a few days – long enough to secure the immediate needs of the survivors of the battle, and the captives freed from the catacombs beneath Tutis, but not long enough to properly protect themselves. They'd fought hard to gain control of the city, and it wouldn't take much for them to lose it again.

Tutis was, in a very real way, the last stronghold of humanity. Before this point, they'd hidden themselves in the Adeo Mountains at the very edge of the known world. And before that? Eleven years of destruction and death had taken place before the survivors were able to pull together enough to form a resistance, a resistance that would die of starvation if they stayed in the Adeo Mountains. These mountains were barren and could not sustain life indefinitely. Losing what they'd gained in the safety of the city was a pressing concern.

"We need to fortify," General Prait said. "We know the Malic'uiel will not let us rest for long. Our army is too weak to survive another onslaught. We must build up defenses outside the city walls; dig pits for their Cadavers to fall into. Should they make it past the pits and reach the walls, make sure they're lined with spikes and other dangers. We can't have them inside this city."

"General? What happens if the Malic'Uiel themselves come? We can fight the Cadavers, but we have no defense against their mind games." The man asking was a recently promoted captain. He'd fought hard in the battle for Tutis, and had shown his determination to save humanity many times over.

General Prait digested the query. Though he was young and newly appointed, he'd earned the general's respect long before. Bronson had shown skill and courage not only in the battle of Tutis but in other battles before then. In this case he seemed to have the right of it with his question. The Cadavers were men and women who'd been turned into monsters by the Malic'Uiel. They still bled and they still died. They could be defended against. But the Malic'uiel? They were beings unlike any he had ever seen. They seemed to move on shadows, and they brought with them darkness and fear, a fear so debilitating many of his people simply froze and were captured or killed while they fought the horrifying panic of their own mind. General Prait had experienced the madness the Malic'Uiel wrought, and it was terrifying.

"We can't let them get close," the general said at last. "From a distance, they can't use their mind games against us. They're most dangerous when they're close. But they can fall under the bow, which gives us an advantage. I want archers stationed along the entire perimeter of the walls. I want the weapons here ransacked and used. Any crossbows will be taken to the top and affixed to the walls. If they come, our weapons will be well established to hit them from a distance. They'll be our primary focus."

Bronson nodded, then cleared his throat. "Is it...safe to stay here, General?" he asked.

General Prait sighed. He knew Bronson was asking the questions they were all thinking. And they were valid questions. Staying in the Tutis in the heart of the enemy's land could be a death sentence for them all, but as the leader of the small pocket of humanity remaining, General Prait had to consider not only their safety but also their ability to carve a life out of this world, to find a way for humanity to not only survive but thrive in the darkness. Humanity could not thrive in the Adeo Mountains.

After they'd taken Tutis, they'd tallied up the number of people remaining; there were less than a thousand. But there were other people out there – hundreds or thousands existed trapped and enslaved in the catacombs of each city. There were also traitors to humanity, marauders that roamed the land outside the city looking for victims to bring to the Malic'Uiel, but they would find no help from that quarter. The people enslaved in the cities...they needed them. Some risks had to be taken to give humanity a chance.

"It's not safe anywhere, Bronson," General Prait finally answered. "We can't survive in the Adeo Mountains. Our food stores are depleted, and the soil is too unforgiving to grow food. We die there, or we take a stand for humanity here. Those are our only choices."

Bronson bowed his head in agreement while another captain, a freed slave named Leland, shoved his way to the front of the group.

General Prait hadn't known him for long, but what he did know about Leland told him that this was a seasoned, hardened man who had seen far more horror in his life than any man should. He looked at everything with mistrust and cynicism, a trait the general usually appreciated. "General," Leland said. "I watched what the woman did. What was that?"

"I don't know, Leland," came the answer.

"Can we trust her? Did she just entrap us?"

"I trust Caden," General Prait said. "And right now, I'm giving Kyra the benefit of the doubt."

Leland's face hardened. "Her body did not die though lightning struck it. She seemed to control the elements. That's what the Phantoms do."

General Prait nodded, worry lines creasing his forehead. "It's also what Caden does, and we know he uses it for good. Kyra's always been loyal to the army."

Leland's gaze flashed momentarily to Caden. There was no mistaking the distrust written there. But he turned quickly back to the General. "She was loyal before she was taken captive and polluted by the Malic'Uiel. And she brought a Cadaver into our midst! Have we let the enemy within our gates?"

Around him heads nodded in agreement. A few men echoed his words, and others instinctively brought their hands to their weapons, their eyes darting to the gates as if they could see through the city to the infirmary where Kyra lay.

General Prait held up his hand to steady the small crowd. "I understand your concern. I share them." He stepped to Leland, gripping his shoulder. "If we have let the enemy in, she will be dealt with. The Cadaver has been locked up. No harm can come from him. I give you my word, I will have the truth and ensure the safety of this city."

Leland's mouth worked as if he wanted to say more, but he nodded, and his posture relaxed slightly. "All right, General. I will trust your judgment."

The general addressed the entire group then. "We sit in a precarious position. The enemy is surely gathering to attack, and I admit we don't know what power Kyra wields. She could be dangerous, as Leland fears. I will watch that situation very closely." He let his eyes wander over them, touching briefly on each one. "Most of you have stood with me this far. Some have just joined but you know the world we are striving for. Continue at my side, as my captains and council, and we will see this through."

The group murmured their assent. The youngest men and women shuffled away to fortify the city as their general requested, while the others – new council members from Tutis – returned to gather more hands for the labor.

General Prait stayed outside the gates, watching the beginning of the fortifications. His hands were clasped behind his back and his lips turned down in what was becoming a perpetual frown. He'd been leading this army for four years. It had started with him, Dr. Bron, and a few others who'd escaped the Malic'Uiel. It had grown over time as they'd absorbed random pockets of surviving humanity into their ranks. Slowly, order had come from the chaos until they had an organized army. He led as the general, and a group of twenty captains helped keep order.

But though he led the army, he was not above them. Their governance was unique – each individual was there by choice. General Prait did not take the role of reprimanding his captains or his soldiers, nor did he control how they spent their time.

They'd adopted the same system for Tutis. General Prait led the city, and a council of twenty supported him in that role. Many of his captains had given their lives during the battle for Tutis. Those men had been replaced by slaves that had been freed when the city was taken. The most influential of these men and women had joined the council and stepped into the role of captain.

Leland had been among that number. General Prait's eyes followed him as he threw himself into the work of fortifying the city. Ignoring the warning blaring from his gut, General Prait joined his men, working alongside them. Leland was a captain, and a trusted member of the citizenry. His gut would just have to learn silence.

CHAPTER 3

In the land of Celebrus, the Master of the Malic'Uiel watched as a single bolt of lightning arced across the sky toward the city of Tutis. He beckoned the Lord of Celebrus forward, gesturing to the lightning.

"They have failed," he said. "The Lord of Passus has lost her. She's with the rest of her kind."

Lord Celebrus watched silently, hands clasped in front of him. While he appeared calm, he found his own fear rising. The Master's judgements were swift and calculated. His position and the position of all the Lords of Spero were at risk. If they could not complete the Master's bidding, they would be banished to Letum and returned to shadow. Most of the human survivors in Spero did not know what Letum was, nor how to reach it. They didn't know other realms existed beyond their own; they didn't know where he and his kind had come from. But they once had – many thousands of years ago they had known. History had been lost to the humans in Spero, but in Letum, memory was long. Their conquest now was a battle begun millennia before. And they'd already lost once.

Lord Celebrus surreptitiously kept one eye on the Master. Spero was theirs, but there was another realm to conquer. And the woman – Kyra – was the key.

When the lightning faded the Master turned to him. Though his demeanor was calm and his voice quiet, Lord Celebrus knew the anger that raged inside. When the Master was calm, nobody was safe.

"Lord Passus has been destroyed," the Master said.

"How do you know this?"

"Because the girl has accessed the power of Lumen. We can no longer take her soul."

Lord Celebrus stepped to the window of the Citadel, resting his hands on the sill while gazing into the distance beyond. His eyes flickered between the scene before him and the Master, who watched him silently. The blue sky and bright sun spoke to tranquility, but a new storm was raging, one that could destroy everything they'd fought for.

"Master," he said again. "If she has accessed the power of Lumen, does that mean..."

"That Lumen is open? No," the Master said, moving to stand next to him. He studied the land before him, but Celebrus knew he didn't see the landscape. He saw the realm of light. "The door to Lumen is closed. Kyra has unlocked their power, yes, but she is untrained – she does not have full access to them."

"Then we must destroy her."

The Master gazed at Lord Celebrus for what felt like an eternity. Finally, he spoke. "We cannot cross the barrier she created. Nor can we destroy her."

Lord Celebrus's jaw dropped. He, the Master, and the other Lords were Malic'Uiel. Not human. They were born of darkness and nurtured in its power. Their forms in Letum were that of a shadow – shapeless masses that moved over the land and kept the darkness in place unless and until they found a human body they could inhabit. Then they took the human's body, consumed the soul, and used its strength to push the darkness ever deeper into the heart, the very core, of Letum. This way, they'd gained control of the realm.

In Spero, the Malic'Uiel had taken the forms of humans and improved them. Without flaws or blemish, the bodies were the pinnacle of perfection. Broad shoulders, rippling muscles, beautifully defined feature, and hair as soft as feathers, the human men had looked upon them as gods and willingly given their souls.

After more than a decade of conquest, with every human falling into submission one way or another, that one woman had managed to resist them, had escaped, and used the light against them, baffled Celebrus. He could not make sense of it. "She...banished us from the city?"

The Master nodded. "The same protection now exists around Tutis that exists along the borders of the Adeo Mountains. Our kind may not enter." He clasped his hands behind his back, stepping away from the window. "Only the Phantoms and Cadavers can enter therein."

"How?" Lord Celebrus asked. "How can one woman stop us?"

The Master glanced at Lord Celebrus. "Do you know nothing?" he hissed. "How have you risen to these heights on so little knowledge? There is always one gatekeeper to the door of Lumen, one woman holds that key. Without her, the line of power ends and the door will remain beyond our grasp."

Lord Celebrus bent his head in confusion. "I don't understand, Master. If there is a gatekeeper, why did we not hunt her before?"

The Master turned to glare at Lord Celebrus, his gaze penetrating until Celebrus trembled in fear. "Do you question me?" he demanded.

Lord Celebrus jerked his head from side to side, mortified that his Master would think such a thing of him. "No, Master," he whispered, bowing in allegiance.

"I have been searching for the means to open the door to Lumen since we entered this hovel they call Spero. We did not hunt the gatekeeper because we made the mistake of thinking these humans were unintelligent swine – a mistake you continue to make." The Master stepped closer, his head a hand-span taller than

Lord Celebrus, who shrunk in his shadow. "These swine kept histories that speak of bloodlines that carry the power of Lumen through their daughters. The human Kyra is the last of her bloodline, and she has stepped beyond our grasp."

Lord Celebrus's face paled as he listened to the words. "Master," he said, his voice shaking. "What would have happened if she died?"

The Master hissed in disgust. "You would know if you'd taken the time to study the histories that exist inside your own city!"

Celebrus dipped his head in acknowledgement, choosing to placate the Master rather than risk his anger. "Yes, Master. I have unwisely chosen to bask in my power, seeing myself above the humans I enslave."

"You *are* above them. But you cannot fully enslave a soul until you fully understand it."

Celebrus swallowed hard, remaining silent.

"If we had killed her the door to Lumen would have been lost to us forever. The light of Lumen flows in her veins; she is the key."

"Then...what must we do?"

The Master paused, head bowed as if staring through the floors beneath him. Finally, he answered. "We cannot send the Cadavers to attack the city and risk endangering her life. For now, we let them think they are safe. I know she is the key that will give us entry to Lumen, but I have not yet discovered how she is to do it. As with the door to Letum, there is a ritual that must be followed." He paced the room, his feet barely making purchase with the floor; he appeared to float above it, like a ghost. Suddenly, he stopped and his head snapped up. "She is the bloodline to Lumen," he said, gazing out the window as if seeing her beyond the space that separated them.

"As you've said."

The Master swung on Lord Celebrus. "Don't you see!" he cried. "We already *own* her. She signed herself away with her own blood. All that she is, and all that comes from her, is mine."

"I don't understand."

The Master shoved Lord Celebrus away. "You are a fool. With the power of Lumen on our side, all the realms will be ours. Lumen cannot stop us."

"But she resists?"

The Master glowered at Celebrus, his irritation at his ineptitude obvious. "Of course she does. She would not be the Countess of Lumen if she didn't. But she is human, and ours. We have many humans that provide children for our armies – children that become our Cadavers. She will do the same, only her child will become far greater than any Cadaver."

The Master's demeanor calmed, and he nodded thoughtfully. "Yes, her mind is powerful, but the flesh is weak. She will bear a child for us. Her daughter will be something we can shape and mold to do our bidding. The mother will open the door and the daughter will carry the bloodline – a daughter that is loyal to us. One who desires to serve us!"

"What then happens to the mother?"

"After she's given us a child, we will have no use for her."

Lord Celebrus nodded. "Dispose of the mother, then the child becomes the key. But how do we capture the mother if she's surrounded herself with the Light of Lumen?"

The Master's eyes narrowed and his face darkened. "She will be delivered to us. Humanity is so easily manipulated. Sow enough fear, and you will always find those willing to betray the people they claim to love. We will use her own people against her."

Lord Celebrus smiled, his angelic face marred by the malice that danced in his eyes. "She will suffer greatly for her betrayal."

The Master nodded in agreement. "She was warned that forgiveness does not come from us; she forgets that she gave us her life. We will take it and use her to achieve our victory."

Lord Celebrus gazed across to Tutis once more. The fear that had clutched his chest was gone. One human, even if she had the power of Lumen, could not destroy the perfection of the Malic'Uiel.

The Master had his plan, and it would ensure victory across all the realms. The Master had also seen fit to entrust Lord Celebrus with this plan. He would serve the Master, he would secure his victory, and in so doing, he would rise to greater heights. The Master would be Lord of all realms, but he, Lord Celebrus, would be Lord of Spero.

CHAPTER 4

The night's darkness had not yet faded when Caden woke and slipped out of his bunkhouse. He walked silently through the streets of Tutis, unwilling to wake the sleeping city. His heart felt calm; for the first time in months, true hope flared in his breast. There was no reason for this hope, nothing but the knowledge that Kyra was no longer a Malic'Uiel prisoner. She was here, with him, instead of there, and she'd been here for nearly a week. While she wasn't awake yet, something in his gut told him her long sleep would soon be over.

He moved silently past the infirmary, knowing she lay safely inside. He would come see her later, but for now he wanted to let himself experience, however briefly, a moment of peace. Heading to the gates of the city, he climbed the stairs that accessed the wall. Light was just beginning to kiss the day as he reached the top of the structure. He sat on the edge of the wall, facing inside the city while he waited for the glowing orb to welcome the morning. As he did, he let his mind wander over where he now found himself and how he'd gotten here.

The city of Tutis was a small city in the land of Spero. Prior to the dark days of the Malic'Uiel it had been a haven for men and women journeying between Miro and Pluvia. It wasn't uncommon for travelers to get caught in storms blowing from the Adeo Mountains; thus, Tutis was erected out of desperation for shelter during unpredictable times. Its wealth had grown quickly, and it wasn't long before Tutis was known as more than just a traveler's respite. Wealth, trade goods, and even secrets traveled through the city on their way to new people and places.

Caden had traveled through Tutis once, as a boy. It was when his family moved from Patriam to Censura, a city cloaked in mystery. It was rumored by most that one could rise to great heights in Censura or fall to great depths. It was spoken of as a land where one's success was determined by more than skills and determination. Alliances built with well-connected individuals were more important to the people of Censura than the ideals of honest trade and loving relationships. The stories hinted at darkness, and whispers flitted on the wind of a city where life had no meaning, where wealth and power surpassed all else. The whispers spoke of individuals vanishing in the dark, of men rising from poverty to wealth in less than a fortnight. This was a city that intrigued some and terrified others. In Censura, survival was a deadly game, one that many could not help but play.

Caden's father, Jace, had always been fascinated with Censura. When a traveling tradesman from that city stopped in Patriam, Jace had been impressed with more than the quality of his wares; the man spoke of a land where competition reigned fierce, where a man could elevate himself far above his station and be worshipped for doing so. Jace saw his playing field in front of him. He'd spoken for years about the stifling solitude of Patriam, and how the ease and simplicity of their life grated at his nerves. The following week their home had been sold and his family was on the move to Censura, where Jace planned to become one of the greatest men in the city. But they had traveled to Tutis first, a business move that Jace had promised would work to their advantage.

When his family reached Tutis, Caden's mother, Sienna, begged Jace to stay in the small city. She loved the quaint beauty it offered. The people were friendly and welcoming. The city had a beautiful view of the Adeo Mountain Range, and it was surrounded by the deep green trees of the Miro Forest. In the east the mountains rose in stunning glory, and to the west the forest stretched endlessly, a rugged world just waiting to be explored. The city spoke to Sienna's soul and beckoned her to stay.

Jace refused.

Caden, still young, had no choice but to stay with his parents. He watched his mother shed silent tears while Jace stomped forward with deaf ears and determined footsteps. This was Caden's first experience with betrayal. He'd stood by his mother, trying to be strong for her, but the seed of resent had been sown in his heart; bitterness toward his father began to grow.

When they reached Censura, Sienna put on a cheerful smile, but as time wore on her smile faded, replaced with a mask of hopelessness and fear. Caden could do nothing as she retreated into herself, worn down by the scowls of her neighbors and the rejection of the man who had once claimed to love her.

Caden's resentment grew. He begged his father to return to Tutis – to anywhere – rather than watch his mother suffer. Jace refused, and Caden's resentment turned to anger. But it was too late for Jace. In Censura, one could fall as easily as one could rise; it wasn't long before Jace fell prey to its dark grip.

A drip of liquid on Caden's hand forced him from his reverie. He straightened quickly, wiping the single tear on his tunic and burying the memories he'd allowed to surface. His childhood was a dark place that he rarely ventured into. Hurt and anger roiled in his stomach. Jace had betrayed those he loved long before he'd betrayed the world.

Breathing deeply to quell the anger, Caden raised his face to the mountains and the rising sun. Pink rays shot through the sky, promising a beautiful day ahead.

It wouldn't be long before the sun climbed above the mountain, turning the sky from pink to blue and waking the world beyond. If he was lucky, Kyra would wake today. Whatever she'd done with the lightning had all but killed her. He'd gone to the infirmary every day, giving her as much of his healing power as he could. It wasn't much at first, as his body still recovered from Gilrich's attack. Caden had lost a lot of blood, and it had taken a few days before his strength returned.

It didn't matter. Caden would do it all again. As it was, Kyra slept day and night, which was a relief to Caden – the alternative was much worse. His body had to knit itself back together as a result of him saving her, but she was alive. That's what mattered. He'd sat next to her for hours and watched her chest rise and fall, grateful for every breath she took. Wherever her mind was, her body was with him, and she would return to him, eventually.

When the first rays of the sun touched the city walls, Caden held up his wrist, letting the light shine on the symbol etched on his skin. The symbol had come out of nowhere, a pale tattoo that seemed to glow with its own light at first but had now faded until it merely shimmered when the sun hit it. It was a simple symbol – a rectangle encasing three circles evenly spaced within it. The middle circle seemed to balance between them, while the other two were inside equally sized triangles, the tips of which touched the sides of the inner circle. He'd seen the symbol many times before. It was the same symbol on Kyra's necklace, it was a symbol he and Kyra had spent countless hours searching for answers to. It seemed to be linked to whatever power Kyra had invoked during her first moments in Tutis.

Before Kyra's capture, the two of them had discussed many times what the meaning or purpose of the symbol could be. The symbol had appeared on the wrist of Em, Kyra's father shortly after her mother, Evia, was killed, and it was etched on city walls. It meant something important, something that could turn the tide of this war. But they didn't know what. The day of Kyra's capture they'd been in Novus looking for any answers they could find to the question of the symbol. They'd found nothing and Kyra had been lost. Months later, the day he rescued Kyra from Passus, it had shown up on his skin.

The symbol wasn't a scar, nor did it hurt when it appeared. It was just...there. He still knew nothing about it. He hoped Kyra had discovered some answers during her imprisonment. She hadn't had the necklace before she'd been taken, and when she called forth the lightning, she'd studied the necklace as if it meant something. Maybe she'd learned something. He hoped so because he had a lot of questions.

When the sounds of the waking city began to reach Caden's ears, he stood, ready to take on the morning. General Prait had commissioned all able-bodied men and women to fortify the city. They had been working feverishly for days, and progress was showing. Beyond the city walls, trenches had been dug to hinder any enemy advancing on foot. These were deep pits designed to deter the enemy and were located on the edge of the forest. They surrounded Tutis like a moat. If the enemy made it past the trenches, they'd find holes filled with traps and snares, hidden in plain sight. Once they came to the walls, they would have to scale them or break down the gates to get inside. Scaling the walls would be no easy task; along the perimeter, deadly spikes jutted out from the base, placed at such an angle that a man risked his life by getting too close. Anybody attempting to climb over would find themselves speared before they ever made it across. These fortifications extended to the gate as well, with archers on guard to protect it, and its own set of traps ready to take the life of any enemy that dared cross.

Cadavers – creatures that were once human but had been manipulated and distorted by the Malic'Uiel – would find it difficult to make it to the walls. Phantoms – creatures who possessed some of the magic of the Malic'Uiel but were not enslaved by them – would likely be unhindered. As they could travel anywhere at will, there would be no stopping their progress into the city. They were the biggest concern. While most in the city felt safe against a potential Cadaver attack, they were all on edge knowing their defenses could not stop the Phantoms. A possible attack by those soulless creatures had many of the citizens discussing a move back to the Adeo Mountains. That, of course, had its own set of problems. Mainly, starvation. The mountains couldn't sustain them. They all knew it. Tutis was their safest bet.

As for the Malic'Uiel, not enough was known about them to know whether the alterations to the city's defenses would hinder their progress should they choose to attack, but the people hoped they would. The goal was to hold back as many approaching enemies as possible, making it easier to defend themselves against those who made it to their gates.

Yes, Caden thought as he eyed the improvements with satisfaction. *Tutis is becoming a much-needed fortress, a safe haven to the people living inside.*

As he walked back through the city to his bunkhouse, he felt a swell of gratitude. For too long, he and those he fought with had hunkered down in the elements, at the mercy of whatever nature wanted to throw their way. Here, in Tutis, they had bunkhouses, supplies, and a proper infirmary where Dr. Bron and her patients were protected from outside elements.

Dr. Bron, for her part, was almost giddy with her new arrangements. "A real infirmary!" she'd cried when first given the building. "With walls, a door. A place for supplies. Cots for more than two!" It was the most joy any of them had seen in a long time.

As Caden moved into the heart of the city he saw General Prait striding toward him. "I've been looking for you," the general said. "Come with me."

Caden fell in step beside him. They moved back the way he had come, toward the storehouses which made up the Cadaver's – Gilrich, he reminded himself, though his mind stumbled over the name – prison. When they stopped in front of his door, Caden stiffened, gaze fixed on the general. "What are we doing here, sir?" he asked.

"We are here to decide what happens to this Cadaver."

Caden glanced at the building, then back at General Prait. "I thought we were keeping him alive."

General Prait gestured to the door, beckoning for Caden to enter. When he did, he found Gilrich's mutilated form kneeling on the floor, wrists bound and chained to the wall behind him. The cloak he wore hung in tatters off bony shoulders, covering a bulging chest, arms that curved unnaturally outward, and legs that bowed backward, almost as if the body itself wanted to be on all fours.

Pity and anger swelled in Caden's breast. Somewhere he knew Gilrich lived inside that twisted body. He'd seen it himself, but unlocking that mind seemed impossible.

Gilrich had loved Kyra almost as much as Caden did, and he'd nearly killed her.

"Caden, it's cruel to keep him alive this way," General Prait said quietly. "You and I both know that if we were kneeling there and Gilrich was able to, he would offer us mercy."

"Is murder merciful, General?" Caden asked, not taking his eyes from his once best friend. The words tasted foul on his tongue. General Prait was right. Gilrich, in his untwisted state, would have removed them from their misery. Caden didn't want to look at the monster, let alone consider that his friend's mind was trapped in that horrid body, a body which slouched forward, hopeless and beaten, while chains dug at his wrists; dried blood caked the shackles.

General Prait flung his arm toward the prisoner. "Is *that* merciful?" he cried. "To torment a man we all loved, to let him suffer on the hopes of one woman? A woman, mind you, who came from their lair and has had her own mind twisted by their games?"

Caden remained quiet, gazing at the monster he'd once called friend. Part of him wanted to end the Cadaver himself, but not out of pity. This anger he felt toward him was irrational, but it was there. He couldn't get the vision of Kyra from his mind, bleeding at the Cadaver's feet. But he also couldn't deny Kyra her request.

"General," he said. "Kyra is here because of me. I'm the one who stole her from the Malic'Uiel. You're right. We don't know the state of her mind. But she is no prisoner to them." He gestured to Gilrich. "If you were in this state and one person believed you could be saved, wouldn't you want them to try?"

General Prait blew his breath out in frustration. "Of course, I would," he huffed. "But damn it, it kills me to watch this."

"I know, General. I'm going to try to wake Kyra again today. I've been healing her bit by bit every day; she's nearly whole. There's no reason for her mind to remain locked. Will you wait until we know more before we make a decision about him?"

General Prait closed his eyes, shaking his head in defeat. "I won't keep him here like this for long, Caden," he said. "Not unless I see proof that what she claims is possible."

"I agree, General."

Caden turned to go, but General Prait stopped him "The men are wary," he said. "They fear Kyra. They know she was in their power. They know who she was before taken captive, and the Kyra they knew did not have the power to manipulate lightning. They fear she will kill us all in our sleep."

"I've heard the whispers, General," Caden said. "I know they fear her. They fear me, too."

"They do," General Prait said, "But you've earned our trust. She hasn't. I trust you Caden. I've always trusted you. But if falls on you to restore our faith in the woman we once knew.

"You have my word it will happen."

CHAPTER 5

With General Prait's conversation playing out in his head, Caden entered the infirmary and strode straight to Kyra's bed. Before taking Tutis, the army's infirmary had been a tent that housed a few small cots, a table where Dr. Bron could mis her herbal concoctions, and little else.

Dr. Bron's new infirmary was much larger. Multiple bunkhouses had been converted to make room for all the wounded. Cots lined the walls of each bunkhouse, offering shelter and providing plenty of room for Dr. Bron to do her work. The cots were filled with men and women still recovering from the battle for Tutis. Some of these individuals were physically wounded, with burns from the Malic'Uiel covering large parts of their bodies, or deep wounds from sword and dagger. They would require care and rehabilitation. Others had succumbed to the fear wrought by the Malic'Uiel, a fear sown in the mind – intangible, but as real to them as the physical world they were surrounded by. These people were physically well but mentally broken, wounded beyond Dr. Bron's ability to repair.

Kyra had been separated from the other patients and kept at a safe distance, tucked into the back corner of the infirmary; nobody knew what kind of power existed inside her, and almost none were willing to venture too close to find out. General Prait, Dr. Bron, and Caden were the few exceptions. All three had known her well before her captivity, and all three harbored hope that she'd been able to fully shed the Malic'Uiel evil, though General Prait was more than wary.

Kyra hadn't moved in days. Her chest rising and falling was the only indicator that life still coursed through her. Every day Caden came here and used his power to heal her wounds. Physically she was much improved, but for whatever reason, she wasn't waking up.

Today, he came with renewed determination. He would visit her mind today. He'd spend many hours healing her body, but wherever she was – whatever kept her unconscious – was not outside of her. He needed to unlock her mind. He'd thought about it all night until it was the thing that made the most sense.

When he reached her bed, he dragged a stool over and sat down. He touched her cheek gently, brushing his fingers over a row of gashes on her cheek. She'd come to the infirmary with these wounds. He'd chosen to heal only her injuries that were life threatening, leaving the gashes to heal themselves. But he'd looked at them every day, and every day his heart ached more at the physical manifestation of the brutality Kyra had experienced.

He closed his eyes, willing his magic to slip from his fingers and into her wounds. He wouldn't leave her with physical scars of what she'd endured. Not if he could help it. His fingers grew warm, heating the flesh beneath them. He sensed her cells knitting themselves back together, connecting once more to close the gashes left by the Malic'Uiel. Her flesh seemed to sigh beneath his fingers. When he opened his eyes, all that remained were pink lines that would fade over time. He ran his fingers along the now healthy skin. If only waking her up was as easy as healing her wounds.

"Kyra," he said quietly, hoping she'd somehow hear him. "Kyra, we need you to wake up."

She remained unmoving.

He glanced at her face, then leaned forward to rest his hand on her head. Closing his eyes again, he willed her mind to open to his. He still wasn't used to it, this ability to plunge into someone else's mind. This, his magic, all of it was the result of a Phantom's attack. The Phantom, Maliel, had been near death, and he'd attempted to implant himself in Caden's mind, choosing to take his body. But Maliel had failed and fled, and Caden was left with his dark magic pulsing inside him. He now tried to use it for the benefit of humanity, but it was magic born on the devastation of the

Malic'Uiel. It was not good magic. Caden didn't quite believe he was good, either. Even now, guilt twinged in his stomach for the violation of Kyra's mind. He shoved the guilt down and pushed forward. Kyra would understand...he hoped.

Letting that thought calm him, he waited while the world around him disappeared until he stood on the precipice of her mind, looking in. His body remained by the bed, leaning toward her. To any onlooking it would look as if he sat quietly next to her with his hand resting on her forehead. Only he and Kyra would share this experience.

He'd been in her mind before, with her permission, of course. She'd wanted him to learn to use his magic with her. The first time he'd experienced her, there had been bright swirls of light and color. It was the most beautiful thing he had ever seen. But now, he saw only faint touches of color, tiny pieces of her soul. Her memories and dreams wisped about inside a gray fog. Here and there they surfaced, but the fog permeated everything. He couldn't connect with any piece of her.

"Kyra," he whispered. "Where are you?"

When the words left his lips, everything froze. The colors stopped swirling and the fog stopped drifting. He froze with it. Last time he'd been in her mind, she'd welcomed him in, fully aware of the choice she'd made. This, the frozen landscape in front of him, was a response to a threat, a danger.

He was that danger.

He took a deep, slow breath, calming himself in an attempt to calm her. "Kyra," he said again. "Let me in. Let me help you." Slowly, motion started again. One memory seemed to reach out, beckoning to him. Unbidden, it washed over him.

Caden was in this memory. He stood behind Kyra, running his hand up her back. He experienced the pleasure that action gave her, the contentment it provided. When he stepped closer and wrapped his arms around her waist, she melted into him.

"Are you happy?" the apparition of himself asked her.

She nodded.

"Does this feel right?" he asked.

"Yes."

A thrill of excitement shot through her – he felt it all – when he turned her body to his, cupping her face in his hands and running his thumb along her jawline.

"Now does it feel right?" the memory asked.

Caden watched her experience, living it with her, as if he *was* her, but his own emotions were riddled with confusion; the two of them had never had this moment together. He'd never held her, in any way. He didn't understand how this could be one of her memories.

He set aside the confusion and watched the interaction.

"Does it feel right?" The memory – him – again.

"Yes," she answered.

His hands moved to her neck, and a touch of fear crept into the memory. Then his hands began to squeeze. He saw himself through her eyes, saw his hands crushing her neck while she fought for air, saw the pleasure he received, the joy he felt at taking her life.

"Now?" the apparition asked.

Her fear welled up around him, swirling into his soul, overwhelming everything. He wanted to run, to escape this awful memory, this apparition, this truth of the monster he was.

"No," she sobbed in the memory, her voice hoarse. Panic gripped at his stomach – her panic – as he lifted her until her toes barely touched the ground.

He was killing her.

"Stop!" he screamed, shoving the memory away until the fog and colors swirled around him again. "That wasn't me!"

How do I know? Her mind spoke to his; the words flooded him with relief. She was in here.

"I would never hurt you," he said. "You know that." And he spoke the truth. Whatever that memory was, he wasn't part of it. He couldn't hurt her.

I'm afraid, she whispered. *Afraid to die and afraid to wake.*

"We need you, Kyra. I need you."

Around him her memories swirled again, energized by the anxiety she felt. Caden felt it too as it gripped his heart. The gray fog rose, enveloping everything in her mind.

"Where is your light, Kyra?" Caden asked. "The beautiful colors, the energy that once existed here, where is it?"

I'm afraid. My soul is lost. I've given it to them.

"Come back to me and I'll prove you haven't," Caden answered.

Kyra's mind seemed to hesitate; darkness grew while her light faded.

"Kyra!" Caden cried. "You've fought this far. Don't give up now!"

Anguish crashed into him, and his mind shuddered as she tried to push him away.

"I'm not leaving with you," he said, gritting his teeth against the effort it took to stay. "I know who you are, and I am not leaving."

I'm not worth fighting for, she whispered, fading away.

"Neither am I," Caden said. "But you fought for me. You fought for all of us."

Indecision fluttered on the edge of his consciousness. She was bending.

Will you help me? I gave myself to the Malic'Uiel. I swore my soul to them. The darkness takes what it his.

A vision of Kyra's master rose in Caden's mind. "We do not forgive those who betray us," the Malic'Uiel said. A second vision appeared. This time her master screamed as her light forced him to succumb.

I killed him, she whispered. *I betrayed my master. I betrayed the darkness. I can never be free.*

"I'll help you," Caden said. "I'll do whatever it takes."

He would. Those were quite possibly the most honest words he'd ever spoken. The moment the words left him he was shoved out of her mind. The fog and colors vanished, and he resurfaced in the physical reality, breathing heavily. His hand clutched her arm, and he forced himself to release her. It was a disorienting experience, entering someone's mind, and it took a lot of energy from him. The effort he'd expended to stay in her mind had depleted him. But when he looked at her face, her eyes met his gaze.

"You promise?" she asked, blinking back tears.

Caden smiled, taking her in his arms. "I promise," he said. "Whatever it takes."

Kyra clung to him, silent sobs shaking her body while her tears soaked through his tunic. "Please don't leave me," she whispered. "Don't make me do this alone."

"I won't. I'll be here, always."

She let him hold her while she cried out months of pain and frustration; the hot tears spoke to the depth of the torment she'd experienced. When they dried, she sighed and pulled away, setting her trembling hands in her lap "I don't know what happened, Caden," she said. "When you took me from them, I felt so sure, so clear in my path. Now it's muddled. Everything is dark."

He took her hand, entwining his fingers in hers. "Would you believe me if I said I know what you mean?"

Kyra's eyes met his, holding his gaze. She looked at him as if she saw him now for the first time, and her jaw dropped when she realized the truth. "The Phantom," she said. "You fought the darkness. The monster you speak of...it's the same as this?"

He nodded. "Similar. I don't have the Malic'Uiel in my head, but I harbor a different monster. I swear to you, you can get through this."

She breathed slowly, in and out. Her body calmed, hands stopped trembling. "I can do this," she whispered.

He let her sit quietly for a few minutes before gently touching her hand. "Aside from the madness inside," he said, a half-smile on his lips. "How do you feel?"

"I feel fine..." she said, and then glanced around, finally realizing she was surrounded by injured men and women. "Where am I?"

"In the infirmary in Tutis. You're safe."

She looked around the room in confusion, then pushed herself up off the cot, walking to the door on the far side. "How did I get here?"

"I brought you here. Have you no memory of it?"

She leaned against the doorframe, brows furrowed as she tried to piece together what had happened. "I remember bits and pieces of it. I remember telling you to bring us here, and I remember somebody telling me to protect the city, but beyond that it's dark."

"Nobody told you to protect the city," Caden said. Her words were just one piece in the mystery he needed to solve, and he listened with interest. She wasn't the only one hearing voices – it was Avalyn's voice that had told him to go to Kyra that day. Avalyn, his dead wife, had saved Kyra's life. He understood none of it, just like he didn't understand Kyra's actions that first day in Tutis.

Kyra nodded, oblivious to his thoughts. "They did," she insisted. "But I don't remember who it was."

"I wonder..." Caden mused, thinking back to that day and how strange she'd acted. She'd moved as if in a trance. "Do you think that has anything to do with the lightning?"

"What lightning?"

Caden frowned. "After you came here, you went to the top of the wall. I don't know what you did, but you seemed to call a lightning bolt to you. Your body absorbed it, then you threw it over the entire city."

Kyra's face paled. "Did I kill anyone?"

"Nobody was hurt, but half the city is terrified of you. General Prait demands to know what happened."

Kyra pushed out of the doorway and into the open air, hugging herself as she gazed at the sun. She seemed to be seeing it for the first time. After a few moments, she started walking down the quiet streets. Most of the citizens were busy fortifying the city, preparing a garden, or taking care of children. Very few citizens had time or opportunity for idleness, which gave the two of them ample opportunity to talk without interruption.

"How can I explain something I don't understand myself?" Kyra asked.

Caden stopped her then tugged at the pendant hanging around her neck, holding it so the symbol was visible for her. "Before the lightning came you held this up to the sky. Do you know what the symbol means yet?"

"Of course I don't," she snapped, jerking it away from him. "Though..." her face softened as she turned to him. "Avalyn gave me this necklace, Caden. You deserve to know. Somehow, she's communicating with us both from beyond the grave. She told me it was the symbol of Lumen, but I don't know what Lumen is."

Caden gazed at the necklace and then glanced at the symbol etched on his arm. So, Kyra remembered. Caden had spoken to Avalyn a few times in the past. He'd shared some of his experiences where she'd come to him in dreams and visions. Avalyn had worn that necklace in at least one of those vision. He had thought she was a product of his imagination, but if Kyra had spoken to her as well... "The night you were taken, I spoke to a woman who said that Lumen is the realm of light. Does that mean anything to you?"

"No."

Caden rubbed his fingers along the faint mark on his wrist. He thought about the symbol and all they'd gone through to find its meaning. They'd seen it shimmering in the sky not long before Kyra was taken. Em, Kyra's father, had· the same symbol on his wrist. General Prait had found it etched on the side of a city. And now a ghost communicated with them both. All the pieces were there in front of him if he could just put them together! He thought over all he knew, and all he didn't know. Finally, the mystery cracked open just a little, and he thought of something he hadn't before.

"Kyra, have you considered that maybe the world isn't quite as small as we think it is?"

"What do you mean?"

"Well, the woman spoke of the realm of light, and Avalyn has been able to communicate with both of us, though I know she's dead. How is that possible?"

Kyra rubbed the pendant between her fingers. "I don't know," she said. "I assumed Avalyn was a figment of both our imaginations, but..." She removed the necklace, holding the pendant in her hand. "She gave this to me, so she couldn't be."

"Exactly!" Caden said, getting excited now. "So there's a realm of light – a second realm, separate from Spero. There's more to this world than we know! We need to learn more about Lumen, about this realm of light."

His thoughts flashed back to a dark memory, one he wished he could forget. But it was a clue to the mystery. Jace, his father, knelt with his hands bound, face battered, silently begging Caden's forgiveness. Darkness swirled around him, and Caden knew something terrible was coming.

That was the night the Malic'Uiel entered Spero; they'd come through methods Caden did not understand, brought to his world by black magic and sorcery. Could they have entered from another realm?

"*If* the realm of light exists," Kyra said.

"If," Caden agreed. "But it's a clue worth following. You ended up their prisoner because we were looking for answers; maybe it wasn't all for naught."

Kyra's shoulders slumped. "We went looking for answers to more than just the question of the symbol." Kyra leaned against the wall of a nearby building, sliding to the ground. "Do you think my father is still alive?" she asked, glancing up at Caden. "He doesn't deserve that fate."

Caden said next to her, mirroring her movements. "I don't know, Kyra," he said. "I expect he is. The Malic'Uiel seem to use their victims fully before discarding them." *Even after discarding them, still they are abused,* he thought but did not say aloud. Caden had seen the waste heaps of the Malic'Uiel. They were nothing more than the bodies of those consumed, piled high against the back wall of the cities. Manipulated, coerced, abused, and then discarded like garbage. There had been a heap of the dead in Tutis, but the army had buried them first thing. It was the least they could do for these Malic'Uiel victims.

Kyra pulled her legs up and rested her forehead on her knees. "I hope my father is alive," she said, her voice muffled. She turned her head to face him. "Do you ever feel like you're being fed just enough hope to keep you going, but not enough to win the fight?"

"What do you mean?"

"I feel like every step we take just gives me more questions and no answers. Maybe we're rats being manipulated by the Malic'Uiel at every turn."

"Maybe," Caden said. "It does feel that way sometimes."

Kyra sighed, leaning her back against the wall. "Where did they come from?" she asked. "What are they, and how did they get here?"

Caden swallowed hard, afraid to look at her. The Malic'Uiel had come through the betrayal of one man. Shem, the man who was the real reason Gilrich had lost his mind to the Malic'Uiel, knew how they had come to be; Caden was there the day they'd come, too. He glanced at Kyra whose eyes were closed as she held her face to the sun. Guilt tugged at his soul, and he shifted his tunic to cover the scar that marred his chest – a single handprint that whispered of dark secrets in his past.

The blood of betrayal ran deep in his family.

"I don't know *what* they are," he murmured. "But I swear to you that I've given my life to destroying them." The image of his father swam before his face, his haunted eyes seeking those of his son. Caden glared at the memory. Peace would come for Caden after the Malic'Uiel were sent back to the hell they spawned from.

CHAPTER 6

I t's strange," Kyra said as she and Caden worked their way through the city. They'd come to an area that bustled with an activity no city had seen in years. Caden directed her steps away from the people moving about. Even still, they all stopped to look her way, their postures tense and faces wearing masks of hostility or fear. Kyra did her best to ignore them. "Tutis looks the same as Passus, but there's an energy here that feels like life. Passus only had death. I feel almost normal."

Caden chuckled. "I know how you feel."

The two of them worked their way to the front gate to see the progress of the fortifications. There were a few guards at the gate who eyed her with trepidation, but they did not hinder their way. When they reached the top of the wall, they stopped while Kyra studied the scene beyond the city. Aside from the trench near the tree line, the earth looked as if one could pass across it safely. Freshly dug dirt was the only hint that something may be amiss; beneath it snares and pitfalls lay in wait. Eventually, the trench would be disguised as well.

"Why haven't they attacked yet?" Kyra asked. "They far outnumber us; their forces are stronger. It doesn't make sense. Why would they leave us alone and give us a chance to fortify?"

Caden clasped his hands behind him, following her line of sight. "I've been wondering the same thing," he said. "Every day I wake feeling like I'm being lulled into a sense of safety, and once I get there they'll attack and slaughter us all."

"They may," Kyra murmured. "They have the means to do so."

They watched the work for a short length of time, both weighed down by a melancholy gloom, but then Caden brightened. Kyra had spent months with them, living inside the enemy lair. She'd be the one person living that knew their secrets!

"Kyra," he said, suddenly animated and hopeful. "Did you learn anything while with them that could be used against them?"

"All I learned from them were their patterns and behaviors."

"Such as?"

"They are most active at night," she said. "The sun is abhorrent to the Cadavers. Darkness is safer. And the Malic'Uiel never sleep. They don't need to."

"But..." Caden said. "We slipped into many cities at night. If they are most active then, how did we move through undetected?"

She shrugged. "They didn't expect to find a human in their strongholds. They sought them beyond the walls of their cities. Inside, there was a false sense of security."

"Even though they captured me while I was inside?"

She nodded. "One human is nothing against the Malic'uiel. In their eyes, you got lucky. For the rest of us, it was simply a matter of being hidden in plain sight. But that changed after we began attacking the cities. They saw their weakness and filled it quickly."

"Which explains why we were overtaken."

She nodded. "They knew we were there the night I was taken. My master told me as much. They wanted to know what we were searching for. We were always prey in their trap."

Caden reached over to take her hand. "I'm sorry," he said. "I've wanted to say it for so long. I'm sorry you were taken that night. I'm sorry I left you behind."

She squeezed his hand, forcing a smile. "I told you to leave," she said. "I remember that much."

"I shouldn't have listened."

She sighed. "It's too late for that, Caden. What's done is done." She turned, moving back down the steps.

"Where are you going?" Caden called.

"You said General Prait is looking for answers. I don't have any, but I can at least try to get him to trust me again."

"First him, and then the rest of the city. They may need some convincing."

Kyra scrunched up her nose as she glanced at the people around her. "Yeah, I kind of figured as much." She put on a brave smile and squared her shoulders. "I'll start with the general."

Kyra found General Prait examining the squat buildings in the cell complex. The buildings were small, less than the length of a man from top to bottom and side to side. She watched as he studied one; he moved around it, pushing on the walls, tugging at the corners before moving on to the next one.

"What are you doing, General?" Kyra asked as she walked up.

He gestured to the building. "Trying to understand how these cells work," he said. "There are no doors. We know they're prison cells, but there were no prisoners in Tutis when we took the city. How do they get the captives inside?"

Kyra stepped to the building. On the side of the structure was an intricate lock. It looked as if a key was needed for entry, but she slipped her finger beneath the lock, pushing a latch aside. A section of the wall slid to the left, revealing a doorway.

"The lock is there to confuse people," she said. "It's a precaution to keep people like you and me out of them. There's a latch beneath it that opens the door. It's actually quite simple."

General Prait peered inside, but Kyra turned away. Seeing inside the cell caused her stomach to twist; she had far too many memories linked to a cell just like this. A moment later General Prait stepped into it, running his hand along the wall opposite the door.

"There are markings," he said. "Lines carved in the wood."

"They're time markers." She didn't need to look inside to know what she'd find. "Indicators of failed hope. When you're in these cells you try to keep yourself from going mad, so you distract yourself by attempting to track the passage of time." She finally turned to catch his gaze. "Do the lines start to fade at some point?"

"Yes. They just kind of...stop."

She closed her eyes, licking her suddenly dry lips. "That was the moment this prisoner gave up hope," she said. "How many markers are there?"

He counted quickly. "Less than ten."

"It doesn't take long for a soul to give up hope," she murmured. "Especially not when the world has turned against you."

General Prait frowned but he left the cell, feeling beneath the lock for the latch. A moment later the door slid shut. "How long were you in one of these?" he asked.

"I don't know. Once I stopped marking the days, time became meaningless. It just...ceased to exist. My life became nothing but endless hours of torment."

General Prait pursed his lips, regarding Kyra with interest. "Walk with me," he said.

She stayed beside him while they walked through the residential area of the city.

"How does it work?" General Prait asked. "Becoming a Cadaver?"

She didn't answer immediately, pausing to gather her thoughts, and to choose her words. Cadavers were, after all, the enemy. And she had been one. She glanced at the general, who waited expectantly. Then she let her eyes move over the rest of the city, falling on the people going about their day. She made eye contact with some; those she did turned away but not before she saw their fear. She needed General Prait's trust. She needed the people's trust. She had to be honest.

"Becoming a Cadaver is a choice," she answered. "One made through coercion after weeks of torment, but it is a choice, nonetheless. In those cells they force you to forget who you are. The people you love turn against you. You become a monster."

"How can they do that?" General Prait asked.

She shook her head. "I don't know. I watched my master do it to Gilrich and I still don't know what he did. Somehow, they connect with the mind. They twist the memories, turning reality into fiction and fiction into reality. Crammed in a dark, cold cell it's impossible to separate what's real from the illusion."

"So..." General Prait said, taking slow, measured steps, his hands behind his back and head bowed as he tried to grasp what she shared. "I've been in the Malic'Uiel grip – their mind game – and had them twist my memories. Is it similar to that?"

"Yes," Kyra said. Her lips flattened into a thin line as memories of her time with them resurfaced. She found herself struggling to breathe, pushing down panic as she fought the remnants of a demon that no longer held her physical body, but still claimed a part of her soul. "It's the same premise as those mind games, but far worse. Because once your relationships are destroyed, and you no longer trust those you love, they change the memories. In that cell, the people I loved tried to kill me, and in response I killed them. I have very clear memories now of killing my mother; they feel so real! I have memories of Caden trying to kill me, of my father wrapping a rope around my neck. Logically, I know those aren't real. But emotionally, they feel very real." She sighed, closing her eyes against the pain. "Eventually, the Malic'Uiel are all the world has to offer. You begin to trust them. You lose so much of yourself, and your mind becomes so twisted, they begin to look like salvation. The tormenter becomes the savior." Her hands clenched into fists and her jaw tightened as the memories continued. "It's been so long since I felt human. Part of me has forgotten how to make decisions, to think critically, to be independent of them. I have to tell myself I'm safe here," she murmured. "Because I know I'm not safe with them, yet there was a sense of security in giving everything I was to them." She wet her dry lips with her tongue then sent General Prait a wan smile. "I know it sounds like I'm one of them. I'm not. Their security was torment in itself, and I had to become numb for it not to destroy me." She sighed. "Still, there can be comfort in the darkness. Pain, when it's all one knows, becomes a very familiar friend."

General Prait stopped walking and put his hand on her shoulder. Around them, people paused to watch. One look from the general sent them scurrying away. "It sounds like you've been through hell."

Her lips turned up in a half smile. "I suppose that's what you'd call it." The conversation caused a melancholy to fall over her. Too many horrible experiences had been relived, so much so that the brightness of the day seemed to dim. One arm wound its way across her chest, a subconscious effort to hold herself together. "I want you to know, General, that I had abandoned the Malic'Uiel ideology before Caden ever came for me. They did me a favor in their torture chamber; they stripped me to nothing and laid my soul bare. I realized when I became nothing that I was capable of anything." She straightened and her arm dropped; light seemed to flood the area around her.

General Prait glanced first at Kyra's face, and then the sun. He would later describe it as a ray that pierced through the clouds to shine only on her.

"The Malic'Uiel lost their power when I embraced mine," she said, a small smile on her face. "My soul, though claimed by them, could not be used by them. In those moments, I knew I was free." That sense of freedom tingled inside her now, a small reminder of who she'd become. She closed her eyes and pulled in a deep breath, releasing it slowly while the tension in her body faded.

General Prait pursed his lips in thought as he listened to her story. He didn't sense any deception, and physically she was as perfect as any other human. Cadavers, he knew, wore their loyalty in the deformation of their bodies. And Phantoms had an inhuman quality that swirled around them. She was neither of those things. Still, she carried a power he didn't understand.

He dipped his head, acknowledging what she'd shared, and began walking again. "Your story of your time with them is credible, Kyra," he said. "But can you explain the lightning?"

She grimaced. "I can't. I wish I could. I don't know what happened or what the lightning was."

"You didn't move as yourself; you almost seemed to be in a trance."

"That's what Caden tells me." She hesitated, biting her lip as she studied her commander. "You wouldn't send me back to them, would you?" she asked, fear pricking at her heart. "I know the people here don't trust me. I can't blame them, but I'm not here to hurt them, I swear on my soul."

General Prait sighed. "No," he said. "I'd never send somebody back to that. If I truly felt you were a threat, I'd imprison you here, like Gilrich, where you could do no harm."

She flinched at the mention of Gilrich's name. "How is he?" she asked.

"He's a Cadaver," General Prait answered. "A monster in our midst. I would say he isn't well."

"We can save him," she said.

Her quiet words revealed a hope he did not share. He folded his arms, leaning against the wall of a building. "Gilrich is a topic for another time. Right now, I need to understand what happened. I need to know what power you hold – I guaranteed the people their safety, and I intend to deliver on that promise."

Kyra remained silent, letting her mind roam over the events of the previous weeks. So much had happened that didn't make sense, so much that left her confused. How to help him understand?

"Well?" General Prait prompted.

She finally met his gaze. "I don't know what happened, General," she said. "With the lightning. All I have for you are my experiences." She gestured toward the outer city. "Can we keep walking?" she asked, all too aware of the people pausing to watch them. Curious men and women gaped at her with fear and anger.

"Of course." They walked silently until he turned her down a narrow, empty street. When they were out of hearing range, she spoke. "As a prisoner to the Malic'Uiel, I chose the life they offered. It was that or death. Sometimes I think I should have chosen death." Her lips curved up in a sad attempt at a smile. "I signed my soul to them. They have records of all those they have killed, and all those they have claimed. Part of me probably still exists with them; I fear it does. But though I wrote my name on their parchment, I never could fully give myself to them."

She held out her hand in front of her fingers, outstretched as she turned it over to see the palm. "My hand is perfect," she said. "This wasn't always the case. As a Cadaver, your body begins to change. The darker my mind got and the more I gave them my soul, the more gruesome my body became. My hands were like claws," she mused, stretching the fingers once more. "The face I have now is not the face I had then. For a while, I embraced them." She yanked her fingers through her hair as her eyes filled with tears. "I imprisoned Gilrich," she said. "I dragged him to his cell and locked him in. I'll never forgive myself for that."

"Shem was at fault for that, not you."

"Does it really matter who else was involved when I'm the one that sealed his fate?"

"I think so."

"I'm not so sure." Kyra shook off the melancholy that wanted so hard to settle over her. It hurt going back to those memories. It hurt reliving who she'd become. "I tell you this in the hopes that you'll see a woman standing before you, an ally to the people, not some Cadaver or some traitor sent from the Malic'Uiel."

"I see a woman, Kyra, but I am concerned that you don't have answers to your first day here. I need to understand what happened."

Kyra chewed on her lip as she reflected on his words. He did deserve to understand, and he would if she did. But she did not. "General," she said. "Have you ever communed with the dead?"

The general's brow furrowed in confusion. "The dead? Spoken to them?"

"Yes."

He shook his head.

"I have. I've spoken with Avalyn, Caden's wife, more than once."

"Caden's dead wife," he murmured. "I know her story."

"Avalyn has a different agenda than the Malic'Uiel. She's come to me multiple time in dreams or...visions. I don't know which. Every time she did, I found more power in myself. The day Caden freed me from them, *she* freed me first." Kyra held out her pendant to General Prait. "You know about this symbol as well as I.

We've discussed it. You thought it meant nothing. I thought it might give us answers. Avalyn told me this is the mark of Lumen. She says it's a symbol of hope. A *dead woman* told me these things. Can you explain that?"

"No."

"Can you explain how a body can be twisted into something dark and gruesome with nothing more than a twisting of the mind?"

"No."

She pursed her lips, one hand on her hip as she studied him. "Can you explain how monsters came from nowhere to destroy our world?"

He shook his head.

"Then you admit we have many questions that have no answers?"

"Yes," he said, the word almost a whisper.

"I have much I don't understand," she said. "I hope someday I will. I do not have an answer to the lightning and what happened the day I came here. But I can tell you that whatever I have inside me, whatever caused that lightning, does not want to cause pain."

"Go on."

Kyra held out her palm again, beckoning for the general to study it. A faint sheen of light bloomed on her hand before fading away. "The day Caden saved me was supposed to be the day they broke me. Obviously, they failed. But there *was* destruction that day.

My master was destroyed, or his soul banished, by me. I suppose he no longer exists."

General Prait's face scrunched in confusion. He massaged his forehead, trying to understand. "What do you mean? And what is that on your hand?"

She spread her fingers wide, palm side up. A faint glow hovered over the skin. "I don't know what the light is," she said. "I just know it saved me. My master was going to take my soul. They'd mutilated my body, and the soul was next. I don't know how it happened, but light came from my hand and engulfed him. It pulled the shadows out of him and he...dissipated in front of me. It saved my life. Then Caden took me from them."

"And brought you here."

"Yes."

"Which brings us to the lightning."

"The lightning that I still don't understand." She sucked in a deep breath, filling her lungs before letting it out in a rush. "The day we came here, a voice was guiding me. It told me to protect the city. I remember nothing beyond that point, but I'm told I seemed aware of what I was doing. The fact that I don't remember scares me. But I don't believe I was acting to cause harm."

She stepped to the opening of the small street and let her eyes rove over the city. Her arms were folded in front of her, a protection against the darkness in the world, as if that could somehow keep it at bay. General Prait moved to stand next to her. She glanced at him. "General, I will be the first to tell you that I don't understand what's happening, and I don't know what kind of danger lurks inside me. I know the Malic'Uiel hold runs deep; I know I've been altered, probably forever. A deep sadness overwhelms me. I'm terrified for what I could become. What if I never fully escape them? But then I look at Caden and I see what's inside me, and I have to believe in what's possible. I'm different than I was, but I'm still here. I still live. I will fight for humanity until my last breath. I know you're looking for answers that I don't have, but I'm asking you to please trust the woman you once knew. Part of her is still here, somewhere."

General Prait nodded while pity tugged at the corners of his lips. "You've suffered, Kyra," he said quietly. "You've been through more than any of us. I do know the woman you were, and I hope the woman you are now isn't so different from her." He pulled her into his embrace. She melted into it as a daughter leans into a father. "Welcome back," he said. "The people are concerned, my men more than most. But I, for one, am glad you are here."

CHAPTER 7

Maliel the Phantom hovered just inside the forest edge, his eyes fixed on the walls of Tutis. From his location he had a perfect view of the city, but he was also concealed from the soldiers stationed along the walls. The land between the trees and the city walls was bare, but Maliel knew better than to attempt to cross it. He was a Phantom, an altered being, but he wasn't dead. He was...trapped between both worlds. Neither living nor dead, not a ghost nor a human, he existed in between those states, and he preferred it. His time as a human had been miserable, but he wasn't ready to die and move beyond the grave. He would take this half-living state for the power he now had.

For days now, he'd been watching these humans. They'd set a fair number of traps. Those traps could harm him, if he were stupid enough to walk into one. *Disgusting creatures,"* he thought, *thinking they're safe from the Malic'Uiel.* He knew, without a doubt, that this safety they had would not last for long.

The Master had sent him to secure the female, Kyra. He'd warned him to proceed with caution – a warning Maliel threw aside immediately. Humans could not withstand the power he held. The only exception was the human Caden, who held a portion of Maliel's power.

Maliel spat in disgust. That night had not gone as planned. Maliel had intended to take Caden's body for his own, as his was weak from Caden's attack. Instead, he'd failed and Caden had absorbed Maliel's power. For the first time in his life as a Phantom, Maliel had been forced to leave a fight and struggle for his survival. The human had nearly killed him. It was sheer willpower – or a desire for revenge – that had kept him alive. Weeks had passed before he felt like his old self. Then he learned that Caden had unlocked the power of the Phantoms.

He glared at the city walls as if he could tear them apart with his gaze. He'd love to see Caden lifeless beneath his blade. Someday, he would. But today, he had to get the woman.

His plan was to transport himself into the city, take the woman, and transport right back out. The human traps, as well as the humans themselves, would be avoided. It wasn't his typical method – he liked to play with his victims. The game of cat and mouse was one of the greatest pleasures he got to experience in his life.

But the Master had forbidden it. His command was to get in, get the girl, and get out. He ground his teeth as anger rose. He'd been one of the first supporters of the Malic'Uiel, celebrating when they'd crossed into Spero and willingly jumping into their service. He'd been rewarded with the power he held now – the power to transport anywhere, to manipulate fire, and draw out the life of man with a touch. They had made him a Phantom, him and many others.

Drunk on power, the Phantoms eventually fought to break free of the Malic'Uiel control; he'd been one of them, but his efforts had been covert and gone under the Malic'Uiel notice. His comrades had been slaughtered and he, along with the remaining Phantoms, became nothing more than magical slaves. He ground his teeth in anger. Someday he would be free of the Master. Until then, he was forced to follow.

He glanced at the noon sun. Taking precautions as the Master demanded, he had decided to wait until darkness fell. The woman would be harder to locate, but there would also be fewer humans about to spot him or recognize that he was not one of their number.

He leaned against the tree, folding his arms as he waited. Today would be a long day.

As the sun fell, torches lit up along the top of the wall. The sentries were still there, as they had been every night for days. The city was never unguarded. Lucky for him, his abilities would make it easy to bypass their 'fortifications.'

The laughter of the guards on the wall floated back to him. He grunted in disgust. Ridding Spero of the human scourge was the best thing the Malic'uiel ever could have done.

He moved silently to the back of the city, transporting himself easily with his magic. He did love this part of being Phantom – the ability to go anywhere his mind wanted to take him made travel very easy.

The gates were guarded more closely than the back walls, a mistake you'd think the humans wouldn't make considering the back wall always seemed to be their entry of choice into a Malic'Uiel city. He moved as close to the walls as he dared, focusing his thoughts on the Citadel. Since he didn't know where the female was, he would have to transport himself to the only location he could visualize within the city. From there, he would conceal himself in the streets or try to pass himself off as a human. The thought repulsed him. He'd shed his humanity long ago and had no desire to pretend to pick it up again.

He sighed, watching the moon rise. The sounds on the wall petered out as the city slipped into slumber. He envisioned himself dragging the girl from her bed and dropping her at the feet of the Master; excitement rose inside at the prospect. He couldn't play his normal cat and mouse game, but he could enjoy her fear, nonetheless.

As silent as a shadow, but far more dangerous, he vanished from where he stood, reappearing in the black gloom of the Citadel. From here he could see beyond the cell blocks and into the city. He slipped between the cells, watching his surroundings carefully for any potential threat. There was no movement. This late, most of the people would be sleeping. Here and there he might run into a guard, but those were stationed on the outer walls. He doubted there would be any person in the city center to bother him. Even if they did stumble upon him, they would be easily dispatched.

Quietly, he slipped forward. His feet made no movement on the ground. One of the benefits of being neither living nor dead was near weightlessness; gravity didn't have the same hold on your body when nature couldn't tell if you were a ghost.

Kyra slept fitfully on her cot, thrashing against the nightmares that invaded her dreams. Something seemed to whisper in her mind: *wake up.* She ignored it – she just wanted to sleep! The whisper persisted, getting louder. *Wake up.*

Go away, Kyra thought. *Torment somebody else.*

"Wake up!" This voice was loud and clear, and Kyra bolted forward.

"Who's there?" she called.

The room was silent. Caden snored lightly on the cot next to her. She'd been given her own bunkhouse, as the other women were afraid to stay with her, but since her experiences with her master, it frightened her to be alone. Caden had moved his cot in with her. He, of course, slept peacefully.

Get out of bed.

She groaned. "Listen," she muttered. "If you're going to be in my head, you may as well tell me who you are."

Caden stirred. "I'm Caden," he mumbled.

Kyra ignored him.

I'm your guide, the voice said. *I'll be here when you and the people around you need help. And right now, you need help.*

Kyra paused. "Why do I need help?"

Go outside.

Kyra obeyed, grumbling. "I've lost my mind," she muttered. "Gone completely nuts."

She stepped out the door of her bunkhouse then stopped in defiance. "Okay," she said. "You've got me out here. What now?"

The voice was silent, and Kyra sighed. "Fine," she murmured, rolling her eyes at the presence that was not there. She turned down the street, walking toward the Citadel. In the dark it was as imposing as ever, casting its shadow over the city.

Careful, the voice said. *It's dangerous.*

"Oh, so you're back again?" Kyra growled.

Shhhh.

Kyra snapped her mouth shut. The voice was driving her crazy, but up to this point it had kept her alive, whatever *it* was. She had to give it credit for getting both her and Caden safely to Tutis. So, she listened, taking extra care as she shuffled up the street.

A pebble clattering to her left caused her to jump, and she whirled toward it. Just as her eyes fell on Maliel, he grabbed her arm, jerking her into his grasp while he clapped his free arm over her mouth, stifling her scream. She knew Maliel. She could never forget his face, or the night he'd ripped her father from her life and delivered him as a prize to the Malic'Uiel. Panic and rage pooled in her stomach. They'd fought so hard that night, she and her father. They'd been betrayed by marauders while they made deals with Phantoms. The marauders gave them victims, and the Malic'Uiel remained unaware of their existence. It had been a game for them all, except her.

"I've been looking for you," Maliel hissed, drawing her attention back to him. "They've sent me for you."

His words sent a chill clear through her body. His arms held her tight against his chest, a chest she wanted nothing to do with. Unable to scream, unable to fight, she fought the urge to vomit. "Yes," he said, his lips tickling her ear as he spoke. "They want you very much."

She knew exactly who he meant. She couldn't go back, not to them, not ever. If she thought she suffered before, going back to them she'd learn the true meaning of torture.

Fear rose like a specter of her master and it took all of her power not to let it consume her.

Maliel chuckled, enjoying her fear. Normally when I take a human, I try to render them unconscious first. It's easier for me, merciful for them. You see? It's painful to travel the way I do. But not you. No," he hissed. "You can feel all of it." His breath was warm on her neck, and a chill crawled down her spine. "The Master awaits your return." His voice dripped in her ear. Fear tightened in her chest until she could hardly breathe. She yanked her head back, cracking him in the face with the back of her skull. Her mouth freed, she tried to scream, but he recovered too fast and shoved his hand into her mouth; she choked on the sound of her own fear. Already her body felt weaker as the poison of his touch seeped into her.

Stop him.

Maliel's body began to shimmer. She fought against him, scanning the city and praying somebody was awake to help. The streets were silent. Desperate, she bit down on the fingers still jammed in her mouth. When he jerked away, she shrieked before he clapped his palm over her jaw again. Their bodies vibrated as he called forth the energy it would take to transport them away. Pain raked across her skin, burrowing itself in her flesh.

Stop him! An image of her, hands outstretched to her master, light flowing from her palm, flashed into her mind.

She finally listened to the voice. Glancing at her hand, there was a glow.

Use it!

The words came with an image. She saw herself gripping Maliel's wrist, willing the light to spread from her body to his.

She obeyed, following the image.

She had no choice; if she went with Maliel, they'd destroy her.

The voice was her only chance.

She twisted her arm and gripped his wrist, hard, concentrating on shoving whatever light she had into his flesh. The moment her light touched him, the vibrating stopped. Blessed coolness rushed over her as the pain vanished.

Maliel grunted, dropping his hand from her mouth and tightening his hold on her body. She sensed him trying to transport out, but his cells would not obey. Anger gripped him. His arms crushed her so tight against him she couldn't take in a breath. It wasn't until the doors around them began to creak open that she realized she'd been screaming. People rushed out to help but froze, their faces twisted in fear when their eyes fell on the light traveling up his body – a light that clearly came from her.

"Kyra!" Caden's voice broke above the din, but she couldn't focus on him. Whatever she was doing was working. Maliel couldn't transport. He couldn't take her.

She felt the light in her body now, and as it left her body an electric current seemed to ripple with it. She realized it was energy. It hummed in each of her cells. She clamped her jaw shut, pushing all of the energy she had into the matter at hand. More of the light pulsed into Maliel's body. It spread up his arm, across his shoulder, and into his chest.

The second it touched his heart, Maliel shrieked and threw Kyra away. She stumbled, landing hard, but immediately shoved herself back up. Caden reached for her, but she brushed him off.

Maliel, panicked, beat his hands against the light, but he couldn't stop it from spreading through his body. "What is it?" he shrieked, eyes wide with fear.

"Light," she said. "Life. The energy of my soul. Your soul is dark. Mine is not."

Around her, the crowd grew. Some of the people covered their faces with their hands, afraid to watch. Others simply turned and fled.

Like a smoldering fire, the light spread, devouring him, enveloping him completely. Kyra watched, fascinated, while it penetrated his skin. It burrowed deep into his body. Darkness oozed out of him. The black vapor she'd puked up many times before in her dealings with Phantoms swirled from him in a wispy fog. Deeper and deeper the light went, shoving more and more of the darkness out. Finally, all that remained was a frail, powerless body.

A human body.

Thin white hair clung to an aged head that seemed to drag the body toward the ground, forcing it to hunch over. Maliel's tunic hung on a skeletal frame. The limbs were shriveled and sickly. His eyes, nearly black, were surrounded by dark circles. They sunk deep into the gaunt face.

Gasps rose from the crowd, and murmurs floated through the air like a ripple.

"What are you?" Kyra whispered, gaping at Maliel in horror.

He dropped to his knees, too weak to hold himself up. One glance at his hands and a tortured wail ripped from his chest. "I'm human," he sobbed. "You've stolen my power!"

Kyra swallowed hard, backing away from the pitiful creature toward Caden. "I only meant to save my life."

He glared at her, hate seeping from his pores. "You've stolen everything!" he screamed. "Taken everything from me!"

More people flowed into the crowd, watching the scene before them with morbid curiosity.

Kyra stopped her escape, glaring at Maliel. "You already took everything from me," she said. She threw her hand out toward the crowd. "You stole from all of us here – taken our loved ones, wrecked our homes. You and the Malic'Uiel plague have destroyed all our lives." She stepped closer, standing above him and gazing down at his haggard form. "You got what you deserved."

Caden was next to her now. He pulled her against him but kept a stony gaze on Maliel. Though Caden seemed still, she felt his body shaking. "You have so much to answer for," he hissed. "I will get all the pleasure in the world seeing you hang for what you've done."

Maliel seethed, but as more and more people seeped into the street, he began to glance around in fear. He knew he had lost. From the folds of his tunic, he pulled out a dagger. Caden rushed forward, but not fast enough. Before he could be stopped, Maliel plunged the blade into his own heart, collapsing on the street with the hilt sticking out from between his ribs. Blood dripped onto the stones beneath him.

If one Phantom got in, many can.

There was the voice again.

"What am I supposed to do about that?" Kyra snapped.

Caden blinked, tearing his eyes from Maliel's corpse. He looked confused. "What are you supposed to do about what?"

She just shook her head. It didn't matter.

He glanced at the body once more, then at Kyra. "How did you do that?" he asked. "With the light?"

She clamped her mouth shut, pressing her hands against her stomach as nausea from Maliel's poison settled in. Her thoughts were not on Caden. They were on the voice. It was right. Maliel wasn't the only Phantom controlled by the Malic'Uiel. The people of the city were not safe, as much as they wanted to believe they were. She had to find a way to protect them.

Kyra's stomach churned as Maliel's sickness worked its way through her body, weakening her system. It was the way of the Phantom to infect its victim with poison. His blackness would have to be expelled, and she knew it.

"I'll explain...when I can," she said, finally answering Caden. She dropped to her knees, weak as the poison raged through her. Fire blazed in her stomach and the world spun. 'Caden," she gasped, grasping for him. The cobblestones beneath her faded in and out of focus. "Help me."

Caden glanced once at her face and knew what was coming. He scooped her into his arms and hurried down the street to their bunkhouse.

Groaning, she curled her body into the smallest ball she could, getting sicker by the minute. The crowd split like a canyon as she moved through it. In the past, Kyra had simply lost consciousness when the Phantom's plague overwhelmed her body. This time, consciousness was not forthcoming.

She wished it were.

Maliel's poison would have to be disgorged. No, it wouldn't kill her, but it would feel like dying as her body expelled every bit of the black magic. A fresh wave of nausea washed over her, and she buried her face in Caden's chest, biting back the sickness.

Caden kicked open the door of the bunkhouse and laid Kyra carefully onto her cot, where she curled back into a ball.

"Are you all right, Kyra?" Caden's voice broke the silence.

She shook her head. The room spun violently from the motion.

"It'll pass," he said, gently rubbing her back.

She only groaned in agony.

"I'm sorry, Kyra." He fell silent, but his hand never left her back, nor did the motion stop.

"Caden," she said through clenched teeth, forcing herself to hold it together. "I think I'm losing my mind."

"Why do you say that?"

She rolled over to face him, digging her knees into her stomach to dull the pain. One hand gripped his leg as if that would steady the room. "There is a voice in my head as real as my own voice. It told me to use my light against Maliel." She squeezed her eyes shut, biting back tears as pain ground in her stomach. "You asked what it was." Her voice shook and she had to pause to breathe between the words. "That's what it was."

Caden's gentle motion had moved to her arm, but it faltered for a moment before he resumed it. "Was it the same voice as before?"

She nodded.

His hesitation spoke volumes. When he finally spoke, he said simply, "There are many questions, and very few answers, but we will figure them out together. Your light removed the curse of the Phantom. It destroyed the darkness. It must be a gift."

Kyra nodded, no longer caring about the conversation or the voice. The sickness was working its way up. She hugged her body tight, wishing she was unconscious, praying Maliel's infection would spread quickly and be done.

CHAPTER 8

Geneal Prait?" Kyra rapped on the wall of his bunkhouse. "Sir? Are you there?"

Days had passed since Maliel's attack and subsequent death. Kyra had stayed close to her bunkhouse, sick with Maliel's poison at first, but even after recovering she received terrified stares when she ventured near others, and she'd decided it would be best to stay alone for a while. The people already didn't trust her; apparently Maliel's death hadn't helped that. But she was also a citizen of Tutis, so she'd decided this morning that she would venture out among them again. They'd just have to learn to accept her presence.

"One moment," General Prait said.

She stepped to the side of the door, waiting. When he exited, he was closing the buckle around his tunic. "Good morning, Kyra," he said, combing fingers through his hair. He stepped to a barrel of water next to the building, splashing it on his face. "What can I do for you?" A folded rag sat next to the barrel. He snatched it up, using it to dry his wet skin.

"I'd like to see Gilrich," Kyra said. "Is that possible?"

General Prait cocked his head, observing the woman before him. "Caden told me you think you can help him."

She nodded.

"How do you intend to do that?"

"I don't know, sir, but I have to try. Just imagine how many lives we could save if we were able to reverse the damage caused to the mind!"

"What if you can't help him?" General Prait asked. "What if his condition is permanent."

"I'm hoping it's not...but if it is, I won't make him suffer longer than necessary."

General Prait scratched the back of his neck then smoothed down his tunic. "Go ahead and try," he said. "But I'd like Caden to go with you."

"Thank you." Kyra smiled, trying not to betray her nerves or give too much rise to her hope. But she'd reversed her condition, so hope rose on its own. She hurried off to find Caden. Like it or not, he was coming with her.

Gilrich had been imprisoned in one of the many storehouses in the city. The storehouses themselves were located past the cell blocks and the bunkhouses, closer to the city walls. When the two of them – Caden and Kyra – stood in front of the building that had been converted to Gilrich's prison, Kyra had to fight to control her nerves. What if she couldn't do this? What if he couldn't be helped?

Just as she touched the door, it swung open. Gilrich's guard stepped out, a scowl on his face.

"Hello, Leland," Caden said. "General Prait gave us permission to see him."

Leland didn't try to hide his disgust. "I don't know why we keep him alive," he snapped. "We're wasting valuable resources on a Cadaver. He barely eats. Most of the food rots – we've cut his rations to the bare minimum." He huffed in anger. "He's no better than an animal, more useless than a dog. Or a rat. I'd prefer a rat to his revolting body."

Kyra bit her tongue and turned away, anger festering in her stomach. She wanted to lash out at Leland but doing so would not help her. She needed friends, not enemies. Caden just rolled his eyes.

When no response came from either of them, Leland huffed and stomped away. "Useless waste of time," he mumbled.

Kyra shot a look of frustration to Caden, who shook his head in response. "Not worth it," he said.

"I know," she muttered. But oh, how she wished it was!

They found Gilrich chained to the back of the storehouse, hands bound behind his back, knees grinding into the floor. "They could have given him some comfort," Kyra murmured, his pitiful state pricking her heart. It hurt to see him this way – or at all. He did not look like the Gilrich she remembered. The pollution of his mind had marred his features. His spine curved painfully, and his fingers formed into claws behind his back. She knew if she could see his legs beneath the cloak they'd be twisted and misshapen. Even his face was distorted, with the lips pulled into a perpetual frown that carved deep lines into the skin. His nose flattened against the cheeks, and his eye appeared swollen, but Kyra knew they weren't, they were just reshaping themselves – the bones around them were reforming and elongating, pushing them past their sockets. If Gilrich continue to be a Cadaver, every part of him would soon be unrecognizable.

"Why is he chained this way? It's clearly causing him pain."

"He fights everything they do. They had to restrain him. If anybody gets close, he tries to hurt them."

Kyra's heart throbbed for her friend. She closed her eyes, breathing slowly to dispel the lump in her throat. She tried to picture the Gilrich she had once known. *Her* Gilrich had been excited about living. His blue eyes would light up with mischievous energy whenever he spoke. He had light brown hair that refused to be tamed, skin darkened by the sun, and wiry muscles that were capable of incredible tenderness when he wanted to show it. Yes, it was a Cadaver in front of her, but that Cadaver had once been her friend.

She settled her breaking heart then moved to crouch in front of him until her eyes were level with his. Gilrich hadn't moved when they entered, but now he raised his face to hers.

He glared at her. "You did this to me," he hissed. "You and those parasites you've betrayed the Master for." He struggled against the chains, fighting to move closer to her. His hands clenched and unclenched behind him, as if he wished to wrap them around her neck.

She nodded, swallowing against tears that threatened to flow. "I did this to you," she said. "I let the Malic'Uiel bring you to this. I'm sorry."

He spat in her face.

She merely nodded, wiping his saliva on her sleeve. "Gilrich," she said quietly. "Can you hear me?"

The Cadaver clamped his mouth shut, eyes oozing hatred.

"This isn't you, you know," she said. "This distorted body and polluted mind." She crept closer, reaching out to him. He snarled, snapping his teeth toward her outstretched fingers. She dropped them, but didn't move back. "Do you remember a time that isn't marred by anger?"

His eyes narrowed. "You have no right to speak to me," he said. "Your betrayal will not go unnoticed. You were warned the Malic'Uiel do not forgive."

"I was. They don't forgive, especially not me after what I've done. But Gilrich," she said, imploring, her hands twisting in front of her. "They wanted me to kill a child. A small boy, so innocent and perfect." She held his gaze, begging him to understand. "I couldn't do it. The child had done no wrong."

"The child was human," Gilrich snapped.

"You were once human, too," she said sadly. "And you will be again, if I have my way."

"You will never have your way!" he screamed, jerking against the chains that held him. The outburst was so sudden she fell back in surprise. The flesh on his wrist tore and viscous blood dripped to the floor as he attempted to reach her, face full of murderous rage. "They'll take you as they took the rest. Humanity must fall so the Malic'Uiel can rise!"

"Gilrich," Kyra cried, hands fluttering over him as if she could stop him. "Please. You're hurting yourself."

"Come on, Kyra," Caden said, tugging her away. "This will do no good. You can try another day."

Kyra allowed him to lead her away, but Gilrich's screams followed them as they left the building.

When the screams faded, she stopped, closing her eyes as she forced her pounding heart back into submission. "It's my fault he's in there," Kyra said. "My fault."

Caden took her hand and pulled her into an embrace. "Just because you put him in the Malic'Uiel cell, doesn't mean it's your fault."

"How is it not?" she mumbled against his chest.

"Shem kidnapped him," Caden said quietly. "He took him to the Malic'Uiel. Shem is to blame for what happened to Gilrich. Besides," he pulled back, cupping her face in his hands. "You were victim to them too, remember?"

"I knew what I was doing was wrong," she said, pushing away from Caden, wrapping her arms around her body while she shivered. "I knew it, and I shoved it down and did it anyway."

"We've all done things we knew were wrong," Caden said, his voice pained. "Maybe we should focus on forgiving ourselves rather than damning ourselves because of it."

"What have you ever done wrong?"

He sighed. "More than you know." He wouldn't hold her gaze as he said this, just looked beyond her, his mind obviously on something far away – probably in the past that he never fully shared with her.

He spoke sometimes as if he carried the weight of some terrible deed. She didn't know what it was, but she didn't believe he was capable of something as horrible as he seemed to think it was. She hoped he would eventually trust her enough to share his secrets with her.

He knew all her dark secrets; she wanted to know his.

CHAPTER 9

The Master of the Malic'Uiel ghosted through the streets of Pluvia, trailed by multiple Malic'Uiel while the Lord of Pluvia kept pace at his side. He'd come to this city less than a fortnight ago, choosing to reside here while he determined the best way to deal with the humans who had taken Tutis.

Pluvia was the closest city to Tutis, and thus afforded him the best opportunity to act, should he decide on a swift attack. However, he needed the girl, and he needed her alive. Attacking the city put her in too much danger. For the time being, she was what stood between the humans and him.

He glanced at the Malic'Uiel next to him. Lord Pluvia, a lesser Malic'Uiel than he, one given charge of this city, was rising through the ranks quickly due to his cunning and capacity to see what others did not.

"The phantom failed," Lord Pluvia said to the Master. "The report was delivered to me this morning. He was directed to bring her to you, and he has not done so."

The Master smiled, a cold, dead curve of his lips. "I expect Maliel no longer walks among the living."

Lord Pluvia's perfect steps hesitated for just a moment. "How is that possible?" he asked, regaining his composure and quickly matching the Master's stride.

"She is the Countess of Lumen. He could not withstand her light."

"But...why did you send him in there?"

The Master sent Lord Pluvia a glance of disapproval. "I sent him there to die."

Pluvia nodded, grasping to understand. "I...see," he mumbled.

"Lies do not become you," the Master said. He stopped walking and faced Pluvia directly, resting one hand on his shoulder. He squeezed just a little too hard, a subtle reminder to Lord Pluvia that this gesture was not that of a comrade. "Maliel was a failure to his kind. He let a human overcome him and take his power. He gave them an advantage and needed to die."

The Master's eyes bore into Lord Pluvia's, demanding he listen. "I need the people to fear the woman. If she shows any power beyond what they have already accepted, I expect that fear will come quickly. As she is the Countess of Lumen and her power has awakened, I knew, should Maliel find her, that she would destroy him using the light of Lumen."

"How did you know this?"

The Master studied Lord Pluvia for many moments. "I am no stranger to the power of Lumen. One cannot destroy his enemies if one does not understand them."

Lord Pluvia nodded, his faced grave; he did not understand, but it was much easier and safer for him to agree with the Master than to show weakness.

"Send the Phantoms in after the people," the Master commanded. "Have them avoid the girl, but take the others in the night. Make sure the people know she is to blame. We will rain fear on them from all sides until they release her back to her rightful Master."

Kyra hurried through the streets of Tutis, avoiding the eyes that watched her. Word of her run-in with Maliel had spread quickly in the days that followed, and the people were not responding well. She'd hoped they'd stabilize but that was not happening. With each retelling, the story had been embellished. She heard the whispers everywhere she went, whispers of a witch that could destroy with nothing more than a touch, a look. The people avoided meeting her eyes, as if they thought they'd drop to the cobblestone as a corpse whose life had been stolen by her glance.

She'd determined not to lock herself away for their fear, but that may have been the easier choice. Some of the people she passed watched her with curiosity, but most scurried away when she got near, naked fear evident in their eyes. None would hold her gaze, and a few were openly hostile. They scowled as she passed, their hands clenching into fists. Twice, she'd had to change course after small groups of men blocked her way. She had a feeling that beating her to death would make them happier than they'd care to admit.

Caden was right. Restoring General Prait's faith in her was easy compared to this. Even men she had known long before her capture now watched her with apprehension.

"I didn't kill Maliel," she muttered, hunching her body and wishing she could make herself smaller than she was. She knew she'd contributed to his death, but it bothered her more than she cared to admit that the citizens believed her a killer. "I didn't kill him. He took his own life," she muttered again, to nobody but herself.

She thought about attempting to see Gilrich, but decided against it. The guards were often belligerent in their fear, and Gilrich hated her. She tried not to let it hurt, but today, right now, it hurt. She couldn't face that in this moment.

Her shuffling steps brought her to the gate of the city. She stopped for a moment to study the large structure. Unable to escape the whispers and stares of those in Tutis, these walls that once promised safety now acted as the cage trapping her on display, exposing her for the world to belittle and hate.

The promise of freedom beckoned to her from beyond. She gestured to the guard. "Will you open the gate for me?" she asked. "Please?"

"No. Nobody is to go in or out unless the General has given word for them to do so."

"This place is a damn prison," she muttered, glaring at the guard. He looked away, refusing eye contact. She wasn't surprised.

Without another word, she spun on her heel and walked away. Rather than return to the smaller prison of her bunkhouse, she headed to the section of the city where the storehouses were located. Fewer people wandered there, which meant fewer eyes on her. She entered the area quietly, scanning for people she might need to avoid. Thankfully, the area was empty. She sighed as she slumped against the wall of a storehouse, sliding down until her butt hit the ground. She took the pendant Avalyn had given her and turned it over and over in her hands.

The mark of Lumen. Was it a blessing or a curse?

"What am I?" she asked the empty street. "A pawn in multiple players games? A servant to forces beyond my control?"

She fought down anger. All these people surrounding her, and none of them could see that she just wanted to be normal, that she wanted to help and support them. She hadn't asked for this power, but they couldn't see that. No, they regarded her as a plague.

She ripped the necklace off, dropping the pendant in her palm to study it closer. The design was simple. A rectangle encased three balls all equal distance apart. The balls on each side of the rectangle were surrounded by triangles, the tips of which touched each side of the circle in the middle. The balls seemed to float in their respective locations. Kyra held the pendant aloft, causing it to dangle in front of her. Hanging there, the long side of the rectangle was perfectly balanced, lining up with the horizon. She studied it for a moment, then reached up and plucked out the ball on the left side. The pendant immediately dropped to the right. Without the ball to balance it, the weight of the entire thing shifted. Carefully, she replaced the piece, restoring balance once more.

Avalyn had shown her this necklace, had spoken of the balance of the pendant and how it could be tipped in one direction or the other. How, Kyra did not know, since Avalyn had died many years ago when the Malic'Uiel had taken her. Died or become a Cadaver. Either way, Avalyn was gone. And yet, she'd spoken to Kyra while Kyra herself was trapped in their grasp – spoken to her and given her this necklace.

None of it made any sense. She'd spoken of the balance inside Kyra, and the forces of good and evil. It seemed to Kyra that only evil was left in this world. Maybe good could be found elsewhere, but in Spero, darkness reigned.

She sighed and replaced the pendant before resting her head against the wall, closing her eyes. It didn't matter. Avalyn spoke in metaphors, and Kyra did not know what balance she referred to, anyway.

Kyra's arms rested on her knees, which were tucked into her body. She'd spend months searching for answers to the very symbol that now hung around her neck. Instead, she'd found imprisonment and torture. Somewhere in the midst of that she'd glimpsed herself as well, but that vision had since clouded over. And after everything she'd experienced, she was no closer to finding the answers she had once sought.

"Maybe it's time to give up," she murmured. "To stop fighting the darkness and succumb." For a time, she had lived in apathy, choosing to feel nothing rather than feel the pain of losing everything. There was almost comfort in that.

The darkness caressed her, resting on her shoulders like a blanket.

Then her head snapped up.

The darkness lied.

There was no comfort in its cloak.

"Give up?" she hissed to herself. "What kind of fool are you?"

Angry shouts from the streets beyond ripped her out of her dark thoughts. She bolted up, rushing toward the noise. Gilrich's prison was near. Those screams could only be coming from there.

When she rounded the corner, she found a group of men huddled in front of the open door. From inside, she heard cries of pain and howls of anger. She rushed forward, shoving her way through the men that blocked her path.

"What are you doing?" she cried, storming through the door to find Leland and a group of soldiers beating Gilrich's shackled body. These men were supposed to be guarding him, not killing him!

Gilrich could not fight back. Instead, he screamed in anger and huddled in a ball on the floor as tears of pain poured down his cheeks. He looked like a black mass, covered as he was in his tattered cloak.

"Stop!" she cried, yanking on Leland's arm before he could throw his next punch. He shoved her away, continuing his murderous deed. "Leland!" she screamed, throwing herself into him with enough force to smash him into the wall. "You're going to kill him!"

He grabbed her by the neck, squeezing her windpipe as he glared. "You didn't see what he did. I tried to give him food, and he attacked me. He's dangerous." He threw her to the floor where she coughed, gasping for air. "Just like you."

Seething, Kyra launched herself at Leland, ripping her dagger from its sheath in the same moment.

From the doorway, voices bellowed, "Leland!"

Leland whirled, but not before her arm wound around his neck and her blade pressed against his throat. Blood trickled down his skin, staining the tunic below.

"I said leave him be," she said icily, her eyes blazing. "I will kill you as surely as you are willing to kill him." She glanced at the men pressed in the room. "Back away or I will shove this blade in his throat!"

The men obeyed, arms raised as they skittered backward to protect their leader. Leland's hands clenched in anger, but he did not move.

"Now," she said, lifting the blade to his chin. Her hand was steady, and her determination unwavering. "Get out."

Leland glared at her, body shaking in rage. "You will see us all dead," he hissed.

"I won't," she said. "I do not want blood on my hands. But you will not have him."

Knowing he'd lost, Leland stomped out of the building. His posse of soldiers followed, leaving Kyra alone with Gilrich. She dropped to her knees, the dagger shaking in her hands. "Are you okay?" she asked the Cadaver.

He didn't move, just moaned in pain.

She wiped the dagger on her tunic, returned it to its sheath, then crawled over to Gilrich, helping him sit against the wall. It looked uncomfortable with his hands bound behind him, but it was the best she could do.

"I'm sorry," she said, slumping next to him, hoping Gilrich was in there somewhere and could hear him.

He didn't take his eyes from her, and though she saw anger in them, beneath that she also saw pain. One eye was bleeding, and bruises blossomed on his cheeks and neck, disappearing beneath the cover of the cloak. She was lucky they hadn't killed him.

"What do you want with me?" he pleaded, his voice shaky and thick with sorrow. For the first time in her experience with Cadavers, she saw the humanity hidden deep inside.

"I want to help you," she said, gingerly reaching her hand out to rest on his shoulder. She peered into his eyes, searching for some sign of her friend. "I want you to find your way back." She spoke to him as if it were the Gilrich she'd once known. She had to see him as such; otherwise, she could only see a Cadaver and her beliefs would falter.

He grunted. "If you want to help me, then kill me." He spat a mass of saliva and blood onto the floor. "Your friend is gone," he said, the hard edge returning. "I'm what's left. So send me back to my master or end my existence. I'm here to serve them, not live in slavery to you."

"I once thought that, too," she said, "but now I know better." She stood and turned to go, pausing in the doorway. That brief glimpse of his humanity had given her hope. She thought about how giving up had seemed tempting for that moment earlier. But that temptation was long gone. If she, who had found her way back, had wanted to give up then certainly he, who was still in the Malic'Uiel's dark grip, would want nothing less.

He deserved her compassion as well as her grace.

"I'll be back, Gilrich. I know you can hear me somewhere in your mind. Know that I am fighting for you. I will see you again."

CHAPTER 10

Shem sat across the fire from Huiel, watching as he stuffed his face with the carcass of a rabbit. The animal had been cooked over a fire, and as the juices dribbled down Hueil's chin, Shem's stomach wrenched in disgust. He set his own rabbit aside. He'd eat when the disgrace in front of him was finished.

"Could you be anymore revolting?" Shem asked, throwing a stick across the fire. It knocked the rabbit from Huiel's hands.

Huiel glared at him, picking up the meat and brushing off leaves and dirt. "I expect I could try," he muttered, biting his teeth into the animal again. "What has you so irritated tonight?" Huiel demanded after ripping off another chunk of the rabbit and loudly chewing it until it was mush in his mouth.

"Nothing," Shem spat.

Huiel shrugged, continuing his attack on the animal in his hands.

Shem kept his dark gaze trained on Huiel. He needed him, unfortunately. But that didn't mean he liked him. He and Huiel had been comrades for a very long time. They'd been in the army together, led by the weakling General Prait who acted more like a father than a general. Shem had spent enough time with the army to know he preferred the world of the Malic'Uiel.

Both men looked up as a third man stomped into the clearing. A beheaded pheasant dangled from the man's waist, and his dagger was stained with blood.

"Found yourself some dinner, then, did ya, Anwill?" Huiel observed.

Anwill grunted, plopping next to the fire as he plucked the feathers from his kill.

"Clean off your dagger," Shem growled to him. "The weapon shows the character of the man. You wouldn't want us think you're a slob, would you, Anwill?"

"Guess not," Anwill mumbled. He left the pheasant in the dirt and went to the nearest tree, plucking off a few leaves which he then used to wipe the blade. They didn't do the job well – streaks of blood were left behind – but he shrugged, shoving it in its sheath. "There," he said, squatting by the fire again. "Happy?" He picked up the bird, yanking the feathers out and throwing them into a growing pile near the fire.

"Where's Falan?" Shem demanded, ignoring Anwill's comment.

"Finding his own bird, I expect." Anwill held the pheasant up, examining his work. Here and there a feather clung desperately to the creature, but for the most part it was clean. "Throw me that stick," he said to Hueil, gesturing to the stick Shem had thrown at him. "That should do for roasting."

Huiel tossed it to him, and he shoved it in the open cavity of the bird's neck. A few minutes later the smell of roasting pheasant filled the air. Anwill settled himself in front of the fire, anticipation lighting up his features. It had been far too many days since they'd had meat in their diet. This was a welcome change for them.

"When's he coming back?" Shem asked.

Anwill glanced up at him in confusion. "Who?"

"Your brother!"

"Oh," Anwill said, turning the bird on the stick. He pulled it away from the heat, checking its progress. A moment later he shoved it back in the flames. "I dunno," he said, finally answering Shem's question. "He's slower than me. Can't hunt as good as I can. It could be a while."

Shem grunted, folding his arms across his chest. "He better hurry," he muttered. "We've got things to do."

Huiel glanced up at Shem. "Plans are changing?" he asked.

Shem nodded. "I've come up with a new plan for us."

Both men straightened, watching Shem intently now. "What is it?" Anwill asked.

Shem smiled in grim satisfaction. "Kidnapping, since it worked so well last time."

Huiel grunted then went back to his meal. This was why Shem kept him around. He never questioned.

When they'd been in General Prait's camp, the two of them had taken Gilrich and used him as a bargaining chip to secure their safety with the Malic'uiel. Their desertion from the army had taken some time in coming. It wasn't until Kyra came up with – and General Prait executed – a plan to attack the Malic'Uiel cities that Shem decided to leave. The plan had left his brother dead, a death which dissolved the last shred of Shem's loyalty to humanity.

He preferred the world of the Malic"Uiel.

Swearing from the far side of the camp distracted the three of them, and they all turned to find Falan pushing his way through the trees. "Damn limbs," he growled. "So thick here ya can't even take a step without trippin' over them." He pushed past the final leafy barrier, snapping the branch in the process. "What?" he demanded when he saw them all looking at him.

"Just waiting for you," Shem said calmly. "Are you about done?"

"Yeah," he mumbled, seating himself next to Anwill. He pulled his own pheasant out of his bag and began plucking its feathers, adding them to Anwill's pile.

"So who are we kidnapping?" Huiel said, turning his attention back to Shem.

Falan's hands froze over the bird; a group of feathers fluttered to the ground. "We're kidnappin' someone?"

"Yes," Shem answered. "A woman that the Malic'Uiel have been after for some time, according to the whispers I've been hearing from both marauders and Phantoms." *Marauders who he and his group had delivered to the Malic'Uiel.*

Marauders wandered freely, bringing victims to the Phantoms in a tentative truce to protect their own freedom, a truce Shem was doing his best to break. He wanted nothing more than to see humanity wiped out, or to see himself ruling those that remained.

"Who is the woman?" Huiel asked again.

Shem couldn't stop the grin from breaking on his face. "Kyra. The Malic'Uiel want her. They even sent Maliel in to get her, but he never returned. He's probably dead."

Huiel scratched his stomach, then leaned forward to rest his elbows on his knees. "Kyra always has that watchdog Caden around. You know what he can do."

"Of course I do. We have to lure her away from him."

"Where is this Kyra?" Anwill interjected. "She wanderin' around like the rest of the free world?"

"No," Shem said. "She's in Tutis."

Falan cocked his head to the side. "You mean, she's in that city with the soldiers?"

Shem nodded.

"How we s'posed to get her outta there?" Falan asked. "She's surrounded by an army!"

Shem glared at him. "Like I said," he answered. "We lure her out. One of you two idiots are going in. The army is always looking for new recruits."

Anwill and Falan exchanged glances.

"Don't worry," Shem said. "They know who me and Hueil are, but they'll accept you easily. Just tell them you're looking to fight the Malic'Uiel."

"What's in it for us?" Anwil asked. "You're askin' a lot."

"Power," Shem said darkly. "If you want more power than anyone, do what nobody else will do. The Malic'Uiel want her. We give her to them, stay in their good graces, and we gain power. It's very simple."

"Fine," Anwill muttered, acting not quite convinced, but when his lips curved in a smile, Shem knew he was won over. "We'll be your recruits."

Shem grunted, poking the fire with a stick and stirring it into life. He saw himself as Caden, manipulating fire with his thoughts. When they succeeded with this, he'd be one step closer to having that power.

CHAPTER 11

The morning sun had just peaked over the horizon as Kyra rounded the corner and marched down the street to Gilrich's prison. She'd spent a lot of time over the past couple of days thinking about their last exchange and, by damn, she wasn't going to sit here and pretend like that Cadaver had any say in whether or not Gilrich found his way back. She reached the makeshift prison and briefly noted that the guard was nowhere to be seen.

Good.

Leland had been reprimanded by General Prait for attacking the Cadaver, though his punishment had been, in her opinion, too light. He'd received barely more than a slap on the wrist – a change of assignment to a different area of the city. The General and most in his council believed Leland's lies about Gilrich's aggression.

Kyra did not.

He was chained so thoroughly he could not have made any such attack. Today, it looked as if Gilrich's guard had either been replaced or removed. She wasn't sure which. No other men were near, nor were there any on the street. Strange, but fortunate for her.

Kyra inched the door open and slipped inside. She and Gilrich were going to have a chat today.

She stopped two steps in. "Who are you?" she demanded.

A young woman rose with some effort. She'd been kneeling in front of Gilrich. When the woman faced Kyra her tunic revealed a rounded stomach, which the woman further accented by placing her hand just on top.

"My name is Dalia," she said, holding Kyra's gaze.

"Where are the guards?"

"They'll be here soon. I requested they bring me more water."

It was then that Kyra noticed the items in the room. To the right of the woman sat a small bowl of water with a rag flopped over the side. Next to the bowl a pile of clean rags waited.

"What are you doing?" Kyra demanded

Dalia glanced at the Cadaver behind her. He watched the exchange in silence. Then she straightened her shoulders, holding her head high in defiance.

"Tending to his wounds," she said. "And if you're here to stop me, just know it will do no good. I will be back, even if I have to come at midnight."

Kyra shook her head, backing down as gratitude pricked her chest. "I'm not here to stop you," she said. She crossed the room to Dalia. "How is he? Leland and his men hurt him terribly."

Dalia knelt next to Gilrich again, wringing out the rag before gently dabbing his face. He did not resist her efforts, but neither did he respond. "His body will heal," Dalia said. "These Cadaver bodies react to injury differently than ours. I was worried he had broken bones, but that doesn't seem to be the case. As far as I can tell he can move his body just fine – or he would be able to, without these chains." She gestured to the shackles. "I'd like to see them come off."

"As would I," Kyra said. "But General Prait will never agree to that."

Dalia sighed. "I know."

The guard returned shortly after with a small bucket of warm water. He set it on the floor next to Dalia's other supplies, then turned and smiled at Kyra.

"We haven't met," he said, holding out his hand. "I'm Bronson."

Kyra blinked in surprise, hesitating for a moment. First Dalia, now Bronson, treating her like she wasn't a plague. Was he serious? His smile seemed genuine. Slowly, she put out her hand. "Kyra."

He chuckled. "I know. Don't take this the wrong way, but I knew you before the Malic'uiel took you."

Kyra's eyes widened. "You were with the army in the Adeo Mountains?"

"Yes."

"But we never met."

He grinned. "I was shy, and a little intimidated by women."

Kyra nearly choked. Sometimes, focused as she was on being a soldier and saving the world, she forgot she was a woman. "Well," she finally answered. "I'm happy to meet you." She held his hand a little longer than necessary, stressing her point. "Truly. Thank you for being kind."

His eyes met and held hers. "You deserve some kindness."

His words nearly did her in; floodgates that would release too many tears threatened to open. She swallowed hard, glancing away before he broke through her defenses. "Thank you," she whispered.

Sensing her discomfort, he turned to Dalia. "Let me know if you need anything else," he said before leaving the room and closing the door behind him.

Dalia continued her ministrations while Kyra watched. "Bronson is a good man," she said. "It's good to have him here with Gilrich."

"Yes," Kyra murmured, trusting Dalia's judgment though she barely knew her.

After Dalia cleaned and dressed Gilrich's wounds, she squeezed out the rags then poured all the water from the small bowl into the bucket. Before she stood, she placed her hand on Gilrich's cheek and used her thumb to stroke the distorted bones. He didn't pull away or fight the touch. He simply held her gaze, and in the pool of his eyes Kyra saw all she needed.

"I'll be back," Dalia said, smiling at the Cadaver. That moment between them changed Kyra's mind. Instead of speaking to Gilrich, she wanted to talk to Dalia.

The two of them left the building together.

"Thank you, Bronson," Dalia said as they passed him.

"Anytime."

Kyra simply smiled at him, but his eyes held hers, again, and her grateful heart beat faster. Here was one man who did not fear her. Relief flooded her body.

Dalia had started up the street while Kyra's thoughts had been on Bronson. Kyra hurried to catch up now. "How long have you been coming here?" she asked when she fell in step behind her.

"I came to see him one day out of curiosity," Dalia said. She kept her hand on her stomach as she walked, caressing the bump but unaware that she did so. "Or anger. Part of me wanted to see him hurt. But when I got here and saw him in that pitiful state, I couldn't be angry. I sat here for hours that day, listening while he screamed at the guards, abusing them with his words."

She chuckled. "Many of them were not unwarranted. They are not kind to him."

"He's a Cadaver," Kyra said. "They see nothing else."

"I know. But I saw something else that day after the guards eventually got fed up and left him alone. I slipped into the storehouse; he didn't register my presence – I still don't think he knew I was there. He was crying. Not wailing or sobbing, just crying. He looked so...broken," she said. "And then I realize that somewhere in that body there was a human, a perfectly good man trapped in darkness."

"There is," Kyra said. "A very good man."

Dalia glanced at Kyra, pity marring her features. "He's your friend, isn't he?" she asked.

"Yes." She sighed. "Or he was. One of the few."

The women continued their stroll past storehouses and into the residential district. The silence stretched on, but it was comfortable. Kyra realized it was the first time since coming to Tutis that she didn't feel like an aberration.

"When is your child due?" Kyra asked.

Dalia smiled. "I am in my sixth month."

"Are you excited?"

"I am," Dalia said. "And saddened. The child will be born without a father. But my baby will also be free, and that means the world to me."

"The father died in the battle?"

"Yes."

"I'm sorry."

Dalia turned and offered a half smile to Kyra. "He was my husband, and will be honored in my child's memory," she said. "He died giving our baby freedom. There is no greater cause than that."

Kyra sucked in a harsh breath, her steps faltering, as the words barreled into her chest. Her own father had been lost ensuring her freedom. She remembered the night Em was taken as if it had happened the night before. It should have been her, but he'd stepped in, and the Phantom had stolen him instead. She'd always hated that he'd given himself up for her. The guilt stayed close, like a badge on her heart, but with Dalia's words she saw a different view. She'd never considered that he might have been glad to do it if it meant she would remain free.

Dalia had stopped walking and waited for Kyra. "You okay?" she asked.

"Sorry," Kyra mumbled. "Yes, I'm fine."

The women fell in step together once more and continued through the city. Dalia ignored the stares and hostility of the others incredibly well. Kyra...tried. She didn't do very well. Those who were the most hostile received a cold glare back, right in their vicious little eyes. A burst of satisfaction flared every time they broke her gaze.

"Dalia," Kyra asked, turning her full attention to the woman at her side. "Why are you helping Gilrich? Especially after you've been enslaved by them. I assume you are one of those freed from the Citadel, and I know the treatment most of you receive from the Cadavers."

"I am one of those freed," Dalia said. "And yes, a Cadaver did guard my cell while the Malic'Uiel determined my fate. This child," she tapped her stomach. "Was not a child by free choice. But I wasn't willing to watch my husband suffer because I wouldn't bear a child, and neither was he willing to watch me. Coercion is a powerful tool."

"Yes," Kyra agreed. Dalia's words stirred up memories of her time with the Malic'Uiel. For a season she had been given the task of watching over the women and children in the catacombs. The men had been locked deep in the underground maze, while their wives were kept in rooms together to raise their children. When Dalia said she was coerced into giving life to the child, she was right.

When the Malic'Uiel had first set up their underground dungeons, they'd done so intending to enslave a portion of humanity and force them to continue producing the slaves that would eventually become with Cadavers or breeders. During the initial onslaught, most people were thrown in the cells surrounding the Citadel, above ground, where the Malic'uiel would break down their minds until they chose the life of a Cadaver. But some were sent to the underground dungeons.

Men who'd willingly joined the Malic'Uiel were initially allowed to maintain their humanity; they were tasked with forcing pregnancy on the women. The Malic'Uiel learned quickly that rape did not go over well.

The women fought back, and they fought back hard. Some of the men were killed, other brutally maimed. The women coordinated and planned their methods of attack, so when they were brought to these monsters of men, they were prepared.

Eventually, the men refused their task.

It was then that the Malic'Uiel found that love could be used for their gain. They found and enslaved married or betrothed couples. First, they separated them, breaking their physical bond but ensuring the emotional connection remained. Then, they'd offer them physical intimacy in exchange for the promise of a child.

The couples refused. None would bring a child into slavery. After that failure, the Malic'Uiel stooped to their greatest weapon: torture. They brought the women to their lovers, chained them in the same dungeon, and forced them to watch while the lovers were tortured. Sometimes they'd chain the men and torture the women. In all cases, the partner had to watch, had to hear the cries of agony as their lover's bodies were brought to the brink of the physical pain they could endure.

Some couples never gave in. They were tortured until death finally gave them relief. Most could not bear it that long. The coercion was effective. In exchange for their lover's physical well-being, the couples agreed to a life of slavery for themselves and to bear children into the same servitude.

It was a terrible choice to make.

Guilt pooled in Kyra's stomach; as a Cadaver she'd grown to love one particular child. He'd helped her find her light. But before that she'd kept the women and children enslaved and turned a blind eye to the horrors they were forced to endure.

It was Dalia's hand on her arm that pulled her back to the present. "Are you all right?"

"Yes. Forgive me." *Forgive me for being complicit in your torment. Forgive me for being among the number that kept you enslaved. Forgive me for being part of something that hurt you so terribly.* She said none of what she needed to say. Instead, she asked, "Why do you help Gilrich?"

Dalia stopped walking and pointed forward. "Look," she said.

Kyra did as directed and saw a garden that the women had planted. Green shoots stood out in stark contrast to the dark soil.

"We were able to bring it back to life," Dalia said. "The soil we thought was dead was only ruined on the surface. When we removed that soil, we found rich, healthy ground beneath." She stepped to the edge of the garden and sunk to her knees, running the dirt through her fingers. "I believe Gilrich is the same," she said. "I've heard rumors that you are going to try to bring him back. After I saw him crying that day, I saw that was possible. So, I help him because I believe that beneath the dead exterior is a rich, healthy interior." She abruptly stood and gripped Kyra's hands. "Please bring him back," she said. "If we can save him, we can save others."

Kyra nodded, gratitude welling inside her. Dalia was the first in the city to see the possibilities Kyra saw. "I will bring him back," she promised.

Dalia smiled and released her grip. "I know you will. Take courage, Kyra, for there are those of us in the city that see good in what you do. I know you are feared by many, but you do have allies among us."

"Thank you," Kyra whispered.

Dalia squeezed Kyra's hand again before stepping into the garden, stooping to examine the growing plants.

When Kyra left, she left with peace. There were others that supported her cause, people who believed in her theories. That was more than she'd ever thought possible.

Dalia had given her hope.

CHAPTER 12

S hem and his comrades kicked dirt over the pitiful fire they'd warmed their breakfast over.
They weren't far from Tutis; they'd see the city
before midday if they maintained an easy pace.
Now, with the sun rising, it was time to move on and
set their plan in action.

When they reached the outskirts of the city, Shem
held up his hand, stopping the group. Little activity
was visible from inside the tree line. The area in front
of the city was fortified with angled spikes that protruded from the ground near the wall, waiting for a
victim. In front of those spikes, nothing but dirt
blocked their way. The few sentries atop the walls
looked sleepy and bored. Shem grunted. "Why don't
they just attack this thing and end it?" he muttered.
"It's not like the Malic'Uiel can't take the city."

Anwill scrunched his nose as he studied the city.
"Maybe there's more happenin' here than we know."

"Hah!" Shem guffawed. "I spent more time with this
sad excuse for an army than I'd care to admit. Believe

me, there's nothing more in there than terrified humans who know their end is coming."

Anwill shrugged. "Guess we'll find out," he said. He straightened his tunic, checking to see that his dagger was in place. "So let me get this straight before I go on and mess everythin' up. I'm s'posed to pretend to be a straggler, somebody lookin' to join and fight?"

"Yes," Shem said. "It's simple enough. They trust humans that come willingly to join the 'cause.'" He rolled his eyes at the sheer stupidity of it all. "You'll get in easy. From there, you have to be my eyes and ears in the city. I want to know all their habits and patterns. I want to know the changing of the guard, what time the city wakes, where General Prait resides – all of it. And everything you can tell me about Kyra. Befriend her if you can. I'm counting on you to find a way for me to get her out."

Anwill dipped his head once in acknowledgment. "Got it," he said. "Eyes and ears. Spy. Get the girl."

"We'll be back in a week, Anwill," Shem said. "Get something useful for me before then."

"I will." He flashed a smile at his brother. "Wish me luck, Falan." Squaring his shoulders, he stepped beyond the tree line toward the city gate. He kept his eyes on the wall, just in case one of the sentries decided he was a good target. His feet made it less than ten paces when they suddenly fell out from under him. Screaming, he flailed, trying to grab hold of anything to keep himself upright. His scream cut short when he crashed into the ground at the bottom of a deep hole.

He groaned, shaking dust out of his hair while he shoved himself back to his feet. "What in the world was that?" he muttered. He glanced up, seeing blue sky above him. To his right and left the hole extended along both sides, then curved and disappeared. This was a trench, and it appeared to encircle the entire city.

"By all that's good and holy..." He swore then jumped, reaching for the top of the trench. "Hey!" he called. "Get me out!" His hands clawed at the dirt at least five hand-spans below the top of the hole. He couldn't reach any higher than that and slid back in. "I can't get to the army if I'm stuck in a hole!" he screeched. His efforts were useless, and he flopped against the dirt wall in disgust. "Shoulda seen that comin'," he said. "I'd have dug holes, too, if it kept the Malic'Uiel away." He tipped his head back, cupping his hands around his mouth. "Hey!" he cried again. 'Get me out!"

From the top of the wall, two sentries stopped their pacing and peered toward the gaping hole. "There's someone in our trap!" they called down to the men at the gate. "Hurry and get the General!"

One of the men below dashed away to find General Prait. Before long, the general, with Bronson at his side, came to the gate. Bronson stayed below while General Prait climbed up the wall to join the sentries.

He saw the opening to the hole immediately. "Did you see it fall in?" he asked the sentry nearest him.

"I did," the man said. "*It* is a *he*. He came out from the trees pretty intent on getting here. The trench stopped him. Do you think we should let him out?"

"I think we should go see what we've caught," General Prait said. He grinned, clapping the soldier on the back. "I, for one, am glad to know our traps work."

The general hurried down the steps, gesturing for his soldiers to open the gate as he reached the bottom. Bronson and two others were recruited to follow him outside, just in case they'd caught an enemy instead of a friend.

When the three of them reached the pit, they peered down into the hole. Staring back was a short, squat man with thinning hair and bad teeth. He stood with his hands on his hips, glaring up at them. "I came here to join an army, but I'm thinkin' of leaving' now. Don't really like bein' somebody's pet."

General Prait chuckled. "Believe me, you are no pet. We'll get you out of there. Bronson, throw down a rope."

Bronson did as requested. The heavy fibers knocked Anwill on the head and he growled. "Careful," he said, gripping the rope to pull himself up while Bronson and another soldier held the other end, bracing themselves to hold his weight.

When he reached the top, he huffed, "Whew!" he said. "Didn't expect to fall in a trap."

"They're not for humans," General Prait said. "They're meant for Cadavers. We haven't had a new recruit in a while. Honestly, I didn't think there were any left."

Anwill grunted, sticking out his hand. "I'm Anwill," he said. "And I heard about ya so I came to help ya fight."

The General gripped his hand. "General Prait." He waved toward the others. "These men are Bronson and Noelle. Porter is the other back that way." He nodded in the third soldier's direction. "We're glad to have you, Anwill."

As they headed back toward the gates, General Prait asked, "Have you seen any other humans recently? Any more ready to fight?"

"Not that I recall, General," Anwill said. "I've been alone for a while." He glanced back at the trees, sending his comrades a farewell smile. He'd made it, just as Shem said he would.

Peering out from the trees, Shem waited until the soldiers had made their way into the city before he tapped Huiel and Falan on the shoulders, beckoning for them to follow him into the forest. "We have one week before we have to be back here," he said. "That gives us time to set things up for ourselves." He grinned at his companions. "I think we can make it safe for us to wander in any part of Spero. The Malic'Uiel need us, and they don't even know it."

Huiel played with the hilt of his dagger, stroking the smooth metal. "How do they need us, Shem?" he asked.

"Do you think we would be setting a trap for Kyra if a Phantom could do the job?"

"I hadn't thought about it," Huiel said. "You were part of the army. It made sense to me."

"Of course, you didn't think about it," Shem snapped. "You just follow. You've never thought about anything."

Huiel's face darkened and anger flashed across his features, but he swallowed it down.

"They need us," Shem said again. "And if they don't now, they're going to. I'm going to make sure of it." He shoved through the trees, picking up his pace. "Come on," he said. "We've a plan to put into action."

CHAPTER 13

T he wind howled through the streets of Tutis, rattling the petrified branches of dead trees – skeletal reminders of the city's previous occupants. Somewhere behind the thick blanket of clouds the moon rose, but inside the city was dark. The guards at the gate huddled by small fires that struggled to stay lit. Those stationed on the walls hunkered down with heads tucked into their chests. Rough blankets wrapped around their bodies were the only barrier they had against the foul weather. The rest of the inhabitants had taken refuge in the bunkhouses, unwilling to step into the wind or brave the dark streets.

Kyra paced the floor in her bunkhouse, stomping across the room.

Each bunkhouse was one small room with a door on the front, window on the back, and bare walls on each side. Tonight, those walls encroached on Kyra like a living, breathing monster.

From his cot, Caden watched her movements. She reached the far side of the building then whipped around, heading toward the door only to whirl around in the other direction when she came to it. A candle burned near the door, offering some light to the space, but it wasn't much. A second candle rested on the floor in the corner opposite the door. They painted shadows on the walls that danced and moved, as if the wood itself was alive.

"It's too small," Kyra muttered, facing the far wall again. "Too small." Her hands fluttered about, massaging above her chest in nervous motion. She whirled back toward the door, forcing herself to breathe as she stomped.

"What's the matter, Kyra?" Caden asked.

She shook her head, keeping up her vigil across the room. "I don't know," she said. "Nothing. But...everything. I feel like I need to run. There's something dark about, and I can't tell if it's in me or out there." She reached the far wall again, groaning as she turned once more.

When she passed his cot, Caden pushed off it, grabbing her wrist and stopping her movement. "Kyra," he said, stepping closer to her and taking her other hand.

Her eyes darted between him and the door.

"Hey," he said, lifting her chin up until her eyes met his. "What's going on?"

"I don't know," she whispered. "Something feels wrong, but I don't know what it is, and I don't know why." She glanced toward the door again.

"You're itching to get out of here, aren't you?"

"Maybe." She met his gaze, imploring. "Do you ever feel like you just need to escape? Like things were better when you had the freedom to roam the forests and hills – when your survival depended only on your skills, and you weren't worried about protecting hundreds of people?"

"You don't have to protect them," he said. "General Prait is in charge. He's got guards and lookouts. We're as safe as we can be in this city."

"I know," she said. She pulled her hands away from his and wrapped her arms around her chest. "But you didn't answer my question."

He sighed. "Sometimes, yes. It seems like an easier life. But we both know it wouldn't be. We'd end up as Cadavers, minds and souls sucked away to serve them."

She shuddered.

"Come on," Caden said, tugging her arm and leading her to sit on the cot. "Sit down. Let yourself relax." He sat next to her, rubbing circles on her back. She wasn't sure if the action comforted her or agitated her even more, but she tried to follow his advice.

After a few minutes her nerves had settled down a bit, but there was a pit in her stomach that ached. She groaned, leaning forward and dropping her head on her knees. "I hate the night," she murmured.

Caden chuckled. "I don't blame you." He'd gone from rubbing circles on her back to letting his fingers trail up and down her spine.

"That feels nice," she mumbled into her knees.

"Good," Caden said.

When a few more minutes had passed Kyra straightened again, taking in one more deep, calming breath. "I'm okay now," she said. "Thank you."

Caden nodded, dropping his hand to rest on the cot behind her.

"But something is wrong," Kyra said. "Some darkness comes into the city."

"Could it just be the night? It's eerie as it is. And the dark isn't kind anymore."

She shook her head. "No. There's something out there." Her gaze was trained on the door, as if she could see right through it.

"How can you be sure?" Caden asked

"Can't you feel it?"

He paused for a moment, but then shook his head. "No."

"I can."

She rose, pulling him off the cot with her as she went to the door. Before she opened it, she stopped. "I can go alone and find out what it is," she said. "But I'd rather you come with me."

He smiled, not letting go of her hand. "I'll come with you."

She nodded then pulled the door open. The wind blew into the bunkhouse, extinguishing the candles and plunging the room into darkness.

"I hate the night," she muttered again before leaving the relative comfort of the building. In the dark, Kyra could just make out the bunkhouses on either side of her, then the darkened areas beyond them where more of the structures stood. She could see little else.

Caden squeezed her hand. "I'm right here," he said.

"I know." She mirrored his action, letting him know it meant something to her.

They left the bunkhouses and headed in the direction of the Citadel. The wind yanked at Kyra's hair, whipping it into her face. She cursed and pulled at the errant strands, holding them in a tail behind her head. "I hate the wind, too," she muttered.

Caden chuckled. "What else do you hate tonight?"

She stuck out her tongue, but he didn't see it in the dark. "Everything."

He laughed out loud at that, but the wind carried the sound away.

As they neared the Citadel the howling in the wind changed, becoming a scream that carried from the distance.

"What is that?" Kyra said.

"It's just the wind. It's getting stronger. We're about to get soaked."

"It's not the wind," Kyra said, following the sound. For a moment it disappeared, drowned out by the howling, but then it carried to them again.

"Come on!" Kyra cried, running toward the sound. As they got closer the scream got louder, but then it stopped and began coming from another direction. Kyra whirled in the new direction, rushing to find the source. But then the scream started from the original direction, and a third joined the others. Caden faltered for a moment when he heard the screams, too.

"What is it?" he cried, racing toward the second scream and ignoring the other two.

"I don't know." She kept pace next to him, a rising sense of desperation and fear clawing at her chest.

The second scream picked up in strength as they neared the bunkhouses on the edge of the cell complex. "In there," Kyra said, charging toward the house that faced the opening to the Citadel. Caden leapt forward, following her lead. She shoved open the door with Caden on her heels, a ball of fire held aloft in his hand. The fire cast light into the bunkhouse.

"No!" Kyra screamed, throwing herself into the middle of the room. There, a Phantom stood. He looked almost human, but his skin was as pale as a corpse, and his feet did not touch the ground. Dark hair framed the thin face, falling to the side of his tight cheekbones. He hovered a hand-span above the wooden floor, a living apparition of death. He grinned; one hand gripped the neck of the man that resided in the bunkhouse. The other gestured to the man's wife, who wailed from the cot she was slumped on. Blood soaked her left arm, which hung limp at her side.

Kyra assessed the situation in the same amount of time it took to take a breath, then threw herself at the Phantom. He easily shoved Kyra aside, laughing. She was wasted no time attacking again, ripping her dagger from its sheath, while Caden launched fireball after fireball at the demon. Kyra was about to strike again when the Phantom's fingers flicked out. Caden's fire blazed into Kyra's weapon. Searing pain kissed her palm as the glowing hilt melted the flesh; the dagger clattered to the floor. The Phantom then whipped the fire into a ball, sending it to hover over the woman on the cot.

Kyra and Caden both froze. The Phantom smiled in satisfaction. "Don't come near me," he said.

Kyra glared at him. "Let them go."

He shook his head, then jerked toward Caden, who'd taken a careful step toward him, hands on his dagger. "Don't even think about it," he hissed. "Or I'll have to kill her." His jaw jerked toward the woman, whose sobs of pain filled the room. "This one," he said, patting the cheek of the man trapped in his grip. "He's already mine."

Caden clenched his jaw, forcing his arms to stay at his side.

"It isn't any fun when you're not allowed to manipulate fire, is it?" the Phantom crowed. Then he shifted his attention back to Kyra. "I wanted you to find me," he said. "It's nice to put a face to the name." He bowed slightly in mock respect. "I am Rajak. I broke the woman's arm." He chuckled. "Mangled it, more like. And I've been holding onto her husband just waiting for you. What woman isn't going to shriek when her arm is in that condition?"

"You could have found me," Kyra said. "Instead of hurting her."

Rajak smirked. "It's more fun this way." Then his face hardened. "I want to know how you killed Maliel."

"I didn't kill Maliel," Kyra said. "He killed himself." She glanced at the woman on the cot. The woman suffered, but she reached her good arm out to her husband, as if she could hold him and keep him with her. Kyra's heart ached. How could she help him?

Rajak scoffed. "No Phantom willingly kills himself. Why would we? We have power over all but the Malic'Uiel." His face darkened and he dipped the fire closer to the woman. She cried out as flames reached for her flesh. "I'll get my answer one way or another," he threatened. "I want to know how you did it."

"I touched him. That's all I did." She held out her hand to Rajak. The palm glowed slightly. "The light engulfed him."

Rajak stared at her, a touch of fear and respect in his eyes. A moment later both vanished and his lips curled back in derision. "You're learning to manipulate the elements," he said. "I guess your soul must be black after all."

Kyra ground her teeth but let the comment roll off her. Black heart, black soul – what did it matter if she didn't hurt people with it? "Let the man go," she said. Rajak shook his head. "I don't think I will."

In that instant, he dropped the fire on the woman, engulfing her body in flames. At the same moment, his grip around the man tightened and they both began to blur. The woman's shrieks tore through the building into the night as the fire devoured her flesh. Kyra lunged for Rajak. Instead, she passed through his body as it disappeared.

Rajak's fading laugh mingled with the cries of the burning woman.

"Save her!" Kyra screamed to Caden. The woman's shrieks grew louder as the flames burned hotter.

"I'm trying!" he cried. He pulled the fire from her body, absorbing it into his own before placing his hands on her melted flesh. He pulled back in less than a minute, defeated, hunched over, mouth a thin line as he fought back tears. "The damage is too great," he said. "I can't heal her."

The woman convulsed on the cot. The fire was gone, and her body cool to the touch, but her eyes rolled back in her head; bits of charred hair clung to her scalp.

Kyra dropped to her knees near the cot. "I'm so sorry," she said.

The woman did not respond. Instead, her body went still and she released her last breath.

"No," Kyra whispered. Her hands fluttered over the woman's body, searching for somewhere to touch that wasn't covered in melted flesh. There was nothing. Instead, she buried her face in her hands, choking on her own sobs. She'd tried and failed to save them both.

Caden knelt next to Kyra, holding her while she cried.

"I could have saved him," she sobbed. "If I had only touched the Phantom."

"I couldn't save her either," Caden said quietly. "I couldn't get the fire off. We are both responsible."

Suddenly, Kyra's head shot up. "There were others," she gasped, tearing for the door. "Other screams. Other people attacked tonight!" She raced through the city, ignoring the wind that ripped at her hair and yanked at her clothes. There were other victims, but how many, and what fate had they suffered?

The dark streets did not betray the Phantoms. They remained as if nothing had happened. But Kyra knew better. She listened intently, straining to hear above the wind as she ran. Finally, she heard the sound of someone crying. She jerked toward it, ripping another door open in the night. Caden's fire filled the place with light. On the floor a young man, hardly more than a boy, knelt, clutching a dagger in one hand while the other arm hung at his side, useless and covered in blood.

"What happened?" Kyra gasped.

The man turned to her, his face streaked with tears. "It came in the night," he said, his voice raspy and broken. "I woke...I thought my arm was being ripped off. There was a Phantom." He sucked in a shaky breath. "He...had my bunkmate. He waited, the Phantom did, just...staring at the door." The boy tried to come to his feet but groaned and slumped back down. "I tried to stop him." His voice was so quiet Kyra had to strain to hear. "He took Axil with him...took him to the Malic'Uiel, I suspect."

Kyra held back expletives as anger roiled in her stomach. "Caden can help your arm," she finally said. It was all she could say. She wanted to scream, to chase the monster down and rip him apart herself.

The boy glared at her, seeming to realize now who spoke to him. "This is your fault," he said. "You brought them here."

Stunned, Kyra just gaped at him.

"Shut up," Caden snapped. "This isn't her fault any more than it is mine or yours."

Kyra just sighed, "Let it go, Caden. He's hurt and scared. He has no one else to blame. Just heal him so we can go."

Caden head bobbed once, but his jaw was clenched tight. He gestured to the cot. "Sit down."

The boy obeyed, but his eyes were clouded in fear. "It's going to hurt," he told the boy. "But I will make it so it heals properly. And then Kyra and I will leave, and you can rethink the stupidity of your last statement."

The boy clamped his jaw shut, closing his eyes and gritting his teeth while Caden pulsed his magic into the damaged flesh of his arm. A stiffening of his body was the only response to the pain. After a few minutes had passed, Caden gently let the arm go to rest on the cot. "It still needs to heal. You'll want to have Dr. Bron bandage it up. But when it's fully healed you won't have any lasting damage."

The boy merely nodded.

Caden turned back to Kyra, his frustration evident.

"There were more than these two," she said. "We have to find the others, have to let General Prait know."

"Let's go."

The two of them hurried to General Prait's quarters, where they woke him and filled him in on what they'd seen. Then they spent the rest of the night searching every bunkhouse and finding all those that had been visited by a Phantom. In every case, they found the same situation: one person was taken, while one was left behind with a mangled arm or a crushed leg.

Caden healed those that he could, but as the night progressed, exhaustion set in and he was forced to stop.

When the sun peeked over the mountains, they met again with General Prait.

"How many?" he asked.

"Twenty-seven," Caden answered.

General Prait groaned, yanking his fingers through unkempt hair. "It was an organized attack. And we have no guarantees it won't happen again tomorrow and every day following until the rest of humanity is gone."

"What do we do, General?" Kyra asked.

"I don't know." His eyes shot to Caden. "Do they have a weakness that we don't know about? Is there any way we can stop them?"

Caden licked his tongue over dry lips, but his eyes were focused on Kyra and his face was pensive. "Maybe," he said slowly.

General Prait followed his gaze. "Kyra?" He arched one brow, looking to Caden for confirmation.

"Yes," Caden said. He choked on the next word as it left his mouth. "Kyra."

Kyra listened to the exchange, trying to ignore the pit in her stomach. She clamped her hands together to stop them from shaking. Of course, she was their weakness. They wanted her. She closed her eyes, shutting off the world and taking deep breaths. *You're safe in Tutis*, she told herself. *The Malic'Uiel are not here, and General Prait won't send you back.* But she couldn't fully believe her own words. He might send her back if it would save the rest.

The general and Caden continued strategizing, but Kyra couldn't hear them anymore. Her heart pounded in her chest, and a ringing filled her ears.

Hot. She felt so hot, and a hand seemed to be pressing down hard on her. She fought to keep her breathing steady, but she really wanted to scream.

An apparition of the Malic'Uiel rose up before her; it was all she could see.

Not real! Her mind screamed.

Too many memories of them lived in her brain, and right now, those memories wanted to consume her, wanted to drag her into their dark depths.

She managed to find one moment of control, long enough to tell the men – in choked, mangled words – that she was going back to her bunkhouse.

She lied.

The second she was out of their sight, she fled. She didn't see the people around her anymore, she just had one lone thought: get away from it all.

Eventually, she found herself huddled against the back wall, safely buried in shadow. Nobody would find her here. Nobody liked to come here. Too much death had lived in these shadows. But she had survived death. It was in these shadows where she allowed herself to fall apart.

Those memories she'd been fighting...they won. She wasn't in the city anymore, not in her mind anyway. She was with the Malic'Uiel while they shredded her to bits in every way imaginable. Her head ached as if they were with her now, ripping apart her mind. Her body throbbed as if it were being physically abused by them.

Not real!

She bit her lip to stop from screaming.

Not real.

The words whispered in her mind.

But now she had visions of the future where General Prait and the people handed her over to them, gave her to the devil to save their own skin.

Hot tears streamed down her face, and her arms clutched tightly around her chest in a wasted effort to hold herself together.

Not real.

Her mind sighed the words in a weak effort to regain control of the panic. It didn't matter. It felt all too real.

Not real.

Those were the last words she remembered before the darkness took her fully, and she slipped into its depths. In that hell, something inside her broke.

Hours later, Caden found her cramped in the shadows of the back wall, trapped in her own panic. He coaxed her into his arms and brought her to their bunkhouse, staying awake for her while she slept. Her sleep was not restful. She tossed and turned. At times, her breathing hitched and froze. Tears made their way down her cheeks, and sometimes she cried out in fear.

But once, she reached for him. He took her hand and she clutched him as if he were the only thing keeping her from slipping off the shores of sanity.

"Stay with me," she breathed. Her eyes were closed, and she lay curled in a tight ball. Half asleep, half awake – in the world of dreams.

"Stay with me," she murmured again, her voice soft and gentle, a woman instead of the soldier she'd been forced to become.

His heart ached to protect her.

So, he stayed. He lay on the cot next to her and wrapped her in his arms. She settled against his chest and finally, blissfully, fell into restful sleep.

CHAPTER 14

A cloud of fear hung over Tutis like a leaden cloak. It weighed down the citizens who moved through the city with faces drawn tight, eyes darting about at every shadow. The woman who'd been murdered was taken from her home to a burial mound outside the city. Many of the citizens formed a progression behind those who bore her body, but that progression stopped once they reached the gates. Caden, Bronson, and General Prait were the only people willing to move past that point. The citizens stayed behind, putting faith in walls they knew could not protect them.

When the gates closed behind General Prait and his small crew, the people returned to their homes, each wondering if they would be the next victim in a world they no longer belonged in.

As the day progressed, the pall grew heavier. Shadows lengthened and the sun fell in the sky. The darkness crept toward them, and the fear rose with it, an invisible force determined to consume them all.

Kyra felt the fear of the citizens, but her thoughts was not focused on that. She stood outside the Citadel, studying its black walls. Her mind kept flitting back to the previous night, to Caden holding her and the safety she'd found wrapped in his arms. She hadn't expected that, hadn't meant to seek solace from him. But she couldn't bring herself to regret it. No, that was a memory she filed away as one to be cherished.

The Citadel.

She snapped her attention back to the matter at hand. The people were terrified; they needed safety. Could this building offer them some protection when others couldn't?

She found an old torch on the wall and lit it before she moved into the structure. The light from the fire fell on the walls, forcing the shadows to dance as she moved deeper. This building was exactly the same as the one she'd frequented while a slave to the Malic'Uiel. She knew the stairs to the left led up to the towers and spire, and those on the right were a path to the catacombs. The building itself wasn't pristine like those she was used to, however. It had been damaged in the battle for Tutis, but it could be made secure for the citizens if needed. It was cold, though, too cold, as if heat could not penetrate the devilish walls. As a Cadaver, she hadn't noticed a lack of heat. But as a human, she certainly did.

She let her feet take her to the stairway on the right. Her footsteps echoed through the building, which groaned in response. She was the first to haunt the place since the Malic'Uiel had lost. Shivers crawled up her spine. Though the monsters were gone, their essence remained. Voices seemed to whisper in the dark, and the light from her torch cast images on the walls that writhed and stumbled like the cloaked demon she'd once been.

She took one step down the stairs, then two, pausing at each step to listen. Logic told her the place was empty, but the hair on the back of her neck hinted otherwise. She took a third step, then a fourth. The darkness grew, creeping up the stairs to lick at her feet. Memories flooded through her: a mother screaming while she stole her child, a young boy clinging to her hand that somehow trusted her despite her monstrous appearance, and a Cadaver – her – sobbing in the corner while a frail human tried to offer comfort. The woman's words echoed through Kyra's mind – *Yea, though I walk through the valley of the shadow of death...*

Kyra blinked back a tear. The woman had no idea how right she'd been. Swallowing hard, Kyra pushed back the memories and stepped into the darkness at the bottom of the stairs. Her torch flickered, the light dimming as a cold breeze twisted the strands of her hair, but the light held strong. Kyra held the torch high, letting the light fill the small chamber. She could almost see herself as a Cadaver crying for relief, wishing more than anything for death. Bile churned in her stomach as she remembered what she'd once been, and what she'd forced Gilrich to become.

She was about to move into the chamber when footsteps echoed from the floor above. She stopped, turning toward the sound. The footsteps stopped, too. After a moment they started again, but this time much softer, as if the person wanted to muffle the noise.

Instead of waiting for the visitor to find her, she turned away from the chamber and hurried back up the stairs. A soldier she'd never met hovered near the top. He stumbled back when she stomped up. His eyes darted about the room while his fingers twisted nervously.

Kyra studied him for a moment, her gut sending off warning signals. "Who are you?" she demanded.

The man straightened, fingers stopped moving, and he cleared his throat. "I'm Anwill," he said. He stuck out his hand. "Nice to meet ya."

She didn't take the proffered limb. "Are you following me, Anwill?"

He shook his head, but his eyes fell when he tried to hold her gaze. "I just saw ya comin' in here and got curious."

Kyra held the torch between them, ready to use it as a shield or weapon if need be. "Why are you following me?"

"I aint! Truly." He licked his lips and stumbled back a step toward the door. "Just curious."

"If you were just curious, you wouldn't be so nervous." Kyra said, stepping closer. She held the torch up
just a bit higher, moving the heat near him; it would
soon be uncomfortable for him. "Again, Anwill, why
are you following me?"

He glanced at the torch, then at her. Fear flashed in
his eyes before he buried it. Finally, his head dropped,
and his shoulders slumped. He stepped back, giving her
the space she wanted. That was when she knew she'd
won. "I was curious 'bout you," he said, almost docile
now. "I wanted to know why the people here are
scared'a ya."

"So you *were* following me."

Anwill nodded.

Kyra grunted in disgust. "I'm not a sideshow. Not
some freak you find in a bazaar."

"I didn't think ya were," he said. "But when they's
talkin' like they are…" He shrugged. "Like I said. Curious."

Kyra rolled her eyes and shoved past him. "Well, go
be curious about somebody else. I'm not here for your
pleasure."

"Hey, wait!" he said, hurrying to catch up. "I didn't
mean anythin' by it. I'm sorry. I'm not great 'round
people."

She stomped forward, ignoring his pleas.

He grabbed her arm, yanking her to a stop. "Hey,
come on!"

Anger rippled through her. "Let me go," she hissed. "Or I'll bash this torch into your head."

He glanced at the solid wood of her torch, then at her face before dropping her arm. "I just wanted to 'pologize."

"Anwill," she said. "I don't want apologies. I don't want people following me around the city because they're curious about me. I don't need to be stalked by some creep that I don't trust." She held out her hand and the palm glowed, pulsing along with her anger. "I may not know what this is, but I know it can protect me because it has done so before. Unless you want me to find out on you what I'm capable of, I suggest you leave me be."

Anwill gaped at her, jaw slack, before stumbling back a step. "Is that how you killed the Phantom?"

Kyra clenched her teeth, curling her hand into a fist. "He killed himself," she snapped, shoving her way through the Citadel entrance. She dropped the torch in its sconce.

Anwill didn't follow her this time. He let her go, but his face spread in a wide grin that she didn't see. She was not only fiery, but she had fire within her. It glowed on her damn hand! And he was going to bring that to the Malic'Uiel.

Kyra marched away from the Citadel and away from Anwill. Anger surged through her body. She'd wanted to hurt him, wanted to punch his ugly face. The emotions were familiar – they'd been her companions for months. She'd felt the same desire to harm him that she'd felt as a Cadaver. She'd wanted the power that came with pain, wanted to hear him scream. She swallowed in disgust and wrapped her arms around her chest. The cavity where her heart should have been seemed empty and dark. She couldn't be sure, but the old Kyra wouldn't have craved that power.

It scared her.

She veered toward her bunkhouse. Maybe Caden could help.

The sun had disappeared while she was in the Citadel and the night's darkness clung to the building like a bloodied tunic clings to a body. She was the only one on the streets. The rest of the citizens were barred in their homes. Each bunkhouse had been fortified, with additional bolts and locks attached to deter a Phantom attack. She didn't believe the security measures would make a difference, but if that's what gave them comfort, who was she to argue?

Part of her wanted nothing more than to protect them while another part of her didn't care. Why did she fight for them when none would fight for her? When she was nothing more than an outcast, a threat...a witch.

The first scream to break the night froze the blood in her veins. Her reasoning vanished with her anger and cold dread washed over her.

They'd come again. She needed to protect the people. Of course, they were afraid of her – she was afraid of herself!

Forgetting Anwill, she raced toward the sound. But a second scream shrieked through the night, and then a third. The terror reverberated off the walls, surrounding her as more and more screams filled the air. They were everywhere. The people were defenseless, caught again in the Phantoms' trap.

After a minute that seemed like an eternity, the screams stopped. Kyra stumbled, nearly falling to her knees; the silence was so much worse than the screams. How many victims had been taken tonight? How many innocent souls were about to be subjected to the Malic'Uiel torment? Forcing her legs to keep going, she shoved open the door to the nearest residence. The inhabitants looked up at her, eyes wide with fear.

"Is everybody safe in here?" she asked.

They nodded.

"Summon the general," she gasped before racing on to the next building. Surprisingly, the occupants listened. One of them slipped out behind her and ran in the direction of General Prait's bunkhouse.

Kyra barely registered the motion, so focused was she on her mission. She burst through door after door. It was easy to spot those who'd suffered tonight. Their faces were streaked with tears and their bodies trembled in fear. The Phantoms hadn't hurt anybody this time; they'd just taken more.

But the night wasn't over, Kyra realized. They could return again and again. The people in the city were nothing more than pigs waiting to be slaughtered. Two weeks of this and humanity would be lost.

When she left the last house on the street, Kyra turned to see Caden racing toward her. "Come on," he said. "The general called an emergency council of his captains. He wants you there as well."

CHAPTER 15

When Kyra and Caden came upon the council, most of the others had already gathered. The group crammed into the largest building in the city, aside from the Citadel which nobody wanted to enter. The building stood next to the infirmary, and had become the city's headquarters – everybody called it simply the Meetinghouse.

It was one room, like most of the buildings in Tutis, and built for nothing more than function. The smooth panes of the wood on the walls and floor were worn to a dull gray color, and the door creaked as they entered. Near the door, a window had been cut into the wall, allowing the light to shine in through the clear glass during the day. Tonight, it was an eye yawning to the darkness. There had been cots at one point, but those had been removed after the army took up residence. A crude table and chair had replaced them. These were shoved near the back of the space to make room for the council. General Prait stood in front of the table, waiting to address the crowd. Kyra stayed near the door, attempting to keep a reasonable distance between herself and the others in the room.

Leland and Bronson were the last to straggle in. General Prait didn't wait for people to get settled before he jumped right in. "This is the second night the Phantoms have come," he said. "We have to find a way to protect these people, and we have to find it now."

"Can we stop them?" Bronson asked, his voice carrying from the back of the small crowd. Kyra glanced at him, but saw Leland glaring at her instead. She turned her attention back to General Prait.

"The only way we can fight them is in large numbers, and even that is risky. Caden is more equally matched than the rest of us, and Kyra seems to have the ability to defend herself against them, but most of us aren't equipped to go against them. They can control fire, they disappear and reappear at will – even their touch is deadly." General Prait shuddered. "I've expelled their poison from my veins. It's not an experience I'd care to repeat."

"What if we left the city?" This voice came from Vailynn, one of the mothers who'd been enslaved in Tutis and had recently joined the city council. "As I understand it, you survived outside before. We could leave, go back in hiding, and regroup."

General Prait tapped his fingers on the side of his leg. "I thought about that," he said. "After last night's attack I considered that to see if it was an option, but it's not. The only place we can find relative safety is in the Adeo Mountains, but those mountains can't sustain life. We've nearly depleted what's available out there. We will starve to death if we go back. Here in the city, we have stores to last us until after the first crops come in, and we can send hunting parties to the woods for meat. There's a chance here. Only death waits for us out there."

"The Cadavers were beginning to hunt us in the mountains anyway," a second soldier added. He'd been with the army for a while and had spent plenty of time in those mountains. "I imagine it was only a matter of time before the Phantoms or the Malic'Uiel made their way to us."

Kyra tried to keep her focus on the general, but her skin felt like it was crawling up her spine. She looked around to find Leland gazing at her again, his face a dark mask of anger. Fingers of cold danced on the back of her neck. Still gazing at her, Leland called to General Prait. "Why don't we give them what they want?"

General Prait turned toward him. "And what is that, Leland?"

He gestured toward Kyra. "Her."

All eyes turned toward her; most of the faces matched Leland's. A few held pity. Kyra's gut twisted in trepidation. Had they called her here just to betray her?

General Prait's brow furrowed. "What makes you think they want her?"

He pushed himself through the crowd. "The Phantom that came that first night – the one she killed – he came looking for her. She was his target, and when he failed, they all started coming. Give them what they want, maybe they'll stop coming."

"Give them what they want, and we all lose," Caden seethed. "If she is their target, giving her up would be the stupidest thing we can do."

"Your opinion carries no weight," Leland spat. "You're nothing more than a soldier, and you follow her like a whipped dog." He folded his arms across his chest, jerking his head back to the General. "If we get rid of her, we get rid of the reason for the threat."

Caden had been offered the role of captain shortly after they'd taken Tutis, but he'd refused the position. Still, he was requested to attend all council meetings because of his in-depth knowledge of the Phantoms. Kyra wondered now if he regretted that decision, since it kept him from putting Leland in his place.

General Prait's eyes narrowed as he studied Leland. "Humans are the threat," he said. "Not *one* human. *All* humans. Whether she goes or not doesn't matter because they'll keep coming. They know we're here; they can come in easily and leave with fresh blood. We get rid of Kyra, we lose one of the few resources we have that can defeat them."

Leland grunted. "We don't know that she didn't invite them in. We all saw what she did when she came here."

JULIANNE KELSCH

General Prait turned his attention to the rest of the room, ignoring Leland's diatribe. His eyes met hers and what she saw surprised her – she saw tenderness. He cared about her. The tension in her stomach subsided a bit. She could trust the general.

"We're not giving them Kyra," he said. "I'm not going to be responsible for the blood of another human being, not when I can keep her from them. I need other suggestions."

"The Citadel is empty," Kyra said. "The catacombs below may offer some protection."

Leland swung toward her. "Dungeons! Half the people in this city barely escaped that place. I survived in them for years. My woman died battling her way out. I will not go back."

"But they may be safe down there," Kyra argued. "At least until we find a way to defend ourselves against them. It's not ideal, but safety in the catacombs would be better than sitting out here every night waiting to be the next victim." She moved forward, coming to the front of the group where she turned to face them. Too many pairs of eyes glowered at her. She bolstered her courage by finding the few that were kind – Caden, Bronson, General Prait. Those encouraging glances helped her ignore the rest of them. "If we can keep the people together, they have a better chance of defending themselves. One individual can't fight a Phantom, but maybe ten or twenty can. The Phantom's have weaknesses. Caden knows that better than anybody. We can learn to exploit them, but we need time to do it. Maybe that will give us some."

General Prait tapped his chin with his knuckles. "I agree that we need time but asking the people to go back into those dark pits...I don't know if we can do that."

"Kyra," Bronson said. "How is it that you are able to fight them? What did you do to the one you killed?"

Kyra glanced at Bronson before holding out her palm and studying the glowing skin. "I don't know," she said. "It was the light. All I did was touch him."

"And what is the light?"

Kyra shook her head. "I don't know that either. It showed up after I escaped the Malic'Uiel."

Bronson stepped to her, gesturing to her hand. "May I?" he asked.

She hesitated for a moment before offering him her palm. He took is in his hand, holding his own palm over the light. For a moment the light shone brighter – not enough for the others in the room to notice, but enough that the two of them did. Bronson's eyes met and held hers, questioning. Her look mirrored his. It was as if he had light to share with hers. When he pulled his hand away the light faded to a dim glow, and her palm felt colder. She curled it into a fist, tucking it behind her back. A small part of her wanted to pull him back, to feel his light again.

"My mother used to tell me a tale," Bronson said, addressing the crowd but staying close to her. "It was the story of a woman who was made of light. Her palms would glow – that's how people knew what she was. They'd glow especially bright when she used the light."

"What did she use the light for?" Kyra asked.

"Healing, mostly. She'd heal the hearts of men."

Kyra's lips pulled up in a half smile. "If I could heal the hearts of men, Gilrich would have returned to us by now."

"The point of the story isn't that she healed others, it's that she controlled the light. Her hands glowed like yours do." He addressed General Prait now. "If we can harness Kyra's power, we may be able to defeat them."

"You're finding truth in a fairytale!" Leland cried. "A child's story. Kyra is no woman of light. She's a seductress. She's seduced you, and Caden, and our esteemed General Prait. If we're not careful, she will seduce us all!"

Bronson laughed. "Seduced? You've lost your mind, Leland. She is no more dangerous than you or me, and we know she can defeat Phantoms because we've seen her do it. Why not take advantage of what she has? We'd be stupid to let that go to waste."

Leland threw up his hands in defeat. "You all disgust me. Fine. Follow the witch. She'll only lead you to your doom." He spun on his heel, stomping from the group and out of the building. Nobody noticed when

Anwill sidled up to Leland, keeping pace with him as he stomped away. The rest of the council already had their attention turned back to the general, who acted as if Leland had never been there. "Bronson has a point," General Prait said. "What Kyra can do may be our saving grace. I think he's right, Kyra. We need to harness what you have." He gestured to Caden. "And you. We have to take advantage of the power you both possess."

Kyra swallowed hard, glancing at the faces of those in the room that hated her. Her palms began to sweat. "I don't know how to use it," she murmured, thinking of all the ways they'd damn her if she failed. "I don't even know what it is. I can't promise this will work."

"We have no options," General Prait said. "We find a way to defeat them, or we all die. You and Caden are soldiers, and you've both worked hard to be the best. So, train together, control these powers you have, be better than our enemies. You two may be our only chance."

CHAPTER 16

They left the meeting in groups, some of the men following General Prait to assess the damage left from the Phantom attack, while others went through the city offering comfort to those who'd lost friends in the night. Kyra and Caden returned to the Citadel, where they studied the outside perimeter of the building.

The Citadel was located in the exact center of Tutis. In a city controlled by the Malic'Uiel, all activity flowed to and from this structure – it was the heart of the city; every movement in or out was the heartbeat. Here, the heart was dead. The Citadel stood as a silent, dark sentinel to the horrors Tutis had witnessed. It was a solid black structure, built of stone and coated in something otherworldly, something that caused it to absorb light. The grounds closest to it lived in permanent shadow, unable to be kissed by the sun.

The building itself stretched to the sky, with four towers rising higher than the surrounding walls. Each tower lined up perfectly with a cardinal direction on the compass rose. Kyra knew from her experiences with them that these towers had huge openings on each side that looked out to the city beyond. From them, the Malic'Uiel would oversee the entire city and keep it running as the perfect destructive machine – an image they loved.

From the core of the building itself, a great spire rose above it all, like a finger attempting to tear open the sky. Birds never flew near the spire, wind never stirred, and clouds gave it a wide berth. It was its own source of death; every good thing in the world fled from it. The spire in Passus was where Kyra had been taken after she'd refused to succumb to the Malic'Uiel conditioning. It was where she'd witnessed the final product of the Malic'Uiel abuse – the sacrifice of a man's soul to the monsters who'd become his god.

She gazed at the spire, but she did not see it. Instead, she saw in her mind a man, a Cadaver who'd willingly served the Malic'Uiel, celebrating as he gave the last of himself to them. The final sacrifice of a human was the gift of his soul. This man had given his. The Malic'Uiel sucked it away, pulling it from his body while he rejoiced. But his rejoicing did not last.

The process had changed him. His body, deformed and mangled when he'd given his soul, shed the physical deformation that represented the deformation of his mind. Bit by bit, awareness crept onto his face.

As the Malic'Uiel sucked away his soul, the color changed from black, to gray, to red, and slowly shifted through other colors until it was pure, bright white.

Throughout this process, the man's body had turned from Cadaver to human – the elongated, curved fingers, the twisted and mangled limbs, the hunched spine, even the flattened nose all returned to a perfect, human state. But it was too late for him. At the end, he knew what he'd become, what he'd done, and the evil that he served. He'd sobbed in sheer mental agony while they ripped the rest of him away.

"It's not a bad idea, Kyra," Caden said, breaking her out of her thoughts. "But there would be no promise of safety inside."

She shook her head, dispelling the horrible memory and coming back to reality. "I know," she finally said, focusing again on why they were here. "It could be worse than it is now, putting them all in one place. But the Phantoms may not expect that, either. If they don't know we're down there, they have no reason to transport themselves inside."

The two of them stood together, shoulders touching. His fingers toyed with hers. Though they hadn't spoken of their night together, they both felt a shift. She knew as well as he: that moment of compassion, of vulnerability, had stripped them both of their defenses; something had changed.

"Eventually they'd figure it out," Caden said. He held out his hand and a ball of fire erupted over his palm. "And if they caused a fire down there..." He let the sentence hang.

"It would be a death trap," Kyra finished. "They block the stairwell, we lose everybody." Kyra held out her own palm, mirroring Caden's movements. "General Prait thinks I can control mine the way you control yours," she said. "But yours is fire and mine is light. How do you control light?"

Caden chuckled. "How do you control fire? It's one of the most volatile substances known to man. It devours and kills mercilessly. Everything can be controlled, once you learn how to do it." He opened his palm wider, and the fireball grew, doubling in size. A moment later it shrunk until it was barely more than a flame.

"How do *you* control it?" Kyra asked, her brow furrowed. She focused on the light, willed it to increase or decrease but it stayed the same. It glowed just above her palm, a pulsing orb no bigger than an apple shimmering in a rainbow of colors.

"I understand it," Caden said. "Maybe that's the difference between you and me." He balled his hand into a fist and the fire disappeared. "It's not the fire I manipulate, it's the energy inside it. I demand that the energy move or operate a certain way, and it does, almost like an extension of my mind."

Kyra dropped her hand to her side. "So if I understood the energy of the light, I could use it?"

"Possibly," Caden said. "It may be no different than fire." His lips turned up in a half smile. "But I had this knowledge forced onto me, where you are navigating uncharted territory. I, at least, understood where mine came from and why. Yours will have to be discovered."

Kyra sighed, "It feels like most of life is something to be discovered. I guess it's a good thing you know where yours came from, but it was a cruel twist of fate when Maliel gave you his darkness."

Caden's smile faded and he sighed, turning away from her. As he did so, his tunic shifted enough to reveal the edge of a scar, one she knew was shaped like a hand. She'd seen the scar before, but did not know its origin. He noticed the shifted tunic and quickly covered the damaged flesh again. "I wish I could say the darkness came from him, but I can't. It was already in me." His mouth set in a bitter smile. "All Maliel did was shine a light on what I knew was already there."

Kyra reached up slowly and pushed the tunic back, tracing the edge of the scar. To her surprise he didn't flinch away, but after a moment he caught her hand and removed her fingers from his chest. The tunic fell back into place. "What is this, Caden?"

Caden did not release her wrist. Instead, he placed her hand over both the tunic, the scar, and his heart. "The scar is a symbol of the evil I harbor, a reminder of the horrors of the Malic'Uiel. It's my motivation to fight every day against them so I can restore what was stolen from the world."

"But where did it come from?" Kyra pushed, tugging the tunic aside so she could see the angry red flesh. "What causes a scar like that?"

"Betrayal," Caden murmured.

Kyra cocked her head in confusion, but Caden didn't offer more.

"Come on, Kyra," he said, stepping away from her and ending the conversation. Her hand dropped to her side. "The night has barely started. For all we know, the Phantoms will come again. It's time to unleash whatever power you hold."

Kyra fell in step beside him, but she wasn't ready to let his past go. "We've spoken of your secrets before, Caden, a long time ago." They'd discussed it briefly, long before the Malic'Uiel had taken her. He wouldn't share with her then, either, but now...she had hoped he'd give her that part of himself since she harbored her own dark shadows.

He grunted.

Not a good sign.

"I can help you shoulder the burden," she said, keeping pace with him as he moved down the street. "When will you open up to me?"

"When we win this war. Until then, my secrets are mine to carry alone."

CHAPTER 17

As they moved down the dark streets, they didn't see two figures watching them. Anwill and Leland both had their eyes trained on the pair.

"I don't trust her," Leland said. "She'll drive us all to our deaths."

Anwill murmured his agreement, but he waited. When the couple turned down a side street, he spoke. "We could get rid of 'er."

"Kill her in her sleep?" Leland said, a smirk on his lips. "You may not be suspect in that murder, but I would."

Anwill shook his head. "Nah, nothin' so gruesome." His eyes darted around the area, then he gestured his head toward the Citadel, striding toward it as he did so. Leland followed suit. Anwill didn't speak until they disappeared inside the monstrous building. "We don' have to kill 'er," he said. "Just get rid of 'er."

Leland folded his arms across his chest, brows curved down in mistrust. "How do we get rid of her?"

Anwill cleared his throat, twisting his fingers together, his shoulders hunching. "I'm about to share some secrets with ya. Ya can't tell nobody. Do I have yer word?"

Leland frowned. "Go on," he said.

Anwill swallowed hard, his eyes gleaming. "I got some people that want Kyra. They're waitin' for me to git 'er. They're goin' to give 'er to the Malic'uiel."

Leland's face darkened, but his lips curved in a cruel smile. "You're here to take her away?"

"Yeah," Anwill said. "I'm s'posed to find a way to give 'er outta here. Or lure her away. I tried to be her friend, but she don't trust me."

Leland snorted. "I can't imagine why. She's not stupid." As much as he hated Kyra, he had to give her a little credit. She had a way of knowing who she could trust and who was her enemy.

Leland's body relaxed and he gripped Anwill's shoulder. "You're telling me you have a way of getting her to the Malic'Uiel without putting the rest of us in danger?"

Anwill nodded.

"And all you need is my help? I just have to help you get her out of the city?"

"Yeah," Anwill said. He flung his arm toward the wall. "We git 'er out there, they'll do the rest."

Leland's face broke in a wide grin. "The witch will be gone and her poison with her. The Phantoms no longer have a reason to target us. We may just be safe here." He sighed. "Wish we could get rid of Caden, too. He's as much a threat as she."

Anwill's tongue darted out, wetting his lips. "Maybe we could," he said.

"How?"

If we're takin' 'er anyway, he's gonna come after 'er. He ain't gonna lose 'er without a fight."

"So we use her as bait?"

Anwill's head bobbed once, and his lips curved crookedly. "Yeah. Bait. We kill him when he comes to find 'er, then my friends send 'er to them."

"Then I kill the Cadaver and we're rid of the witch, the phantom, and the monster," Leland said. He stuck out his hand.

Anwill gripped it, unwilling to let go when Leland pulled away. "A few days," he said, squeezing tight to stress his point. "That's all we got."

"And all we need. I'll meet you here tomorrow, same time. Come with a plan."

Anwill nodded, releasing the hold.

"Make sure your friends are ready when we are. It won't take long."

"They will be."

CHAPTER 18

The remainder of that night was quiet. While the citizens of Tutis huddled in their bunkhouses, ever fearful of another attack, General Prait, his captains, and many soldiers patrolled the empty streets. They stayed in groups, weapons drawn, on high alert. But their vigilance proved unnecessary.

It wasn't until the dawn broke that they returned to their own bunkhouses, exhausted after the long night. Most slipped into a dreamless sleep.

But not Kyra. She fell into her memories.

The Citadel towered above her, a black prison silhouetted in the moonlit night. She darted from the structure, glancing behind her as she ran. No Malic'Uiel had spotted her yet, but that didn't mean they weren't there, waiting in the shadows. Her feet hit the cobblestone streets far louder than she wanted – the sound bounced off the surrounding buildings, a traitor to her presence.

She couldn't get caught.

She wouldn't get caught.

Breathing hard, she pushed her body to move faster, begging her limbs to take flight. Somewhere in the distance a faint wailing caught her ears.

An alarm.

A second alarm picked up the sound, then a third, the wailing growing ever closer. Adrenaline surged through her body, sending her soaring across the cobblestone. But it wasn't fast enough. The streets to the left and right spewed Cadavers; they filled the area in front of her, behind her. They closed in, surrounding her, but still she pushed forward. Yanking her sword out of her sheath she cut through the masses, shoving bleeding bodies aside as she fought her way through. The city wall loomed ahead. Her rope dangled from the top, beckoning her to freedom.

The Cadaver came from her side – she saw him in her vision – but she wasn't fast enough to get out of the way. He slammed into her, knocking her to the ground. Her head cracked on the cobblestone. Pain rippled up her leg and through her body, while the world tipped off kilter around her. The Cadaver leered at her while his clawed fingers dug into the flesh of her arm. Something about him was familiar – his eyebrows curved up and his lips were slightly offset from his nose. Even distorted, those features were still visible.

Suddenly, it hit. Like a brick to her stomach, she stared at the face in horror.

The Cadaver was her father.

Kyra screamed and jolted awake, her hand clawing at the wall for support. She blinked rapidly, trying to dispel the image, but she couldn't because it was tied to a memory. The dream had changed some of the details, but that night was clear in her mind.

She'd gone with Caden and Gilrich to infiltrate the Citadel. They'd known it was a suicide mission, but they were desperate for answers, and they'd gone in search of the symbol. Caden and Gilrich made it out. But that night marked the beginning of Kyra's torment.

The face in her dreams was real. He had held her captive while her friends escaped.

The tears that had been a dream were now very real, and they slipped down her cheeks unbidden. Logically, she'd known her father, Em's, fate, but some part of her had hoped he'd been able to fight them off, as she had done. She'd hoped his mind had protected him against them. But the dream triggered the memory, and she now knew his fate. Em, her own father, had been there the night she'd been taken; he'd dragged her into enslavement.

She let the tears fall silently, her heart aching at the torment she knew he'd endured. What memories had they given him? Who had she become for him? She knew they would twist her in his memories, make her into a monster.

She ground her teeth, digging her fists into her eyes. In some respect, she was responsible for his captivity.

He'd sacrificed himself to ensure her freedom – the Malic'Uiel would turn that act against them both. It was how they corrupted the mind; the people you loved became your enemy.

She swung her legs off the cot, resting them on the floor of the bunkhouse. Closing her eyes, she gripped her knees, holding her body rigid as the mental torment burrowed deep inside. She willed it to go with the rest, to hide itself deep where she wouldn't have to experience it again.

After a few minutes of intense breathing and focused effort, the pain had reduced itself to a quiet ache, no more potent than what she felt on a normal basis.

She sighed and let her body slump over. Her father was a Cadaver. He'd lost his mind to them.

Shoving herself off the cot, she slipped out of the bunkhouse in search of Gilrich. Knowing Em's fate only fueled her determination to free Gilrich's mind from their grasp.

Outside, the sun was high in the sky. She squinted at the bright light, surprised that she'd slept at all with her memories tormenting her. She groaned and shoved away from her bunkhouse toward Gilrich's prison. Those memories were buried now, and they would stay buried!

When she approached Gilrich's door, the men guarding his building stepped aside. They were new guards. They'd changed since Leland's attack on her friend. They eyed her with mistrust, but did not attempt to hinder her. She paused for a moment inside the entrance to let her eyes adjust before closing the door. Light streamed in a window on the side of the building, and candles on the opposite end lit the space, casting out the shadows.

Gilrich glanced up when she entered, but otherwise ignored her. His head dropped into his chest, and he sat slumped against the wall. His hands were still bound behind him.

"Gilrich," Kyra said quietly, coming to kneel in front of him. "Can you hear me?"

The Cadaver grunted but didn't say anything.

Kyra sighed. "Gilrich," she tried again. "Please talk to me."

He lifted his head and glared at her. "I told you. Gilrich is dead."

"No. He's not. I know he's in there. He has to be."

The Cadaver eyed her with some curiosity. "Why do you care so much about this Gilrich?" he said. "What's it to you if one more human is gone?"

Kyra's lips twitched up in a sad smile. "Gilrich was my friend. And a kind soul who didn't deserve this fate. He was genuinely good, and to be honest I don't think there are many people like him left."

He grunted again, and his head cocked to the side as if he were studying her. Or maybe he was studying himself. A flicker of recognition flitted through is eyes, but it quickly vanished. Then he snorted.

"You're a good liar," he said. "But not good enough. You humans – there's always an agenda. Even if it's just to make yourself feel better. You know it's your fault Gilrich is lost."

He straightened up and a cruel smile broke on his cracked lips. "I remember that day. I remember looking up and seeing you with Master Passus." He chuckled, though there was no humor in it. "He knew who you were. The human, Gilrich, he was in control of the mind. He hoped you'd save him. But you didn't. You threw him in that cell and destroyed him." The Cadaver caught her gaze and held it.

Fear and anger churned in her stomach. She *was* at fault. She *had* taken him to the cell.

The Cadaver continued. "But you destroyed him long before he ever came to the Malic'Uiel. You pitted Caden against him. You turned the General against him. You conned Shem into taking him prisoner and stealing him from the life he knew." The Cadaver shook his head in disgust. "And now you come trying to save him. You humans are despicable."

The Cadaver's words landed hard in Kyra's gut, as painful as if somebody had punched her. They made her sick; it wasn't a sickness fueled by guilt but by anger. She glared at the Cadaver, seeing the gruesome body in front of her, but beneath it feeling the soul that resided within. The Malic'Uiel had stolen her friend and turned him against her. Her mouth worked as anger rose; her jaw clenched, and fists grew tight.

"I did none of those things," she hissed. "Caden loves Gilrich as much as I. General Prait cares for Gilrich as if he were his own son. And Shem..." She chuckled mirthlessly. "Shem is the worst kind of evil – he's a man who betrays his kind for his own gain. I wouldn't put my enemy in Shem's hand, let alone someone I cared about." She leaned forward until she was nearly nose to nose with the Cadaver. "And if you think I'm going to give up on Gilrich, you're wrong. I know he's in there. I know your polluted mind has him trapped away somewhere. I was one of you, remember? I know how this works! And I will free Gilrich from the shackles you have bound him with."

The Cadaver kept her gaze, holding her stare as long as she held his. Then he started to laugh. A small chuckle at first, but it grew until his laughter roared, filling the entire space. The sound was unnerving because it was the laughter of one who knows he's going to win. "Hope!" he cackled. "That's what you exist on. You and your hope. It will be your undoing!"

Kyra's eyes narrowed. She thought of Dalia. The woman had been through hell, but she lived for a future none of them could see. She saw Dalia's hands cradling her bulging stomach, smiling tenderly at the small kicks of her child, hopeful even though the baby's father was dead. She would raise the child alone in a world determined to destroy it, but that wasn't the future that Dalia saw. She saw one where the child would thrive. Her hope gave her something to fight for.

Through clenched teeth Kyra spoke. "It is hope that gives humans the strength to keep going." She pushed herself to her feet, gazing down at the Cadaver in pity. "It is hope that sees us through the dark times." She stepped to the door and quietly opened it, but before she left, she stopped, glancing back at him. "And it is hope that reminds us of the light, even though the darkness reigns. Gilrich is still in you. You know I am right. You fear him. He will find his way back."

CHAPTER 19

A s Kyra returned to her bunkhouse, she passed Dalia. "Are you going to see Gilrich?"

Dalia nodded. "Yes. I come every couple of days. I think it's good for him."

Kyra paused, watching her friend for a moment as a thought took root. "Dalia," she said. "How does Gilrich treat you?"

Dalia shrugged. "He doesn't. He's usually very quiet when I'm there. I give him food. I tell him about my life. He rarely responds."

Kyra's teeth tugged at her lips, and she tapped her chin with her fingers. "I wonder if you can help me," Kyra said. She fell into step with Dalia, heading back toward Gilrich's prison. "Gilrich believes that I have harmed him. The Malic'Uiel have turned me into his enemy. You...you're not his enemy. He has no memories of you that are painful, nothing that has been twisted into a lie. And you're genuinely good." Kyra began speaking animatedly, her hands trying to draw a picture of what she saw possible. Dalia could be the tool she needed. "I can't free him," she said. "At least, not yet. Not until he doesn't see me as somebody coming to harm him. But you...you can!"

Dalia's brows turned down and she looked at Kyra in confusion. "How am I supposed to free him?"

"By bringing him back to the light. Help him find the truth in his memories. Dalia, talk to him about more than your life, about the life before the Malic'Uiel, about what has been and what could be. Give him the truth."

"I'm not sure how..." her voice trailed off. She glanced at Gilrich's prison, and then at Kyra, whose faced was flushed with excitement. "You really think I can help him?"

Kyra nodded quickly. "I do. And I'll be learning what I can to help him as well. I know we can save him, because something saved me. I was once him."

"How did you come back from that?"

Kyra chewed on her bottom lip. "I'm not sure. I've tried to understand it, but it's difficult. No matter what they did to me, there was a part of me that couldn't accept the lies. My soul rebelled, and they saw it. They tried to force me to become what they wanted. My master," she sent Dalia a sick smile. "That's what they were to me. He...forced his way into his mind and obliterated everything that I was. I can't explain how or what he did, but I was nothing. A body without a mind and barely a soul."

Dalia's eyes were wide. "Did it hurt?" she whispered.

"Yes. It was horrible."

"I'm so sorry." She lay her hand on Kyra's arm, as if by touching her she could portray just how deeply she felt.

"There are worse things in life. I've seen them. What they did..." She thought of the time she'd seen them steal a man's soul. "There are worse things," she said again. "And when they took my mind, they took the darkness with it. They took it all. That's when I knew. I did not have to be what they said I was."

She shook off the memories and gripped Dalia's hand on her arm. "We just have to help him see who and what he really is. He's not lost in there forever. He just thinks he is."

Dalia rubbed her stomach absently, smiling when the baby kicked her hand. She nodded. "I'll do my best."

CHAPTER 20

While Kyra and Dalia discussed Gilrich's future, Caden opened the gates of Tutis and slipped out. Every day he went outside the city to monitor the traps and pitfalls. Sometimes he made adjustments or small repairs, but mostly he just checked to make sure they were all in working order. Today, he made his normal rounds, then decided to do an additional check around the walls of the city.

He traveled around the circumference, staying close to the city while scanning the areas closest to the wall for any possible chink in their defenses. Above, looming over him, wooden spikes of uneven lengths planted a hands width apart crowned the top of the walls. Below, similar spikes had been dug into the ground. Between then, nothing existed to stop an advance if an individual were to make it past the pitfalls and traps. Still – he glanced up again – getting to the walls would be the beginning of a whole new set of problems for invaders.

Near the back of the city he stopped, pausing in respect as his eyes fell on a mound near the forest edge. This was a mass grave, opened just long enough to give the most recent human inhabitants of Tutis a proper burial. Many of them were dead long before General Prait and his army took up residence – these men and women had already given the Malic'Uiel the final piece asked of them, they'd given their souls to fuel the Malic'Uiel lusts. Caden shuddered at the thought. Their bodies had been discarded in a decaying heap pushed up against the back wall of the city.

Others had lost their lives during the battle that secured Tutis. These were men of the army, and members of the enslaved citizenry. Those who remained had mourned the passing of those they knew as well as the passing of those who'd been lost to darkness. But the grave served as a reminder, however small, of what they fought and why.

A faint green sheen covered the mound. Life continued to go on, even though the bodies beneath it were no longer living.

Caden slumped down near the city wall, sliding until he sat on the dirt, resting his arms on his knees. It was quiet here, and somehow peaceful, although the peace was intermingled with a sort of melancholy. He closed his eyes and let the rare moment of peace flood through him.

A face appeared in his mind. A beautiful face, one he adored. His wife, Avalyn, smiled gently at him.

"Caden," she said. She reached for him, cupping his cheek in her hand. Her skin was warm and soft. *"I need your help."*

Caden kept his eyes closed, letting the vision take place. He knew he wasn't asleep, and he knew he wasn't dreaming, but he was afraid if he opened them he'd lose her. "Of course, Avalyn," he said. "I will always help you."

Avalyn emerged in his vision, fully, her body clothed in white, supple material and radiating light. *"Darkness encroaches on Kyra,"* she said. *"It's trying to take her. I can't communicate with her, but I must."*

Confusion settled in Caden's breast. "I don't understand," he said. "Are you not simply my imagination giving me relief?"

She smiled but a hint of sadness played around her lips. *"No, my love. I am not your imagination; nor am I hers."*

Caden listened in silence as Avalyn continued. *"You and I know Kyra is far more than she realizes. You've seen her soul, as have I."*

A vision flashed in Caden's mind of a place filled with light. The grass glowed a brilliant green, and rivers sparkled like diamonds. Great cities gleamed white, radiating their own light. Then the memory of his experience with Kyra's mind surfaced, and he saw many of the same features. Her mind seemed to emanate light; she'd been filled with it.

The memory faded and Avalyn was there again.

She's wrapping herself in fear," Avalyn said. "She doesn't realize it yet, but she is. The darkness is taking her. Hope is fading, though she fights it. She hopes for Gilrich, but is losing faith in herself. You must help her navigate those waters or all will be lost."

"I don't understand," Caden said again. "Why is she different?"

Avalyn said nothing as a new image surfaced. The image was a woman singing to a young babe.

> *Rest your eyes in sleep, my love*
> *I am here to guard you*
> *Find the joy in dreams, my love*
> *I am here to guide you*

> *Let your fears away, my love*
> *I am here to hold you*
> *When you wake, you'll find me*
> *Watching over you*

The child lay quietly, watching her mother with eyes full of adoration. The mother stroked the child's soft cheek, then took the child's hand. The infant's eyes began to droop. Her tiny fist wrapped around her mother's finger as the woman continued...

> *Take your toddling steps, my love*
> *I am here to catch you*
> *Share with me your voice, my love*

I am here to hear you

Discover who you are, my love
I am here to love you
As you grow, you'll see me
Watching over you

As the song faded, so did the image.

"This is Kyra's mother," Avalyn said. *"She was the gatekeeper to Lumen – in Spero's histories her title was the Countess of Lumen. This role is passed from mother to daughter. It comes with specific gifts given through Lumen to the child. Those gifts lie dormant unless necessity requires they appear."*

"Gifts?"

Avalyn nodded. *"The power of light,"* she said simply. *"Once unlocked by the Countess, they can be taught to others."* She stepped closer, gripping Caden's hand. *"But this power only exists where light is allowed to thrive."*

"Which is why the darkness fights so hard for Kyra," Caden said, his mind connecting the pieces. "It needs to extinguish her light."

"Yes."

"If darkness takes her, then what?"

"Then humanity will fail. Kyra holds the fate of humanity in her soul."

"She has no idea," Caden whispered, his heart catching in his throat.

Avalyn nodded. *"She can't hear it yet – she isn't ready to know the truth – which is why you must help her. I am her mentor. I'm to guide her, for my soul as well as the others. But with the darkness swirling around her, I can't get through."*

Caden clasped his hands together across his knees, determination taking root. "I'll help her."

"I know you will." Avalyn sighed and touched Caden's hand. "You are her protector, Caden. That mark you bear is the mark of the protector. There is always one set apart to keep the Countess safe. Em became that after Evia's death. Now the role has fallen on you."

Caden knew if he opened his eyes and twisted his wrist back and forth, he'd see light shimmering off the symbol stamped there. "I would have protected her anyway," he said quietly.

"I know," Avalyn said. "You love her." She gripped both of Caden's hands tightly, holding his gaze. "Don't be afraid to show her."

"I do love her," Caden whispered. He held Avalyn's face in his mind for a long time, memorizing every beautiful feature. "I'm sorry," he said. "I haven't forgotten you."

Avalyn pushed Caden's chin up to face her. A single tear slid down her cheek. "Don't be sorry, Caden," she said. "I am already lost."

Her hand dropped and the vision faded. The light faded with her.

When Caden opened his eyes, he found himself gazing at the pale green mound, sitting in the same cold dirt. But something had shifted, and he knew it. He and Kyra had been seeking answers, and Avalyn had given him some. Kyra had more of a role to play than she knew. He believed it, but she would have to learn. And the symbol? It *did* mean something. It spoke to more than they knew. He would trust that, for now, and he would trust Avalyn.

He would protect Kyra and keep the darkness at bay.

CHAPTER 21

The Master ghosted down the steps of the Citadel tower in the city of Celebrus. He'd left Novus to return to Celebrus, which was a city once renowned for its knowledge. This is where humanity had reached its height of advancement. Now, if all went as planned, what he kept here in Celebrus would help him unravel the last thread holding humanity together.

He continued down the tower, moving through long hallways and twisted corridors until he reached a stone door that remained closed to all but him. Upon nearing the door, he touched a lever to the right and it swung open.

The room he stepped into was circular, with a table in the middle and a second, smaller table set to the side. Torches surrounded the perimeter, giving the room an acrid smell while lighting the interior space.

The Master moved to the center of the room, where a woman lay on the stone table. Her eyes were closed, and her chest rose softly, slowly. He studied her face;

the skin was smooth, the features serene. Silver hair gleamed in the torchlight, the tresses tangled and matted on the table. Every few seconds her lips twitched or her eyes fluttered beneath their lids, but beyond that she was motionless and unaware.

After a moment, the Master moved to the second table near the wall. This table held vials of liquid. Some were clear, while others were a smoky gray. He took the clear liquid, along with a glass funnel, and brought them both back to the woman. Forcing her jaw open, he slipped the funnel into her mouth, pouring the liquid down bit by bit. At first, she choked on the liquid. He tipped her head back slightly and the choking stopped. The concoction slid down her throat into her body where he needed it to be. Ribbons of it dribbled down the side of her mouth, landing like tears on the stone beneath her.

Satisfied, the Master returned to the table and grabbed a vial of the gray liquid. He swirled it briefly as he stepped back to the woman's body. Again, he tipped her jaw open, pushing the glass funnel into her mouth to the back of her throat. He administered the gray liquid in the same manner as the first.

The woman heaved as the liquid slipped into her throat. She gurgled and choked, her body instinctively repelling the Master's offering. He clamped her mouth shut, forcing the liquid to stay inside. As it slid into her stomach, her body convulsed, chest heaving and arms spasming at her side. Slowly the liquid worked its way through her system. Her body succumbed to the poison and the twitching stopped, the convulsing ended.

She lay completely motionless once more. Her lips no longer twitched. Her eyes no longer fluttered, and her features once again became serene. Her skin was flushed and warm to the touch. Life flowed in the veins, but her mind was trapped inside a useless body.

Kneeling next to her, the Master grasped her hand in his, closing his eyes as if in prayer. After a brief moment, his mind slipped into hers. There, he stood on the precipice of her soul and watched. Light swirled around him, and he followed it, floating after it until it led him to a scene he'd witnessed many times. He let it unfold around him, observing silently, looking for details he had missed.

In the scene another woman, one he now knew as Kyra, gazed down at the mark of Lumen in her hand. It dangled from her palm on a thin chain. She appraised it for a moment, then brought it to hang around her neck. Bending on one knee, she bowed her head. One hand clutched the pendant while the other gripped something that lay in the space beneath her. That particular area was in shadow.

The Master moved closer, brow furrowed as he studied the shadows beneath her. They did not separate and reveal the secret of what lay beneath, but he knew whatever hid in those shadows was important to Kyra, and to Lumen.

Suddenly, light burst from Kyra's hand, engulfing her body and the shadows surrounding it. But the light was too bright. The Master could not see what she'd touched.

He ground his teeth, jaw clenched in anger. This vision had been repeated for him many times, always with the same result. The missing piece was vital to his success, for this was the moment Kyra opened the door to Lumen. He needed to be there with her, needed her to open it for him. But he was missing information, missing pieces. No matter how many times he'd seen the vision, he could not see how she opened the door, nor did he see what happened beyond the light. His knowledge was tainted and incomplete.

He pulled himself from the woman's mind, frustrated at his inability to obtain the rest. Releasing her hand, it dropped back on the stone, as useless as her vision. He bent closer, face a breath away from hers. "You cannot hide the truth from me forever," he murmured. "I have your body. I have your mind. As I have gleaned the secrets I've needed thus far, so I will take the answers I seek."

The woman remained motionless, unresponsive. She could not hear him. Her mind was not present. But her soul was a window he could use to see many things; he had used it to uncover the secrets of humanity.

No matter.

Seeds of fear were being sown against Kyra inside the human stronghold. He was patient. Eventually they would restore her to her Master, and then he would exact all he needed. She would open the door to Lumen and lay bare the path for him that would result in his victory over all the realms.

CHAPTER 22

The third night of Phantom attacks loomed on the horizon. As the sun hastened its deathly crawl into darkness, the people in Tutis, terrified and trapped, found refuge in the storehouses and buildings, rather than the bunkhouses. They gathered in groups, cramming ten or more in each building. The hope was that the Phantoms would search the bunkhouses first, find them abandoned, and assume the people had fled the city. If they decided to search the city, the people would be warned by groups of soldiers hiding in the shadows, waiting for signs of an attack. Should the Phantoms attack the storehouses, the people could better defend themselves if their numbers were high.

Kyra hovered near the outer buildings, keeping a close eye on all who entered while the remaining stragglers slipped into their shelter. As the last door closed, she went to find Caden, who was staying outside with some of the other soldiers. She had volunteered to watch through the night with the others, but she couldn't say it was out of kindness; spending the night crammed in a storehouse with at least nine others, most of whom did not trust her, did not sound appealing. She'd take the fresh air, solitude, and uncertainty over that any day.

When Kyra left the area, she didn't see Anwill slip away in the opposite direction, toward the back of the city where no soldiers would be stationed. He was supposed to meet Shem today, and he couldn't be late. He had valuable information to share.

After exiting the city, Anwill skirted past the burial mound and danced his way around the traps set for intruders. He'd made a few friends in this city, and they'd let him know where he could safely walk without falling into a pit or coming to some other demise. The information was incredibly helpful.

When he reached the forest edge, Shem was waiting. Anwill greeted him with a grin, but Shem did not return the gesture.

"What have you learned?" Shem asked.

"They're scared," Anwill said. "The whole lot of 'em. Phantoms have been attackin'. Put 'em all on edge."

"Of course they're scared," Shem snapped. "They were scared long before I ever left."

Anwill chewed on his nail, then spit it into the trees. "Yeah, but it's different this time. They're movin' the people into the storehouses, sleepin' 'em in there, putting a bunch of 'em together. They think it'll give 'em a leg up when the Phantoms attack again."

"When they attack again?" Shem perked up in interest.

Anwill nodded. "Couldn't stop 'em the last two nights. Not even Kyra. Took almost thirty people and killed a woman the first night. Second night the number was higher. They know if this keeps up for long there'll be nothin' left."

Shem folded his arms, tapping the fingers of his right hand on his biceps. "So, if the Phantoms go directly into the bunkhouses as they've been doing, they'll find nothing?"

"Yeah."

"And they're grouping them up now. So, if the Phantoms should, say, light the buildings on fire instead of taking the people, they'd be in trouble?"

Anwill's head bobbed, and he grinned again. "Sittin' ducks."

Shem's lips twitched as he fought back a smile. "What else?"

"Kyra's alone a lot. She stays away from most the people. They're scared of her, too."

"Caden isn't."

Anwill shook his head. "No, but he don't act like her watchdog neither. He's with her a lot, but he don't guard her or nothin.' She's alone plenty."

Shem leaned against the tree while he studied the city. "Why are they afraid of her?"

Anwill leaned closer and his voice dropped in awe. "She killed a Phantom," he said. "I weren't there to see it, but as the story goes she pulled the power right outta him. Turned him into a frail old man."

"Interesting," Shem murmured, stepping closer to the forest edge. "That's why they aren't sending a Phantom to get her. It's probably why they want her so bad." He swung toward Anwill, face stretched into a grin. "This is good. She's isolating herself."

"We're gonna bring her to ya," Anwill said. "Lots of people in there don't trust her. They think if she's gone, they'll be safer."

Shem's eyes widened in surprise, then a smile curved on his lips. "Well done, Anwill," he said. "We need allies on the inside."

"We have one, and workin' on more. Our plan ain't clear yet. Still some kinks to work out. But we'll have her within a week. Til then, you'll have to wait here."

Shem grunted. "I'll leave Huiel and Falan. When you get her, there'll be a trail for you to follow to find them."

Anwill cleared his throat. "We're gonna set a trap fer Caden, too. You gonna miss that?"

Shem's face darkened. "Don't kill him until I get back."

Anwill grunted. "What are you gonna do?"

"Secure our footing in this war," Shem hissed. "Just do what I said. This will all pay off in the end."

As Anwill returned to the city, Shem slipped deeper into the forest. Huiel and Falan were waiting for his word. They both perked up when they heard him coming.

"Good news?" Huiel asked.

Shem nodded. "Good enough. Kyra's isolating herself, which'll make it easier to take her. Anwill's planning her kidnap. And I have some information I think some others will want. You two stay here and wait. I'll be back soon."

CHAPTER 23

K yra and Caden hunched beneath the shadows of the walls surrounding Tutis. The night brought a light rain that permeated everything. The clouds hid the moon, blocking all light from that quarter. Aside from the rain, no sound could be heard inside the city; the people were huddled in storehouses, and the soldiers guarding the streets had been directed to stay silent. The city appeared abandoned. But inside, hundreds of people waited, holding their breath in the hopes that the Phantom scourge might pass them by tonight.

Alone and concealed beneath the shadows, Kyra and Caden, both part of the night watch, worked to draw out her power. Their primary goal this night was discovering her strength. They'd chosen this particular location because the parapet hid them from view. Playing with fire and light in full view of the city would achieve the opposite of what they intended. So, they hid where the Phantoms would not see them.

They'd begun practicing as the sun fell beneath the horizon. Hours had slipped by unnoticed as they worked to draw out Kyra's power. Hours of practice with no results. Kyra's lips were pressed in a thin line, and though she said nothing, Caden knew from the way she breathed – deep, focused, intentional – and the way her hand trembled when she held it out that she was getting weary. Soon, they'd have to stop.

But not yet. She was determined to make something happen.

"Okay," Caden said. "Let's see your palm."

Kyra stretched out her hand, studying the faint glow. It was white with a blue edge to it.

"This time when you try to make it bright, don't think of it as a light separate from you. Think of it as an extension of you. I am not separate from this fire. Its energy is one and the same to my own. Think of your light the same way – it's simply an energy derived from inside you, one that you get to control."

Kyra bit her lip, concentrating on the light. She imagined it growing, becoming a ball like Caden's fire. Her eyes narrowed and she held her breath, thinking not of the light now but of the smallest bits of energy that created the light. She visualized it dancing and moving. But the exercise proved to be futile.

"It's not working," she said, her mouth pulling into a frown. She glared at the light, begging it to do something, anything! All she achieved was for it to dim. She dropped her hand in frustration. "I'm not even sure this can be controlled."

Caden pursed his lips, rubbing his chin as he did so. "I know it can be controlled. I've seen you do it."

"You're referring to a day I don't remember," Kyra said. "How do you know it was me in control that day? Maybe the Malic'Uiel manipulations hadn't faded like we thought."

Caden studied her, his gaze serious. "It wasn't that," he finally said. "This was nothing like what they do. Whatever it was, I don't believe they were part of it." He moved closer and reached for her hand, smoothing out her palm. The light responded to his touch, growing stronger. His face lit up. "Did you see it glow brighter just now?"

"Yes," she said. "It did the same thing when Bronson held his hand over mine. Maybe it's activated by others."

Caden gently smoothed her fingers out. "Try again?"

She nodded, aware of his touch more than anything.

He let his palm hover above hers. Her light flared for a brief moment, and then vanished. Her brows furrowed and she widened her palm, willing the light to return.

Nothing happened.

She ground her teeth in frustration. "Useless," she snapped.

Caden shook his head, closing her fingers into a fist. "Stop trying for just a few minutes. Rest. You're trying so hard to fix the problem, you won't be able to see a solution. Let your mind clear for a bit."

Kyra sighed and let her arm drop. She leaned her head against the wall, closing her eyes and sliding down until she sat on the cold cobblestone. "I'll never stop trying to understand this...or myself."

"I would hope not."

They lapsed into silence with Kyra lost in her thoughts, grappling with her fears and frustrations, while Caden couldn't help but think of the conversation he'd had with Avalyn earlier, about the darkness that fought so hard for the exhausted woman in front of him.

He sensed it now – that darkness Avalyn spoke of – sensed it swirling around her. It was a chaotic energy, one that brought confusion. He stepped back a few steps, away from the space surrounding Kyra.

The confusion lifted.

He returned to his place near her, and so did the chaotic, frenzied energy.

Kyra glanced at him, eyebrows raised, unaware of his experiment. "What was that?" she asked, letting her eyes droop closed again.

"Testing something." *Maybe,* he thought, *the dark chaos is what's stopping her from accessing the light.*

"Kyra, do you remember the day you escaped the Malic'Uiel? Remember how sure you were that we would be fine? I thought we were lost, but you had the most serene countenance I had ever seen. I swear, you emanated light." He'd never seen any person more pure, more sure of who they were and their place in the world.

"Would you believe that day is one of my better memories?" she said, a smile playing at the edge of her lips. "I felt so free. And it wasn't because I was no longer captive." She opened her eyes and found Caden's. "There were no shadows around me. I'd lived in darkness for so long, but that day..." she sighed. "All there was was light."

No shadows. Those were her words. He couldn't suppress a smile. This could be it – the answer to their problem.

"You were extraordinary," Caden said. "And when we came to the city, and you called down the light from the sky..." He shook his head, voice tinged with awe as he remembered. If only she could see it, too. "Your soul – that beautiful creation I've seen in your mind – that's what I saw. The few moments I was privileged to glimpse into your mind, I saw who you could be unencumbered by darkness. And somehow, that day, you were. The light was a gift for the rest of us." He moved to kneel in front of her, gently gripping her shoulders. "It wasn't that you controlled the light, or that you cast some unexplainable spell over the city. The light *was* you. Using it the way you did was just another part of you; it was you – uninhibited, raw, and unleashed. And it was extraordinary."

Kyra blinked rapidly, and her eyes shone, but she held is gaze. "If that was me," she whispered, "How do I find my way back?"

He smiled, shifting the tiniest bit until his fingers stroked her cheek. "By believing that you can. By seeing yourself the way I do, and letting it be true. Let me be the lens through which you view yourself. The darkness couldn't hold you then, and it can't hold you now. I know you feel it – the hopelessness, the pain, the fear – not only for yourself but for the rest of us. That weight, it is the weight of darkness. I believe you will gain power over the light when you allow yourself to be free of it." He moved closer, taking her face in his hands, his thumb brushed gently over her lips. "You are an incredible woman with gifts that may save mankind, but you have to let yourself *be* that."

Kyra swallowed hard, keenly aware of a lump forming in her throat. How had he spoken the words her soul cried out to hear? She leaned into his palm. "I'm afraid," she whispered.

"Of what?"

"What if I can't do it? What if I never learn to understand or control it? What if I hurt the people I'm trying to save?" Her voice hitched and she paused. After a moment she said, "How can others rely on me when I'm unable to rely on myself?"

"Believe," Caden said. "I'll believe in you when you think you can't. I'll hold you together when you're falling apart. Because you can do this. And I'll be here every step of the way. On the days when you don't think you can do it, I'll be here reminding you that you can. Just like I am now."

His hands slid down her arms until his fingers slipped into hers. His gaze dropped for a moment and his teeth tugged on his bottom lip. "I know you're a soldier first, Kyra, and that your focus is on saving your father – and humanity in the process. I understand why you want to free Gilrich's mind; if you can save him, maybe you can save others, maybe you can free Em." He inched closer, knees touching her legs now. "But do you think...maybe you can allow for more in your life?"

Kyra's breath caught in her throat. Around her, the world faded. In this moment it was just the two of them blanketed in the comfort of the night. He was so close that his warm breath fanned her face. She could close the distance between them in less than a heartbeat, her lips on his...

Her eyes widened. Never in her life had she had the thought of kissing someone. So focused had she been on being a soldier that she hadn't allowed other thoughts to come into play. Sure, Gilrich had joked about it before he'd become a Cadaver, but there was nothing romantic for her with Gilrich.

Caden, however...

For reasons she didn't fully understand, her heart pounded in her chest. She couldn't tell if it was from excitement or fear.

"Kyra," Caden whispered. He reached his hand up, turning her face toward his. His thumb stroked her bottom lip. "I'm right here."

Kyra swallowed hard, holding his gaze as her mind flew in a million different directions, all of them centered on the man in front of her.

He'd been her companion, her confidante since she'd returned from the Malic'Uiel. He'd taken care of her, watched over her, stayed by her side while others turned against her. He'd coaxed her into returning to reality, held her while she cried and suffered, picked her up when she felt she couldn't carry anymore. All of this just in Tutis.

Her mind flew then to the memories of their time together before she'd become a Cadaver, sifting through so many weary days and dark nights until she locked in on his time in the sick tent after a Cadaver had nearly killed him. She'd stayed by his side far more than necessary. At the time, she'd justified it a lot of different ways, but in reality she'd just been drawn to stay. She hadn't understood why she couldn't leave him, why it mattered so much to her that he live. Her conversation with Gilrich that day stood out:

"I wonder," Gilrich said. *"Would you mourn like this for me?"*

She'd been crying. Her answer had been horrible. *"I don't know. Would I?"*

Gilrich had tried to comfort her then, wouldn't leave her to cry alone. Then he asked, *"Do you wish it was me lying there?"*

She couldn't answer him honestly, and she'd refused to be honest with herself. If she had been honest, maybe she would have understood a few things – Gilrich obviously understood more than she did.

He left her with one final question. *"Right now, you're afraid of losing him. He's clinging to life, and you can't stand it. Why is that?"*

She couldn't answer Gilrich's question at the time – she wouldn't even look to see why. The ramifications of the question filled her with fear. That was uncharted territory. It was dangerous to go in there because once she did, there was no going back. That day, she'd chosen not to understand.

But today, today she understood.

Both hope and concern gripped her heart as a future unfolded in front of her, one she'd never allowed herself to see. She and Caden together, building a life, maybe even a life worth living. He clearly felt more than she'd realized, and she cared for him far more deeply than just a friend. They could love one another – they could be happy.

But one day they would lose.

Fear crashed over her.

One day the Malic'Uiel would come for them. One, or both, would be left broken while the person they loved was destroyed physically, emotionally, and spiritually. Her heart had shattered when Evia, her mother, was killed. She'd repaired pieces of it, but those pieces were ripped away when Em, her father, was taken. There was no patching it together after that. It beat to keep her body alive and that was all she would allow it to do. Maybe it wanted more with Caden. She could see that now. But her heart couldn't take another loss. Worse, she didn't trust herself not to be the one to leave him in pieces.

The wall pressed against Kyra's back, both comforting and claustrophobic. It spoke to safety, but it also barred her in. Her legs ached to run, willed her to escape before she broke him as she'd broken Gilrich. But there was nowhere to go. And he deserved an answer. Could she allow for more in her life?

He waited for her response; a quiet calm flowed from him, and his gaze never left her face.

"I can't," she finally whispered. "I want to, Caden, I do. Or rather, my heart wants to. But I can't risk opening that part of myself again."

"I won't hurt you," he said, his voice a whisper, mirroring hers.

She tried to swallow the sand in her throat, attempted to moisten her tongue, which felt an awful lot like a desert. *"You're* not the one who will hurt me. Nobody wins in this war. The Malic'Uiel make sure of it. If I let my heart go where it wants, I'll lose you. I'll have to watch them turn you into a monster. And I can't."

Caden leaned back on his heels, studying the cobblestone beneath his knees while rubbing the scar on his chest, the one that looked like a handprint. He lurched to his feet and paced away, hand pressing again and again over the scar. He turned back, hesitated when he glanced at her, then went back to pacing. He almost looked like he would flee, but then he whirled back and dropped in front of her.

"What if I told you the Malic'Uiel can't destroy me?" he said. "I'm sure they can cause my death, but they cannot turn me into a Cadaver. I suppose they could have made me a Phantom at one point, but I don't think that's possible now, either."

Kyra frowned. "How could you be immune to them?"

Caden tugged on the collar of his tunic, and his cheeks darkened in shame as he pulled back the material to reveal the scarred flesh. "Because of this. They gave this to me. They can imprison me. They can destroy my mind. But I cannot become a Cadaver. They are bound by their own oath." He smoothed the tunic back into place, covering the ruined flesh. "That's all I'm willing to share about this. It is my greatest point of shame. But I am immune."

Kyra's eyes flitted to the scar, then back to his face. Her mouth dropped as she considered what he was saying. Why would the Malic'Uiel swear an oath not to harm a human? Humans were not only their prey; they were their slaves, and their source of life. They fed off their souls. Why would they give one amnesty?

Panic edged its way into her breast. Who was Caden if he'd forced an oath from their lips? What kind of person knelt in front of her now?

The wall against her back was a trap. She couldn't get space to sort through this. All she could do was gape at him and pray he was the man she knew him to be.

CHAPTER 24

Kyra's hesitation seemed to darken the night around them, as if her very emotions caused the shadows to fall.

A sad smile formed on Caden's lips while he watched the emotions run across her face.

"Who *are* you?" she finally asked.

"I'm Caden. I'm the man you know. I tell you this part of my secret tonight because...I love you. I've loved you for a long time, and if I want to have anything with you, you deserve to know."

"*What* are you?" she whispered.

He sighed. "I'm a man trying to right the wrongs of so many others."

Her brows raised, but her face told him she did not find that answer satisfying.

"I don't know what I am," he said. "Half man, half Phantom. Maybe half man, half monster. I've been a monster for a long time now, long before the Phantom ever got to me."

"Caden," she said, exasperation creeping into her voice. "You can't be cryptic with me. First you ask me to open my heart to you, then you tell me you're immune to the Malic'Uiel – no, that they've sworn an oath not to harm you. An oath. With a human! And then you tell me you're a monster." She cocked her head to the side, shoving him back the tiniest bit. "You're asking me to trust you with everything but giving me very few answers in return."

Caden rose to his feet, pacing in front of her. "I don't know *what* I am," he said. "But I know *who* I am. I was a boy when the Malic'Uiel came to our world – realm, whatever you want to call it. One night I was taken from my home, in the middle of the night. I woke up to somebody clamping a dirty hand over my face, then a musty sack over my head. I couldn't scream and there were too many to fight. I didn't know what was happening, or who they were.

The men who kidnapped me held me in a cell for three days. They didn't unbind my hands, nor did they remove the sack. For three days I lived in darkness – in terror – I knew they were going to kill me. The cell was cold, and the floor was just dirt. Or rather, mud. Water seeped down the walls. I couldn't lean against them without the water soaking into my tunic. I did it a few times, when I was desperate for sleep, but it was so cold."

He spun on his heel, facing her while pleading for understanding. "I curled up in the middle of that cell. I wasn't alone. Rats came and went, sometimes biting at my feet or fingers. I couldn't see so all I could do was scream and try to scare them off. I was so scared for what those people would do to me." Caden pressed his clenched fist into his forehead, as if he could shove the memory out of his brain. "I wish now they would have just killed me."

"What did they do?" Kyra asked. Grief pricked at her heart, grief for a child she hadn't known who'd had an experience no person should ever have to endure. Three days in a cell like that would shape a child forever.

Caden went rigid; his hands dropped to his side and his jaw clenched in anger. "They used me to re-open the barrier between our world and theirs. Or rather, they coerced others through me." His head rose and when he faced her there were tears in his eyes. "If those men would have just killed me, let me starve to death or let the rats eat me alive, the Malic'Uiel never would have made it here. They couldn't have found their way through. But they needed me, and they kept me alive. And now our world is destroyed. Because of me."

Caden dropped to his knees, his legs buckling in defeat. "And that's why I tell you I'm a monster. I've always been. I was the catalyst that caused all of this." His hand fluttered toward the darkness surrounding them. "There would be no Phantoms, no Cadavers, no Malic'Uiel, if not for me."

"You were a child," Kyra rasped. "You can't believe that of yourself."

"But I can, Kyra. I was fourteen. Old enough to find a way to stop them. Old enough to know what I caused. You blame yourself for Gilrich, for the loss of his mind. It doesn't matter whether we were in control or not, does it? We caused hurt to others."

Kyra nodded, a lump forming in her throat. He was right. She blamed herself because at the end of the day, she was responsible for Gilrich. While she didn't believe Caden should carry the blame for the destruction of the world, she could understand why he did.

"You told me once that you were going to carry this secret to the end of the war. What changed?"

Caden's lips formed a wan smile. "You. I want you to know who I am. I want you to know *what* I am. Know enough, at least. But I didn't tell you everything; I just told you what mattered. I won't tell you the rest."

"Do I want to know the rest?"

Caden shook his head. "No. You don't."

They both slipped into silence, which stretched on. It wasn't uncomfortable, just melancholy. Both of them had devils they were battling. "We're losing, aren't we?" Kyra said.

"I hope not," Caden answered. "I won't consider us lost until all humanity is dead or destroyed."

Kyra shook her head, reaching to touch Caden's hand. "I don't mean humanity," she said. "I mean us. You and me. We're losing to our own demons."

Caden's hand closed around hers, and he brought it to his lips. "Only some days. We're fighting an internal battle as desperate as the external one. We're going to have those days where the battle is fierce." He reached and grabbed her other hand, bringing them both to his lips. "Tomorrow we'll start the battle again, and tomorrow we'll be winning. Because we woke up. Because we chose to live. Because we believe we're better than the voices that say we're lost."

Caden's words washed over Kyra like a soothing balm. She chose to wake up every single day. And every day she fought the war of her mind and the war of her world. The people in the city feared her, but she wanted nothing more than to protect them. She could run, live on her own, and escape it all for a while, but she chose to stay because she believed something better was possible.

Caden was right.

Somewhere inside she harbored power. Maybe just a small seed, but it was there. She would cultivate it, would discover its source and control it. She pulled in a deep breath, closing her eyes so she could truly feel the cool air as it rushed into her lungs. Life existed in that small movement. She envisioned the air swirling in her as she envisioned the light Caden spoke of swirling in her mind. She imagined it rushing through her veins to fill her entire body.

Life existed in the light.

Understanding began to prick at her consciousness. When she'd been imprisoned, she'd found the light – in the middle of her own hell and suffering, stripped away, she'd found it. And in that, she'd found life – her life. The light saved her.

Her eyes popped open. The more she embraced the light and separated herself from the fear, the more she embraced life. She stretched out her palm again. It glowed as it had for weeks, but now the light swirled in intricate patterns, dancing and jumping away from her skin and around her hand. Tendrils of it twisted up her arm.

Caden watched the light with awe. "What happened?" he asked.

"I...I think I'm starting to understand," she said. A giggle burst from her lips as the light flared toward Caden. "The light is life," she said. "I just have to find life – I have to live!"

Caden held out his palm, mirroring hers. A ball of fire exploded over it. "I carry death in my power, and you carry life."

She nodded, holding her hand above his. The light reached toward the fire, encompassing it until it consumed it entirely. When she pulled back, Caden held a ball of light.

"Yes, but life overcomes death." She grinned and her eyes flitted to his. "I don't know how to control it yet, but I can see it. I know where the path begins"

"And I'll help you find where it ends."

She shook her head. "I don't think we have to find where it ends. I believe we decide where it ends."

"Then I'll walk it with you."

"At my side?"

"Always."

She laughed out loud as the light flared, twisting around both of their outstretched arms. "Maybe I can't embrace us yet," she said. "But maybe I can learn."

He laughed with her, gathering her in his arms.

She sighed into his embrace. Her heart beat against his chest, happy, and for the moment, content in his arms.

"Can you learn to love me?" he asked.

"I already do love you, Caden. You'll just have to help me unlock my heart."

"Can I kiss you?" he whispered.

"Not yet," she said. "But ask again sometime. Eventually I may say yes."

CHAPTER 25

Kyra and Dalia made their way through the streets of Tutis. Miraculously, the city had experienced three days of respite, with no attack from the Phantoms. The relief the people felt was palpable, evident by the mere fact that fewer people shied away from her, and one or two even ventured to make eye contact, without hostility driving the action.

Dalia's child seemed to be strong and healthy. Twice, Kyra had felt the baby kick beneath her fingers. Dalia's hand rested on her stomach, protecting the unborn child she carried.

"How's the baby doing?" Kyra asked.

Dalia glanced up. "Wonderful," she said. "Every day the kicks get stronger. I think it's a boy. It must be with how much he moves!"

Kyra laughed. "Maybe it's just a really determined girl."

"Maybe. I'm happy either way." Her hand rubbed gentle circles on her stomach. "I'm looking forward to meeting him...or her."

"I can only imagine," Kyra said. "Yours will be the first child born in freedom in many years. I hope that's a good omen."

"It is," Dalia said. "It has to be, otherwise what's the point?"

"I ask myself that a lot," Kyra murmured.

After a few moments of silence Kyra asked. "Have you visited Gilrich within the last day or two? I plan to see him today, but wonder if you made any progress?"

Dalia nodded. "Yes, I visit him daily. He's talking to me more. He holds my gaze now, and he doesn't look angry when he does. For a long time, he wouldn't look at me, and he only grunted when he spoke."

Kyra beamed. "That sounds like progress!"

"It is," Dalia said quietly. "To some degree. I haven't been able to get him to see you any other way, though. There's been no progress there."

"I'm not surprised." The disappointment wasn't as sharp as Kyra expected. Unlocking Gilrich's mind would take time. She stopped walking and turned to her friend. "Do you think maybe I should let him be for a while? I can't help but feel like I'm making things worse."

Dalia cocked her head to the side as she considered, and her hand continued rubbing absentminded circles on her growing stomach. "I think you should continue to visit him. Somewhere in his mind he knows it's because you care – he must know."

Kyra glanced toward Gilrich's building and her nose scrunched up in dismay. "I keep hoping he knows, but sometimes it's hard to keep hope alive. He's so angry, so determined to stay the way he is. The Cadaver wants to live."

Dalia nodded and moved toward the building again. "So does the man." As she walked, one hand supported her back. "I'm starting to feel the weight of this baby," she said with a laugh. Then the smile faded. "Maybe Gilrich would open up to you if you stopped trying to change the Cadaver."

"What do you mean?" Kyra asked, falling back into step beside her, her hands clasped behind her back.

"When I visit Gilrich, I don't have any reason to be there other than to make sure he's okay. I'm not trying to change the Cadaver. I don't even hate the Cadaver, though I know I probably should. It's just me and whatever creature is in front of me. Maybe you should try accepting what he is before forcing that to change."

Kyra bit her lip, and she eyed Dalia with worry. "But if we don't change the Cadaver, we'll never have Gilrich back."

"We may never have him back anyway."

That thought twisted in Kyra's gut. She knew she might never get him back. But to accept him as a Cadaver, to see that monster day in and day out, to know Gilrich's mind was still there, and leave it? Everything in her screamed against it, but Dalia, from everything she could tell, used both her head and her heart. She was intuitive, and understood things on a different level than most. She connected with the people around her in ways Kyra had never seen. Kyra had a deep trust in her. "Maybe you're right," Kyra said.

Dalia smiled, touching Kyra's arm briefly. "I don't know if I'm right. I just know what you're doing right now isn't working." They were outside the building now and she gestured toward it. "Go inside. Keep visiting him. Keep loving him. Maybe something will change."

As Dalia turned to leave, Kyra climbed the steps into the building. The nearby guards were engaged in a haphazard knife-throwing contest. Neither of them was winning, but they both ignored her, which suited her just fine.

Inside the building Gilrich remained as always, chained to the wall, unable to move more than a step or two. Somebody had brought him a pillow and a small blanket. Probably Dalia.

"Hey, Gilrich," Kyra said as she closed the door. "How are you today?"

The Cadaver watched her, choosing to remain quiet.

Kyra sat in front of him, staying just out of reach. She studied his face, searching his eyes for some sign of her friend. A monster glared back.

"Do you remember the first time we met, Gilrich?" she asked. "I'd just come through the Land of Desolation and found the army. You were the first man I saw." She smiled at the memory. "You were so confi-

dent – arrogant is how I took it. You were kind. And
that made a difference for me, even if I didn't show it
that day."

Gilrich grunted.

"You became a great friend," she said. "One I ad-
mired." She leaned back on her hands, gazing at her
friend. "I didn't recognize you at first when I was a
Cadaver and they brought you to me. I didn't know
who you were. But even as a Cadaver, I knew you
were somebody I could trust."

"It's not wise to trust a Cadaver."

"No," Kyra mused. "It really isn't. But I couldn't
help it. It's part of who you are."

"Not anymore."

"Dalia says I should accept that you are a Cadaver," Kyra said. "Accept that you may never change."

"Dalia has more sense than you."

Kyra chuckled. "I believe she does." She leaned forward, holding his gaze again. "But here's the thing,
Gilrich. I was a Cadaver. My mind was theirs, too, but
it's not anymore. I found freedom. I know you can find
it, too. I'm not trying to change you; I'm trying to free
you from the world they've trapped you in. I know
how hopeless that world is. I know what it feels like to
have everything you love destroyed and turned into
the enemy, to have love become hate, to experience a
pain so deep and so vast the only thing you can do is
wrap yourself in apathy – to stop feeling anything be-

cause if you don't, the pain will kill you. Apathy as a means of survival. It's a horrible way to live."

Girlrch's eyes didn't flinch from her. His tongue shot out and licked parched lips. "Maybe theirs is a world of apathy, but at least it was a world that I was free to reside in. You have me in chains here."

Kyra eyes his bonds, knowing he was right. "The people fear what you may do to them."

"As they should," Gilrich said. "You and I signed away our souls to the Malic'Uiel. I am bound to serve them." He glared at her. "As are you."

"You can walk away from that," Kyra breathed. "I did." She held out her hand, showing him her palm, which glowed faintly. "You can find your life again. A different life than the one you've been conditioned to crave. The one the Malic'Uiel leave you with does not bring joy. It's empty and requires the suffering of others to sustain it. The one I found brings so much more."

Gilrich studied her palm. He seemed drawn to it. His breathing calmed, becoming soft and even. His shoulders relaxed. And when he glanced at her face, for a moment she saw *him*. She saw Gilrich looking back.

She smiled and his eyes darted away. The rapid breathing returned. "Go away," he hissed. "Take your light and leave. I want no part of it."

Kyra crept closer, kneeling in front of him. Slowly she brought her hand to his face. He tried to turn away, but he couldn't stop her. He had nowhere to go.

Gently she placed her palm to his mottled cheek. "I'll bring you back to me," she said. "To Caden. To the general. We need you."

Gilrich refused to hold her gaze, but she saw tears in his eyes.

Something had shifted today.

She'd seen it.

Gilrich was coming back.

CHAPTER 26

Tutis was spared a fourth night, and then a fifth. At first Kyra felt relief, but as the days passed with no sign of the enemy, foreboding began to grow in Kyra's breast. The Phantoms were coming back, of that she was sure...so why weren't they attacking now? What game were they playing, and how could she counteract their move?

"Something is wrong," she told Caden. They were resting in their bunkhouse after spending the dark hours on the night watch. "They're changing their plan, I'm sure of it."

She held out her palm in front of her, reminding herself as she tried to coax the light to life, that it was part of her. The worry in her chest made it hard to demand anything of it, however. The ribbons and swirls sparked for a moment then faltered, returning to the faint glow she was used to.

"Struggling today?" Caden asked, moving to sit next to her on her cot.

She nodded. "I can't seem to find the light right now."

"You're worried about Tutis," Caden said. "For good reason. My gut tells me you're right. I know they're coming back – everybody knows."

"It's not that they're coming back that worries me," Kyra said, dropping her palm in her lap. The lack of response from her light frustrated her and she curled her fingers into a fist. She didn't want to see it anymore. "What worries me is that they're going to change their methods. They're not going to give us a chance to adapt to them. They'll play this game of cat and mouse until they've taken everybody. Tutis will be a dead city once more, and all hope for humanity will be lost."

"As long as we have you, we have hope for humanity," Caden said, taking her hand and smoothing out the fist. He wove his fingers through hers.

Kyra sighed. "You say that. I hope you're right."

"Have you heard the voice lately?" Caden asked. "The voice that guides you?"

"I haven't heard it for weeks." Kyra's exasperation was plain.

"Hmmm," Caden pushed himself off the cot, moving to stand near the small window. He gazed into the streets. "Empty today," he observed. "The people are afraid."

"They don't know where to turn for safety," Kyra said. "Do they follow General Prait's lead and stay here, or do they flee? Whispers on the street tell me that many of them are thinking of going back to the Adeo Mountains."

"I've heard that, too," he said. "There's a rift happening."

"Unfortunately. But I can't say I blame them." Kyra flopped backward on the cot, letting her eyes sweep the ceiling. "We need to unite them. The division is only causing harm."

"Mhmmm," Caden murmured. He continued his tenure at the window, gazing outside but his thoughts were far from the view he was fixed on.

"Caden?" Kyra asked, pushing up on her elbow. "Where are you right now?'

He blinked and turned back to her. Red flooded his cheeks. "I was thinking about Avalyn."

"Oh," Kyra said, her face falling. She rose to her feet and to stand behind him, resting her cheek on his shoulder as her fingers trilled down his arm. "I'm sorry you lost her."

"She's still here," he said, tapping his temple. He turned and smiled, tapping Kyra's as well. "And here."

Confusion clouded Kyra's features. "I've never met her. She's not in my mind. I have no memories to hold her."

Caden smiled. "You have more than you think. Avalyn speaks to me, too, Kyra, as she speaks to you."

Kyra rocked back. "What are you saying?"

"The voice you hear is Avalyn. She told me herself. She needs you to find her...for all of us."

Kyra blinked and her face paled. "I'm not sure I like the sound of that," she whispered. "You're telling me I speak to the dead?"

"I'm telling you you have a role to play in this. So do I, and so does she. She can help you, but you have to let her in again."

Kyra swallowed hard, trying to get rid of the feeling of sand in her mouth. *I speak to the dead? What kind of creature am I?* She fought against the knowledge, all too aware of an all too familiar fear creeping in and, worse, of the darkness flaring up to take her. She knew now that the darkness was a cloak of protection, and it had been since she'd found her way back from the Malic'Uiel. She feared it, but she understood it enough to find some comfort in it. She could wrap herself in that cloak, walk away, and never look back. She could escape all this uncertainty.

Stop it! This voice was all hers, and it screamed at her. *This is not you! That cloak you crave will kill you. Quit acting like the child who lost her mother, and step into the woman that destroyed her master – the one who pulled a Phantom's power right from his body – be the woman all enemies fear!*

Kyra listened to that voice, her own voice of reason, and her resolve grew.

Whoever or whatever was speaking to her now was right. She had to shed every bit of the cloak of fear and embrace what could be. She squared her shoulders and sucked in a deep breath. Who cared if she spoke to the dead? It didn't matter what kind of insane things happened inside her head. She had two choices at any given moment: cower in fear of the unknown until she returned to the Cadaver she had been. Or embrace the unknown with open arms and allow the discovery of what could me.

Memories pricked at her conscience, and she saw herself in the chamber of the Malic'uiel, an observer this time instead of the key player. The Master had tried to force her will, and instead, he woke something inside her, something great and glorious. The light exploded from her and consumed him – whatever it was had forced her Master to succumb to the same suffering he'd caused for others. She hadn't feared death that day; she had welcomed it. Nor had she been afraid of those who controlled her life. No, she'd shed their chains and stood against them. *That* was who she had to become.

"Well?" Caden said, peering into her face. He saw far more than he ever let on, and she knew it. That's why he studied her the way he did.

"I can't live in fear anymore."

"No. You can't. Neither of us can."

Before the moon rose that night, the people were safely tucked away in the storehouses. As with the previous three nights, soldiers hid in the shadows waiting for an attack. Kyra and Caden took up their post under the parapet, waiting with the rest of them, but secluded so Kyra could spend more time working with her power.

Tonight, for the first time, she felt nothing but a sense of calm. The conversation from the morning had stayed with her throughout the day and she'd allowed the peace it brought to flood through her. The light responded to the calm inside, and tonight its tendrils not only flowed up her arm, they swirled around her entire body – an array of colors dove in and around her: pinks, blues, purples, greens, yellows. They buzzed through her veins like bolts of lightning.

Caden watched this display, his grin growing wider with every passing second. "It's beautiful," he said, reaching out to let the light swirl around his hand. "I've never seen anything like it."

Kyra laughed. "That makes two of us. I think I'm starting to understand how it works, though. When I focus on a specific location on my body, the light moves to that area. If I focus on my entire body, the light surrounds me."

"I wonder..." Caden murmured. A second later fire ignited on both of his hands. "Can it be controlled the same way my fire can?"

Kyra sent the light back to her palm, where it lay dormant until she was ready. "What do you mean?"

"Remember how I told you that my control of the fire isn't magic so much as it is an understanding of the energies that create fire?"

"Yeah, I remember that."

"Light is made up of its own energetic structure. I can send this fire away from my body or suck it into my body. I can command it to engulf any of my targets or pull it away from a burning object. But it isn't done by focusing on the object or location; I do it by telling the energy to do what I want it to do. It listens and responds."

"Interesting," Kyra said. "You think light would operate the same way?"

"It makes sense that it would."

"How do I find out?"

Caden held his fiery fist toward her. "Try to replicate my fire in your light. Close your eyes and feel the light in your body. That's how I began practicing. I let myself feel the energy."

"Okay," Kyra said, closing her eyes as he suggested. She brought her attention to her palms first. Caden was right, there was an energy there. The electricity she'd been experiencing seemed to hover just over her skin. Cut off from sight, the rest of her senses were forced to enhance. The light hummed over her while her skin remained solid.

"I can feel it," she said. "The energy. It's in my hand."

"Is it anywhere else?" Caden asked. "Search for it in the rest of your body."

She went back to the energy buzzing on her hand, then followed where it led. Lines of it shot up from her palm, twining over and around her skin, humming inside her. A smile broke on her lips. "It's in my veins," she said. "My blood." She focused on her heart, listening for the thrum of energy there. It pulsed from her chest along with her heartbeat; the energy rippled from her body in waves. Her eyes popped open. "It's part of me," she whispered. "It truly is life."

Caden hopped a little on the balls of his feet, excitement pulling him toward her. "Now…" He held his hands out again. Flames licked at his flesh but burned nothing. "Can you mimic me?"

Kyra bit her lip in concentration. She found the hum of energy again then focused on individual pieces of it. She just had to feel the source. For a moment, she felt it, but search took effort, and she couldn't maintain it. Her breath came in short bursts, eyes narrowed as she concentrated on the energy coursing through her.

Mimic Caden's fire!

She pushed harder, demanding the light move. It shifted around her but wouldn't respond the way his fire did. Sweat broke on her forehead and her frustration mounted. It had to be possible!

Suddenly, she lost control. The light burst out of her, engulfing them, the parapet, and the surrounding buildings before snapping back to her body.

She gasped, doubling over with her hands on her knees. So much for being discreet. If they were lucky, nobody saw that. "I must be doing...something...wrong," she said between breaths. "You make it look easy."

"It is easy," Caden said "Now. It wasn't always."

She leaned her head against the wall, closing her eyes while she sucked in great gulps of air. "That's exhausting."

He chuckled. "It's only exhausting until you realize the energy is no different than any other part of your body. It's just as easy as controlling your fingers." He wiggled his fingers at her. "Just like that. You've just found a body part you didn't know you had, and now you get to learn how to use it."

Kyra rolled her eyes. "An invisible body part. Perfect."

"I'm serious."

"I know you are." She straightened, holding out her palm. "I'm going to try again."

He folded his arms, waiting.

But as she was about to close her eyes, a ball of fire exploded from within the city.

CHAPTER 27

B oth Caden and Kyra whirled toward the explosion, and then bolted forward, all practice forgotten. The Phantoms had come again, there was no question about that. As they neared the storehouses, a second ball of fire filled the night sky, this one nowhere near the first. Kyra veered toward the second while Caden pounded toward the first, racing down the street away from her. She glanced at him once, long enough to see him turn the corner out of her sight.

Smoke drifted toward her, but it got thicker as she neared the source of the explosion. She coughed, covering her mouth with her sleeve. People poured from the storehouses, choking on the thick smoke. Some of them were crying, others screamed and clutched one another for support. Flames licked at the walls and roofs of multiple storehouses.

Kyra stopped short when she found the source of the explosion; horror wrenched in her gut. She'd found a storehouse completely engulfed in flames. The door was bolted shut, and the bolts melted into a mass of metal. Nobody could get out. Inside, people screamed, pounding on the door, the walls. Hands flailed from the small window, clawing at the air, desperate for escape.

The light in her veins hummed, surging stronger and stronger. It grew, whirling and dancing up her arms and around her body. It wanted to save those people.

And so did she.

She took one step forward when an explosion inside the building obliterated it. The force of the blow threw her backwards. She landed hard, her head cracking against the cobblestone. Stars exploded in her vision. She gasped, dazed, trying to fill lungs that wouldn't take in air while the world spun, and her ears rung. The faces of the people around her were masks of horror. Heat blazed over her skin. Then, she saw the first Phantom.

One after another they dropped into the city. People fled in every direction, desperate to escape. They stumbled over one another, crying in fear. But it was useless. The Phantoms were quick and thorough. They dropped in, yanked their victims away, then vanished as quickly as they had come.

Screams filled the night in every direction – except for the burning building. Those screams had stopped.

Kyra's lungs finally opened, and she sucked in a huge breath, choking immediately on the smoke. But her burning lungs still managed to find relief. Reorienting herself, she lurched to her feet and half stumbled, half crawled toward the building, trembling as she gaped at its remains. Nobody could survive that. They'd be lucky to recover any bodies.

Just as quickly as it started, it was over. The Phantoms were gone, along with their victims. The storehouse was a pile of ash, along with its inhabitants. The buildings closest to it were piles of rubble. People stumbled about, dazed and bewildered. Others screamed for water or help.

She hadn't been able to save them, any of them. Not the people trapped in the building, or the victims snatched by the Phantoms. She collapsed on her knees in front of the building's ashes, unaware of the tears that flowed unhindered. Around her, pounding footsteps spoke to the panic that gripped the people rushing around her. The wails of those who'd lost loved ones filled the air. All Kyra could think of were those who had been taken, and those who'd been killed.

She hadn't been able to stop them.

Grief rippled through her body.

Just before she pushed herself to her feet, a man – one of the many people running by – stumbled into her. Their bodies tumbled to the ground, with hers pinned beneath his. "Hey!" she yelled, accusing, but that was as far as she got before he shoved a wad of cloth in her mouth and clapped his hand over it. Anger flared when she saw Leland grinning down at her.

He moved swiftly as he pulled her to her feet and yanked her arms painfully behind her back. Anwill materialized in the madness and bound her wrists before Leland released them. Leland prodded her forward while Anwill stayed close behind, probably concealing the rope that bound. Leland's dirty hands never left her mouth. In the panic of the night, nobody noticed or cared as they dragged her away.

"Come on," Anwill said. "We have to hurry 'fore they figure she'd gone."

"We'll be rid of her long before they do. You know they want her." Leland's voice, growing in her ear, had a dark, menacing edge.

Panic crept into her chest. The Malic'Uiel – they were taking her back to them!

The light energy she'd felt so strongly while facing the fire surged through her again, demanding that she use it. It roared in her chest like an animal – no, like another being, another mind, gaining strength and power. The energy grew until she knew she'd explode into a million bits if it didn't find release.

When it finally forced itself out of her, she screamed – a primal, bloodcurdling sound that she could not control. The gag disintegrated as an explosion of light threw her and her captors to the ground. Her hands flew free as the light obliterated the rope, but not in time to stop her body from slamming against the cobblestones. The breath whooshed from her lungs. She lay there, momentarily stunned. Her body trembled all over, but the hum of that power buzzed through her, and she greedily lapped it up, coaxing it into her veins.

The sound of groaning broke her out of her shock, and she looked around to see both of her captors – one still in a daze, one struggling to his feet. Anwill, on one side of her, lay flat on his back, hands clenched into fists, shaking uncontrollably. His clothing was torn, hair disheveled, and a trickle of blood dripped from his head onto the street. Leland attempted to stand on the other side of her. He was a little better off, trying to push himself up on shaking legs.

Kyra scrambled to her feet and whirled to face him, hands outstretched while lightning arced between her palms. "Don't come near me," she warned.

Leland straightened to his full height, fingers twitching, and jaw clenched. Hate and fear battled for dominance in his eyes.

She held his gaze, pushing back the flood of anger and sadness that rushed through her. She'd known Leland hated her, but she hadn't thought he would try to get rid of her.

"Why, Leland?"

Leland's eyes narrowed. Her heart sunk as the hate in his eyes won out. "Because I won't let humanity lose at the hands of a witch."

Sadness pricked her heart. "If only you knew how much I am trying to help. I may not understand what I am, but I know I have the power to win." She held out her hand, showing Leland the light that danced on

THE RISE OF SPERO

her palm. "This light protects life," she said. "It didn't come to me to destroy what's good."

Leland ignored the light. Instead, he spat at her feet. She didn't have to imagine how much he wanted her dead. Hate oozed from every power of his body. He glanced to his side, where his dagger lay not far from where he stood.

So focused was Kyra on Leland, the greater threat, she didn't see Anwill until he was almost on top of her, barreling toward her like a storm. She dodged out of the way, distracted just long enough for Leland to crack his fist right into her temple.

She stumbled backward while the world spun off kilter. Darkness crept in at the edges of her vision. Fearing she would lose consciousness and wake up a prisoner – or not wake up at all – she willed the light to slither from her hands and encompass her body. When she felt its energy encasing every piece of her, a shield of lightning that would bring her no harm, she allowed herself to stumble to her knees, gasping, fighting to hold onto consciousness. The energy pulsed around her, her shield, her protection.

From behind, Anwill rushed to grab her, but when his body hit the shield, he was thrown back. A sickening crack followed as he crashed into the corner of the building. She jerked toward him just in time to see his body crumble to the cold cobblestone.

Leland stumbled back, shocked and terrified. His focus shifted between his broken comrade and the woman he'd chosen to make an enemy.

Rather than face her, he turned and fled.

Alone, Kyra let the energy slowly fade until it was in her hands one more. Head pounding, she eased herself to her feet and shuffled to where Anwill lay. Carefully, she knelt next to him, testing the inside of his wrist for a pulse.

There was none.

She sighed and let her head drop into her hands. She hadn't meant to kill him, hadn't wanted to kill him. She only wanted to protect herself.

A tear dripped on her palm and then another. Soon she couldn't stop the sobs; they wracked her body, ripping from her throat, uncontrolled and broken. She didn't stop crying until she heard pounding and moans – the sounds of a body being beaten.

Leaving Anwill, she ran in the direction of the sound. Maybe she was at fault for Anwill's death, but she could at least try to save the living.

When she rounded the corner, she found Caden mercilessly beating an already broken man.

She screamed and sprinted toward him, shoving him off the beaten body. One glance told her who his victim was: Leland.

"Caden," she said. "Look at me!"

Caden's eyes were wild, and he tried to shove her aside. His one focus was on Leland.

"Caden!" she screamed, gripping his shoulders. "You're going to kill him!"

Finally, he blinked and lucidity returned. "He deserves to die."

"You can't kill him, Caden. Not like this. We will let General Prait deal with him."

Caden stopped fighting her, but his hands were shaking. Rage rippled off him in waves. "He would have killed you!"

"He would have. But you know more than anybody in order to fight the monster you can't become the monster." She pressed her palm against his chest, covering the scar that lay beneath the tunic. "Isn't that what you're teaching me every day? Isn't that the choice you've been telling me I get to make?

From behind her, Leland coughed. His breaths were raspy. "I'm not a murderer," he said. "Not like you two. You're going to see us all slaughtered in our beds." He coughed one more, spitting blood onto the cobblestone. "I'm doing what's best for the rest of us. The two of you be damned."

Caden covered Kyra's hand with his, pressing it over his heart. The muscles in his jaw were taut, and his eyes darted between Leland and her. "If he had killed you, we would all be lost." His whole body trembled. Flames licked from his fingers, reaching toward Leland.

"Control it, Caden." She stepped closer, pressing the other hand to his cheek. "Nobody controls the monster better than you. You don't need to do this."

Slowly the flames pulled back, bit by bit, until they disappeared. "You don't understand, Kyra. If you are lost, I have no reason to keep going. The monster would win."

The silence that followed weighed on them both, oppressive and suffocating.

Caden's hand over Kyra's was like a lifeline right now, a portal to a world she had once understood, one that had tipped off its axis in the last few moments. She had killed a man, and she'd only just stopped Caden from doing the same. What were they becoming?"

Finally, Caden pulled her against his chest, holding her tight in his arms. His hand came up, winding itself in her hair. "I...can't lose you, all right? I can't."

She lay her head against his chest, content to let him hold her. "I'm not going anywhere."

Behind them, Leland cursed. "You'll kill us all."

"Get out of here, Leland," Caden snapped. "Scurry away before I finish this." To prove his words, the tendrils of flame returned, reaching toward him.

Leland hesitated for just a moment before lurching to his feet and limping down the street.

"Are you okay, Kyra?" Caden asked when Leland was gone. He took her face in his hands, gently brushing his fingers along her temple where Leland's fist had made contact. "I'm sorry I didn't get here in time."

Her eyes fluttered closed when his lips followed his fingers. He placed a gentle kiss on the bruised skin. "I'm sorry," he said again.

"I'll be fine, Caden. But Anwill is dead."

Caden groaned. "What happened?"

"My light..." she trailed off. "It was an accident. They wanted to take me back...to...to..." She shuddered, wrapping her arms around her chest. "I can't go back." The words were a wounded plea, torn from a broken soul.

Caden stiffened next to her, lips flattening in anger. "That was their plan? To give you back to them?"

"Yes."

"I'm glad he's dead. I should have killed Leland, too."

"It would be worse for both of us if you did."

"Maybe." His eyes flitted down the street where Leland had fled, as if he wanted to go after him.

She slipped her hand in his, keeping him anchored to her side. "We have to be better than them, Caden. We can't give in like they can."

"Can't we?"

He turned the full force of his gaze on her now, and his demeanor changed. In the space of a moment, she knew he wasn't talking about Leland anymore.

She fell back a step, heart suddenly pounding.

"Kyra..." he said, stepping after her. "I..." he paused, hands clenched into fists. He reached her then pulled back, hesitant and unsure. She felt his uncertainty in her own beating heart. Did she want this? Did he?

But when he straightened, and his smoldering gaze found her own, her heart quieted. He closed the distance between them in one step.

When his lips found hers, the world stopped.

Time vanished.

Spero disappeared.

His fingers wound in her hair, and he breathed her in as if she were life itself. She clung to him, suddenly desperate for his contact.

Her shattered heart started beating again.

When he broke the kiss, she nearly protested, but then his lips moved to trail down her jaw and neck instead. Fire ignited everywhere his lips touched her skin. And she didn't fight it. Didn't stop it. She wanted nothing more than this, than him, right now and forever. Her light flooded around them, encompassing them in its own embrace.

Finally, he sighed and time restarted. She remembered where they were, what they were, and the body that lay in the street beyond them.

But for the moment, it didn't matter.

He pressed one more gentle kiss to her lips. "I'm sorry," he said. "I didn't want to hold back anymore."

She smiled, and brushed her thumb over his lips. "I didn't stop you."

"I'm glad."

She let her eyes close, let her mind wrap around the beautiful memory of this moment, knowing that soon they'd have to face a much harsher reality. When she opened them again, he was watching her. "I just...don't want to forget this experience," she said. "It's mine to cherish." Then she took his hand and squared her shoulders. "You ready to face this all again?"

He nodded, squeezing her hand in his. "I'll be by your side every step of the way."

CHAPTER 28

While it was tempting to stay in the moment of bliss they had found, Kyra and Caden knew they couldn't. They had to face the reality of what the night's attack had brought not only to Tutis, but to Kyra.

They left the scene of Anwill's death hand in hand, as much for support as anything. They both knew that this death – since it was caused by Kyra's power – would come back to them, reaching beyond the grave, a ghost whose sole purpose was to hover over their lives and siphon away the moment of peace they'd found in each other.

It would come, of that there was no doubt. There would be consequences for his death.

But tonight, as much as that weighed on them, there were other damages that needed attending.

As they returned to the storehouses, to the pile of ashes that was once a building, the scene of horror reemerged. Kyra hesitated and then stopped. They'd made mistakes tonight, but maybe Caden had done some good. "Were you able to help anybody, Caden?" she asked, her voice betraying the hope she was afraid to feel.

"No," he said, his grip tightening on hers. "I wish I could say otherwise."

"Me too."

The picture unfolding before them was one of utter devastation. People stumbled by in a daze; their eyes were glazed over, hands limp at their sides. Some of them held their arms tight around their bodies, as if that one act might keep them from crumbling to pieces. General Prait and members of the council moved among the people, comforting where they could, sending others to Dr. Bron for help when they couldn't. The words General Prait spoke made their way to Kyra. They sounded hollow. "It'll be okay. We'll figure this out. I'm sorry he's gone."

Generic phrases. General Prait had no comfort left to give.

"How did you know Leland had taken me?" Kyra asked Caden, her voice quiet so the others wouldn't hear.

"Dalia. She saw them take you."

Kyra nodded. Of course. She hadn't seen Dalia in the chaos, but she was one of the few allies she had in the city. None of the others would have noticed or cared.

"Can I ask you something, Caden?"

"Of course."

Kyra kept her voice low so the people around them wouldn't hear their conversation. "Why were you willing to kill him for me?" She didn't need to say who; he knew.

Caden grunted. "I snapped tonight," he said. He bent, picked up a piece of charred, smoldering wood and threw it onto the pile of rubble that had once been a building. "I've watched him abuse you, watched him poison this city against you. When she told me he took you, I lost it. I saw red and wanted blood." He ran dirty fingers along his chin, leaving a streak of soot and blood. "Leland has no idea the damage he almost wrought, not for myself but for humanity. His life is meaningless compared to yours."

Kyra groaned. "No life is meaningless! Isn't that what we're fighting for? The value and sanctity of life?"

"Yes, but you don't realize how imperative you are to this. That light you carry inside you is more than a parlor trick." He turned to her, shaking her shoulders as if he hoped to wake her from his nightmares. "You are the key to winning this thing."

She brought his hand up to her face, resting her cheek against his palm. It was a warm comfort on a comfortless night. "I can't be the key if what I do or who I am causes others to die, no matter how bad they are. I don't fully understand this light, but I do know that it is life. If it causes suffering and pain – and death –" she stumbled on the words. "Then I believe...it would seem..." She bit her lip, trying to clear her thoughts. Finally, she asked, "What happens when light becomes the post that others are judged by? Who are we if life becomes death?"

"I don't..." his brow furrowed, hand dropping to his side. "I'm not sure what you're saying."

She threw her hand out to encompass the damage surrounding them. "These people have a right to fear us. Leland, as much as I dislike him, believes he is right to fear and hate what he doesn't understand. Can we blame them? What we carry is unnatural to the human world, and I can't fully control mine! One miscalculation, one moment of lost control, and we could leave a trail of death behind us. Do you understand? *They* get to be run by fear, *they* get to let anger control them. *We* don't."

Her eyes swept over the devastation in front of them, resting for a moment on each person still hovering in the night. "We are their protectors, Caden, whether we asked for this or not. Maybe it's time we let go of our concerns and start focusing on them, truly. Not on being heroes, not on discovering what we are, but simply on being there for the last of humanity." She stepped away from him to help a young child who had stumbled near them. As the child ran off, she glanced at Caden. "I am not humanity's last hope. *They are.* This child is, along with all the others. Those who aren't here. Those who are trapped in dungeons beneath the cities or locked in the prisons of their own minds." She wrapped her arm around Caden's waist as he moved next to her, pulling her close. "We can't let anything like tonight, with Anwill and Leland, happen again. We do not have the grace to lose control."

Caden sighed, pressing his lips against her temple. The area throbbed in response. Leland's fist had left a mark. "You're right," Caden said. "I let my anger take hold of me."

"And I let fear. But no longer. You and I have to rise above this."

"We will," Caden murmured.

"And we have to stop the Phantoms," Kyra said. "I've been letting the others lead, hoping General Prait will find a solution. They can't stop them, so we must. This is the last night the Phantom scourge will find its way into this city."

CHAPTER 29

K yra didn't sleep at all that night. The second the first light of sun touched the morning she left the bunkhouse. Most of the people were still sleeping, exhausted after the carnage of the previous night. She moved lightly, careful not to make a sound as she scurried past the city's buildings.

When she came to the gates of the city, she found a soldier guarding them. Her steps faltered and she hung back in the shadows until the soldier moved enough for her to see his face. Relief washed over her. Bronson was this morning's guard. He was one of the few she could trust; she would have no problems with him.

Her way clear, she hurried toward him. He whirled at the sound of her footsteps, hand hovering over his weapon. But when he saw it was her, he relaxed, dropping his arm. His face broke into a smile.

"You're up early," he noted.

"Couldn't sleep."

He drifted toward her. "That makes two of us."

"Up all night thinking about the attack?"

He nodded. "Trying to solve the problem of how to stop them."

"That makes two of us."

He chuckled at her use of his phrase, but then the humor faded. "I think last night was worse for you than me."

She sighed, shoulders slumped in discouragement. "You heard?"

"I spoke to Dalia. She told me a few things."

Kyra kicked at the pebbles at her feet, mouth pulled down in a frown. Dalia only knew half the story, the part where two men kidnapped an innocent woman. The rest, well, that would get out. Before day's end the entire city would know all of it. She shuddered, thinking of Leland's hand clamped over her mouth while she choked on the dirty rag. Unbidden, nausea roiled in her stomach. She hadn't let herself think about it last night, but now...now she did, and she wanted to scream as the memory washed over her.

Bronson tucked a finger under her chin, nudging her head up until she faced him. His eyes widened when he saw that hers were pools of tears.

"I'm sorry, Kyra," he said, his voice as gentle as a caress. "I want you to know that. What they did to you – it was wrong. I thought their torment was bad enough, but this..." His jaw clenched and his shoulders tensed in anger. "Let's just say I hope they pay for what they did."

Kyra turned her head away, unwilling to hold Bronson's gaze, not after what had happened with Anwill the previous night.

"They did," she whispered. "At least, one of them did."

She shrugged away from him. "I'd like to get outside the city, just for a while. Will you open the gate for me?"

"Hold on," he said, grabbing her arm. "What do you mean?"

She shook her head brusquely. "You'll learn, I'm sure."

"Kyra, what happened?" He didn't release his hold on her, but it wasn't an aggressive grip. He turned her body to face his. Reluctantly, she complied.

His hands on her arms were surprisingly gentle and warm. He brought them up to her shoulders, leaning down so he could peer into her face. "Please, tell me?"

She wanted to bury parts of last night with the rest of her painful memories – bury them and forget them. But that couldn't happen, and she knew it. Anwill would be counted among those who were dead. Leland, who the citizens and the council trusted far more than she, would tell his side of the story and conveniently leave out his part in it. Of course, she wouldn't hide her part in it, either. She would make sure the whole truth was known. Then she'd be left to whatever mercy the council felt like bestowing. She imagined it wouldn't be much.

But Bronson...she trusted him.

"Anwill's dead," she whispered.

Bronson straightened in surprise. Then he took her hand, turning it until the palm faced up. Bits of light swirled above her skin, glowing brightly in the morning shadows. "Did this have anything to do with it?"

"It had everything to do with it." She pulled her hand away, closing the light in her palm. "They were going to take me back to them. To the Malic'Uiel!" She shuddered. "I didn't mean to use it against them. Anwill, he attacked me from behind. The light responded. I don't even know what happened. But then he was dead." She fell silent. After a moment she straightened her shoulders and shook off the memory. "What's done is done. I know I'll face the council later. But right now, I just need to get outside."

He put his arm on the small of her back, gently pushing her toward the gate. "Of course. I'll speak to General Prait, see if I can mitigate the damage."

Her eyebrow shot up in surprise. "You believe me?"

"Of course I do. And I'll do what I can to help you." He pulled the heavy door open. It creaked and groaned on its hinges, but it responded to his action. Then the land outside stretched out in front of her – the most beautiful, welcome sight she'd ever seen.

"Thank you," Kyra said, briefly resting her hand on his arm. "Truly, for being my friend." She slipped out the gate. "I won't be gone long."

He smiled before closing the heavy barrier.

With the gate shut behind her, Kyra stayed as close to the wall as she dared, staying out of the way of the defensive spikes and, hopefully, away from the prying eyes of soldiers on the parapet as well. She wanted to be away from everybody, so she headed for the burial mound, knowing that most of the citizens stayed away from it. Even the soldiers on the walls, when forced to patrol near it, averted their eyes, unwilling to look at or acknowledge the loss of life in front of them.

As she came to the burial mound she slowed her pace, approaching the dead with respect. Tall grasses and wildflowers grew over the mound, spilling into the land beyond. She ran her fingers through the grasses as she walked, letting the silky blades caress her skin. The abundance of life shooting forth from what should have been an area of death filled Kyra with hope. Her eyes roved over the land surrounding the mound and the city; the vision of new life was everywhere. A green sheen covered the ground, promising a fertile field within a few months' time.

When she'd first come to the Malic'Uiel cities, the land was dry and barren. Life could not exist where the Malic'Uiel walked. The forests and trees beyond were able to sustain life, but the cities and the immediate areas surrounding them were desolate sentinels of a time gone but not forgotten.

Somehow, Tutis was no longer bound to that fate. Despite the fact the city had lain in waste for years, life had found its way back again. If this land had come back, maybe they could restore Spero to the world it had once been.

Stopping at the base of the mound, Kyra sunk to the ground. She hadn't come out here just to escape the city, though the peace beyond the walls was a welcome respite. No, last night's events had made it clear that it was time for her to stop living in fear of what she was, and instead embrace what was possible. But she couldn't do it alone, and though Caden was a great help and support, he didn't understand what she was or what she was capable of any more than she did. But maybe she could connect to somebody who did.

Kyra lay all her hope now in Caden's dead wife, Avalyn, a woman speaking from the grave.

As she settled into the grasses she closed her eyes, listening to the wind that sighed around her. The smell of warm earth and fresh growth enlivened her senses, and somewhere nearby an insect buzzed. She hoped it was a honeybee – they'd always made her happy, the way they embraced the flowers and spread the pollen to the next and the next, bringing life to their beautiful blooms. To her, honeybees were more proof that life after apparent death was possible.

She could have lain there for hours, listening to the peace around her, but after a few minutes of tranquility she tuned out her senses and focused instead on her mind. Avalyn had always spoken through her as if she were just another voice in her head, so it made sense that her mind was where she would find her.

Avalyn? Red flamed her cheeks for a moment. This did not feel natural; she was talking to the voices in her head. Some would say this was a sign of madness.

She gritted her teeth, ignoring the thoughts that bounced in her skull. If this was madness, then so be it. *I need your help, Avalyn. You told Caden if I would listen, you'd be there. It's time for you to be here.*

She squeezed her eyes shut, trying and failing to ignore all the thoughts in her head. She'd really done it. She'd gone mad. 'Silly' or 'stupid' didn't begin to describe how she felt right now. Thankfully, nobody could see inside her mind – with the exception of Caden – so if anybody happened to be watching, all they'd see was a possible witch lying in the grasses while the sun soaked her body.

"Open your palms to the sun."

Kyra bolted upright, eyes flying open. She realized in that moment that she hadn't believed Caden, not really. But now the voice was back, and she had to wonder if he was right.

"Avalyn?" she said, talking to the air in front of her.

"Caden talked to you, then?"

Avalyn's voice rippled through her like a shock. She shouldn't be surprised, not really, but this was the first time she'd attempted to talk to the voices in her head. Up until now, she'd harbored a secret belief that the voice guiding her was her own – some smarter, better version of herself.

Of course it wasn't.

"Yes," she remembered Avalyn's question. "Caden talked to me." She certainly looked crazy now. Her eyes darted to the parapet. It remained empty, thank heaven. "Why am I opening my palms to the sun?" she asked, while obeying Avalyn.

"The sun is light, and you harbor light. Wouldn't it make sense that it would benefit you?"

Grudgingly, Kyra nodded her head. "Yes."

"I need you to listen to me, Kyra, Avalyn said. *I've been trying to guide you this far, but there's so much you must understand."*

"Hold on," Kyra said. "I'll tell you where to start. I want to know what this light is. I have power that I don't understand and can barely control. Nobody knows what it is or where it came from, least of all me, and everybody is afraid of it. I can't say I blame them. Any magic that exists in Spero came from the Malic'uiel, and all they bring is devastation and death."

"That's not entirely true," Avalyn responded. *"Magic has existed in Spero since the world's conception. Most of us simply aren't aware of it. The Malic'Uiel brought a different kind of power with them. It's true that their power brings death. But the power of light has always been here. It's available to any and all who are willing to seek it out."*

"If that's the case, why does nobody know about it?"

Avalyn's sigh was like a breath on the wind. *"Sadly, history is too often lost. There were those in Celebrus who knew of the power of light. The great libraries and halls of learning had scrolls and books dedicated to the subject, but very few people ventured deep enough to find the truth. A few individuals passed the knowledge down generation to generation. Most of these people never spoke openly about magic, for a number of reasons. For one, most considered stories involving the power of light to be fairy tales of sort, so if they did share their secrets they were rarely believed. And most of the knowledge was kept secret because there are always those who seek to abuse power. Like the Malic'Uiel, they hunt for men and women they can dominate. They thrive on the control, on the fear they can sow in others, but more than that they thrive on extorting the gifts and talents of others to further their dark ends. And this is why, after the knowledge of light faded away in history, the few that carried it within never sought to retrieve it. But it has always been there for anybody with a mind to seek the truth.*

Kyra pushed herself to her feet, brushing off her backside before pacing away from the mound. "So, you're telling me the information was intentionally hidden from the rest of us?"

"To some degree, yes. But even if the knowledge of the power of light was kept from mankind, the power itself was not, and that's what you need to understand. There are many reasons you were able to discover it,

not the least of which is that the power never left. Any individual willing or able to dig deep into their mind, to go beyond the ordinary thought processes, will find the power of light. It is simply understanding that there is more to themselves than they realized. The more an individual accepts who they are, the greater the power becomes.

Kyra stopped her pacing, a frown tugging at the corners of her lips. "If the power is available to anybody, why does Caden think I am somehow the key to turning the tide of this war?"

Avalyn's voice went quiet, and Kyra detected almost a hint of sadness. *"Because there are those set apart as a conduit for the light between the realms – those whose ancestry binds them to it. Yes, others can find their way to that power, but some hold this most sacred gift. Their power is heightened far above the rest, and is capable of much, much more. Your mother was one of those bound by blood to the magic, and when she died, that role passed to you.*

Kyra froze, foot paused in midair before dropping heavily to the ground. "Did my mother know?"

"Yes. Your mother knew many things, none of which she was able to share with you. You hadn't yet come to an age where those secrets were yours to bear."

The knowledge settled in Kyra's breast, making it hard to breathe. She'd known her mother had secrets, but this...if Evia had only told Em what she'd known, maybe Kyra's life could have gone differently. Kyra's hand dropped and she sucked in a deep breath, hoping the air would expand her chest, which suddenly felt too tight. Avalyn's words only created more questions. But she didn't have time to ask them all; she didn't have time to learn an entire history that had been forgotten. Somehow, in the course of a day, she had to figure out how to use this light to stop the attacks that were decimating humanity.

"How do I use this? How do I control it?"

"Believe – and accept – who you are. All of it. The good and bad. Think back to the day your master succumbed to your light. Who were you that day?"

"I don't know who I was," Kyra whispered. "I was nothing. I'd been nothing for so long. It didn't matter what happened to me at that point."

"Keep looking," Avalyn said. *"I can't give you all the answers you need. Not yet. I wish I could, but my role in this is simply to guide you, to teach you the small pieces I know and help you uncover not only the truth of what you are, but the keys to a future that you hold."* Avalyn's voice grew more and more quiet. *"I must go,"* she said, her voice little more than a faint whisper. *"Keep your mind open. I will guide you through this."*

Her presence slipped from Kyra's mind, leaving a hollow emptiness.

This was new. In the past when 'the voice' had spoken to her, Kyra hadn't felt it fade, hadn't sensed it as an entity different than herself. She filed that information away for later scrutiny, along with all the knowledge Avalyn had just shared with her. Now, she just had to figure out how to use the information she'd been given to stop the Phantom scourge from taking any more of her people.

She took one last breath of the fresh, free, clean air outside the walls before turning back to the city. She'd gotten some of the answers she sought, though they'd only opened the door for more to plague her. For now, it was time to do as she'd told Caden she would and protect the inhabitants of Tutis.

As she slipped back into the city, a pair of hooded eyes, hidden in the shadows of the wall, watched her. When the gates closed, he spun on his heel and wove his way around the traps to the forest. The witch had no right to be in his city. He had a job to complete, even if his ally was dead. There were men waiting to take Kyra from Tutis, men willing to release the citizens from her bewitchment. Leland would make sure they accomplished their goal.

THE RISE OF SPERO

CHAPTER 30

The gates of Tutis thudded to a close behind Kyra. Bronson no longer stood guard at the gate, but as she walked by, she smiled at the soldier who'd replaced him.

"Good morning," she said.

He grunted in answer.

"Or not," she muttered to herself.

When she neared the center of the city, a seasoned soldier stepped next to her and grabbed her elbow, pulling her along with him. "General Prait needs you," he said.

"Is this about last night?"

He didn't offer a response, nor did he let go of her. She jerked out of his grasp, glaring at him in defiance. He reached for her again, but she sidestepped him. "I'll follow you to General Prait," she snapped, "but you won't drag me there like some criminal."

General Prait waited for them near the back of the meetinghouse. Caden hovered near the door, along with Bronson. Most of the council was there as well.

Behind the General, a body was covered in one of the rough blankets that most of the inhabitants slept with at night.

General Prait straightened as the meetinghouse door closed behind Kyra. His eyes roved over the waiting group. Tension buzzed in the air. He rested his gaze on Kyra for a moment and then on Caden. For the first time, Kyra noticed worry lines etched in his face. His mouth hung in a frown, and his shoulders hunched as if the weight of a Cadaver's cloak dragged him down. Pity bubbled in Kyra's chest. In many ways, the man really did carry the weight of the world on his shoulders.

"Come up here, Kyra," he said. "You too, Caden."

The two did as commanded. General Prait gestured to the body behind him. His movements were slow, as if his own weariness was trying to drag him to the grave.

"I need to know all the details of what happened last night," he said. "And I want to know what caused Anwill's death."

Kyra stepped forward, mouth open to speak, when a commotion from the back of the group caused her to turn. The door shoved open, and Dalia pushed her way in; her hand rested protectively over her stomach.

"This is a council meeting," General Prait said. "Dalia, you are not supposed to be here."

"Please, General. I know I'm not supposed to be here, but it wasn't her fault," she said, breathless.

"They were taking her. I watched them take her. I was too far away and couldn't stop them."

General Prait hesitated for the briefest moment before gesturing for her to come to the front with the others. "You can stay. I'll get to you in a minute." He swung back to Kyra "But I want to know what happened to Anwill."

Kyra faced the General, holding out her hands to draw attention to the light in her palm. All she could do was tell the truth. "It's my fault he's dead," she said. "I didn't mean to kill him, but Dalia's right. In the chaos last night, Leland and Anwill attacked me. They bound my hands, gagged me, dragged me away from it all." She swallowed hard and balled her hands into fists; it took a lot of effort to keep her hands from trembling as she relived the kidnapping. "They were trying to return me to *them*."

Next to her, Caden's body was rigid – one hard line from head to toe. Though he looked calm, she knew from the set of his mouth that rage churned inside.

She turned her head and pushed her hair out of the way so General Prait could see the side of her head where Leland's fist had made contact. "Leland hit me. I thought I was going to pass out. It took a lot to stay upright. I was afraid if I lost consciousness I would wake up as a Malic'Uiel slave again, or not at all." She held her hand up, demonstrating the electricity that arced in the light. As the seconds passed it grew stronger and the light grew brighter until she finally closed her fist, encasing the light in darkness. "I knew the light would protect me. I forced it around me like a shield. When Anwill tried to grab me, he hit my shield instead and it threw him back." She dropped her arms and let her hands hang limp, leaving her exposed to the judgment of the General and his council. "I never meant to kill him. He hit the wall of the building and didn't move after that. I swear I was only trying to protect myself."

General Prait chewed on his lip, his arms folded across his chest. He reached out and grabbed her chin, pushing her hair just enough for him to see the bruise Leland had left on her face. "Leland hit you?" He examined the bruise, which bloomed up the side of her face, down to her cheekbone, and crept into one eye. "Punched you, by the look of it."

"Yes."

General Prait's eyes narrowed. "Where is Leland?" he barked to the group.

"He hasn't been seen this morning."

General Prait snapped his fingers at the soldier who'd brought Kyra in. "Go find him. We need to get to the bottom of this."

The soldier dipped his head once then raced out of the room.

"Caden," General Prait demanded. "Were you there for this attack? Did you see it?"

"No. I found Leland running from her shortly after. When I confronted him, he admitted she had killed

Anwill. He also admitted he intended to get rid of her. She is speaking the truth."

"Her version of it. Nobody here can speak for the dead." General Prait swung to Dalia. "You watched them take her?"

"I did. Even if there are no other witnesses, their intentions were clear. They took her in the middle of the chaos, when nobody would notice another missing person or care enough to stop and help. They didn't try to help the rest of us, they didn't try to put out the fires. They just took her and ignored everything else."

As Dalia spoke, the room erupted in a buzz of conversation.

"Your light killed Anwill?" General Prait asked again.

Kyra nodded. "It was unintentional."

"Does it matter?" An elderly woman named Emira shoved forward to the front of the group. Her mouth pulled down in a bitter frown, and thick, graying hair framed a thin, pinched face. Kyra recognized her as one of the new council members – she'd once been imprisoned in Tutis and had helped the other women who were enslaved with her. She'd nurtured and cared for them. Her bitterness surprised Kyra.

"You killed Anwill with your power," she snapped, jamming a gnarled finger toward Kyra. "Whether intentional or not doesn't matter. What you do is dangerous and puts us all at risk."

"But allowing a kidnapping murderer to roam our streets is any less of a risk?" Bronson cried, moving to stand between the two of them. "You'd take a man with a murderous heart over a woman who was defending herself against such a man?"

Emira scowled. "I'd take a man I understand over an unpredictable, out of control witch."

Around them the others nodded their heads, in agreement with the councilwoman. And suddenly Kyra knew the reason for this meeting. It wasn't that General Prait didn't trust her or didn't believe her, this meeting was for the others. Their fear was becoming dangerous, and she needed to put them at ease, otherwise her safety was at risk. General Prait hadn't brought her here to prove that she was guilty of some crime. It was to appease them.

"What would you like me to say?" she called to the group. "You were right. I was not controlled. But I didn't attack Anwill with this light. I used it as a shield. He chose the attack, and the consequence."

"You chose the consequence!" This voice bellowed from the center of the crowd. Kyra knew him. He was called Jonas. He'd fought beside her in the army before she was taken. He'd trusted her once. "You chose to use your light. Your choice left a man dead."

"A man who was trying to harm her!" Dalia fired back. "Why is she the one on trial here, when the others were responsible for what happened? At what point did self-defense become a crime?"

"You are not part of this council," Jonas bellowed. "Your word has no weight here."

"And you will not defend her!" Dalia cried. "None of you will, so I will. No, I am not part of this council, but this woman needs allies, and I am one of the few she has. All she has ever done is try to help and protect this city, but the rest of you refuse to see that. You cling to your humanity, terrified of losing it to the Malic'Uiel, but you can't see that by damning the innocent you lose your humanity anyway!"

Jonas' face darkened. "The woman you defend so willingly," he hissed through clenched teeth, "uses magic planted inside her by the Malic'Uiel."

"They didn't plant it there," Kyra snapped. "It's just part of me. It's part of all of you, too. Or at least, it could be, if you were willing to allow yourselves to be greater than you are."

Her statement rippled through the crowd. Some of the council gaped at her, others grew red and angry.

"I told you she was a witch." Leland's baritone voice carried over the group. They turned as one body to see him hovering near the back. None had noticed him slip in. A mass of bruises covered most of his face, and his lip was split and swollen. He glared at the four standing near the General. "What she does is not natural to humanity. What *both of them* do is not natural." He waved his arm toward Caden and Kyra. "And now she's telling you that you harbor the same evil?" He snorted, pushing his way through to the front.

"She's working for them, sowing seeds of destruction in front of us all, but we're too stupid to see it. The Malic'Uiel have not launched an outright attack against us because they don't need to; they have her doing their work for them! If we listen to her, we'll soon find that her friend Gilrich," he spat the word as if it was a disease, "isn't the only Cadaver walking among us."

General Prait pounded his fist on the table shoved against the wall. "Damn it, Leland, that's enough! Everything you're saying is conjecture. You have no proof to back any of your claims."

Leland whirled toward the General. "Proof? Are you blind? The Phantoms did not begin their attacks until the night one came for her. In the shadows, he came to scheme with her to find the easiest ways to take us."

"She killed him," General Prait said. "She did something none of us have been able to do."

"So?" Leland's hands balled into fists, but he clenched them against his side, as if determined to keep himself from striking her. Kyra kept a close eye on him – she wouldn't be surprised if he tried to attack her again, even with all these people watching. "Since when do the Malic'Uiel protect their kind? They don't care who they kill or how they kill them. And that Phantom, the one she supposedly defeated, was one of their followers. Who says he didn't come here as a sacrifice, to gain whatever glory they believe they're getting from these monsters?"

"Again, Leland. You're grasping here."

"You're a damn fool!" Leland's body shook, and pulsing veins stood out on his forehead. He shoved his face into General Prait's, nearly touching his nose. A trembling hand pointed to Kyra. "String that woman up before she destroys us all!"

"Yes!" The cry came from the midst of the crowd. Others soon followed.

"Do it!"

"She's a traitor!"

"She's one of them!"

"She can't be trusted!"

General Prait had lost control. This wasn't a meeting of rational minds. This was a bloodthirsty mob seeking her death. Standing tall in front of them, she forced her shoulders back and kept her gaze upon them. If murder was their agenda, then they would know that she, the woman they hated so much, would not cower to them.

But looking from face to face, she noticed a few that watched her carefully, not with hate but instead with curiosity and pity. Not all among them were her enemies.

General Prait grabbed Leland's tunic, hissing into his face. "I will not sentence her to death on the fears of a damaged man, and I will not let you continue to abuse her. Your words have shown me the truth: what Kyra said is true. Anwill's death was an act of self-defense. From this moment forward, you have no power in this city. You are no longer a part of this army. I grant you the freedom to stay in Tutis, but under watch; I will not sentence you to death on the outside. But if you touch her again, you will find yourself back in the prison from which you were freed." He shoved Leland away and faced the rest of the crowd. "Those men and women who are walking among us with murderous hearts, willing to give into their impulses, will find themselves quickly judged and imprisoned in the tunnels beneath the Citadel. There are many enemies beyond our gates. I will not tolerate an enemy within our midst as well."

"But you let her walk free among us?" A council member near the front cried. "You put us all at risk because you are unwilling to consider that maybe she's the enemy? If you make these decisions alone then what is the purpose of this council?"

General Prait glared at the man. "Kyra's power will be dealt with in another form, not here. You are set apart to be a council – to lead this city with reason and logic. That is not what is happening here. Too many here are all emotion and no logic. We will reconvene to address the issue of Kyra's power when the council can operate as it was intended. For now, those of you who fear her give her a wide berth and leave her be. Those of you who have courage in your hearts, listen to her and seek to understand what she is and what her experiences have been. She's the only one to have walked among the enemy and survived. There must be something to be gained from that."

The council grumbled among themselves – many sent her glances of pure hate – but they held back.

"You have no right," Emira said. "No right to remove the council from this decision!"

General Prait whirled on her. "When you became a council member you swore to lead with integrity, to listen with logic and remain levelheaded in any situation. That is not what is happening here! We will not meet again until you are ready to act in the station you have been given." He glanced at Kyra then at Leland, who fumed in silence. "This meeting is finished," he snapped.

The room roiled with a dangerous energy, but the council listened. They left the room in twos and threes. Some of them stopped to spit at Kyra's feet.

Bronson's face was grim. "I did not expect that," he said. "They're out for blood."

On her other side, Caden had his arms folded across his chest, jaw clenched shut. "They won't have it," he said. "Not hers."

Kyra let out a shaky breath. Bronson was right. They wanted her dead. "I wish I could say I was surprised."

Bronson gripped her shoulder, holding her gaze. "While you have many enemies among us, Kyra," he said. "You also have friends. I will stake my life on what you have. I've seen the power of light, and I've seen the good it can create. I'll defend you until my dying breath." He stepped to Caden, holding his hand out to shake in agreement. Caden took it, gripping it tightly. "I know you protect her, Caden. I won't leave you to do it alone anymore. If it's just the two of us, the two of us will make sure she remains unharmed."

As Bronson spoke, a few more soldiers, hesitating just outside their small circle, stepped into the space. One of them spoke. "We don't believe what Leland is saying," he said. "Something in me tells me that we need you, Kyra, so we will defend you as well."

Kyra's glance touched on each of them. It fell on the soldiers that volunteered their services, on Bronson, Dalia, and finally Caden. This small group of people was willing not only to give her a chance, but to defend her at all costs, to believe and have faith in something that none of them understood. Her chest constricted and her throat tightened as a rush of emotion filled her body. "Thank you," she whispered.

General Prait stepped to the group then, gently grasping Kyra's elbow. "What happened today is not good for this city," he said. "The council is divided, our leadership weak. I made a promise that I would get to the bottom of this. Kyra, we need to make sure what you do isn't going to harm the people here." He gestured to a small group of men and women to the right. "These are people I trust to look at this logically, to suspend fear and emotion and find the truth. Caden,

Bronson, Dalia – you three should be part of this as well."

The three nodded.

To Kyra, General Prait said, "We will determine whether what you have can be safely managed, and then we will bring the council together again. You will need to demonstrate for us now, and you may need to demonstrate later for the council."

Dalia smiled, taking Kyra's hand. "They're going to see the incredible person I know. And when they're done, you'll be free of this burden."

Kyra nodded, forcing a sick smile before following General Prait to the waiting group. This was it – her reckoning. After today, she would either be embraced by most of the city, or be deemed a witch or a sorceress, something to be feared and abused. If the latter, who knew what her fate would be?

"Don't hide the truth of who you are." Avalyn's voice slipped into her mind; a still, comforting presence in a world of chaos. *"Remember the day you escaped, and who you were then. Show them who you are."*

CHAPTER 31

N ear the back of the city wall was an empty, open space. It had once been the location of the Malic'Uiel waste heap, which was nothing less than a pile of dead humanity who'd given their souls to sustain the Malic'Uiel life. Because of what had once been housed here, most wouldn't venture into this part of the city.

This was where General Prait and the group he trusted took Kyra. "We don't need an audience for this," he said.

When they had all gathered, he gestured to Kyra to come to the front of the group. There was plenty of space between her and the wall, and a large gap between her and the group waiting to assess the danger of her skills.

"I want you to replicate what you did when Anwill was killed," he said. "Can you do that?"

Kyra nodded. "I think so." She focused on the light, willing it to course over her body as she'd done before. It flooded through her, bringing the warmth of a caress. Like a comforting blanket, it covered her; the more she embraced the light, the more she understood it as an extension of herself. The light encased her body, shimmering and dancing in an array of colors. Lightning arced and raced around her. This, this was right. This was what she needed to embrace. She was so sure of that in this moment...but one glance at the watching group told her that they were not reassured; they were terrified.

General Prait seemed the most certain, and even he pulled back as if he wanted to bolt. But she watched him draw in a deep breath before he stepped toward her, hand outstretched. "This is what killed Anwill?"

"Yes," she said. "Or at least, it was part of it. When he tried to grab me, it threw him back against the corner of the building. I believe the impact is what killed him."

"May I?" General Prait asked, gesturing to the protective shield. The apprehension on his face told her he did not want to advance.

But she knew, as well as he, that somebody more than herself had to prove that this was safe. "Of course," she said. "I can't promise it won't be painful." She held out her arm, bringing a small part of the light toward him.

General Prait proceeded with caution, moving his hand through her shield until he took hold of her wrist. Instead of forcing him back, as the light had done to Anwill, it moved to embrace him, swirling up his arm as well as hers. The light buzzed with a new energy as it pulled from General Prait and mixed with her own. A feeling of safety, of protection settled in Kyra's breast. The light was reading his intent; he wanted to protect her.

"You're not a threat," she said in wonder. "The light is a giver of life. I imagine the shield only stops those who would hurt me."

General Prait pulled away, a frown on his lips. He dropped his arms to his side. "Try to hurt me with it. I want to see if you can wield it as a weapon."

Kyra nodded, concentrating on the light as it swirled from her hand. She sent it toward the General. It enveloped his body almost as a mist of light.

"Does it hurt, General?" she asked.

"No," he said. "It prickles a bit, and I can feel it on my skin, but it's doing no harm."

Closing her eyes, Kyra envisioned the light restricting and turning on him, becoming the weapon he wanted to see if it could be. The light pulsed around him and tightened closer to his body, but then it stopped, refusing to go further.

"I can't move," he said. "It's like my body has no mobility."

Kyra beckoned the light to return. "I can't hurt you with it, General. It knows you're no danger to me."

A small murmur erupted from the crowd, but the words were too faint for Kyra to hear. All eyes were fixed on her, and on the light swirling around her. Nobody saw the dark shadow creeping along the buildings behind them, nor did they hear as an arrow was fixed to a bow. The twang of the arrow's release was the only indicator of danger, but Kyra whirled to the sound on instinct. Her light flared around her; the arrow meant for her heart disintegrated the moment the light touched it. A loud whoop broke the night before anybody could react, and two soldiers barreled toward her. The first held his sword high, determined to bring it down on her skull. Caden jumped to defend her, but she thrust out her arm, demanding he stop. When the sword hit her shield, the light arced around the assailant, throwing him back. The second attempted her assassination with a dagger, but the result was the same.

Within seconds, both lay unconscious on the cobblestone street. General Prait's group gaped at her, mouths drawn tight in fear.

Kyra pulled the light back into her, bringing it close to her body once more.

"Heal his heart." Avalyn was here again.

"How do I do that?" Kyra whispered.

"Remember, I told you to find the woman you were the day you destroyed your master. Find her, and you'll know how to do this."

Kyra knelt next to the first man, heart pounding, palms sweaty. Avalyn had a lot of faith in someone who barely understood what she was. But she had faith in Avalyn. She closed her eyes, letting her mind go back to the day she'd escaped the Malic'Uiel, back to the conversation with Avalyn that had given her freedom.

General Prait rushed up to her, gripping her arm as she reached for the man. "Don't!" he cried, his voice breaking.

"I won't hurt him, General," she said, imploring. "Trust me."

General Prait hesitated, his anxiety almost palpable. Then he dropped her arm and took a halting step backward. "Don't hurt him."

"He's safe."

"They've taken your identity," Avalyn had said that day. "They've taken everything from you. They've fought to destroy you. And yet, after all that is gone, what is left?"

And that's where Kyra had understood. "I am left," she'd responded. "I am whoever I choose to be."

Her soul revisited that moment; peace flooded through her as it had then. All of the fears she harbored, her concern over the trial she was now a participant in, even the guilt she felt over Gilrich faded into the background. "I am whoever I choose to be," she whispered to herself.

Gently, she lay her hand on the man's still form. The light responded to her call, as if eager to heed her wishes. It was a part of her, and she let that part course through the man's body, wiping away the stain of darkness, healing the man from the that plagued him. She felt him inside the light, felt his fears and emotions, his joy and his sorrow. And bit by bit, the fear and anger that held his heart captive disappeared. When she pulled the energy back into herself, she left a clean, unbroken soul in her wake. She understood now, with perfect clarity, what the light was capable of.

The man stirred beneath her touch. He would be fine. She moved to the next man. Kneeling before him, she sent her healing balm through him as well. His body was harder to cleanse – more resistant to the power. She sensed, as her light moved through him, that he felt safer in darkness.

The light brought knowledge with it, and she knew now that men had a choice. Before, their only option had been darkness and death. Now, she'd awakened their light. They could embrace it and begin to heal, in time becoming the best version of themselves, or they could reject it and allow the darkness to take them. Either way, the choice and the consequences of that choice would be theirs.

When her light faded from the second man, she stood before the group. Her arms hung at her side, defenseless and open. "You may fear what I am," she said. "But I know who I am, and it doesn't matter what you decide today. I will restore the land of Spero. I will bring light hope...*life* back to a world that has forgotten what it means to feel these things."

She stepped into the group. They parted for her as the sea parts to the bow of a majestic ship. Silence was all that followed, but she had no fear of what she left behind.

"Go to the city gates." Avalyn's instructions were clear, and Kyra did not question why she should follow them.

At the gates, Avalyn continued. *"Go up the stairs to the top of the parapet."*

Kyra stepped onto the stair but hovered there as a memory erupted from the recesses of her mind. She gripped the side of the wall, keeping her balance as the day she'd come to Tutis began to reveal itself to her.

She'd experienced this before.

Taking one step, and then another, she found herself at the top of the wall, staring over the vast expanse beyond.

"You know what you have to do."

"Yes, I do." She took the necklace that she always wore and studied the symbol dangling from her fingers. She was beginning to understand, in far greater detail than she ever had, what this symbol meant. Avalyn had told her it was a balance of power, and she was right. The middle circle represented humanity, while the outer circles were darkness and light. Kyra let the pendant dangle from its chain and removed one of the spheres from its place in the rectangle. The weight of the other sphere forced the opposite side of the pendant to succumb to gravity; it tipped like a scale weighed down on one side.

"I must restore the light," she said, replacing the ball she had taken.

"*Yes,*" Avalyn said. "*No matter what it takes.*"

Kyra nodded, replaced the chain around her neck, and clasped her hands together as if in prayer. She slowly raised them above her head. The light seemed to dance inside her, as if it knew what she would call it to do. When she separated her palms, a ball of light rested between them. It expanded as she opened her palms more and more. Finally, she threw her arms wide and the ball exploded out from her, encompassing the entire city. It shimmered and danced, an array of colors more dazzling than the stars. As it faded, she smiled.

She understood now what she'd done when she'd come to Tutis – she'd commanded the light to protect it from the Malic'Uiel, to create a sanctuary where they could not come. Now she had done the same against the Phantoms. Their kind would no longer have entry into the city.

When she returned to the bottom of the steps, she found Caden watching her.

"The Phantom scourge is over," she said.

He just held out his hand, eyes alight with wonder, and pulled her into his embrace. "I saw you," he whispered.

"Of course you did. Everybody did."

He shook his head. "No. *You.* Your soul. Just like I've seen in your mind. I saw it now, and it was extraordinary."

She just smiled, and when Caden tipped her chin up and bent his lips to hers, she did not pull back.

CHAPTER 32

A lone, sneaking along like a fugitive, Leland crept out of Tutis. He'd been stripped from his place in the army and put the previous day. Since then, his guards had barely taken their eyes off him. He'd finally been given a sympathetic guard; they'd agreed to turn a blind eye while he left the city. He told them he just needed a break from being constantly watched.

He lied.

Now, he made his way across the open space between the city and the forest, careful to avoid the watching eyes of the guards on the parapet. He bypassed the traps he helped set, focusing on a secluded spot just inside the tree line where Shem waited for him.

This was his second time conversing with Shem. The morning after Anwill died, Leland had met with Shem's group, keeping them apprised of the plan's developments. The death changed nothing except their strategy. They still intended to remove Kyra from the city and deliver her to the Malic'Uiel.

Shem leaned against a tree with his arms folded across his chest, the scowl on his face a clear indicator he was not happy. "You're alone," he said. "I thought you were going to bring me Kyra. Thought you said after you sent someone in to tip off the General, you'd be able to get her out of there. 'They'll lock her up. Soon as they do, she's as good as ours.' That's what you said." His eyes narrowed. "You want the witch gone or not?"

Leland ignored Shem's bitter mood. "We have to change our strategy. General Prait is defending her. He doesn't think she's a threat."

Shem grunted in disgust. "The General's a fool. He always has been. He's run by emotion, and never looks at logic. He always refuses to see the danger in front of him."

"She claims she's protecting the city," Leland said. "I overheard her telling Caden yesterday the Phantoms would no longer be able to get in. This was after she cursed the city again with her 'light' or whatever this pollution is."

Shem shoved off the tree, stepping closer to the edge of the forest while he peered at the city in front of him. "That was her, was it?" He mused, alight with interest. "No wonder they want her. She's an anomaly." He glanced at Leland. "Do you have friends in there? Allies we can trust?"

"I can get some."

"Do it. We're going to have to go in and get her. We're going to need help."

Leland stepped next to Shem, mirroring his stance as he folded his own arms across his chest. "And how do you propose we bring her out? You can't get near her. Anwill and I tried that – only one of us now breathes."

Shem tapped his fingers against his arm, mouth pulled down in a frown. "You're saying she's untouchable?"

"That's exactly what I'm saying. Whatever dark magic the witch holds protects her from attack."

Shem's scowl deepened. "What if she's weakened in some way?"

Leland flopped back against a tree, then grabbed a leaf and began pulling it apart in tiny slices. "What do you mean?"

"Can you drug her?" Shem swung to him. "Dr. Bron can do all sorts of things with herbs and plants. She has one particular concoction that's supposed to cure pain, but that's not the only thing it does. When taken, a person becomes very easy to control."

"You've used this before?"

Shem shrugged. "Let's just say I know it's effective."

Leland grunted. "Say I get this concoction in her system? You're saying she'll just be willing to walk out?"

"That's exactly what I'm saying. She'll follow wherever you lead."

The last shred of the leaf fell at Leland's feet as a sinister grin broke on his face. "Then that's what we're going to do," he said. "You all just keep waiting. One way or another, we will get her out of Tutis."

CHAPTER 33

K yra woke to the sound of quiet rapping on her door. Early morning sunlight filtered through the small window of the bunkhouse, though part of it was blocked by the shadow of whoever stood at the door. For a moment, she wondered if General Prait and his advisers were on the other side; she didn't know what had happened after she left. She certainly hadn't followed their directives to stay and finish proving she wasn't dangerous. Strangely, she wasn't concerned about it. She'd done what she'd done, chosen the right course for herself; now it was up to them. She would adjust accordingly.

The rapping began again. Rolling off her cot, she moved to the door so it wouldn't wake Caden. Opening it, she found one of the soldiers who had attacked her the previous night. He yanked his hat off his head, rolling it over and over in his hands.

"Ma'am," he said. "Can I – May I –" His eyes dropped for a moment before returning to meet her gaze. "Can I talk to you?"

Behind her, light snoring rose from Caden's corner of the room. They couldn't talk here, not if she wanted to let him sleep. She nodded to the soldier then stepped out of the building and closed the door behind her.

"Go ahead."

The soldier swallowed hard, and his fidgeting increased, the hat spinning faster. "First, I want to – I need to –" he dropped the hat, flustered. He stared at it, and she wondered if he would simply run. But then he squared his shoulders and met her gaze. The hat stayed in the dust. "I'm sorry," he said. "For what I did. Last night. I've never been more ashamed of anything in my life than I am right now."

Kyra stooped and picked up the hat, holding it out to him. He gave her a grateful smile.

"I thought you were hurting the city," he said. "Thought you'd bewitched us, ensnared us somehow. Leland said you had. He had so much proof, so much that made sense..." His voice trailed off. He beat the hat against his leg; puffs of dirt fell to the ground. "I didn't think I was the kind of person who would murder an innocent, but I almost did last night. I am so sorry."

She studied him, noting the manner in which he held himself – hunched slightly, making himself smaller, as a child who expects to be whipped. He jammed the hat on his head. "Anyway, that's all I needed. I'll go now."

"Wait." She held out her hand to stop him. "I understand why you did what you did. I don't hold it against you. It's Ezra, right?"

"Yes."

She gestured to the hat. "It's a little crooked," she said, chuckling just a little in hopes that it would ease his discomfort.

He blushed but quickly straightened it.

"I know that fear is a powerful motivator," she said. "I understand what drove the aggression."

"Maybe so, but it doesn't make it right."

"No, it doesn't. Still, I as much as anyone understand the dangers of unchecked fear. I don't hold last night against you."

Ezra sighed in relief. He finally smiled a genuine smile. "Thank you," he said.

She thought he would leave now that his conscience was clear, but he didn't. He remained where he was, chewing on his lip. It was clear he had more on his mind.

She pushed away from the bunkhouse, gesturing for him to follow her down the street. "I imagine you're wondering what happened last night," she said, not as a question but a statement of fact.

"Yeah." He didn't move to follow.

"Walk with me?"

He hesitated a moment, but finally fell in step beside her.

They moved through the sleeping streets, making their way to the small garden Dalia frequently attended. At this time of day, it would be abandoned and any conversation they had wouldn't disturb the sleeping residents.

When they reached the garden, Kyra held her palm out to Ezra. "Look at it," she said. The light was so familiar now as it swirled around and through her fingers. This morning it danced in the hues of the sunrise – deep purples, pinks, and pale orange.

Ezra blinked, mesmerized. "What is it?"

"It's light," she said. "What is light to you?"

He scrunched up his nose, as if the question was more complicated than it seemed. "I don't know. Light is the sun…it is warmth, comfort, the promise of something new." He paused, tugging on the edge of his tunic in discomfort. "But in your case, I thought it was death. I thought the light was a sign of betrayal, of a different kind of promise – the promise of destruction."

Kyra let the light flare out from her hand and swirl around Ezra's body. He flinched, but he didn't move, instead allowing it to envelop him.

"Do you feel the life in it?" she asked.

He shook his head, eyeing the light with a mixture of curiosity and trepidation. "Maybe I could if I understood it."

When she dropped her hand, the light faded away from him. "You are wondering what I did to you last night," she said. She stepped closer to the garden, letting her gaze trail over the fertile ground, pleasure bubbling inside as she saw the fruits of labor nearly ready to be picked.

"When we came here, this plot of ground was dead," she said. "At least, we all thought it was. But Dalia and her incredible group removed the decay. They took out the damaged pieces, digging deep enough to find fertile soil. They removed the signs of the damage, and despite the horrors the land has seen, we see life growing from it. Because of their work, the damage no longer suppresses the potential." She glanced at the sun, whose rays lovingly caressed each of the plants. "They exposed this land to the light, and to life, and now we have this before us." She spread her hand over the supple garden before turning back to Ezra. "In a way, I did the same for you."

Ezra worried his lips with his teeth, one eyebrow raised in confusion. "What do you mean?"

"I knew you wanted me dead last night because you fear what I am and what I am capable of. I also know you harbor those fears from the damage that has been brought against you by the Malic'Uiel, the Phantoms, and even some parts of humanity." She set her hand on his arm and let it rest there. "All I did was send a new idea through your body and give it the opportunity to heal from the pain and trauma that it harbors. The light that I have…" she shook her head, shrugging her shoulders in the same moment. "It's life. It's cleansing. It's a new beginning. I simply gave you the chance for a new beginning, and reminded your heart and soul of the person that exists in spite of all the pain, through all the pain, and because of all the pain. Do you understand now?"

Ezra dropped his head, hands clasped together until the knuckles were white. "Is that why I feel so different?" he whispered. "Like...there are things that I should hate, that I could hate, but they don't have any weight anymore?"

"That's exactly why you feel that way."

His questions brought clarity to both of them. She'd felt what she was doing when she'd sent her light through him, she'd understood it on a soul level as it was happening, but putting it into words made it more tangible. "All I did was give you the opportunity. I let your body, your mind, and your soul experience a new idea, but you're the one that chose to take it even if you don't realize that's what happened. You could have wrapped all that fear and pain and hate around yourself and held onto it, and my light would've done no good. So, you only feel the way you do now because you were ready and willing to embrace a life where you're not defined by those experiences. You've chosen to redefine yourself."

Ezra nodded, and when he glanced at her she saw nothing but joy. He gripped her hand. "Thank you," he whispered. "I...I've never felt so free. I promise from this point forward I will be your ally. I will do all I can to defend you against those who would hurt you."

She smiled, but sadness pricked at her heart. "I fear you may be defending me against most of humanity, then."

"Then so be it."

Shem blew gently on the tiny spark he'd coaxed to life. Treating it like a fragile child, he added dried grasses to the spark; a flame ignited and devoured his offering. He added more grass until he had a small fire. The flames flickered and danced, reaching for more fuel. In front of him, a heap of dried, cracked wood, at the base of which he'd piled a mass of kindling, waited for that flame.

Shem had left his small band near the city waiting for word from Leland, who'd returned to gain more allies and try to rebuild some trust for himself in Tutis. They'd begun devising a new plan over a fortnight ago. But there was something he needed before they could spring the plan into action.

He glanced at the western horizon. The sun had slipped out of view and the creeping shadows of evening spread to encompass everything around him. If his plan worked as he hoped, he would never have to waste time building a fire again.

The time was perfect.

In one quick movement, he brought the hungry fire to the dried kindling, feeding its insatiable desire. It leaped up, caught hold, and ravaged the wood as thoroughly as war ravages a kingdom. A dark smile crept onto his face. The ravages of war were devastating in such a glorious way. He watched the flames as they raced across his gift, growing in height and power. As these flames were, so he would be.

The fire engulfed the mass of wood, and he continued to toss more on until the flames shot high in the air. The heat blazed out, reaching toward him. Satisfaction wormed its way into his gut.

Yes, this was exactly what he needed.

Waiting, he clenched his hand into a fist, just imagining the feel of the power coming *from* him. The night deepened and the darkness overcame every bit of light left behind by the sun.

It was almost time.

"Well," a voice said behind him. "Death is not something you fear, I believe."

He whirled to the voice, reaching for his weapon on instinct.

"That will be useless against me." A Phantom stood behind him, mouth curved in a lazy grin. He bowed slightly. "I am Ramuk, and I suggest you leave your weapons be, or this will be so much worse for you." With a flick of his fingers, Ramuk pulled the flames toward Shem. They snaked around him, not touching him – yet – but showing the extent of the Phantom's power.

"I have no intention of using my weapons against you," Shem said, moving his hand away from his blade.

"Excellent! Then this will be painless." Ramuk flicked his fingers again and the flame leaped away from its base toward Shem. It twisted behind him, forcing him to take a few steps closer to his enemy. He did so without hesitation, almost eagerly. Ramuk cocked his head to the side. "You don't fear me."

"No. I want something you have. My name is Shem. Perhaps you've heard of me?"

Ramuk's brows rose in amusement. "Heard of a meaningless human? No. I have heard nothing of you."

"I'm not your average human," Shem snapped, frustrated at being unknown. "I've worked with your kind before. I can help you rise in the Malic'Uiel's good graces."

Ramuk studied Shem, intrigued. The fire pulled back a bit. "You know, I could just take you to the Malic'Uiel and be rewarded by them."

"You could. But we both know what they want, and only one of us knows how to get it."

The Phantom stilled, and the fire pulled back, hovering at a safe distance. His calm demeanor was betrayed by the eager glint in his eye.

"Yes, I do know what they want."

"I can get to her."

Ramuk paused for the briefest of moments – long enough for Shem to know he'd piqued his interest.

"I've heard the attacks on the city have stopped," Shem continued. "Why is that?"

Ramuk shrugged, too casually, and the fire flickered behind Shem, a silent reminder that the Phantom was in charge here. "That information matters not to you."

Shem chuckled, settling himself into a casual stance. "You can't get in, can you?"

From the narrowing of Ramuk's eyes, Shem knew the answer.

"She's been in that city for weeks," he said, pushing his advantage, "And the Malic'Uiel have made no approach. Your kind attempted and failed. But now the attacks have stopped. The logical conclusion is that, somehow, they can't get to her."

"What do you want?" Ramuk asked, no longer hiding his interest.

"I want the power you hold, but as a human. You give me that, and I'll give you her."

"That's not possible. Humans cannot hold this power."

Shem shrugged. "If you don't give it to me, I'll find another who will."

"I could take you to the Malic'Uiel right now and this conversation would be over." Ramuk's hand twitched, as if he might do exactly that.

"And I would ask the same of them. I'm giving you the opportunity to be their hero – to bring them the very thing they crave."

Ramuk licked his lips; in his face, Shem saw naked greed. The woman's life meant nothing to him, but to the Malic'Uiel – oh yes, he could be elevated above the others, revered, respected...feared.

"I just want the power to manipulate fire," Shem coaxed.

"I give you that, and you bring me her?"

"Yes. I have men in the city. I'll bring her to you."

Ramuk straightened and a dark smile slid across his lips. He held out his hand, as if in agreement. Shem, nearly giddy with his success, gripped it hard. The moment their skin touched, he gasped as a shock of pain bolted through him, and then a sickening weakness pulled from his very veins.

Ramuk's smile twisted. "You asked for it."

CHAPTER 34

A fortnight had passed since Kyra's conversation with Ezra. In that time, nobody in the city had bothered her and, for her part, she didn't bother them. Her demonstration to General Prait and the few that he trusted had helped her gain favor with them, but it hadn't swayed the opinion of the citizens or, from what Caden told her, the council. As a result, most of the citizens continued to avoid her, choosing to wrap themselves in their fear rather than see what stood in front of them, and the council continued to fight about her role here.

She knew her tenure in Tutis was shaky, so she did her best to blend into the shadows, to let them forget she was there, if they could.

She'd found in the past two weeks that the vegetable garden Dalia worked so faithfully was one of the most peaceful places in the city. During the midday hours there were always people milling about, but the early morning and evening hours were quiet. Very few people ventured that way.

This night, Kyra found herself at the garden, as she had every night since she'd banished the Phantoms. She sat among the plants, careful not to harm any of them, and let her eyes rove over the city in front of her. Dalia and her friends had worked magic on more than just the soil. The promise of new life seemed to sprout from all around the area, not just the garden. The parts of the city closest to her seemed more alive, as if the tendrils of hope reached out and breathed life into everything nearby.

She had been at the garden for some hours when her peace was interrupted by approaching footsteps, and the cacophony of many voices speaking at once. She turned toward the sound while a dreadful sinking settled in her gut.

General Prait and most of the council rounded the corner, almost marching, clearly on a mission. General Prait walked hunched forward with heavy footsteps. The group came to a stop in front of her; the sudden silence was nearly as loud as the previous chaos. All eyes fell on her, all mouths clamped shut in angry lines. The one exception was General Prait, whose face held remorse, pity, and guilt. "I'm sorry, Kyra," he said. "I can't protect the wants or even the freedom of one at the expense of many."

Kyra studied General Prait, and then let her gaze wander over the group in front of her. "Forgive me, General, but you'll have to explain further."

General Prait glanced at the group behind him. "The *council*," he said through clenched teeth, "has determined that you are a danger to the citizens of Tutis. They will no longer allow you to wander freely in our streets."

Kyra stood, brushing dirt off her backside. Her thoughts flicked to the Malic'Uiel. As far as she knew, they still wanted her. If humanity abandoned her... "I'm to be banished, then?" she asked, formulating a plan even as she spoke to stay out of the Malic'Uiel grasp. "What if I refuse to go?"

"We are not demanding you leave the city," General Prait said. "In fact, you can't leave the city. They want you under guard where you can be watched."

"So I'm to be a prisoner."

"I'm sorry, Kyra." General Prait's face fell but he shuffled forward in shame, reaching out to take her arm.

She stepped back, out of his reach. "What about the others?" she asked. "Leland and those who have conspired to hurt me. Will they be imprisoned as well?"

"They'll be required to stand their own trial." General Prait refused to look at her, refused to meet her gaze. "Their fates will be determined then."

Kyra tried to swallow the ball in her throat, but to no avail. Her eyes touched on the people in front of her, holding their gaze one by one. After only a moment, each gaze dropped; none could bear to look at her. "You know I am innocent," she said. "And harmless. Yet you continue to damn me for the things you fear. What I have can help the city."

Emira barked at her. "That's what you claim, but your power caused the death of a human, and you've admitted yourself that you can't control it." Her eyes were cold, and her mouth pulled down in a perpetual frown. "As such, you are too dangerous, too volatile. For our protection, you must be removed."

Kyra licked her lips, which were too dry for her liking. She rubbed the fingers of her hand together, sensing the light. It responded like an old friend. She studied the light as it jumped and danced. It flared, reaching out to those who sought to take her. They cringed away from her, completely done in by fear. For a moment, she wondered what would happen if she let it consume them. Quickly she closed her palm and dropped her arm to her side. She would not hurt them to protect herself.

"You know you can't take me by force," she said. "This power you fear will also stop you from making me a prisoner. What if I refuse to go?"

"Then we send Dalia in your place," Emira said.

Kyra gasped. "Dalia? She's nearing the time of her delivery. You wouldn't imprison a woman so close to childbirth."

"We will do what it takes to make our city safe."
She folded her arms across her chest, glaring at Kyra.
"We have to control you somehow, and if that's what
it takes, that's what we'll do."

"General," Kyra demanded. "You aren't really going
to let them do this!"

"I tried, Kyra," he said. "I spoke for you, gave you
all the space you needed to learn to control this, but at
the end of the day it's not my decision alone. I am no
king. If I were, you would be free. But I am simply the
mouthpiece for all that remains of humanity, and it's
my job to enforce the decision of this *council*." He spat
the word as if it were toxic. Which, to Kyra, it was. "I
don't want to send Dalia in your place, and I don't
want anarchy in the city. You can stop both. I ask
that you come with me willingly."

The crowd in front of Kyra was growing impatient.
They shifted on their feet, pressing closer, faces growing uglier every moment with hate and fear. She was
all too familiar with that fear...and the darkness it
brought. Her fingers twitched; the light danced happi-
ly. It would be so easy to free herself from this fate.

"Let's go!" one of them shouted, his voice higher
pitched than it should have been, breaking on the last
word. He cleared his throat, eyes darting about. "The
verdict is set."

"She's not going to come," another one said.

"Then we force her."

* 314 *

A rumble started to build in the crowd. Kyra backed away. Lightning swirled up her arms and around her chest. Then she heard somebody cry, "Go get Dalia!"

From the back of the group, two men broke off, hurrying in the direction of Dalia's bunkhouse.

"No!" Kyra said. The light extinguished, along with any hope she had of freedom. "I'll go. Just leave Dalia be."

General Prait's shoulders slumped even more. She wondered if he'd wanted her to fight. Instead, he beckoned a man from the crowd to join him. They stomped into the garden. General Prait avoided the plants, while the other man crushed them to get to her. He carried her chains. Grabbing her roughly, he yanked her wrists forward and snapped the iron shackles in place. She gritted her teeth, pushing down a rising anger.

Her eyes shot to the General, imploring, but he simply looked away. The man attached a chain to the shackles. "She's not going anywhere, General," he said.

General Prait, tears in his eyes, took the chain from the soldier. "Get out of here," he snapped. "All of you. We don't need an entourage for this."

A few of them cried out in protest, but one look from General Prait silenced them. After a moment, they all slunk away. When they were gone, he turned to Kyra. "I am so sorry, Kyra," he said quietly. "I fought for you in that council. I did everything I could.

I've seen what you can do. It's no more dangerous than Caden, and we welcome him freely. They refuse to bend, and if I don't do this, we will have war in this city."

Kyra remained quiet while multiple emotions fought inside her. Anger welled up in her heart, anger at him for his cowardice and them for their fear, but compassion also pushed its way into her mind – compassion for General Prait and the difficult choices he had to make. "Would you really have let them take Dalia?"

"I couldn't have stopped them. These people are gripped with fear and it's making them do unreasonable, stupid things. If I'm not careful, we'll fall into anarchy. We can't afford that."

Kyra sighed and part of the anger ebbed away. "I may understand, but it's not right.

"It isn't." He set his hand gently on her shoulder. "Let's get this over with."

The streets were empty as he escorted her away from her freedom. As they neared the storehouses he hesitated for a moment, glancing at her in sorrow, before leading her to Gilrich's cell.

"He's going to be your new bunkmate," he said grimly.

Kyra gaped at him. "You can't be serious."

"I wish I wasn't."

She pulled back against the chains. "General, you can't leave me with him. He'll kill me!"

General Prait finally stopped and looked at her. His face was one of utter defeat. "I tried, Kyra. They're out for blood. I'm losing power in the city; I've never seen anything like it! The enemy I now fight is within."

She dug in her heels, tugging against the chains that he used to pull her forward. "I'm not going in there. Chain me to the wall of the building. Leave me as a sideshow for the rest of them. Don't damn me to this fate."

"You must. Or Dalia will face worse."

"You're telling me that this is the sentence? This is the punishment for what I am? To be locked away with a Cadaver who thinks I am his mortal enemy?"

"Yes."

"I thought it was to be taken off the streets, to lose my freedom." She flung her hands in the direction of Gilrich's prison. The chains rattled with the motion. "This is a death sentence."

"I won't let it be."

"You couldn't stop them from passing judgment. What makes you think you can save me from this?"

General Prait's body seemed to shrink in front of her. He knew what they were doing was wrong, but he did nothing to stop them.

"You've chosen cowardice, General."

At that, he snapped. His nostrils flared and his anger finally exploded. "You're right!" he yelled. "It is cowardice. It goes against everything I am as a human, as a leader, to imprison the innocent, to do this to a girl who I love almost as much as a daughter." He stomped in front of her, pacing, throwing his hands up as he spoke. He didn't release her chains. "Kyra, I have no defense against this. It is the blackest mark on my soul. I have seen some terrible things. I have done some terrible things. But I have never intentionally harmed the innocent." He whirled toward her and threw his head up, holding it high. "You are right to damn me. I will never ask forgiveness for this."

"Then why do you do it?"

"Because they will hurt those who you love – they'll take Dalia first. She will suffer for your supposed crimes. Bronson will be next. Then Ezra. They can't touch Caden; he'll burn them alive. But you see what their plan is? It's them or you. They won't kill the humans, of course, but eventually they'll get to Gilrich and they will kill him. It won't be a merciful death. The fear is all consuming, it's all they know." He took the chain and wound it around his hand, over and over, barely aware of the motion. "I'll let you choose, Kyra," he said. "You know their plan. I can't stop them. All I'm doing now is trying to mitigate the damage. I'm so sorry you're the collateral."

Kyra had been right. It was cowardice, from all of them. It was the darkness and ugliness of humanity. It was the horror of the Malic'Uiel but it came from the hearts of humanity, from the people she was trying to save.

Her light could do many things, but she didn't know how to use it to wipe away this stain of darkness. She let it flare in her palms, let it wrap itself around her body, a protective, comforting presence. Inside, her heart broke.

General Prait looked as if he wanted to weep when she finally nodded. "I'll follow where you lead," she said.

And she did. He led her up the steps into the hell that was to be her new torment. Gilrich was slumped in the corner, but he stirred when they entered, watching them both with interest. General Prait led her to the opposite wall, fastening her shackles in the same manner as Gilrich's, with her hands behind her.

"I'm so sorry," he murmured. He didn't hide the tears that slipped down his cheeks. She'd never seen him cry, but she knew she watched his heart shatter today.

General Prait paused just before he left the building. "Gilrich is tightly bound. He can't hurt you. And I'll have guards that I trust stationed just outside to protect you. This imprisonment will not last. I know how precarious this situation is for you. Right now, I appease them. But not for long. No, let me create safety for the others and you'll be out of here." Before he closed the door, he stopped. "Keep fighting, Kyra. You still have friends on the other side. We're fighting for you, too." He left, closing the door softly behind him leaving Kyra face-to-face with the Cadaver.

CHAPTER 35

W ell," Gilrich said, not trying to hide the snide grin twisting his already contorted features, "it seems you've fallen from grace."

Kyra ignored him but anger bubbled in her chest. Anger at Gilrich, anger at General Prait, anger at the stupidity of the people in the city. It rose like bile, clawing for release. Anger, fear, frustration, pity, even compassion – they all fought for power inside her. She wanted to cry, scream, lash out, explode. But she couldn't. She wouldn't. Breathing deep, she focused on the emotions, studying them as if she were watching herself instead of living them. She let herself feel each one, and then let it go. Eventually, the anger subsided and she sighed, pulling her knees up to her chest while her back did its best to rest against the wall. It was difficult with her hands shackled behind her.

"It seems you're right, Gilrich," she said, acknowledging him for the first time. "They fear what I am, just like they fear what you are. I guess we aren't so different after all."

Gilrich grunted, then snorted. Soon he was downright laughing, chortling at her expense, his body shaking with amusement and forcing the chains to rattle.

"Oh, shut up, Gilrich."

He only roared harder.

When his laughter eventually subsided, he slid himself forward as far as his chains would allow, inching his body closer to hers. "Now you know what it feels like," he said. "Being chained to a wall, hated by everybody around you, no freedom. Hated because you're different." He spat, and the spittle landed on her chest. The small spot soaked into the fabric of her tunic, staining it a darker shade of brown. "I always knew what it felt like, Gilrich. I never wanted to imprison you here, but they wanted to kill you, and I couldn't let them do that."

Gilrich grunted, slumping back against the other wall. "Because imprisonment is better than death," he said, and in that moment, she understood exactly how he felt.

He would have preferred death.

Her heart nearly broke.

She shook her head sadly, turning her body sideways so she could lean against the wall while her hands dangled behind her. "No. Imprisonment is not better than death. I know that more than anybody in this city. But you're in a prison of a different kind and you don't see it. And I still want to help you."

"Ha!" Gilrich said. "You're talking about the prison of my mind."

She nodded.

"I'm not a prisoner in there," he said. "The Malic'Uiel just gave me the truth. All they did was take away the human failing, weaknesses, and fears. They showed me the truth of what they're doing and who they are. They freed me from my own flaws. That is not enslavement."

Kyra shrugged. "I thought that once, too." She curled away from him into a ball against the wall and let her eyes close. Since she was stuck in here, she might as well rest. She would follow their directives for now, but her tenure here would not be long – not if she had anything to do with it. She'd give General Prait and Caden their chance to make things right in the city. But if they failed, she would find a way to free herself from this prison and all the shackles humanity had placed on her.

Caden stormed into General Prait's bunkhouse, shoving the door so hard it slammed against the wall and rattled the small window next to it.

"You made her a prisoner?" he demanded, chest heaving, hands balled into tight fists. "After everything she's done? After she's put her life on the line over and over and over to protect the people here, you chain her up like a Cadaver!"

General Prait barely glanced at Caden from the chair he was slumped in. Age was catching up to him, and his sallow skin and sunken eyes spoke to the pain he felt at the betrayal. "Caden." He closed his eyes and let his head rest against the back of the chair. "You have no idea how hard I fought for her. They wanted to kill her. They want to see her blood run, convinced somehow that spilling it would save them."

Caden yanked his fingers through his hair and stomped to the table. "She has done nothing wrong! If it weren't for her, everyone in this city would be dead. And to take her when I was not here to stop it!" Caden slammed his fists on the aged wood. "How could you be such a coward?"

General Prait flew to his feet, knocking his chair to the ground. His face was a mottled red, and he thrust it toward Caden. "I know she isn't a threat! But we are up against not only a council of men and women who believe she is, but an entire city! She eventually stopped the Phantom attacks, but why didn't she stop them when they first started? Why did she wait until we'd lost so many of our own to their attacks? And why did the Phantoms attack after she came here? For that matter, why did her power leave one man dead? These are the questions being asked. These are the fears that plague every single person in this city. I don't have answers for them," he snapped. "And no matter how hard we tried, she couldn't give us any. Like it or not, Caden, all the people here have seen is damage caused by what she does. They refuse to see anything else. To them, she was sent here by the Malic'Uiel to lure us all to safety and slaughter us in our sleep."

"You know that's not the case."

"Of course I do!" General Prait kicked the table in front of him, knocking it sideways. "But *they* don't. They needed her where they could control her."

"They need her where she can protect them." Caden's voice had fallen and was creeping up on menacing. "She is all that stands between them and the monsters they fear so damn much."

General Prait sighed and dropped his head in his hands. "I know she's not what they think she is," he said. "I don't intend for her to stay locked up long, but for now there's nothing we can do. Tutis is unstable. We're all that's left of humanity, and we're crumbling. All the people see is somebody with unexplainable power – power that must come from the Malic'Uiel. The men of this army that knew her before she was taken know she didn't have the power of light or the ability to pull lightning from the sky or send electricity over her body. What conclusions do you think they should draw?"

Caden, breathing hard, glared at General Prait. "I'd expect them to remember the woman that was, to recognize that she is the only person who ever escaped the Malic'Uiel, and the only person to ever single-handedly destroy a Phantom! I would expect them to see the truth."

General Prait reached behind him, fixing the chair he'd knocked over and then dropped into it again. "Caden," he said, his voice strained. "You expect defenseless people to trust what they don't understand when the things they don't understand are the reason their world is what it is today. You expect them to operate outside of fear when all they've known for the last fifteen years *is* fear. There is no other way for them to be but terrified of forces that don't come from humanity."

"I won't leave her there, General."

"Yes, you will. Kyra went willingly because the council decided that if she didn't go, somebody she cared about would go in her place. If you free her or she somehow chooses to walk away, Dalia will be wearing the same shackles that Kyra wears now."

"You can't imprison the innocent!"

"I know," General Prait whispered, closing his eyes as if to shut out the world for just a moment. "And yet, we already have. I couldn't get them to see reason. I tried. I tried so hard. You and I have to work with them to restore hope and, if we're lucky, logic. Until then, it's not safe for Kyra to walk free in our streets. And the reason you weren't there when the decision was made? The council felt you were too emotionally attached. They chose to operate in secret; you were intentionally left out. I am sorry."

Caden's jaw clenched; if he'd been able to, he would have spit fire. This all made sense to General Prait, but that made little difference to Caden. He could only see that he was living in a city of idiots, with people too stupid to see the gift they had in their midst. He spun on his heel and stomped from the room. Maybe General Prait was willing to let a council of fear rule the city, but Caden was not. Kyra was the key to their salvation, and he wouldn't see her locked away like some Cadaver.

He had one destination in mind: Kyra's cell. He stomped through the streets aware of nothing except Kyra and her freedom. He marched past the bunkhouses, past the people, leaving them for the unpopulated area of the storehouses. So focused was he on the injustice of her imprisonment that he didn't notice Leland until he spoke. "Not too happy with this turn of events, are we?" Leland gloated.

Caden's head snapped up.

Leland sauntered out of a side street, mouth split in a malicious grin.

"Go to hell, Leland," Caden said. He noticed that they were alone, and for the briefest of moments he considered doing away with Leland entirely.

Leland chortled. "One of us will go to hell, but I doubt it will be me."

Caden whirled, gripped Leland by the throat, and shoved him against the nearest building. "You did this," he hissed. "You and the lies you sow. I should have killed you that night; if it weren't for Kyra, I would have."

Leland's face turned a deep shade of purple, but he managed to smile. "It was worth it," he choked out. "Do you think she's there by accident?" He tried to shake his head, but couldn't with Caden's hand pressed against his windpipe. "I have friends on the council."

Caden shoved harder, completely cutting off airflow. "You deserve to die."

"So do you." This voice came from behind, cutting through Caden's memories to a time when a fourteen-year-old boy watched his father die. He dropped Leland, who choked and gasped for air. Slowly he turned to face his accuser. "Shem," he hissed.

Shem bowed. "Did you miss me?"

Caden, blinded by rage, ripped his sword from its sheath. Within seconds, fire engulfed the blade. "You're no better than they are!" he screamed, arcing the blade down toward Shem's skull.

Shem neatly parried, laughing at Caden's anger. "I've seen this somewhere before," he said. "But where?"

Caden swung and Shem dodged again, almost laughing. "I remember," he said. "Your father acted the same way before they took him. You know his fate, of course."

Caden ignored Shem's barbs, slicing the sword down again and again. Shem easily dodged the attacks, dancing out of the way before the blade ever made contact. Finally, Caden froze as realization dawned. "You've...they've altered you," he said, incredulous.

Shem smiled, but it was dark and loathsome. Fire of his own erupted on his palm. "Yes, well, they needed a human." He threw a ball of fire at Caden, who rolled out of the way. Attack after attack followed until something shot into Caden's side. Huiel came out of the shadows, grunting in satisfaction.

Searing pain rippled through Caden's body. Glancing down, the shaft of an arrow stuck out from beneath his ribs. He slumped to the ground, clutching at the wound. Gasping, the air he fought for refused to give relief. He collapsed on the opposite side, staring down the street, which seemed to sway in front of him.

"Let's go, men," Shem said. The three spun away, racing in the direction of Kyra's cell.

Caden tried to crawl after them, but his body wouldn't listen. It was as if his flesh had fused to the cobblestone.

Avalyn, save her, he thought before slumping into darkness.

*

CHAPTER 36

K yra's sleep was fitful. Her shoulders ached and her wrists throbbed. Memories pushed to the surface, crowding themselves into her dreams. In them, Caden and her father laughed at her, the way they'd done in her twisted memories given by the Malic'Uiel.

"Do you love me?" Caden asked, his voice mocking while his hand pushed against her windpipe, choking the life out of her.

"Stop," she rasped. "You're hurting me." She wanted to claw his fingers away from her throat, but she couldn't pull her hands free; something had them bound.

He snarled and squeezed harder.

"Caden!" she tried to cry, desperate now as her lungs screamed for air. She tried again to free her arms, but it was useless.

Panicked, she jolted awake to find Shem looming over her, fingers squeezing her throat. His hair, blonde and disheveled, hung over black eyes that gleamed with hate. His broad shoulders filled her vision, pushing against the tunic that was too tight for the muscles beneath. Veins in his arms ran under his skin like rivers. Sweat beaded on his flesh, dripping down to his fingers, which remained locked around her neck. She glanced frantically around the room, noting Gilrich in the corner, jerking angrily against his chains. His eyes were fixed on her face.

"Shem," she tried to speak, but no air could make it through. Fog settled in her brain, and the room shifted in and out of focus.

"What are you doing?" From the doorway, Leland yelled at Shem. "We're supposed to get her out of here, not kill her."

"I'm not going to kill her."

Their conversation seemed distant, and Kyra had to focus to understand the words. They had to get her out of here – to where? Her eyes fluttered closed as her body and mind screamed for oxygen.

"Shem!" Leland cried. "Give her the poison and let's go. I don't want to carry her out of here any more than you do."

"Shut up, Leland," Shem growled. "She deserves this. She's the reason my brother is dead."

Kyra's head spun, but Shem's face stayed in focus. Malice dripped from his features. He would enjoy killing her. Maybe even enjoy it enough to risk the wrath of the Malic'Uiel.

His face began to fade, as did the room around her. Somewhere, somebody screamed at Shem to stop. Her body slumped. *How ironic*, she thought, *that this is how I will die – trapped with a Cadaver, and murdered by a human inside the only safe human stronghold.* As she thought those words, another thought came with them: others had tried to kill her, and they had all failed. Light pricked at her consciousness – a reminder.

She'd be damned if she let Shem destroy her light. With the last of her strength, she pushed the light from her hands, begging it to cover her body. The second her light touched Shem's fingers, he jolted back as if she'd struck him.

She gasped, dropping against the wall as she gulped in air. Her wrists twisted painfully against the shackles, but she could breathe. Black spots swam in her vision until her brain soaked in the life-giving air.

When her vision cleared, Shem filled her view. He picked himself up from the floor, dazed. Leland gripped his arm, tugging him upward. "You were supposed to drug her while she was defenseless!" he screamed. He jerked him to his feet, panicked.

Shem stood on shaky legs, but then his gaze swung back to her, and all of his hate came with it. His hands erupted in flames as he stalked forward. "Quit your blubbering," he said to Leland. "We aren't leaving without her."

"We're going to get caught," Leland hissed, resuming his place as lookout.

Shem chuckled, fully recovered. "Do you really think they can stop me?" In one swift motion, he flung his hands toward Kyra. A ball of flame barreled toward her. She threw more energy into her light, doubling the field around her as she ducked down into it. The fire fizzled against it. Shem flung another fireball, and another. Faster and faster they came, the force of them knocking Kyra back bit by bit. Her body trembled against the exertion, and the shield of light flickered.

Shem's eyes darkened. For one moment, he pulled the fire back. Then he hurled it against her with so much force that it threw her into the back wall, slamming her head into the hard wood. She slumped to her knees, fighting to keep from throwing up or blacking out. Her light fled back into her body.

The next fireball hit her in the chest. Shem immediately followed, sucking the flame from her body before it could kill her. Before she could react, he knelt on top of her, digging a knee into her chest while his hands forced her mouth open. She choked and gagged as he forced a bitter liquid down her throat, and then held her mouth shut before she could spit it out.

Warmth filled her chest, flowing into her stomach and down her legs. Slowly, the fight left her until she sat motionless. Shem immediately moved to action, gripping the shackles that bound her. The metal around her wrists melted under Shem's touch, pearling on her skin until it trickled down in molten ribbons. The pain seared into her, and she registered her own screaming, but it was as if it came from somebody else. She tried to make sense of what was happening, but she couldn't understand it. It was as if she'd been locked away in her own mind.

Shem laughed at her pain. "I knew I would enjoy this," he said, forcing the flames to grow hotter.

"Shem," Leland snapped. "I didn't sign up for torture. Get her and let's go."

"Fine," Shem growled, yanking Kyra to her feet. He dragged her to the door, crossing in front of Gilrich as he did so. Without warning, Gilrich propelled himself from the corner and slammed into Shem's chest. Shem groaned, dropping to his knees as he gasped for air.

"Run, Kyra," Gilrich hissed.

She blinked, her mind slowly processing the words. *Run, Kyra.*

Run.

That meant something.

After what seemed an eternity, it sunk in. She bolted for the door. Leland grabbed her arm and yanked her back inside the building.

Run.

She needed to run.

"I don't think so," he said, holding her tight against him. "Shem, let's go." He hurried from the building, pulling Kyra along behind him.

Run!

Kyra's mind screamed the words, but her body wouldn't respond. Her feet shuffled along with her captor. The need to run faded, replaced by a hazy confusion.

They passed the two guards that had been watching the building; their faces kissed the dust and blood formed a halo around their heads.

She glanced back at the building and saw Shem pull the door shut before melting the bolts and setting the wood aflame.

When he caught up with them, he smiled at her. "Your little experiment will burn alive now."

My little experiment? She studied Shem in confusion. *Experiment? What is my experiment?*

When Gilrich began screaming behind the ruined door, she almost understood what Shem meant. But it wasn't enough. Shem dragged her away before she could make sense of it.

They ran through the streets of Tutis. Kyra followed willingly, obeying every command.

"Who did you use that poison on before?" Leland asked. "I didn't think it would work."

"Gilrich," Shem said.

Leland's eyebrows raised. "You're the one who led him to the Malic'Uiel."

Shem shrugged but his face split in a smile. "He had the same tonic in his veins that is now in hers. He went willingly enough after that."

When they reached the back of the city wall, there was a rope dangling from the top. "Get up the rope," Shem commanded her. "Your master waits."

She nodded and gripped the rope. The burns from the molten steel tore as she strained her muscles. When she tried to pull her body up the rope she groaned; pain ignited on her wrists, but she fought against it and began tugging her weight up. Shem's mouth contorted into a smile. "Oh, I've waited so long to see you suffer."

The rough fibers of the rope dug into the burns on her skin, tearing at the damaged flesh. From the top, Huiel beckoned her up. But her hands were slick with blood. She tried to hold on, but it was impossible; she slid back down and collapsed at the base of the wall. "It hurts," she whimpered.

"Damn you, Shem," Leland snapped, grabbing the rope and wrapping it around Kyra's waist and legs. "Hang onto the rope," he said. He left her then, shimmying up the rope ahead of her. She held onto the thick fibers and waited.

Waited for...what? She didn't know. Her mind was a muddled fog.

"Shem!" This voice echoed down the street. Both Shem and Leland whirled toward the sound. Kyra heard it but didn't acknowledge the new voice.

"Pull her up!" Shem called to the two men on top of the wall. Fire erupted on his palm while he faced his new threat.

General Prait and Bronson stood at the end of the street. Behind them, five soldiers waited with arrows drawn.

"Let her go," General Prait demanded.

Shem chuckled and the flames rose. The men gaped at him in fear. "I don't follow the commands of men," he said. "I follow the commands of gods!" His arm whipped out, sending a fireball blazing down the street. The men leaped out of the way, running for cover.

"Take him out!" General Prait screamed. "Don't hurt Kyra!"

From down the street a volley of arrows flew. Some were burned up in Shem's fire while others missed their target and clattered harmlessly on the cobblestone.

"Get her up there!" Shem called to Leland. "Go!"

Leland began pulling her up, inching higher with every passing second.

Shem backed toward the rope, but his fireballs didn't cease. They crashed down the street one after the other, igniting the surrounding buildings. Smoke churned as the fire devoured the wood.

"Don't stop, men!" General Prait cried, ducking out of the way again and again as he moved down the street.

Bronson paused for a moment, studying the battle and his opponents. Shem's focus was on the general and the men firing at him. Unnoticed, Bronson slipped behind the burning buildings.

Kyra reached the top of the rope and Leland dragged her onto the wall, then unfastened the rope. Just after he threw it back down to Shem, he shrieked and stumbled to his knees next to her. An arrow protruded from his leg. Leland glanced at Kyra, then down at Shem. "I'm not going to stay here and die," he muttered. Huiel didn't wait for more than that. He fled down the side of the wall using a rope they'd left dangling for themselves.

Leland glared at Kyra. "I hope they slaughter you both," he said before following Huiel to safety. She watched Leland limp away after Huiel, blood staining the ground beneath him.

Inside the city, the battle raged. General Prait and his men gained on Shem despite the blaze surrounding them. It finally occurred to Shem that he was going to lose this encounter. Glancing up, he saw Kyra's leg dangling off the top of the wall. He needed to get up there with her.

Pulling on the power given him by the Phantom, he gathered the magic together inside him until it couldn't be contained any longer. Fire exploded from his body, racing down the street in a plume of destruction.

Men screamed as the heat melted their flesh.

Shem gripped the rope, scrambling up after his prey. But he didn't see Bronson, nor was he aware of the arrow Bronson released until it found purchase in his ribs.

Shem bellowed and slipped from the rope. He landed hard on his back; his breath expelled in a huff and he lay, momentarily dazed, gasping for air. In his peripheral vision Bronson ran toward him. He ground his teeth in frustration. One last glance up at Kyra's dangling leg and he knew he was going to lose. His prize, his promise of power, so close but impossible to take.

He sent his thoughts to the forest beyond and told his body to go there. The flesh shimmered out of focus until he disappeared.

Bronson pulled up short, skidding to a stop where moments before Shem had lain. Not waiting for the others, he climbed up the rope to find Kyra at the top. She lay still, breathing fast, her eyes wide open but focused on nothing. The skin on her wrists was melted and charred, the flesh torn from her hands. Bones, tendons, and fat were the only things visible on her palms. The front of her tunic had burned away, and the visible flesh was a mass of blisters. To top it off, a garden of bruises bloomed on Kyra's throat, perfectly matched to a man's grip. Tears filled his eyes when he saw her, and anger settled deep in the pit of his gut. To hurt a woman this way – that would take a special sort of monster.

"Oh, Kyra," he breathed, his fingers brushing the wounds on her wrists. She inhaled deeply, clenching her eyes against the pain. "I'm here to help you," he said. "Can you move?"

She nodded.

Taking extra care, Bronson scooped her into his arms. She whimpered but made no other sound.

He held her close, running with her along the top of the wall until he came to the steps that would lead them down.

By the time they reached solid ground, Kyra had passed out, which was a relief to him; better blessed darkness than fiery pain.

When they reached the infirmary he laid her on a cot, handing her over to Dr. Bron's care. Kyra's body trembled even though she remained unconscious. Dr. Bron said nothing, just got to work bandaging her patient.

When Kyra was settled, Bronson left the infirmary and found somewhere to be sick over what Shem had done.

CHAPTER 37

Kyra drifted in a dark fog, her body and mind weightless. A single point of light shone like a beacon, carving a path in the darkness. Curious, she focused on the light. She immediately began drifting toward it, her unspoken desire the only requirement for her to move.

The light began to take shape, spires and pillars rising out of the mist. Materializing in front of her, a gate blocked her way. She hovered at the gate, peering into the space beyond. A gleaming road paved in stone that seemed to emanate its own light led the way to a large city, whose lustrous buildings both absorbed and reflected the sun. All of the buildings were built from light-colored stone – whites, creams, and pale grays. The city itself appeared to wind around a central point. The pillars and spires Kyra had seen rose up from the center of the city. A white gem gleamed from the top of the highest spire, breaking the light into hundreds of scintillating pieces.

"It's beautiful, isn't it?"

Blinking, Kyra tore her eyes from the breathtaking city, realizing that this voice – Avalyn's voice – didn't startle her at all. She had been aware all along of a second entity. Avalyn hovered near, her eyes on the city and a small smile on her lips. "One of my favorite visions."

"Yes, it is beautiful," Kyra said. "What is it?"

"Tutella. It is the city that guards the doorway to Lumen."

"So Lumen is real, then?"

Avalyn nodded. "Very much so. As much as Spero and Letum."

"Letum?"

Avalyn smiled, taking Kyra's hand and pulling her back from the gate. "It's time you learn the truth, Kyra," she said. "We believe you're ready."

"We?"

Avalyn gestured forward. A second point of light separated the darkness until Evia, Kyra's mother, materialized in front of her.

Kyra gasped; unbidden tears sprung to her eyes. She rushed forward and threw her arms around her mother while the tears escaped, staining the shimmering cloak covering Evia's body.

Evia laughed softly while gentle hands stroked Kyra's hair. She smelled like sunshine and lilacs and Kyra breathed her in, experiencing safety for the first time in years. Her mother's body was soft and curvy, beautifully feminine. Kyra was a child again, protected in her mother's arms.

Suddenly, she stiffened, pulling herself away. "I'm dead, aren't I?" She glanced around in awe. "This is where the dead go? I never imagined..."

"Kyra," Evia said. "Shhhh. You're not dead."

"Then where is my body?" Kyra demanded.

Evia chuckled. "You are very much alive – though in some pain – in Spero. I called your soul here, and Avalyn's."

Avalyn dipped her head in acknowledgment.

"Avalyn's soul?" Kyra whipped around, gaping at Avalyn. "But..."

Avalyn waved away her concern. "Listen to Evia. She'll explain everything."

Kyra turned back to her mother, who led her to a row of boulders that lined the trail outside the city. She gestured for her to sit before following suit.

"Let me start by sharing with you the history of the world that you know." Evia waved her hand and the fog in front of them formed into an image: three spheres in a row, encased in a single rectangle. The spheres on the sides were each housed in a triangle, whose tips met and held up the middle sphere.

Kyra's hand automatically moved to her throat, where she found the necklace Avalyn had given her.

Removing the chain, she held the pendant up to the image. They were the same.

"You've been looking for answers to this symbol for a long time," Evia said. "The symbol represents the creation and balance of three realms: Lumen, Spero, and Letum. They are, in essence, the realm of light, the realm of hope, and the realm of darkness. Thousands of years ago the three realms existed as one and were inhabited by three peoples: Humans, the Illi'Crepus, and the Qui'Lumine. The Illi'Crepus were creatures of the night, the Qui'Lumine were those who lived for the light, and humans were of the twilight, neither day nor night. All three existed in peace, and the realms flourished for it."

Evia waved her hand and the symbol disappeared, replaced by an image of a single orb floating in the heavens. This orb pulsed and a rainbow of light bloomed from its core. "This world was once called Vita," Evia said. "In the world of Vita, the Qui'Lumine were guides and mentors, guardians of knowledge. They helped humanity unlock their full potential. Humans were creatures of emotions – joy, anger, passion, and love. They were beautiful to behold, and the Qui'Lumine lived among them to experience emotions they themselves were not capable of." She waved her hand again and the vision dissipated, replaced by a new orb – it was a deep purple and glittered as if it were covered in a million stars.

"The Illi'Crepus were creatures of the night. They brought beauty and magic to the darkness; the stars shone in the night sky just for them. For many years the Illi'Crepus brought balance to the world by tempering the Qui'Lumine's quest for knowledge with industry and growth. They used the wisdom of the Qui'Lumine to improve the world around them. They challenged themselves to be better, stronger, more powerful. Humanity enabled both peoples to experience life on a level they were not capable of on their own, for the darkness and the light existed inside the humans; they were a link that married the three. Their unity created perfect harmony."

Evia waved her hand once more and the vision changed again. This time both orbs floated in front of them, but both seemed dim and weak. "As the years progressed, a new darkness awoke, one that did not create beauty. Inside this darkness, the Malic'Uiel shaped themselves into existence." Again, a wave of her hand and the vision changed. Now the orb did not glitter with stars. It seemed stained with an inky blackness. "The Malic'Uiel were Illi'Crepus who fell prey to the lust of greed and power. They believed they could transform humanity from the natural weakness of flesh, to create a perfect, more powerful species. But in order to do so, they enslaved the minds of humans and destroyed their ability to think for themselves – to reason, to feel, and to love."

Evia stopped, head bowed in sadness. "Thousands of people were destroyed before the Qui'Lumine realized what was happening. Thousands of Illi'Crepus were lost to the Malic'Uiel plague. Humans fled in terror from the Malic'Uiel, desperate to save their minds. But the Malic'Uiel advanced and the scourge of darkness polluted the light, dimming even the brightest of the Qui'Lumine."

Evia motioned toward the fog and the image shaped itself into something new. A dark mist collided with and then swallowed up cities and lands that had once shone as brightly as the city behind her. Eventually, the single orb was a whirling chaos of black mist. A single spark shone inside the mist.

"What is that?" Kyra whispered, moving closer to the spark.

"This is where your history begins," Evia said, reaching into the black mist and pulling out the spark. "Amid the chaos of the battles between Malic'Uiel and Qui'Lumine, a child was born. The mother was a being of light, and the father was human; they were the first to find love by truly witnessing the soul of the other. This Qui'Lumine was the first Qui'Lumine to experience love in the unconditional, raw form humanity did; somehow, the human male unlocked the heart of the Qui'Lumine woman.

"The child, Layla, was half human, half being of light. As such, the power of light naturally flowed through her veins. She had the greatest teachers a human could ask for – her mentors were the most advance of all Qui'Lumine, of humanity, and even of the Illi'Crepus. All peoples found hope in this little girl."

Evia returned the spark to the swirling orb and gestured for Kyra to watch. Slowly, the spark expanded. Everywhere it touched, the blackness dissipated.

"The child brought light and hope back to Vita. She moved among the world, unlocking the light that existed within those who approached her. But by the time she reached adulthood, Vita was locked in a fierce battle for domination. Half the world fought for light, freedom, and love, while the other pushed for darkness and unbridled power."

Another wave of Evia's hand had the image reforming once more. The single large orb broke into three pieces, each a sphere of its own.

"At the height of the fiercest battle, Layla stepped onto the battlefield and commanded the light to her bidding; the darkness could not touch her, and so it cowered beneath her. None could stop while she tore open a door to a new realm, the one we now know as Letum. She broke the world in three, separating the Qui'Lumine and the Illi'Crepus from humanity. In her power, the Malic'uiel could not exist and thus they were destroyed. But none could stop the course set by the Malic'Uiel. The destruction was too great, and Vita could not return to its previous state. The Illi'Crepus – the people of darkness – retreated to Letum, where they built a new world for themselves.

Layla and the other survivors knew that humanity and Qui'Lumine could not exist in harmony without the balance provided by the Illi'Crepus, so the Qui'Lumine willingly stepped into the third realm, the realm now known as Lumen. Humanity was given the remaining world, which became the realm of Spero. Layla stayed in Spero with her people. The doors between the realms were sealed, only to be opened for the souls of humanity passing between the realms to continue their sojourn beyond death."

The mist once again became the symbol Kyra was so familiar with. "The three realms continued to bring balance to one another, each one influencing the other in their own way." Evia gestured to Kyra's necklace. "May I?" she asked.

Kyra nodded, handing over the small chain. Evia dangled the pendant from the chain and removed the sphere on the right. The weight on the other side caused the pendant to drop, hanging out of balance. "As long as the night and dark remain in balance, harmony exists and the realms are safe. But though the Malic'Uiel were destroyed, their darkness was not entirely rooted out, and those roots grew over thousands of years. This darkness seeped into Spero and overtook the hearts of men and the balance began to erode. Once it tipped in the favor of darkness, the doorway to Letum was able to be reopened. The Malic'Uiel returned on the invitation of those who'd embraced their ways."

She returned the sphere to its rightful place, and the pendant leveled out, hanging horizontal once more. "Balance can be restored, but only one can do it." Evia handed the pendant back and nodded her head toward Kyra. "You are the Countess of Lumen, the last remaining descendent of Layla, and you have awoken the light within. Half being of light, half human, you are the key to restoring harmony."

Avalyn stepped forward. "Caden is your guardian, your protector. And he's the only human to harbor the darkness of the Malic'Uiel without being polluted by it."

"We believe that the two of you can restore the balance," Evia said. "Caden is more than protector to the Countess of Lumen. He is the darkness, and you are the light; your fates are intertwined."

Avalyn held her wrist out, revealing a shimmering tattoo that mirrored Caden's. "The mark of Lumen sets apart all those who are bound to the Countess," she said. "I was taught the true history of Lumen from a very young age, and as such I am your guide. My role is to help you find the true essence of the power you carry."

Kyra glanced at the mark, then at her mother. "Father had the same mark."

Evia nodded. "He was my protector, though he never knew that aspect of our relationship. And he was yours, until Caden found his way to you."

Kyra chewed at her lip. "How is it that I'm communing with the dead?"

"There is much for you to learn, Kyra," Evia said. "Focus on mastering your power. For now, leave the questions regarding the dead to the dead."

Kyra started to protest – that answer did not leave her satisfied – but Avalyn stepped closer and smiled, taking Kyra's hands in hers and squeezing them in encouragement. "I am not dead," she said. "The Master of the Malic'Uiel knew my role when he found me; he knew the meaning of the mark. My body is in his control, but I won't give him my mind. I reside in Spero with you."

At this, Kyra's jaw dropped. "You're alive?"

Avalyn nodded. "Just enough. I wouldn't call it living."

Kyra's thoughts flew through the realms to Caden, whose love for his wife had not diminished with time, and whose love for herself had grown. Anxiety rose in her breast. If she was bound to Caden, and Avalyn was still alive...pain crashed into her, and she nearly crumbled under the weight. Caden was not hers, could not be hers. And though she thought she'd resisted giving him her heart, she realized now that she already had. It was his long before her time with the Malic'Uiel.

"You needn't worry," Avalyn whispered, reaching for Kyra's arm as if to offer encouragement.

Kyra pulled away, shaking her head in dismay. "He loves you," she said. "He loves me! I..." She swallowed, trying to force down the lump in her throat.

"Kyra!" Evia said, grasping her daughter's arm. "You are the light and Caden holds the darkness. You are bound by something far stronger than most. Trust that, and let it guide you."

"I don't know how," Kyra whispered. "I fear what I am."

Evia's voice softened. "Avalyn will help you as often as you need. It's time you embrace who you are." She stepped back, letting her hands fall to her sides. "Caden needs you," she said quietly. "Spero needs you. You must go."

As she said the words, the realm of Lumen faded until only darkness remained. After a moment, a dull ache filled Kyra's throat. The ache soon flared into fiery pain.

Kyra woke screaming, clutching at her throat, unaware of the tears streaming down her cheeks.

She blinked and frantically studied the room. It was so dark, where was the light?

When she realized she was in the infirmary, she forced herself to breathe normally, forced her hands to flutter to her side. Slowly, memories resurfaced of her time with Shem until she understood the source of the pain.

Fighting it would do no good. Instead, she lay back, shut her eyes as tight as she could, and counted her breaths, giving her mind something else to think about.

CHAPTER 38

W hile Bronson fought for Kyra's life, Dalia fought for another. She had planned to see Gilrich, but when she turned the corner to his building, she found flames licking up the sides of the structure. Not thinking about anything but Gilrich's safety, she ran to the building and peered through the window. Inside, he struggled against his chains while flames reached to consume him.

Dalia hurried up the steps to the storehouse, yanking on the door. It wouldn't budge no matter how hard she pulled it. Shutting her mind against the death lying at the door of the building, she yanked a dead soldier's blade from his sheath and attacked the door and handle with the weapon. Over and over, she beat it with the blade, forcing the wood to splinter until it finally cracked around the handle. She kept beating until the door finally gave way to her demands.

The moment the door opened, smoke billowed from inside; heat wrapped its deadly tendrils around her. She stepped back long enough to suck in a great gulp of air before charging inside. Staying low, her eyes stinging from the smoke, she pushed herself toward Gilrich, skirting around the flames that rapidly filled the small space. Gilrich slumped in a corner, head lolling to the side. She took the sword and beat it against the chain binding his wrists together. The metal tried to withstand her attack, but the chain was old and brittle. Eventually, it snapped in half. For the first time in months, Gilrich's wrists were free.

Flames snaked closer and closer to her feet, devouring the floor of the building. Her chest ached and she was forced to suck in a breath, sending burning smoke into her lungs. Her body spasmed in response, forcing the smoke out in painful coughs. Ignoring the burning in her lungs, she wrapped her arms around Gilrich's chest and dragged him across the floor toward the opening.

Behind her, where Gilrich had been moments before, wood cracked and popped. The corner of the roof collapsed on itself. She screamed and pulled harder. "Come on," she groaned. "You have to help me."

Under her grasp, Gilrich stirred. His feet began pushing toward the exit. Relieved, she looped her arm around his back, supporting his weight. Together they stumbled from the building, collapsing on the cobblestone in a heap.

Dalia rolled onto her back while hacking coughs filled her lungs. Her hand cradled her bulging stomach. She shouldn't have done it, shouldn't have put her baby at risk, but she couldn't let Gilrich die. With one hand on her stomach, she groaned and rolled to the side, forcing her body back to her knees. Gilrich struggled next to her, lying on his side while his freed hands gripped the cobblestone. His cheek dug into the street and wracking coughs tore at his body.

She inched closer to him, gripping his shoulder. "Are you...okay?" she gasped.

Instead of responding, he sucked in breath after life-saving breath. After a few breaths, he nodded. She let her head droop until it rested on his bicep while tears of relief dripped down her soot covered cheeks. The brief shot of adrenaline she'd had faded, replacing itself with an overpowering weakness. Her hand trembled on his shoulder, and her breaths came in ragged gasps.

Chaos reigned near the wall of the city. Men screamed and flames shot into the sky again and again. For now, they remained unnoticed, but Dalia knew that wouldn't last. The fear the citizens harbored would not stop them from turning on the one Cadaver in their midst.

After Gilrich's breathing calmed, she forced herself to her feet, legs trembling. "Come on," she said. "We have to get you to safety."

Gilrich grunted, but pushed himself up and followed her lead. Together they stumbled down the street, each one supporting the other until the streets around them were empty. The Citadel gleamed in front of them, a haven instead of a prison. "In there," Dalia said. "There are places you can hide."

They hobbled forward, but as they neared the cell complex Dalia cast a glance backward and saw a still form lying in the street. "Oh no," she murmured, clenching Gilrich's arm. "It's Caden."

He glanced back. "So?"

She eyed him sharply. "He's hurt. We have to help him."

He grunted again. "We could just let him die."

She dropped her arm, stepping back as if he'd burned her. "Should I have let you die?" she snapped. "I could have, you know. Everybody else was going to. I could have let you burn with that building."

"And if you had, it would have been the end of me, that is all."

Dalia glared at him, one hand on her hip, the other cradling her stomach. "I got you out of there because I know somewhere in there is a good soul – a person. Not a Cadaver. Not a tool of the Malic'Uiel. A human being with blood and flesh, a heart and soul." She stepped closer, putting her hand once more on his arm. "Are you going to tell me that I was wrong? That your humanity is truly lost?"

Gilrich held her unflinching gaze, but it wasn't for long. When his eyes dropped, they did so in tears. "No," he whispered. "You aren't wrong. If you were, I'd have killed you. That's what the Malic'Uiel would have had me do."

"That's what I thought. We're helping Caden."

"We're helping Caden," Gilrich murmured, following her lead.

When they reached him, Dalia sunk to her knees. She gently touched the arrow still embedded beneath his ribs. "Caden?" she whispered, nudging his shoulder. She leaned down, pressing her ear against his chest. "He's breathing. Can you help me get him to the infirmary?"

Gilrich nodded, easily scooping Caden up. Dalia's eyes widened. "You carry him like he weighs nothing."

"I'm a Cadaver," Caden grunted. "You think I am human, but this body no longer is."

Dalia squared her shoulders and hurried forward. Maybe his body wasn't human – it didn't even look human – but his soul still was.

"You can't go in there," Dalia said as they neared the infirmary. "I don't expect Dr. Bron is alone, and if any soldier sees you, they'll clap those chains right back on your wrists. Set him outside and conceal yourself. I'll let Dr. Bron know he's here."

Gilrich followed her commands and dropped Caden in front of the infirmary. He groaned as the arrow shaft brushed against the wall, pushing against his flesh.

"You could have been gentler about it," Dalia muttered.

He shrugged.

She glared at him. "Hide." She didn't wait for his response, but ducked inside instead. It wasn't long before she reemerged with Dr. Bron at her side, followed by a soldier. Dr. Bron and the soldier hoisted Caden up and carried him inside.

Dalia waited until they were out of sight before starting back down the street. "Gilrich," she hissed into the shadows. "Let's go."

Gilrich stepped out from behind the building, falling in place next to her.

Her detour with Caden did not change her plans, and when they reached the Citadel they hurried inside, letting the darkness swallow them whole.

Many hours later, ash fluttered in the air like snowflakes, stirred up by the evening's gentle breezes. Some of it settled in Dalia's hair, on her shoulders, and on the Cadaver whose arms were wrapped around her still form.

Dalia now slept peacefully, snuggled against Gilrich. At first, he'd hesitated at the close proximity, afraid of the touch, afraid he might hurt her or that she'd wake up and realize she slept near a monster, but when her head dropped onto his lap, all those fears fled. Somehow, this woman had no fear of him. Gently he lay his arm across her sleeping form. His eyes adjusted to the dark easily, and the peaceful silhouette of the angel in his lap awakened something he hadn't felt in a long time.

He brushed his fingers along her arm, feeling the sensation of pleasure stir in his chest. Her hair covered her face, so he pushed it back, studying her feminine features. Her body was not deformed as his was. The smooth lines and curves spoke to the perfection of her humanity. His hand drifted to her stomach. There, life kicked and moved beneath his clawed fingers. She was the essence of life, creating it by her very being. Gilrich had never seen anything more beautiful.

Once again, sensation rose in his chest, but this time it caught in his throat. This was a primal, protective instinct. He knew in that moment he would give his life to protect this woman and the child she bore.

And it was then that he realized Kyra had been right all along: his humanity was still there, buried beneath anger, pain, and the ideals of a dangerous Master.

Hope for a new future bloomed in his soul.

CHAPTER 39

Caden seemed to exist in a space of nothing. Bits of his past drifted in the nothing to haunt him before slipping away – fractured images that brought pain and regret to torment him – trapped in his own mind.

In the near suffocating blackness of his own suffering, his father rose like a ghost, holding Caden's gaze with cold, tortured eyes. Seeing this face, an icy sickness gripped Caden's soul. After a moment, the image began to fade, but a rush of energy filled the space and Caden was pulled into the one memory that would haunt him until he died.

It was cold. So cold. Caden shivered alone in a room with a dirt floor, decaying walls dripping with moisture, and rats as his only company.

They were not good company.

His hands were bound tight with a rough cord that dug into his flesh. He'd been thrown into this place with a sack over his head, but he'd managed to tear that off. It was now a dirty heap in the corner of the room.

Not that it did him any good. There was nothing to see, and no way out. He had no idea how long he'd been here – his guess was at least three days. In that time, he'd been fed three meager meals, and given just enough water to keep him alive. Nobody had spoken to him. Nobody explained why he was here. They'd just thrown him into this hell and walked away.

There was one entrance to the room he occupied. The door itself was locked from the outside, and he knew from experience there were guards stationed beyond it. Whoever had brought him here wanted to keep him here.

Voices from beyond his prison piqued his interest. These weren't the first voices he'd heard since his capture, but one of them sounded familiar. He pushed himself up and crept to the door, pressing his ear against it to listen.

"I told you, I want no part of this." The voice – a rich tenor – washed over Caden like a healing balm. He nearly dropped to his knees in relief. That was his father's voice! Surely Jace was here for Caden.

"You did say you wanted no part of it," another voice answered. "But we reached the point of no return long ago."

Caden recognized this voice as well. The man was a friend of his father's. They called him Honri. He was scarred on the side of his face. The scar pulled at his flesh, forcing every smile on his lips to curve down into a grimace. But it wasn't the scar that filled Caden with dread every time he saw him. No, it was the man's eyes. They were cold and dead. Even if his mouth could turn up in a smile, it wouldn't matter because the eyes were nothing but glassy windows to a blackened soul.

Caden's brief moment of hope drained away. Nothing good followed Honri.

"It's never too late to turn back. Please," Jace pleaded. "Don't do this, Honri. You don't know what you're unleashing on this world. Nobody does." Jace's voice was desperate. Caden had never heard such a tone come out of him. Normally he was boisterous, loud, even intimidating. This was something else entirely – shaky, breathy, almost as if he spoke through panic.

"Whatever comes out of that doorway will be an improvement to what exists now."

"You don't know what's through there!" The words rose in pitch, the desperation clawing out of Caden's father.

Honri did not care. "Ahh, but I do, Jace. I very much do, and I welcome it."

"Why?" Jace demanded.

Caden had no idea what they were speaking of. But it didn't matter – Jace wasn't the kind of man to stand against other men's evil. He was the kind to turn a blind eye. 'Let people do as they may' was his motto.

Even if it hurt people. Since coming to Censura, it was especially if it hurt people. 'That's just the way of Censura,' he would say, as if that justified deplorable behavior.

Sickness rose in Caden's stomach. If his father was standing against something Honri wanted, it must be truly, truly terrible.

There was a pause then Honri's voice dropped and he said, "Because it will end the suffering in this world. It will end *my* suffering."

"People are going to die! Thousands. Millions!" Jace's pleading voice was ragged and breathless, touching on panic.

"People die every day, Jace. Every. Single. Day. You've killed some yourself. Since when does death bother you?"

Caden pressed his ear harder against the door, as if that would somehow help him. It didn't help the sickness in his stomach, or the fact that he wanted to drop to his knees in anguish. But it did make his father's answer come to him unmuffled and clear. "Since I watched an innocent woman die at my hands."

Caden's eyes closed; his head spun and it was difficult to breathe. He'd suspected his father was a murderer, but he'd hoped – oh how he'd hoped that he wasn't! But he was. And from the sounds of it, he would be again.

After a brief pause Honri finally said, "Nobody's innocent, Jace. Not one human is free of offenses and immorality. What we do today will cleanse the world."

"They may not be spotless, but where does forgiveness come in?" His father's voice had dropped in pitch, no longer desperate, but weighed down with sorrow.

"You're a fool, Jace," Honri snapped. "You and your ideals. There was a time when you shared this vision, when the cleansing of humanity brought you pleasure!"

"You speak of things I regret." The voice was so low Caden had to strain to hear.

"Yes, well..." Caden heard two sharp snaps of a finger, then the sound of scuffling feet, and somebody groaned. "Today your vision becomes a reality," Honri finished.

"I won't help you," Jace said. "You need a willing sacrifice – somebody with a penitent heart. I am anything but willing."

The chuckle in Honri's words had a dark, menacing edge. "I thought you'd say that," he said. "But you see, Jace, I know what you care about."

Caden froze.

"Leave her be!" Jace cried.

Caden scrambled away from the door. Jace thought they'd meant his wife, Caden's mother. But he didn't know Caden was locked in this horrible room. They meant him!

From the other room he heard Honri, "Bring in our guest."

Frantic, his eyes darted about the room once more, praying in vain for an escape. Their footsteps approached. He ducked behind the door, preparing to attack. But it was futile. He threw himself at the first man he saw, barreling into his stomach. Both fell to the ground. There was a second man. He yanked Caden up, dragging him into the next room. The two men kept Caden between them, holding his arms tightly. They had no need to. He couldn't escape anyway. His hands were still bound, and the exit to the room was blocked.

He noticed immediately that the room was small and circular. Stone walls glistened with moisture while beads of liquid slipped down, catching in the seams between the stones. The stench of mold and decaying wood fought with the smell of smoke from freshly lit torches. Steel swords speared the earth between small candles, spaced evenly to form a slightly smaller circle than the room; all of the hilts leaned toward the center, where Caden found Jace.

For a brief moment, he caught his father's eyes, but he found no hope there. Jace was stricken, face a frozen mask of horror. Bound in the center of the room, on his knees, each ankle tied to a post driven deep in the ground, he could do nothing for his son. His hands were also tied behind his back. Dark, wet hair clung to a bloodied forehead.

Caden was not a scholar, but neither was he daft. The room was set up for some kind of ritual, and his father was the sacrifice.

Jace's choked voice carried to him, and tears slid down his cheeks, carving a path through the blood. "How did you find him?" he asked, pleading once again with Honri.

Honri waved the question away and began pacing in front of Jace. "When you found the information we needed, Jace, I realized we had quite a predicament. You're right that we need a willing sacrifice, and we need somebody with a penitent heart. Now, where would I find somebody with a penitent heart willing to sacrifice themselves to this cause?"

He chortled, glancing at the men around him. "It's quite obvious nobody here is penitent!" The men chuckled with him; the room seemed to sway with an excited energy. They wanted whatever was coming.

"It really was quite a conundrum for me," Honri said. "A willing sacrifice? Who would open the door to Letum? What kind of individual would ever allow themselves to be the source of the world's cleansing?" He stopped pacing and spun toward Jace. "And then you up and had a change of heart. The world you fought for, you suddenly fought against. And I knew I had found my penitent heart."

He crouched until his face was level with Jace. The mouth, already scarred, twisted in a mutilated smile. "Who better to open the door than the man who dis-

covered its secrets? But I still had to convince you."
He gestured to Caden.

And in that moment, the scene in front of Caden reframed.

Jace was not the sacrifice. *He* was. His knees went slack, and he nearly dropped.

"I know just how to do it," Honri continued. "Caden loves you. He would do anything for you – even if it means sacrificing himself. Will you do the same to save your son?"

The words hung in the air like the gavel of a judge, ready to drop at any moment.

Caden studied Honri. He saw the slump of his shoulders, the malice that drew his lips down in a permanent sneer, and the hollow soul that looked out from the eyes, and he knew that neither he nor his father could give Honri what he wanted. He would not be the sacrifice. He would die first. That thought, somehow, bolstered him and gave him courage. He held his head high and proud. "Whatever he wants you to do, Father, don't do it."

Honri's eyes narrowed into slits. "Such a young hero."

"Don't do it, father. Let us both die."

Honri crossed his arms and gazed down at Jace. "Sacrifice yourself, Jace, and I'll let your son go." He snapped his fingers and one of the men stepped in front of Caden. He held a small, sharp blade in his hand. Caden glanced at the blade then squared his shoulders. He would die courageously.

A small nod from Honri and the man gripped Caden's head, positioning the blade above one ear, pushing just enough into the flesh to draw blood. The sting of the blade and the trickle of blood down his neck caused his courage to falter, but only for a moment. His body trembled, but he did not cry out.

Another nod and the knife pulled away. "Or you can wait," Honri said. "We'll take your son apart, one piece at a time. First, he'll lose his ears, then his fingers, his toes. We'll skin him alive, bit by bit. Days, maybe weeks, will pass. He will feel it all. But he won't die. We'll keep him alive as long as we need. His screams will torment you until you beg to open the door to save you from your own suffering. Then he will die, and maybe you'll understand what I'm doing this for."

Jace turned a tortured gaze to Caden.

"Let them kill me," Caden whispered, though fear clutched his heart and he fought to hold back his own tears. Could he bear the torture? Would he scream for mercy and beg his father to do as they asked so he could have a quick death?

Jace didn't seem to notice that tears dripped down his cheek. He looked at Caden as if he saw a little child in front of him, instead of the almost man that Caden was at fourteen. "My beautiful boy," Jace whispered. "My child." His eyes closed and he swallowed hard, choking back a sob. "I'm sorry, Caden," he said. "I am so sorry."

When he opened his eyes, his jaw clenched in resolve. The tears stopped flowing and he held Honri's gaze. "Let him go, Honri," he said firmly. "He will not die for my crimes. I will open your door. On one condition."

"What condition?"

"You swear an oath, in your blood, that he won't be harmed."

Honri's jaw dropped in shock. "I can't make that oath! I won't have that power once the door is opened. You know that!"

"Then you get whatever is coming through that opening to make the promise for you."

Honri's body seemed to shrink, hunching in on itself as his eyes darted around the room in sudden fear. "I can't ask that of them," he whispered.

We will swear an oath. The voice came from nowhere, whispering through the room. Caden shivered as cold dread settled over his heart. The voice was everywhere and nowhere, inside his head and out; his very soul shrunk away from it.

"Swear it," Jace demanded. "Swear the oath!"

We swear it. We, the Malic'Uiel, lay no claim to your son's living body. He will not be physically harmed by us.

"And you?" His head whipped to Honri, whose eyes darted about the room in fear.

"I swear."

"In blood?"

"In blood." Proving his point, Honri pulled a small knife from inside his boot and pressed the tip into the palm of his hand. The flesh opened and blood spilled down his fingers. He held the blade in the bleeding hand out to Jace, waiting briefly while his men freed Jace's bound wrists. Jace took the blade then gestured to the men to bring Caden.

They roughly shoved him to his knees in front of his father, keeping their hands pressed on his shoulders so he wouldn't run.

"Open your tunic," Jace commanded.

"Father, you can't do this," Caden pleaded. He knew those words meant death for both of them, but the voice that was everywhere and nowhere had left him sick to his stomach, as if simply hearing it had tainted his soul. Whatever it was, it was not good for any of them.

"I'm sorry, Caden," Jace said, not meeting his son's eyes. "This will keep you safe. When all the world is in chaos, you will be safe." He reached forward to grasp Caden's shoulder, as if in encouragement. He finally met his eyes; Caden saw endless sorrow and guilt in their depths. Then Jace moved his hand to Caden's tunic, flipping it open. Caden jerked away, anger swelling in his gut. "Don't touch me," he snapped. "You're a traitor."

Jace ignored the outburst, gesturing to the two men. "Hold him," he said. They moved quickly – in one swift motion Caden's chest was bare and his arms jerked roughly behind him, knees still pressing into the soft dirt.

"Father, don't!" Caden screamed, fighting against the men that held him.

His cries were ignored. Jace did not hesitate to slice a gash four fingers long above Caden's frantically beating heart, using the blade still stained with Honri's blood. Then Jace dropped the blade and grasped Honri's hand, holding it out to the shadows lurking in the corners of the room.

"Father...please..." Caden begged, his voice catching on the words. He knew the pleading was useless. His father was a monster who betrayed all that was good in the world.

"Swear your oath!" Jace screamed to the darkness.

The shadows swirled forward, licking at the blood that dripped from Honri's palm before following the trail back to his hand. Honri trembled as the hand turned black. Jace then pressed the lifeless, blackened palm against the wound on Caden's chest. Caden flinched as piercing cold seeped deep into his heart. Beneath the hand his flesh began to tingle, and then burn as the gash sucked in the congealed blood from Honri's wound, sealing itself closed and leaving a throbbing pink scar the shape of the hand. Branded forever as the son of a traitor, and the conduit for evil to pour into his world.

The men released Caden, but he barely registered that they'd left his side. The room faded in and out of focus, and his ears seemed full of rushing water. He felt as if he'd been swimming in a cold lake and had slipped beneath the surface, weighed down, down, down while the water grew heavier and heavier above him. Light, hope, and the desire to live slipped away.

Then something snapped inside him and suddenly he was back in the room, every detail a stark contrast to the drowning he'd just experienced. He heard his father saying, "I had no choice, Caden." Jace's hand was on his shoulder again, as if Caden wanted the touch.

He shoved him off.

"I won't let you die because of me," Jace said.

Rage rippled through Caden. "You should have let me die. That would have been mercy!"

"I couldn't watch them torture you," Jace said, voice gruff with sorrow. "I couldn't live with your death on my conscience."

"You're a coward." Caden shoved himself to his feet. Honri and his men stepped back, watching the interchange with impatience. Caden was not to be touched by any of them now that the oath was complete. But though he could leave, he didn't. He glared at his father, unable to hide his disgust. The dark stain of betrayal and loss seeped into his soul. A darkness took root that he didn't understand and didn't want to see. Surrounded by these horrible men, betrayed by one he'd loved, he wanted to scream, to cry, to rip those swords out of the ground and cut them all to pieces.

But he did none of those things. Hands balled into fists, shoulders tense and hunched, he fought to hold himself together. "They're going to kill you now," he said to his father. "You'll die, and your conscience will be free. But I will live with this on my conscience forever. How can I be a man in this world when my *father*," he spat the word, "betrayed it?"

"You'll find a way," Jace said. "This is the last time you'll see me, Caden. Know that I always loved you."

"You don't do this to those you love."

"Get him out of here." The command came from Honri. "We have work to do."

"Don't touch me," Caden snapped as the men approached. When he turned to leave, he noticed Honri bend to Jace's ear. It was meant to be a whisper, but Caden heard the words. "I'm glad it's you, Jace. I never did like you."

Another ripple of anger pulsed through Caden's stomach. The last thing he heard his father say was in response to Honri's gloating. "Go to hell, Honri."

"Oh, I'm already in hell!"

The door closed behind Caden, and the light from the room snuffed out. He was in a dark corridor. Not

THE RISE OF SPERO

too far from him a set of stairs led up and, if he was lucky, out.

But he didn't leave. He needed to know what was coming. The door was so old the wood was swollen and decaying. Parts of it had rotted away, leaving small holes he could peer through.

He stayed to witness.

Jace was now bound fully in the center of the room, wrists tied so tight behind his back his shoulders looked almost ready to burst from their sockets. He was bare chested, the tunic in shreds on the floor. Honri stood in front of him for a moment, and when he stepped back Caden saw a symbol dug into the soft flesh above Jace's heart. Blood did not flow from this wound. Instead, the shadows began flowing into it, slowly at first, but after a moment, the shadows plunged into the open flesh. Jace gasped in pain as he fought to maintain control of his body. But the darkness grew and sucked the flesh in around it. Small pieces of his body began tearing away, pulled into the force erupting inside him.

It became too much.

Jace couldn't hold out against the pain. He began shrieking – a terrible wailing sound straight from the pits of hell. More flesh ripped away exposing sinew, lungs, a heart beating strong. Bones began snapping, tearing gaping holes in his body as the vortex sucked them in. The men in the room watched in horror, terrified now of the powers they were unleashing. But not

Honri. He screamed in pleasure. "Take him! Take this man's soul and join us!"

Jace's body, no longer able to contain what it housed, ripped apart, sucked into the blackness. The sudden stillness was unnerving. Where before his shrieking had filled the room, now a heaviness descended. Where Jace had knelt, a dark, roiling mass now shuddered – a black mist rapidly gaining density.

Caden watched, sick with dread, as the mass began to form, pulling itself together, growing in height until the shape of a man began to emerge – a man unlike any he had ever seen.

Standing a head taller than those in the room, the man's body was a perfect line from head to toe. Slender fingers trilled across the new torso and sinewy muscles rippled beneath pale, flawless skin. The pink lips, full and plump, parted slightly to inhale the dank, now metallic air. Blonde hair, messy and tangled, fell just below the eyebrow. He tossed his head, shaking the errant locks aside.

Honri gaped at him. "Who are you?" he whispered.

The man fixed his gaze on him. Immediately, Honri dropped to his knees, holding his head and screaming as if he were being tortured. "No!" he shrieked. "Please...don't!" He stumbled backward, hand flailing in defense. Darkness rolled off the perfect man in waves, filling the room with a palpable evil. Abruptly, Honri's screaming stopped. He blinked as he focused on the room, as if he'd forgotten where he was. Then his gaze fixed once again on the being he'd welcomed into Spero.

"I am the Malic'Uiel," the man said. "I come to rid this realm of imperfection, to give all who seek it respite in me, to make this world great once more."

Honri nodded desperately, his body trembling. "Then do it," he whispered. "We welcome you."

"Turn away from me, Cadaver. You are not worthy to see my glory. Only those willing to shed themselves of imperfection shall look upon me."

"I am ready, Master," Honri begged. "Give me your respite."

From behind the closed door, Caden witnessed the exchange between the Malic'Uiel and Honri. He wanted to leave; he wanted to run screaming in terror from the evil they'd unleashed, but he could not. He was responsible for this monster in his land. Hands trembling, stomach heaving while cold sweat broke out on his neck, he watched and waited, learning this new enemy.

The horror of his father's death permanently branded in his mind, he fought to regain control as anger boiled inside. *Kill Honri,* he thought to his new enemy. *Rip his body apart the way he did my father.*

Yet despite the anger, when Honri began screaming, he couldn't watch. He couldn't stay to witness his destruction as well, so he fled, chased by the agonized shrieking of a man's soul tearing from his body.

Caden jolted awake, gasping at the pain of the memory; it throbbed in his chest. The flesh above his heart – the Malic'Uiel brand he wore – felt as if it was on fire. He cast his eyes around the room, massaging the old wound, expecting to see the Malic'Uiel standing in front of him. Instead, he saw Kyra lying on a cot across the room. Other men and women lay on cots as well. Slowly, his heartbeat slowed. He knew where he was. Remembering Shem and his arrow, Caden clutched his ribs. The arrow was gone, replaced with a bandage.

Dr. Bron ducked into the infirmary. "You're going to be fine, Caden," she said, glancing at him. "The arrow didn't hit anything vital." She stepped to a small table and picked up the barb, examining the tip. "Poisoned, though. If Dalia hadn't found you the poison would have killed you." She set the arrow back down. "As it was, it knocked you out pretty good. You've been asleep for hours."

Caden grunted and swung his legs off the cot. "What happened to Kyra?" he demanded.

Dr. Bron sighed. "She wasn't as lucky as you. Shem got to her." She shook her head in disgust. "She never should have been chained in that damn building like an animal. We left her defenseless and she paid the price."

Caden shuffled over, his breathing shallow. The arrow may not have pierced anything vital, but that didn't mean it didn't hurt. When he glanced at Kyra, he felt the same rage boil up that he'd felt when his father died.

Dr. Bron had bandaged her, but the bandages didn't hide all the damage. They were stained with her blood and needed to be changed. But what he noticed the most were the bruises along her neck, which were a dark, angry purple – bruises that matched the shape of a man's hand. Shem had tried to choke the life out of her. Caden's hands shook at his side, betraying his barely controlled rage. He would help to heal her, but Shem...there would be no mercy for this. He contemplated all the ways he could murder that man. All of them involved significant amounts of pain.

"Shem has a lot to answer for," Caden said through clenched teeth. "If I'm lucky, I'll get the chance to kill him myself."

"You won't be able to get to him. He vanished from the city. Pulled a disappearing act like the Phantoms. Leland was with him. Nobody knows where they've gone."

"Doesn't matter," Caden snapped. "He can't run forever."

Dr. Bron sighed. "We have bigger problems right now than Shem."

Caden glanced at the doctor, waiting.

"General Prait is dead," Dr. Bron said. "Shem's fire killed him and a dozen other men. We have no leader, and the people are calling for Kyra's blood. They think sacrificing her to the Malic'Uiel will remove the target from the city."

"You can't be serious!" The fire in his body flowed through his veins. He clenched his teeth, fighting to control the rage. "When did insanity become the ruling force of humanity?" he hissed.

Dr. Bron shook her head in sorrow. "When fear became the motivator."

CHAPTER 40

Celebrus was a ghost town. Shem and his companions moved through the empty streets, escorted by four Cadavers leading them forward and four following behind. Shem marched with faux confidence, head high, eyes full of arrogance while they scanned the city. Inwardly he cursed Bronson and those who'd thwarted his plans. If they hadn't gotten in the way, he'd be in this city delivering Kyra to her rightful Master. As it was, his ribs were on fire, and every breath sent sharp, stabbing pain into his body. Worse, he'd failed the Master, and failure was not tolerated by the Malic'Uiel. He made an effort now to show that he was stronger than pain and incapable of fear, but it was all bravado and he knew it. Gritting his teeth against it all, he continued his march. Damn Bronson and his arrow. Damn those men that stopped him. Damn General Prait and the whole of humanity.

His thoughts continued in this vein while the Cadavers led them deeper and deeper into the city.

Shem's companions did not share his grit. Huiel and Falan stayed close behind him, as if he could protect them from this place, while Leland made up the rear. Leland's eyes darted about the city in fear. He was in the heart of the enemy's stronghold; one order from the Malic'Uiel and his life would end. But Shem spoke as one who knew the Malic'Uiel. He had assured him there would be safety in exchange for his allegiance to them. It was a safer bet than returning to Tutis or trying to survive alone in the treacherous lands of the Marauders.

Still...

Leland limped behind his companions, hurrying to keep pace, but he kept one eye on the trailing Cadavers. If Shem's word was powerless, Leland could become one of them.

When they reached the Citadel the Cadavers halted, motioning for them to stay put. One of them darted inside the structure, only to return moments later with a Malic'Uiel, whose shrouded head and cloaked body stood taller than any of the four men. Leland glanced only a moment into the darkened hood before dropping his eyes to the ground. Fear quaked in his stomach.

"Follow me," the Malic'Uiel commanded, turning back into the Citadel. Beneath the cloak his feet didn't appear to move; instead, he seemed to float on a black mist. Darkness emanated from him, engulfing any light that came too close. Leland hesitated outside the entrance, hovering in indecision. He glanced behind, hoping for one last look at freedom, and instead saw four Cadavers, hunched over and mutilated, with repulsive grins polluting their already horrid faces.

Freedom was an illusion; he'd given up the freedom of humanity when he'd created his partnership with Shem. Gulping, he took one last look at the evening sky, then ducked into the Citadel.

They wound their way up flight after flight of stairs. The way was dark, and they stumbled. Finally, after far too long, they reached a circular chamber with windows facing each of the cardinal directions on the compass rose. Glancing out the west window, the last bit of color from the setting sun met Leland's vision. Instead of seeing the beauty, he saw the light swallowed up by darkness as the souls of men were swallowed up by the Malic'Uiel. The darkness settled over him as heavy as a leaden blanket. He turned away. There was a plan in place, Shem had told him; his soul would be spared.

The chamber was inhabited by more than a dozen Malic'Uiel. They stood in a loose circle. The being who'd led the four men left them near the entrance and moved to take his place in the sphere, which surrounded what appeared to be a Phantom, reduced to chains.

"Ramuk," Shem said in a whisper so quiet Leland almost didn't hear. Leland's eyes shot to Shem, who kept a nervous watch on the Phantom.

From the edge of the circle, a Malic'Uiel turned to face them. He stood at least a hand span taller than the others, and his gaze fell directly on Shem. No words were spoken, but Shem approached the middle of the chamber as if he'd been summoned, slipping through a gap in the circle to stand near Ramuk. The Phantom spat at his feet as the circle of Malic'Uiel closed around the two of them.

"Ramuk," the leader said, his voice a deep, pleasant bass. Leland started in surprise. He'd expected the voice to match the Cadavers' voices – raspy or guttural, the kind that hurt to hear. Instead, he found himself drawn to the voice. "You have taken it upon yourself to act on your own bidding."

"I believed I could bring you the woman you desire."

"You presume to know my mind?"

Ramuk, trembling, bowed his head in submission. "No, Master. I...I acted out of turn."

"And you gave this human your power."

Ramuk seemed to shrink before them, cowering in fear. "Yes." His voice nearly failed him.

The Master swung on Shem. "You made an attempt on her life."

Shem, trying to keep the appearance of confidence, shook his head. "No, I merely harmed her. I had no intention of killing her."

The Master stepped closer, towering over him. "There is only one God in this realm, human, and you are not it. You were given an otherworldly gift by this traitor, and yet even with that gift you failed to achieve your objective."

Shem's confidence wavered. His shoulders stooped, and his hands trembled, though he clenched them together to stop it. "Forgive me, Master. I have failed, as you say. Kyra is not without allies."

"Nor are you," the Master said, gesturing to the human companions behind him.

"As you say."

"There are consequences to every action, human," the Master said. He straightened and swung to Ramuk. His hand shot out, gripping Ramuk's neck. Where his fingers touched, Ramuk's skin rotted. The diseased flesh spread to cover his entire body. All the while, Ramuk screamed and shrieked as if the skin were being peeled from his bones. The decay wormed its way into his muscles and sinew; before long, he vomited dark crimson blood. He bled from his mouth while the rot devoured the rest of his flesh. The shrieks faded to whimpers, then to nothing as his body twitched in life-lessness.

As the death spread over Ramuk's body, Shem's face became more and more ashen. When he lay motionless – the body too gruesome for the others to look at – Shem did not peel his eyes away.

Leland watched the entire scene from his corner, stomach churning in horror.

Shem had brought them here to die.

As the sounds of death faded, the Master removed his hood, revealing the man beneath.

Leland's jaw dropped. Never before had he seen such perfection. His eyes drank in the Master as a desert drinks in the rain. Every feature on the flawless face played beautifully with the other. The high cheekbones perfectly complemented a strong jawline and smooth neck, both of which hinted at rippling muscles hidden beneath the rest of the cloak. Pale, golden hair that looked as soft as silk brushed the smooth forehead.

This was the Malic'Uiel? This, who humanity called monster and a scourge? This was what humanity should strive to be! He found himself drawn closer, hovering near the edges of the circle. His companions, as captivated as he was, stayed at his side.

The Master gestured to two Cadavers waiting near the entrance, who hurried into the circle and stood on either side of Shem. The movement brought Leland back to reality. Trepidation filled his heart while Shem eyed the Cadavers nervously.

With a glance from the Master, the Cadavers gripped Shem's arms and forced him to his knees, then tugged his arms back until his chest was raised to the Master. He grunted in pain and the wound on his side began to seep blood. Shem's rapid breathing and pale face betrayed his fear. His arms were taut behind him, stretched almost to their capacity.

Another nod from the Master and a third Cadaver entered the circle. He carried a curved blade and a glass vial balanced on a small tray. The blade was a deep ebony and absorbed the light surrounding it. The Master gripped the blade, nodding again to the Cadavers, who tugged harder on Shem's arms. This time he screamed as his shoulder gave way to the pressure, popping out of the socket.

The blood drained from Leland's face and nausea churned in his stomach. Glorious and beautiful as the Malic'Uiel were, he began to understand why they were considered monsters. Was he to be next?

The Master hovered in front of Shem, then ripped the blade through his tunic. The fabric gave way, revealing the bare flesh of his chest, which rose and fell in the control of fear; Shem was near hyperventilating. Without warning or preamble, the Master slashed the blade twice above Shem's heart. Shem gasped and jerked against the attack, but the Cadavers held him fast.

The wound wasn't deep, but blood immediately began dripping down the exposed chest. Then, something else – a black, viscous matter – began to ooze out with it. That's when Shem began to scream. His shrieks filled the chamber, echoing off the cold stone. The wounds on his chest bubbled and frothed as the black matter mixed with his blood. The muscles and sinew surrounding the cuts turned on itself, becoming a flaming red, then yellow, and finally green as it decomposed in front of them, eating the healthy flesh and replacing it with death. The smell of rotten meat filled the chamber; Leland fought to stop from dry heaving.

Through it all, Shem's screams never wavered, never stopped. His body thrashed and writhed against its captors, but it was clear the spasms were not in accordance with Shem's will. His eyes rolled back in his head, all the muscles in his body tight, and still the flesh continued to rot. Soon, a small hole opened up, which grew in size until the bones of his ribs were exposed and beneath them, his beating heart.

It was then that the Malic'Uiel put his hand out, covering the now gaping wound. The bleeding and oozing ceased, replaced by a gray mist that flowed out from around Shem's heart. The Master opened the vial and the gray mist flowed in until the vial was filled with its dark swirl.

Sweat beaded on Shem's forehead, but lucidity returned, and he watched the Master with eyes full of fear. The Master ignored everything but his work. From the edge of the blade, he wiped off Shem's blood. A dark red bead clung to his finger; he dropped it into the vial of gray mist. Then he replaced the stopper and handed both the vial and the dagger back to the Cadaver at his side. Silently, he held his hand against Shem's chest until the gaping wound began to close, knitting itself back together.

Shem's breathing slowed, and his body loosened just a bit. Maybe he wouldn't die today.

When the Master removed his hand, the wound was fully closed, but there remained a scar on his chest in the shape of the Master's hand. He nodded once more and the Cadavers released Shem, who slumped to the floor.

"You have chosen a course you cannot return from," the Master said. "You were given an extraordinary gift by the traitor Ramuk, a gift he had no right to give. As you now hold a part of my power in your soul, so I now hold a part of your soul in exchange. I own you and you have already failed. For every failure beyond this point, I will take more of your soul until I carry it all. You will not become as a Cadaver, nor will your fate match the rest of humanity, most of whom serve the Malic'Uiel. Should you fail in the tasks given you, your betrayal will merit the destruction of your soul far beyond anything you can comprehend."

Shem groaned at the Master's feet, but he nodded. "Yes, Master," he said. "Thank you, Master."

The Malic'Uiel gripped Shem's wounded shoulder and pulled him to his feet. Shem bit his lip to stop the cries of pain. "Do not fail me again," the Master said.

"No, Master."

He released Shem then and gestured to his companions, who shuffled fearfully into the circle. "You have sworn allegiance to me through this human. Your fate is tied to his."

The circle of Malic'Uiel tightened, making all hope of escape a futile wish. The Master retrieved his blade

and then, one by one, cut each man's tunic and band-
ed his chest with two small strokes. The flesh did not
destroy itself for these three, but the wounds did fester
until the print of the Master rested above their hearts.

Leland's head swam and panic gripped his soul. He
could not go back. He could never return. He'd not
only betrayed mankind but himself. He was now a
servant of the Malic'Uiel.

As if reading his thoughts, the Master swung to
him. "Should you achieve the tasks given you, great
glory awaits. I am a master of mercy, and those who
serve me well are well rewarded."

Leland nodded, but the words did not dispel his
panic.

The ritual complete, the circle of Malic'Uiel reopened. With a wave of his hand, the Master dismissed
his newly recruited servants. The men shuffled from
the room. Shem clutched his damaged shoulder and the
others remained quiet, unable to dispel the darkness
that now clung to them.

Shem had enslaved them all.

CHAPTER 41

Satisfied with the enslavement of men whose selfishness drew them to him, the Master left the tower determined once more to unlock the secret that would give him entry into the realm of Lumen.

Slipping into the room where the woman with silver hair lay, he looked down at her still body for a moment before moving to the table to retrieve the vials he used to keep her sedated. He administered the first vial, a tonic designed to give life to her body. Then administered the second, a toxin created to keep her in his control, to bend her body to his will. When he finished administering the poisons, he knelt next to the table, gripping her hand while his mind slipped into hers.

Standing on the precipice of her world, he gazed at the landscape before him. Memories swirled in and out of each other, colorful ribbons tying her life to so many others. Among them, muted but visible, future events reached out to the memories, some taking hold and some not. Those that bound to a memory became the present, and then the past.

He knew the landscape of her mind almost as much as he knew his own. His was a much darker landscape, of course, housing the memories of thousands of souls. He preferred his to hers, but these forays into her mind were necessary to achieve dominion over all the realms.

Talking in little more than a whisper, he spoke into her soul's landscape. "Your mind will open to me today," he said. "For your heart is weak, and I know how to make your mind succumb."

The woman's mind remained unchanged, as if his words had disappeared into nothing, but the Master knew better. She knew everything he spoke. Hers was a human mind, weak, and for the most part, malleable. He'd explored every recess of her mind, every memory, every premonition. The only secret she'd been able to hide from him was the secret to opening the door to Lumen. But today he would try something new. Today, he would show her the true cost of holding onto her secrets.

He stepped from the precipice he stood on, his aura darkening every one of the memories that he touched. They flitted away as if they could protect themselves from him. He chuckled. After all these years she still believed her mind was hers.

Get out. The voice was hers and the memories around him shuddered, reaching toward him. He smiled to himself. This was new. He sensed an underlying fear. Ignoring the voice, he continued across the plain, shoving against the memories that reached out to stop him. They flung themselves at him, encircling him in a chaotic dance as they tried to impede his progress through her mind. Faster and faster they came, a swarm of emotion wrapped in a cloud of brilliant colors. Surrounding him, he began to feel what she felt. Her fear became his, her worry gripped his heart, her agony screamed in his mind. She attempted to push herself into his presence, his being...his very soul. His steps faltered, struggling against the overwhelming weight of her mind. When he began to experience her weakness, he'd had enough. He threw his mind into the fray, ripping apart the memories that stood in his way. Those he destroyed ceased to dance, and instead fell away fading into a dull gray. Red pain arced through her, and the scream that filled her mind gave him shivers of pleasure. The rest of her memories faltered as she pulled them back, afraid to lose more of what she believed mattered, afraid to lose more of her identity. Humans were too easy. They put too much stock in ideals, identities, and individuality. But soon, all realms would realize the truth of what he sought.

It didn't take the Master long to reach the vision that held the secret she hid from him. As he'd done every other time, he reached his hand into the vision, letting it engulf him until he became part of it. He saw the woman Kyra, and he saw himself as he always had.

Kyra stooped into a black mist, the same mist that hid the secret.

"Show me," he said.

My secrets are not yours to take.

"I own you," the Master said.

That is where you are wrong.

The silver-haired woman, Avalyn, he'd learned, materialized in front of him, her soul's manifestation of the body that housed it. She shimmered before him; a faint glow surrounded her form. Her silver hair floated as if she were underwater, and the eyes that held his pierced through him into his prison of souls. For the first time in his existence, he felt naked.

"Get out of my head," he said, shoving against the light she bore. He fought to hold his ground, while his instincts urged him to step back, to protect himself.

She ignored his demand, watching him steadily. Her light did not stop its assault against him.

But he was the ruler of darkness. He clenched his jaw and wrapped his darkness around both of them, crushing her light until it was nothing more than a dull glow. She did not react, doing nothing more than gaze at him. Despite both of them being wrapped in his darkness, he could not shake the feeling that she saw far more than he wanted.

No matter. He had a mission to accomplish here.

While facing her, he sifted through her memories until he found the one he sought. The faces in this memory were familiar to both of them. Avalyn, of course, was a participant. But so was her lover, Caden, the very same man he, Master of the Malic'Uiel, had made an oath with prior to entering the human realm, the man who made his dominion possible. He plucked the memory from her mind and lay it out before her. In the memory, she and Caden vowed to be one in body and flesh, till death do them part. She shone in that moment, radiant with joy.

Avalyn's eyes flitted to the memory now, but aside from that she did not react.

"I believe this was the moment love stole your heart," he said.

She ignored the comment but continued to hold his gaze.

He sought another memory, laying it out like the first. The memory had her attacking a Phantom to save her lover, who bled from his stomach. She screamed while the Phantom ripped her away from him. "And this is the moment you lost love."

"I didn't lose it. I was stolen from it."

"Be that as it may," he said. "This man..." he gestured to the memories.

"Is protected from you. Do not think you can use him against me. If you could, you would have already done so."

He chuckled. "He may be protected by our own oath, but his new lover is not."

Her eyes narrowed as he pulled up an image of Kyra, taken from Avalyn's own visions. "You dream about this woman," he said. "You know she has taken your lover from you."

Avalyn straightened and her chin arched forward. "She can't take what is freely given."

"Oh!" he smiled, clapping his hands in mock joy. "So self-sacrificing! So, you are willing to suffer while they live in the bliss of lovers."

"I am dead to this world," she said. "After my body is free, I will be bound to Lumen."

"Ahhh, yes," he said. "But you see, Kyra and Caden will not be. She has willingly signed over her soul, and his soul remains bound to my oath. Lumen will not welcome them beyond its gates."

She gazed at him steadily, choosing not to answer.

"I can release them," he whispered. "I can renounce the oath given to him, and strike her name from my records. Their souls will be free of me."

"The oath you gave swore not to hurt him," she said. "It made him invincible to you. Why would I wish its release?"

His eyes darkened. "Because no man bound to a Malic'Uiel is truly free. Do you think the oath I gave spared him?" He chuckled. "Look into my mind. You'll find those who have been bound to my oaths."

Avalyn hesitated while he waited. She glanced at the memories of her time with Caden.

"Can you live in the realm of Lumen while he rots away with me?" the Master asked. He spread his arms wide. "I will show you his future."

Slowly, she stepped forward, reaching her mind toward his. When he pulled her into his landscape, she gasped, dry heaving in the darkness.

"Glorious, isn't it?" he said.

Surrounding them, the millions of souls he and his followers had taken cried in anguish. Some wandered the landscape with listless eyes and clouded minds while others huddled in grief, knowing they'd chosen an eternity of torment. Her light faded, unable to shine in his mind's landscape, and the ghostly image that she was seemed to tremble.

He led her beyond these souls, past the lost minds, descending deeper and deeper into his abyss. She held her arms around her body, as if that alone could protect her from his darkness.

Finally, he stopped, gesturing to a wall that stretched along the edge of his mind. Chained to the wall were hundreds of men and women. These souls were physical, as if the Master somehow held their bodies. Blood stained their wrists, dripping down their outstretched arms from chains digging into their flesh.

Avalyn gasped, reaching toward the shackled creatures.

"You cannot free them," he said. "They made this decision willingly. Come." He gripped her arm and dragged her along the edge of the wall until he found the man he wanted. "Look at him," he said.

Avalyn gaped at what she saw. This man hung from the wall by his wrists. His feet did not touch the ground, so the full weight of his body caused the chains to dig into him. Both of his shoulders jutted out at odd angles. His face was bruised and battered. Blood seeped from his lips and from gashes in his cheek and temples. His body was naked, covered only in the bleeding stripes of lashes. Worse, every bone seemed disjointed or broken. A few of his ribs pierced out of his flesh.

"What have you done to him?" she whispered.

"He made a bargain with me," the Master said. "His life in exchange for his son's. He gave us entry to Spero. Didn't you, Jace?" The Master grinned, clapping his hand on Jace's shoulder. Jace winced, but the moan that escaped his lips had no power. "I've reserved the space next to him for Caden," the Master said, gesturing to an empty set of chains hanging near Jace.

"This will be Caden's fate?" Avalyn whispered, horror washing all color from her lips.

Jace lifted his head, and his pleading eyes gripped hers. "I'm...sorry..." he gasped.

"You've damned Caden!" she cried.

He nodded, tears dripping down his cheeks. "I only...meant...to save him." Each broken word was torture in itself.

The Master stepped back, admiring his work. "Kyra will not suffer as Caden will," he said, "though her suffering will be beyond that of many others. She broke her oath with me. There are consequences for that."

"If I show you my secrets, you'll release them both?" Avalyn demanded.

"I will."

"What happens to me? Do I take the space next to Jace?"

The Master turned to face her, for once in earnest. "No. I cannot bind you as I would him. You carry too much of the light of Lumen."

"But I will be your slave," Avalyn said, trembling fingers reaching to brush Jace's shackles.

"I cannot enslave you," the Master answered. "I cannot hold light."

Avalyn met Jace's eyes one more. His silent pleading nearly broke her. "Take me away from here," she said, swallowing back tears.

Seconds later the two stood in Avalyn's mental landscape once more. She held her body tight, still trembling from the journey into his world.

Grief washed over her, grief and heartache at the future Jace had damned Caden to. Her soul was bound to Lumen, and his to Letum. When they died – and they both would surely die – they would be separated. She would go to a world of endless light and he to a world of desperation and torment. Hope seeped away as blood seeps from an open wound. The light of her soul dimmed. She knew it when the brilliant colors of her mind's landscape began to fade.

The Master glanced around. A malicious smile curved on his lips. He would surely win.

"I..." she began, choking on the words she knew she needed to say. She, alone, could free Caden. She could reverse his fate.

But she could not. She would not betray the world.

"I..." she tried again. "Will not..." But just before she finished the words, a deep peace fell over her, one she recognized as peace from the realm of Lumen.

Do not be afraid, seemed to whisper with the peace. *The door must open. It is time to trust Lumen.*

The words were not enough. She could not give Lumen over to the Malic'Uiel darkness.

The words came again. *The door must open. Trust Lumen. There is no other way.*

The peace did not fade as she gazed into the vast blackness of the Master.

Trust Lumen.

She'd trusted Lumen thus far, and she would continue to do so. "I will show you what you need," she whispered. *I will trust Lumen,* she thought. "But I must know you've freed them first."

"Of course." The Master conjured up a new vision for her. First was the scroll Kyra had signed. Before her eyes, the name disappeared. Second, an image of Caden as a young boy, tormented with anguish, crying outside the door while he watched his father die. The handprint that claimed him festered, an ugly red brand that marked him as a traitor. As she watched, the print faded.

"My mark no longer claims him," the Master said. "Caden is free."

"And Kyra?"

"I have no claim to her, either."

Avalyn nodded, stepping back from the vision she'd so carefully hidden. The black mist faded. There Avalyn lay, unconscious at Kyra's feet. Caden crouched near, clutching her hand, his fingers tangled in her silver hair.

The Master looked up in surprise. "You?" he demanded. "And Caden?"

"Kyra cannot do it without us. She is the key, but we are the lock."

The Master's eyes lit up. "How perfect!" he crowed.

Avalyn sighed and her image began to fade. The Master hurried from the vision, pulling himself from her mind, back to his body in the room that was her prison.

He gazed down at her now cold body, grinning in delight. She'd done it. She'd betrayed her kind, as Jace had done, all in the name of love. He bent down, kissing her hard on the lips, overcome by corporeal human joy. "You, my darling, have given me what I need."

Scooping her off the table, he carried her away from the room. While he'd been in her mind, his Cadavers would have gathered to attack Tutis. She would come with them, and with her sacrifice he would finally gain power over the realm of light.

JULIANNE KELSCH

CHAPTER 42

Under cover of darkness, Dalia slipped from the Citadel. Her hand cradled her bulging stomach, which was noticeably tight. Walking took some effort, and it wasn't long before she breathed heavily in her hurried pace. For now, nobody suspected that she harbored Gilrich inside the Citadel, and she intended to keep it that way. Everybody assumed he had died in the fire. Most of them seemed relieved by that fact, considering his status as a Cadaver. She wasn't inclined to change their minds.

Shem's attack had left the city in open panic. With no general to lead, the citizens were entirely ruled by fear. Dr. Bron had found men she could trust who vowed to stay with Kyra night and day, guarding her from those citizens who believed their salvation was her death. Kyra was recovering – largely because of Caden and his healing abilities – but she had not regained her former strength yet.

The attack was weeks past and the fear in the city had not lessened. If anything, it gained in strength.

Fearing for Gilrich's safety, Dalia had taken to sneaking around the city at night to secure food for Gilrich while most of the citizens were holed up in their homes. While she was safe from the citizens, she may not be if they discovered her secret. It wasn't a foolproof plan, but it was all she had.

Tonight, she hurried past the infirmary, seeking out the garden she had worked on for so long. Her stomach tightened more, and she groaned, forced to stop while she breathed through the sensation. Her time of delivery was coming. That thought filled her with fear, more fear than Shem's attack ever had. How could she deliver a child in a city on the brink of upheaval?

After a moment, the tightening passed and Dalia moved on, burying her fears as deep as she could. She had one focus right now, and that was to raid the garden and return to Gilrich and, for the time being, to safety.

As she neared the garden she slowed, scanning the darkness for signs of movement. Though most of the people should have been sleeping, there were always those that were restless or too afraid to close their eyes. The garden was an open space, which left her more visible than she liked.

Seeing nothing, she crept forward, eyes darting around. A shimmer to her left caused her to freeze and she glanced over to see a dancing light. The light flared, growing in size until it cast its glow on Kyra, who watched Dalia with interest.

Dalia hesitated, then changed direction and headed toward her friend.

"I thought I was the only one willing to step into the darkness," Kyra said.

"Sometimes the darkness isn't the most terrifying thing out there."

Kyra chuckled in derision. "Maybe. I've been consumed by true darkness before, though. It is terrifying." She glanced at the moon that shared its light with the city, and then she opened her hand and let the dance of light begin again. "This isn't darkness tonight," she said. "Not really."

"No," Dalia mused, cradling her stomach once more as the tightening began again. "I suppose this wouldn't be considered darkness. Not after that. Where are your guards?"

Kyra shrugged, trailing her fingers as the light bounced between them. "Probably looking for me. I couldn't bear to be confined with them any longer. They are the only people in this city who don't hate me, but they watch me like I am a god, as if I am somehow exalted above them. What they don't understand is that it's not my abilities that I cherish, or those who are great without cause. It's the humanity that I love, and my humanity is all I am holding onto."

"You give them hope," Dalia said. "There's precious little of that to be had today."

"You're right. Humanity has very little hope." Kyra sighed and her arm dropped, the light extinguishing.

Dalia didn't fail to notice. She placed a gentle hand on Kyra's arm. "How are you, Kyra? You seem different tonight."

Kyra almost smiled, but that faded as the light had. "To be honest," she said. "I came out here for Gilrich. He was my friend, and I left him to die. But before I did that, I brought him here and let them shackle him like an animal. And before that, I let the Malic'Uiel use me to destroy his mind. And now I've lost him, and I feel like a piece of my heart is broken." She sank slowly to her knees, running her fingers along the velvet leaves of the plants at her feet. "I think I came here because this was the promise of life and renewal. I just wanted to bring him back, but now I've lost him forever."

Dalia knelt next to her friend and wrapped her arms around Kyra's shoulder. She hesitated for a moment, weighing the risks of sharing her secret. It was dangerous...but Kyra had always shown that she loved him.

"If Gilrich were here, what would you do?" Dalia asked.

Kyra leaned back on her heels, her glance flitting to the moon that bathed them in light. "Set him free," she whispered. "Let him choose his own path."

Dalia nodded and then stood, pulling Kyra up with her. "Walk with me."

Kyra followed more for the companionship than anything. There were no judgments with Dalia, no requirements, no expectations. Just a quiet acceptance that seemed to reach out from her and wrap around Kyra's heart. It was soothing.

They moved carefully through the streets, staying in the shadows, avoiding the few people who'd not yet gone to bed. They snuck around as though they were criminals. But when they reached the Citadel, Dalia did not hesitate as she disappeared into the building.

Kyra followed her inside. "What are we doing here?" she asked.

"You'll see." She led her through the large room in the entry and up several flights of stairs. Memories descended on Kyra like a wave of locusts, blurring the future and bringing her previous existence forward. She'd climbed similar steps with a little boy, Caden, in tow, after she'd ripped him from his mother's arms. Kyra's stomach twisted. She and Dalia climbed higher, and the memories of her final day with the Malic'Uiel grew stronger. Promising to protect young Caden. Almost succumbing to darkness. Gilrich, stabbing the knife again and again into her belly.

Before they reached the top of the Citadel, Dalia veered to the left and led Kyra into a small room off the main stairwell. There was no window here to let in the moonlight, so a small torch lit the interior. When they entered the chamber, Gilrich turned toward them. His gaze stopped on Kyra and his lips turned down in a scowl; his eyes darted to Dalia in confusion.

Kyra froze, her jaw hanging. He stood taller than he had before, his spine nearly straight. The Cadaver cloak clung to his body, but it didn't hide the changes happening beneath.

"Gilrich is not lost," Dalia said. "In fact, he becomes more human every day." A happy smile lit up her face as she reached for his hand and intertwined her fingers with his.

Glancing at his hands, Kyra saw that his phalanges no longer had the appearance of grasping claws. Arthritic fingers, maybe, but the deformation seemed to be lessening.

"What is she doing here?" Gilrich demanded.

"I felt she deserved to know you were alive," Dalia answered.

Kyra gaped at her friend, blinking back tears that threatened to come. He was alive!

"Get her out of here," Gilrich growled.

And he still hated her, but that didn't matter. He was alive. His lungs breathed, his heart beat, his mind had thought. She wanted to weep for joy.

"I said, go," Gilrich snapped.

"Wait," Kyra said, hand outstretched as if she could somehow bridge the chasm between them. "I'll go, but not before you hear me out."

Gilrich's glare darkened.

"I just...want to say that I'm sorry," Kyra said. "I've been sorry for a long time. I never meant to bring you here and have them hurt you. I never meant to cause you more pain." The tears slipped down her cheeks, but she didn't wipe them away. They were part of her ability to feel, and she was grateful for them. She sucked in a breath and her voice dropped. "I'm sorry I let the Malic'Uiel do to you what they did to me. If I could take anything back in my life, that would be it. I would tell them to kill me rather than be the one that betrayed you."

She stepped closer, carefully, aware that he may very well want to hurt her – she wouldn't blame him if he did. "I told Dalia if you had survived the fire, I would set you free. I would let you go find your own path. Whether that path is with humanity or whether it's with the Malic'Uiel is your choice." Her arms dropped to her side, and she stood before him – no defense, no hiding. "We were wrong to imprison you, and I had no right to force you to change after what I did to you. I will help you get out of the city if that's what you want."

Gilrich studied her as if she were a puzzle he couldn't quite put together. And then he looked at the woman at his side. "I won't leave the city. Not without Dalia. I won't take her away from its walls and have her and her child unprotected."

Dalia smiled and squeezed his hand tightly. Gilrich rested his hand on her swollen middle. His eyes lit up for a moment, and then he smiled, and Kyra saw the man she had once known. "He's kicking again," Gilrich said.

Dalia nodded, placing her hand over his. "He likes you."

Gilrich turned back to Kyra. "If you want to make it right for me, Kyra, find a way for me to stay with Dalia as a free man – or Cadaver, or whatever you want to call me. But free."

Kyra swallowed against the joyous lump in her throat. He was coming back – she could see it. The being before her was more man than creature. Dalia had done it. She had done what Kyra could not.

Heart bursting with hope, she nodded. "I'll do everything I can, Gilrich." She turned away from them, suddenly aware that he'd called her by her name, naturally, speaking almost as equals. In his own way, she knew he trusted her. Right now, that meant everything in the world to her. She could have her friend back.

CHAPTER 43

C hoose your master, now." Shem spoke the words with relish. Oh, how he loved the power! In his hand was the finest dagger he had ever held; the blade rippled with fire, which lit the face of the man who cowered beneath the weapon.

Behind Shem, the full moon lit up the landscape, casting long shadows that reached outward, ready to solidify the world's plunge into darkness.

The man jerked his head up in desperation, eyes flicking to the fiery blade. "I'll serve whoever you want, whatever you want. Just don't kill me."

Shem flicked the blade toward a group of men cowering behind the first. "And them?"

The man's head bobbed again, jowls trembling. "They serve who I serve; they stand with me."

Shem straightened, sheathing the blade. "No," he said. "They stand with the Malic'Uiel."

As the man scrambled to his feet, putting distance between him and Shem's blade, Shem addressed them all. "The Malic'Uiel are ready to take the next step in the cleansing of the realms. All who oppose will be cut down by the Cadavers marching behind me. Those men who join us will share in the glory of conquest. No longer can men roam as marauders, paying for their freedom at the price of a human or two. You either join us or you join the rest of humanity in death. We march on Tutis."

Shem turned away from the group of marauders, who gathered their weapons and supplies and fell in step behind him. One man hovered in indecision. "You choose death, then?" Shem said.

"No," the man stuttered. He shouldered his pack and gripped the hilt of his blade. "I serve the Malic'Uiel."

Kyra's light fled from her fingers, rippling toward Caden, who pushed against it with his fire. Fire and light collided, grappling briefly before the light consumed the fire; all that was left was a puff of smoke. Once the fire was gone the light rippled further, forming a ball that grew in size as it neared Caden. Just before it reached him, the ball disintegrated and the light reappeared on Kyra's hand.

"Impressive," Caden said, grinning. "Before long, you're going to be able to overpower my fire anytime."

"It's not your fire I'm worried about," Kyra said.

"Shem's fire, then."

Kyra nodded. "Again?"

In response, Caden held out his hand and a small fireball erupted on his palm. Kyra smiled, following suit. He couldn't help but notice the scars on her hands and wrists, scars left by Shem and his fire that melted metal. Caden had used his abilities to heal her, but she'd refused to let him remove the scars entirely. "My body has seen war," she'd said. "These are marks of the battles I have fought."

The two of them sparred again and again, as they had for many days, lighting up the back wall of the city. Bronson and Ezra, Kyra's self-assigned guards, watched from behind them. No other citizens milled about, choosing to remain a safe distance from Kyra, whom most considered the enemy.

The daylight began to fade and a crisp, pink sky filled the void. As the shadows lengthened, the fire and light seemed to gain power.

From the darkened streets a figure stepped into the light of the dance. Caden saw the man and froze, his fire exploding against the back wall. "I thought you were dead," he gasped. Another fireball formed on his palm as he watched the intruder, who eyed him with mistrust.

"I would have been, if not for Dalia."

"You look..." Caden whispered.

"Human?" Gilrich answered.

Caden nodded.

Gilrich crossed to Kyra. Caden's fireball rose in size, but Kyra held out her palm, shaking her head to diffuse him. "What's the matter?" she demanded of Gilrich.

"It's Dalia," he said. He wrung his fingers together and his face pinched in worry. It had only been a week since she'd seen him, but in that time he'd lost all traits of the Cadaver. His fingers no longer looked arthritic, and he held himself tall with a spine that was straight and proud.

Tears sprung to Kyra's eyes as she gazed at her old friend. "You're back," she whispered. "I missed you."

Gilrich shrugged off the words. "Can you come with me?" he asked.

"Of course."

The five of them worked their way quietly through the streets, following Gilrich to the Citadel. As they neared the building Kyra spoke. "You took a risk coming to get me," she said.

"I didn't have a choice," Gilrich answered. "She needs help that I can't give."

Caden's eyes kept trailing to Gilrich, studying the man who had been his best friend. He shook his head, glancing away, but moments later his gaze would be back on Gilrich's face. "The people here will have to reconsider their prejudices against him when they see he's human," Caden muttered to Kyra. "A Cadaver can be killed easily, but this…" he shook his head again.

When they reached the Citadel they found Dalia in the main entry, groaning in pain. She gasped as her hands cradled her stomach. Kyra went to her and gripped her hand until the pain passed then she turned to the men that were with her. "Bronson, she needs blankets and hot water, and something soft to lie on. Ezra, go get Dr. Bron." Her guards hurried away, and she turned back to Dalia. "How long between the pains?" she asked.

"Not long. They're consistent and getting harder." As she spoke, her jaw tightened and she began to moan again, curling over her stomach. Gilrich hurried to her side, hands fluttering as if the motion could somehow help.

"Support her through it," Kyra said to him. "When it passes, help her lie down and let her rest against you. Talk her through it. Help her relax."

He nodded and wrapped his arms around her while she leaned into him, moaning against his chest.

It wasn't long before Bronson returned with scratchy blankets, a few flat pillows, and a pail of water. "I thought Caden could heat the water here," he said.

Kyra nodded. "That's fine. Help me make a bed for her." The two of them quickly spread out the blanket and propped the pillows up for Dalia to lie on. While they worked, Gilrich helped her to the floor, where she lay against his chest. She labored with him; through each pain he spoke quietly in her ear, urging her to relax, to breathe, reminding her that she wasn't alone.

When the bed was ready, Kyra went to Dalia. "You ready to move?" she asked.

Dalia shook her head, eyes closed tightly shut. "I don't want to move," she gasped. She moaned again, clenching her teeth as another contraction started.

"We'll stay here, then," Kyra murmured, holding Gilrich's gaze.

His head bobbed once. "We'll stay here."

As the minutes crept past the hour and into the next, the contractions grew stronger. Kyra went back and forth between pacing to the door looking for Dr. Bron, to kneeling by Dalia's side and helping her through each pain. Time ticked on and Dalia's pains grew closer.

"Where is she?" Kyra whispered to no one in particular, glancing once more at the door.

Outside, voices rose and somewhere in the distance a woman screamed.

Dalia glanced nervously toward the noise, but Kyra took her face in her hands and redirected her focus. "Whatever is happening out there is out there. What you're doing here is far more important. Let us worry about that. You worry about this."

Dalia nodded, panting through another contraction.

Finally, Dr. Bron hurried into the Citadel. She breathed heavily, as if she'd been running. When she saw Dalia she swore under her breath, but her eyes didn't linger on her. Instead, she ran to Kyra and grabbed her arm. "Kyra, you have to get out of here."

Kyra shook her off. "I can't leave her."

"You have to," she said. "They're going to kill you."

"What!" Dalia cried.

Gilrich wrapped his arms around her, pulling her closer. She sobbed as another contraction pulled her into its grip.

A moment later a group of men stormed into the building. They dragged Ezra with them. His face bled from a gash in his forehead, and he surveyed the scene in panic through one good eye. The other was swollen and bloodied, and the left side of his face was a bruised, mottled mess.

Kyra jumped to her feet. "What are you thinking? She cried. "What did you do to him?"

The men ignored the words, tossing Ezra aside in their rush to pull her away from Dalia. A group of them also surrounded Caden, who responded by igniting a fireball on his palm.

"Stop!" Dalia cried. "Don't take her!"

Kyra's light rippled from her fingers and traveled up her arm, swiftly moving over her entire body until she was encased. "Don't touch me," she snapped.

"I'm sorry," Dr. Bron said. "I tried to stop them. The Cadavers are at our borders, and the Malic'Uiel just beyond. They are demanding we give you and Caden up to them."

"You can't touch me," Kyra hissed to the men who surrounded her.

"You're right," one of the soldiers said. "We can't. But we can kill one of them or you can come with us." He dipped his head once and half of the men trained their arrows on Gilrich, the other half on the woman laboring at their feet. Before Kyra could respond, more men flooded into the building.

Kyra's light bloomed out from her, reaching toward the men threatening Dalia. Next to her, Caden's fireball doubled and then tripled in size. The heat surged menacingly.

The soldier chuckled. "You can't protect her from us all, nor can you protect everybody you love. First it will be the Cadaver, then Dalia, then Ezra over there, followed by Bronson. One by one we will kill them all, until you can't take their deaths falling on your head. Or we can just take you, and no one will have to be sacrificed over you."

"Between the two of us, we can stop you," Caden said. "None of you are a match for this."

Behind them all, Dalia's sobbing filled the space. She groaned as another contraction surged.

"She will be dead before your fire kills us all," the soldier said. "I promise you, no matter how many of us you fight off, you will lose more than we do today."

Dalia's groan became a scream as the contraction piqued. This was not good for her. No woman in labor should be subjected to this.

Slowly, Kyra pulled her light back, allowing the shimmer to fade. This man had murder in his heart. Judging by the looks on the faces of the others, so did they. She wouldn't be their reason for making good on their murderous promises. Nor would she be the reason Dalia suffered more than she needed to during her labor. She closed her fist on the light until it went out.

"All right," she said. "I will come with you, but you will leave this building and you will let Dalia and Gilrich alone."

Caden's jaw clenched in anger, but he followed her lead. "Are you sure about this?" he demanded.

"I'm sure in this moment it's the right thing to do."

He dropped his fist to his side, seething in anger.

Kyra turned from the men and knelt at Dalia's side. Dalia was between contractions, and she watched the exchange in agony, not caring that the tears dripped down her cheeks. Kyra squeezed her arm gently. "I wish I could be with you for the birth of your beautiful child," she said. "But I'm putting you in danger. Gilrich will get you through this. I will keep you and your baby safe. He or she will be born free of the Malic'Uiel pollution."

Dalia gripped Kyra's hand and nodded while sobs hiccupped in her throat. "Promise you'll come back to meet my baby?"

"I promise," Kyra said. She leaned forward, kissing Dalia's forehead. Dalia's skin was covered in a sheen of sweat and her face flushed. When Kyra pulled away

Dalia clenched her teeth and leaned into another contraction, moans rising unbidden while the contraction gained in severity.

Kyra turned to the men, her eyes flashing anger. "I'm keeping my end of the bargain, now all of you get out and leave Dalia in peace before I find out what my light is truly capable of."

The mob glared at Kyra, but their feet shifted nervously, and they shuffled out of the building; nobody wanted to see Kyra make good on her promise.

Kyra left the Citadel with Caden at her side. As she left, her light began dancing on her fingers, and Dalia's moans turned to cries of physical and emotional agony.

Kyra faced the gate and the Malic'Uiel beyond. Though she appeared to be their captive, determination settled in her breast. She had destroyed her Master and she could destroy the others as well. She had a promise to keep: Dalia's baby would be born free.

THE RISE OF SPERO

CHAPTER 44

Outside the Citadel the air seemed to vibrate on waves of panic and fear; it was palpable and heavy. People ran to the front gate, many of them brandishing weapons. Some of them had the look of warriors – soldiers who would defend humanity to their dying breath. Others had the look of defeat, carrying their weapons sloppily as they slogged toward the gate. To them, the war was already lost.

As Kyra stepped out of the building and into the people's view, they began whispering her name. The words spread from mouth to mouth like the wind in a storm, growing in pitch and power as it did so. It was not a comforting sound, and it was mingled with other words: witch, sorcerer, traitor, Cadaver. She hadn't known before then that her own name could hold such fear. In response, she commanded her light to grow; the comforting warmth rippled over her body and shimmered around her as a barrier to the people surrounding her. The men who'd taken her captive shied away from her, holding their arrows trained on her instead. She knew, if she chose to act, that their weapons would be useless against her. But those arrows wouldn't be useless against Dalia or Gilrich, so for them she went willingly.

Caden walked at her side, muttering threats and curses. His fire wove around his body like a ribbon. She'd never seen it act that way before, and he didn't seem to be aware of the change. It reached out beyond him, grasping for the soldiers surrounding them. The men recoiled from it, turning their faces from the heat. But it didn't touch them. Caden's eyes flicked between his fire and the soldiers, a grim smile on is face, and Kyra realized he knew exactly what he was doing. His display was a show of power – a reminder that he and Kyra were not the captives the soldiers believed them to be.

Their progression through the city seemed to reach the ears of all the citizens of Tutis. Little by little they joined the progression, slinking out of their doors and sliding into the streets behind the outcasts. At first, they joined in a small trickle, but as they moved through the streets the trickle grew into a stream of humanity trailing behind them.

Kyra glanced behind and her face darkened. All these people were people she had tried to protect, people Caden had tried to protect, and yet here they were willing to sell two innocent souls in exchange for a moment of safety. Somehow, they had deluded themselves into thinking that the Malic'uiel would leave them be once they gave up the 'witch.' Kyra knew better. These people were sadly mistaken. The moment their protection was gone, the Malic'Uiel would swoop in and take what remained of humanity.

She jerked her head forward, willing the anger that seethed to stay contained. Her light coursed around her like a storm, waiting for her to unleash it. And she would unleash it, but not on these fools who walked so blindly into their doom.

By the time they reached the city gates the crowd had swelled from tens to hundreds. The soldiers lining the wall glanced down from their posts and their eyes widened at the crowd. Many of them brought their focus back to the Malic'Uiel, their faces betraying a wide range of emotions – everything from fear to relief to hope to guilt. Most of them wouldn't look at Kyra or Caden, choosing instead to avert their eyes or stare at their feet.

The procession stopped in front of the gates and Kyra's would-be assassin dipped his head once, motioning to the soldiers who guarded the entrance. A moment later, the gates began to creak open.

All sound ceased. Every eye was trained on the gate, waiting, watching. Fear was palpable in the air. It settled in the heart of every man, woman, and child like a thick blanket of fog, polluting the air, distorting the senses of humanity.

The gates slowly opened, their hinges groaning in protest at their forced use. When they swung aside to reveal what stood on the other side, a whisper of fear rippled through the people like a shock of electricity. The land between the city walls and the tree line was bare and empty, the traps and snares untouched. But standing along the forest edge was the leader of the Malic'Uiel. On each side, two other Malic'Uiel. Behind them, more of the demons streamed from the trees. And to the side of them all were row after row of Cadavers. They pushed forward, a dark mass of distorted humanity, less than the length of a man from the first row of hidden pits. These Cadavers not only surrounded the city, but their distorted bodies stretched into the forest and beyond. The city's defenses would not be enough to stop them, should they advance.

The Malic'Uiel leader gazed at the people in the city. Those who found themselves caught in his gaze trembled and quaked, crying as fear stole their memories and twisted them into monsters.

"We are here for the girl," the Malic'Uiel called. "She has much that we desire, and she has given herself to us; we have come to claim what is ours."

With that phrase, a low murmur broke out in the crowd. Kyra heard various voices rising above the cacophony.

"She is a witch."

"She has betrayed us."

"She lied."

"It's her fault we have their army at our doors."

"Traitor."

"Monster."

"Witch."

"Demon."

"Sorceress"

The murmur grew into an angry rumble and the people pushed forward, as if they wanted to shove her out the gates and into the arms of death itself.

Above the din, one voice rang out. "Stop!" it screamed.

The crowd shoved aside as Bronson pushed his way through. When he neared Kyra, the soldiers surged in around her, cutting off his access to her. Bronson's face flashed anger and he ripped a dagger from his belt. "You've lost your minds," he said. "Without her, you would all be dead, and yet here you all sit ready to damn her and Caden to the worst fate imaginable."

He swung around to face the crowd, shaking in anger, the dagger trembling in his grasp. "Every one of you would rather die than face the torments of the Malic'Uiel," he screamed. "You'd beg your best friend to slit your throat before you gave yourself up to the Malic'Uiel – you'd murder the ones you love rather than have their souls destroyed by the Malic'Uiels fears and manipulations. Yet Kyra, the only person to escape their grasp after experiencing their torment, you willingly give to them? You offer her up like a sacrificial lamb for what? Your peace? Your comfort? Your safety?" He spat out the words as if they were poison. "You, who she has served again and again. She's protected you, fought for you, bled for you, and been willing to die for you, and you offer her payment like this?" His hand swung out to encompass Kyra surrounded by the angry soldiers. "You willingly give up the innocent for naught." Bronson's arms dropped to his side and his eyes narrowed. His voice dropped in pitch, steadied, and the next words he uttered gripped the hearts of his listeners, sowing an entirely different kind of fear. "After this," he said, "the Malic'Uiel won't need to use their games on you. Yours are the souls that will be lost."

Silence descended on the crowd. Many of them looked away, and some began shuffling backward. Bronson turned back to the soldiers, shoving his way through them. They parted without protest, stumbling back as if in a daze. "You may be willing to give her up to them, but I am not." Turning to Kyra, he gripped her arm. "I stand with you now, and to my death if need be."

Kyra gazed at him in surprise. She hadn't expected anyone to fight for her. After a moment, she smiled, gently pulling his hand from her arm. "I would not ask you to," she said. "Humanity needs a leader, one who will not be swayed by the emotions of fear and anger. Whatever happens to me, you must stay and lead them."

Bronson's jaw tightened. "I will not lead murderers."

"Kyra."

The soft voice floated across the open space between the forest and the city. It wove itself around her like a caress. When she turned toward the sound, the leader of the Malic'Uiel stepped forward. "We have a place for you here with us," he said, gesturing to those behind him. "We come to bring you home."

"I am home," Kyra said. "I belong with humanity."

"And yet, you are so much more than humanity."

Kyra cocked her head to the side, studying the creature she had feared so much. "I am only what I choose," she said. "No more, no less."

The Master chuckled. "Then why does light swirl around you like a beacon, and yet the rest of humanity stands in darkness?"

Glancing behind her, Kyra found the eyes of the people on her. She frowned, turning back to the Master. "We have a lot more to learn."

The Master held out his hand, beckoning. "Come home with us, Kyra, and we will bring these people no harm."

Kyra balked at the outstretched limb, eyes narrowing in distrust. "Your words carry as much weight with me as the words of a gnat. If I leave this city, you'll destroy these people the moment I am past the gates."

The Master remained silent for a moment, then his hands lifted to the hood covering his head and he

JULIANNE KELSCH

pulled it back, revealing his face. The collective gasp told Kyra the action was not lost on the people; none had looked upon the Malic'Uiel's chosen form before. He smiled and his lips parted in a gentle smile, belying the evil that simmered beneath his attractive appearance.

"Yes," he cooed, addressing the people now. "You fear me so much, and yet, you need not fear. I have come to save humanity from itself – to cleanse the world of evil." His arms dropped to his side, and he turned the palms toward the people, open and trusting. "When I was welcomed into your world, it was for the purpose of ridding Spero of the pain so often caused by humanity. All of you have suffered at the hands of those you call brother; before I came, brother killed brother, spouse turned against spouse. Some of you saw the horrors of humanity and turned to me to solve it."

He twisted his body to look behind him and gestured to a man hiding beneath the cover of the trees. Shem stepped forward, coming to stand beside his new master. The Malic'Uiel put his hand on Shem's shoulder, smiling at him the way a father smiles at the son he loves. "Shem saw the vision of humanity and welcomed me here. As such, he has been rewarded." He swung back to the people. "Many of you see the vision as well. I invite you to embrace what I am creating – to embrace a life free of pain, of suffering, of condemnation. All I ask in return is that you serve me." He pointed at Kyra, and Caden next to her. "Show me your willingness to serve by delivering them back to me."

He fell silent and a murmur erupted behind Kyra. Bronson swung to face the crowd, dagger outstretched. "Do not listen to him!" he cried. "Every word he speaks is a lie. You've seen the Cadaver Kyra brought here. Does that look like freedom to you? That's what he promises!"

"He promises freedom from pain!" a man cried.

"He promises our suffering will end!" shouted the woman next to him.

"A life without fear!"

"Freedom!"

"Peace!"

Kyra turned to face the crowd, her eyes blazing. "His promises are delivered only by a life of servitude. Do you want to live in bondage? Do you willingly give up your freedom for the peace he claims to offer?"

She stepped toward the crowd and her light surged out, forcing the soldiers back. "I've been his chattel! I've experienced the 'freedom' he speaks of. It comes at a heavy cost." Her head snapped up and she locked eyes with the man who wanted no pain. "The removal of pain came when I was willing to give myself to him completely – when I chose to feel nothing. Nothing! No light, no joy, only the desire to do his will." She took another step forward and the light surged again, shoving the crowd back. "You've all seen Gilrich! You saw what I did to him, my best friend. I dragged him to his destruction because I listened to the promises of that monster." Her hand flung out behind her to encompass the Malic'Uiel standing at the clearing's edge. "There is no freedom nor peace in what he offers."

Her voice dropped and she became deadly still. "I have witnessed the destruction of a man's soul," she murmured loud enough for the crowd to hear. "While in their grasp, I brought a man to them who had willingly given his soul. He served them for many years. When they were done with his service, they took what he had given. They pulled his soul from his body to fuel their own." Kyra's voice hitched on the last word, and she chewed in her lip, trying to dispel the image. "The horror of that moment will stay with me until I die, and likely beyond. Before he died, that man knew exactly what he'd done, and he saw the destruction in his actions." Her voice became husky, and her hands clenched into fists at her side. "It is the worst thing I have ever witnessed. Believe me when I say you do not want the promises the Malic'Uiel offer."

"But we will survive!" one woman cried out.

Kyra shook her head sadly. "No. Survival is not what they offer. You will not survive."

Don't make them choose, Avalyn's voice spoke quietly in her mind. *It is time you let the light guide you. Go to him.*

Kyra swung back to the Malic'Uiel, confusion etched on her features.

He stared back at her, a delighted smile on his face. "Caden," he called. "I have a gift for you."

CHAPTER 45

K yra's glance shot to Caden, who stiffened at the mention of his name. Behind the Malic'Uiel, the Cadavers parted while a woman with silver hair was pulled forward, her wrists in chains. When she reached the front of the group she sunk to her knees, unable to go further. Her face was a deathly pale. The Cadaver that led her forward handed her chains to the Malic'Uiel, chains that were useless; she could not have run.

"Avalyn," Caden whispered, his voice twisted in anguish.

She lifted her head until her eyes met his and then she smiled.

Tears streamed down Caden's cheeks, and his fire reached beyond him...reaching for her. Kyra's light swelled as well, as if it wanted to encompass her.

"We have to go to her, Caden," Kyra said. "We can't stay here anymore."

"I know," Caden whispered. He looked as if he wanted to bolt across the clearing and gather Avalyn into his arms.

"Malic'Uiel," Kyra called, stepping forward. She held her hand out toward him and willed the light to suck back in until it was just a ball on her palm. "I will come with you, but my protection stays with this city. Do you understand?"

The Malic'Uiel cocked his head to the side as if he was unclear. "Your light comes with you," he said.

"It does. It's part of me. But this city stays under my protection. You will not get what you want."

At this, the Malic'Uiel grinned. "I only want you."

Kyra clucked her tongue at the blatant lie. "You want so much more than me," she murmured.

"Be careful, Kyra," Caden said quietly. "He is a master of manipulation."

"I know," she said. "But I am the Countess of Lumen, and I wield the power of light."

"And you are human," Caden reminded her.

"Yes," she said, finally turning to smile at him. "That's why I have to do this. I think I'm beginning to understand. I have to show the rest of humanity what's possible; I have to *be* the light."

"You can't do this, Kyra," Bronson said, speaking quietly so only she could hear. "You can't give yourself to him."

She set her hand on his arm, imploring. "You've trusted me this far, Bronson. Can you do so once more?"

Bronson chewed on his lip while his glance darted between her and the Malic'Uiel. "I'm coming with you."

"No. The people need a leader. I'll find my way back." She didn't wait for his response. Moving past him she stepped out the city gate. Caden fell in step beside her. While the two moved as one, Caden looked at nothing but Avalyn. It was as if she pulled him to her and he could see or do nothing else.

As they neared the waiting army, the Malic'Uiel beamed in pleasure.

In the very center of the city, in the Citadel far removed from the scene unfolding at the gates, Dalia gripped Gilrich's hand while sweat dripped down her forehead. On instinct she had lowered to a squat, with Gilrich supporting her weight. Her groans turned to bellows as the head of the child in her womb nudged into her birth canal. Her body contracted again and again, demanding that she push the child through. Between contractions, she leaned against Gilrich, panting and crying. "I can't do this," she sobbed. "I can't."

Gilrich, his head pressed to hers, holding her through the physical pain and grief, gripped the back of her neck. "You can, Dalia," he whispered through clenched teeth. "You can. This baby will be the first born into a new world."

Gritting her teeth, Dalia screamed as another contraction built pressure and broke against her body.

"You can," Gilrich whispered as she pushed once more.

When Kyra and Caden reached the Malic'Uiel, Caden immediately dropped to Avalyn's side. They'd crossed the distance between the city walls and the forest, safely avoiding the many traps and pitfalls. The wind rustled the leaves in the forest behind her enemy. For a moment, she allowed herself the memory of traveling through different forests with her father, both of them safe. Somehow, those memories brought her joy. But he was gone, and she was here. Kyra let her eyes rise to meet the Malic'Uiel. "I did not come to serve you."

The Malic'Uiel just smiled, reaching to pull his hood back over his head. "You came to save her," he said, pointing to Avalyn. "I think you know how to do that."

Kyra nodded, "You want me to open the door."

"I want you to open the door." His silky voice slithered from the cloak, and this time her stomach churned.

"You want Lumen."

He dipped his head in acknowledgment. "I want to rid all realms of pain."

Kyra's eyes flashed anger. "You want to bring all realms into your dominion; you don't care if people suffer."

"I seek perfection. Suffering is a byproduct of imperfection."

Kyra glared at the Malic'Uiel. "You're a liar. I will not give you access to Lumen. You can have me, but Lumen you will not have."

The Malic'Uiel sighed, shaking his head as if in sadness. "Your master said you could not see the world I am creating."

"He is my master no longer."

At this, the Malic'Uiel chuckled. "You think you've destroyed him? Oh no! You simply sent him back to Letum. His essence remains there, rebuilding strength. He will be back, as we all have come back." But then, his eyes flashed anger. "You betrayed him. You betrayed us all."

Kyra's head rose almost imperceptibly and her back straightened. "I saw the future you are creating," she spat. "And I chose not to participate in it."

"And for that, Avalyn will die."

Before Kyra could react, he jerked on the chain holding Avalyn, dragging her body across the ground until she lay at his feet, her silver hair matted and dirty while blood dripped from her wrists and tears slid down her cheeks.

"Avalyn!" Caden screamed.

The Malic'Uiel ignored him and instead reached for Shem's hand, slashing a blade across his wrist before holding it above Avalyn's heart. The blood dripped onto her chest where the shadows began to converge, burrowing through the clothing. When they began digging through her flesh, she couldn't hold back the screams.

"Stop!" Caden screamed, barreling into the Malic'Uiel and knocking the creature back. "You won't take her!"

The Malic'Uiel chuckled. "Kyra knows how to stop this," he said.

Caden swung to Kyra. "Stop him," he cried. "Don't let her die like this."

"Open the door, Kyra, and her suffering stops," the Malic'Uiel said, a cruel chuckle on his lips.

Avalyn's screams rent the air, gaining in pitch and severity.

"You're asking me to betray Lumen!"

"No," the Malic'Uiel said, manic laughter twisting the words. "I'm not asking."

Kyra gripped Caden's shoulder, holding him back while they both stared at Avalyn's wrenching body.

"I can't betray Lumen," she whispered.

"You have to help her," Caden begged. "There must be another way. I watched my father die like this. I can't watch my wife die this way as well. Use your light to stop this."

"I can't betray them," she said again. She clenched her fists as rage built in her chest. For a moment, she considered letting it take her. But then she remembered Avalyn's necklace and the balance it represented. She gripped it in her palm, closing her eyes in concentration.

Her light flared out from her, twisting and whirling as it arced around and out from her body. When it grew beyond her, she hurled it at the shadows attacking Avalyn. It struck them like a lightning bolt strikes the night sky, parting them in an instant. The moment the shadows dispelled, the light wrapped around Avalyn. Her screams stopped but she lay motionless on the ground, her face gray, arms and fingers twitching. The front of her tunic was covered in red, viscous blood. Inside the hole the shadows created, her heart was visibly beating.

"I can't heal her," Kyra said to Caden. "You have to."

The Malic'Uiel glared at Kyra. "You betray me again," he said. "Without your submission, the city does not have your protection." He flicked his hand and the Cadavers surged forward, racing across the clearing to the waiting city. Some were taken by the traps, but many more surged behind them. "Your light may keep us out. It may keep the Phantoms out. But it will not stop my army."

Shrieks from the city preceded the twang of bows as arrows flew into the attacking army. Cadavers screamed as the deadly weapons struck them. Some cried out as they fell into the many pits dug into the ground while others shouted in triumph when they reached the walls and began climbing, only to be impaled by huge spears as the wall's defenses knocked them back.

Still, they surged forward, wave after wave. More screams broke out as the creatures died. It wasn't long before the wails of dying men joined the death cries of the Cadavers. The metallic scent of blood mingled with dirt and sweat assaulted Kyra's nostrils. And yet they kept coming. The city's defenses could not hold them long.

Desperate, Kyra flung her light far beyond her, throwing it over the city. Her body trembled with the exertion, but she held her ground, willing the light to stop the incoming army. She felt it tremble as the Cadavers ran into it only to be thrown back. Arrows and weapons disintegrated when they touched it. The light flickered as if it would go out, but she closed her eyes against the pain, begging it to hold. When she opened them, she glared at the Malic'Uiel; sweat poured down her neck and her legs quaked, but she did not falter.

"I. Serve. No. Master," she screamed.

He glowered at her. "You will serve me!" He flew at her as darkness and shadows poured from his body and the bodies of his comrades. Inky blackness spilled from the forest, swirling around them both until she was engulfed. She could see nothing but her own light protecting her body. She heard nothing. And she felt nothing. It was as if she'd been suspended in the nowhere of time and space. Still, she willed her light to hold and protect the others.

Eventually the sound of the Malic'Uiel wailing broke its way through the darkness. His shrieks tore at her mind, ripping open long-healed wounds, unearthing long-buried fears and memories. All that she'd become with the Malic'Uiel raged forth from the depths she'd buried it in to consume her again. She screamed against the onslaught, remembering her light, remembering why she fought. The memories flooded open, every one attacking her at once. She experienced them all as one: she murdered her mother, buried her father, destroyed Caden, consumed Avalyn, and ripped Gilrich from a life of freedom into a life of anguish. Her mind screamed at her that these memories were lies created by a dark master, but in their onslaught she couldn't see the lie, only the truth they wanted her to see.

Gilrich.

Her mind focused on the memory of her friend. Gilrich wasn't a Cadaver any longer. He was human with flesh and blood, a soul that felt anguish and hope. His face lingered in her mind, reminding her that all was not lost. She gritted her teeth, holding on to him.

In the midst of the onslaught, peace descended on her like a blanket of snow. Though she saw nothing through the blackness surrounding her, she sensed much with her mind. Her light held strong, protecting those she loved and those who'd fought to hurt her. In the darkness, she saw the door to Lumen shimmering before her, and she saw Avalyn standing there, an apparition that faded in and out of focus. Avalyn smiled and some of the blackness cleared until Caden came into view, frantically working to heal Avalyn's heart.

"Open the door," Avalyn said. "Lumen knows what's coming. They are ready. Your light will be the salve that heals this world. But you must open the door. It is humanity's only chance."

"They'll die."

"You have help on the other side."

Kyra hesitated in indecision. Everything in her screamed at her to leave the realm closed to the Malic'Uiel, but Avalyn had guided her this far. She trusted her with her life.

"I can't do it alone," Kyra finally hissed, exertion forcing her to her knees.

"I know. That's why I'm here."

Kyra's eyes flicked to Caden, who had stopped his ministrations and now gaped at them both.

"You'll die," Kyra whispered "It requires too much energy. You're weakened so much as it is. I fear you don't have enough."

"I may not make it through, but you will live," Avalyn answered. "And that's what matters."

"No," Caden croaked. "I can heal you. I can't lose you again!" His jaw clenched in determination as he clapped his hands once more over her body lying motionless on the ground. His eyes stayed fixed on the apparition of her soul. "Please, Avalyn," he cried. "There has to be another way."

Avalyn stepped to Caden, and her image sharpened, pulling into focus. She knelt next to him, looking for a moment at her still body. "Caden," she said. "Does that body look as if it lives to you?"

"It could," Caden cried. "I see the heart beating!"

"Caden," Avalyn said again, this time cupping his cheek with her hand and pushing his chin up to face her. "We cannot sacrifice humanity to save one life."

"But I already lost you," Caden sobbed, pushing his healing magic into her heart again and again. The flesh surrounding the wound knit itself together and began forming over the area. It was pink and healthy, pulsing full of life. "Don't leave me again."

Gently, Avalyn placed her hands over Caden's, stopping his fire. Then she leaned forward and brushed her lips against his cheek. "We will see each other again," she whispered. She brought her hand to his face, holding his gaze for mere moments, but to him those moments were eternity – an eternity that ended much too soon. Before a tear slipped down her cheek, she pressed her lips to his, once, twice. When she pulled back, she smiled. "Goodbye, Caden, I will always love you."

Stepping back, she left him crying over her body while she went to Kyra. "You have to do it now," she said. "We don't have much time." She took Kyra's hands, closing her eyes, and brought her forehead to Kyra's. It was only a brief moment, but it was enough. Avalyn had shown her what she needed to do.

Kyra inched closer to Avalyn's body while the apparition of Avalyn's soul slowly faded. Taking the necklace from around her neck, Kyra returned it to Avalyn's, clasping it beneath her hair.

"I need your help, Caden," Kyra said quietly. "It requires all three of us."

"I can't do it," he sobbed. "I can't help you. She's healing. I can't stand by and watch her die."

Kyra took his palm in hers. "She's dying, Caden. Her life dims as we speak. I can feel it. The Malic'Uiel has woven his poison too deep."

Caden shook his head in desperation, gripping Kyra's hand as if she could pull him from the hell he was in.

"Please, Caden." Avalyn's hand fluttered to grip Caden's. The hold was weak. Her breaths was shallow as she fought through the pain her body had endured, but her eyes did not leave his face. "It's the only way," she whispered. "You have to let me go. Everything will be okay."

It was Avalyn's plea that finally broke him. Sobs tore from his chest, but he managed to choke out two word. "All right," he said. He bent forward, pressing his lips against hers one last time. "Goodbye, my love," he whispered. He stayed that way for a moment, letting silent tears fall on her cheeks. Finally, he turned to Kyra. "I'm ready."

Kyra knelt next to both of them. She closed her eyes, pressing her hand lightly on Avalyn's chest above her heart. Her other hand held Caden's.

Everything stilled.

It was as if time stopped around Kyra while she gathered her strength. The light that she'd been using to hold the Malic'Uiel at bay fled back to her, gathering in her chest. When she opened her eyes, the light glowed from her skin and hair. The mark of Lumen illuminated on Caden's wrist. A moment later, the same mark shone above Avalyn's heart.

The darkness dispelled, pushed away by the light emanating from Kyra's form. The light expanded to engulf the Malic'Uiel, the surrounding army, and the city. All life was caught in its grasp. Lightning raced across the sky, crashing into the darkness over and over until all that was left was a gray mist. Then the lightning gathered together into an electric orb that hung above Kyra. The mark of Lumen shimmered on its surface.

Everything stopped. Hearts slowed, time stilled, and the very air refrained from pulsing. Wind ceased and animals froze mid-motion. Then thunder cracked and the orb shattered, sending a bolt of lightning into Kyra's chest. Her body arced with the electricity, rising off the ground until it was suspended while the energy surged through her and into the symbols that Caden and Avalyn bore. The wind picked up, whipping across the waiting people. Thunder rumbled before barreling into the hearts of men.

When it looked as if Kyra could take no more, the energy exploded out of her, knocking the enemy off their feet, shaking the walls of the city. And there, hovering in the now clear sky, was a door born of light. Lightning surged around the frame and light poured through the opening – a blinding, piercing light that both cleansed and purged.

The Malic'Uiel drank in the sight of the door, eyes heavy with lust.

Kyra dropped to the ground, nearly unconscious. Caden lay near, head slumped against Avalyn while his arms held the lifeless form of his wife; his shallow breathing was the only indicator of life.

The now silent people of the city gaped at the door, shock and horror written on many of their faces, hope written on others.

In the height of the stillness, the sound was broken by the screams of a woman bearing down for the last time, followed by the cry of a newborn baby.

CHAPTER 46

I t started as a low hum, the sound of wind whispering through the trees. The people glanced around nervously, hearing the sound but feeling no movement in air that hung as heavy as fog. Without understanding why, nobody spoke – the silence was almost reverent.

But the sound increased, and the wind came, slowly at first but gaining in force and severity. Soon the trees bent beneath the force of the gale, nearly bowing at the feet of the Malic'Uiel. The rushing wind clawed at the hair and clothes of the people and tore at the cloaks covering the Cadavers. Branches ripped from the trees and were hurled into the Cadaver army – those that couldn't get away fast enough were bludgeoned with them. People shrieked, running for cover beneath the walls of the city, but their shrieks could not be heard above the screams of the wind.

Light descended over Kyra and her two companions, protecting them from the onslaught of the gale. But all around them, chaos raged.

From the east, darkness rode on the waves of the wind, racing toward the door of light suspended in the sky. All watched in horror as the darkness plunged into the door, forcing the light back where it had come and enveloping the world in darkness. The wind shrieked on, and the darkness kept coming until it was so thick it was suffocating.

Through the darkness, streaks of light began to appear. They cut into it, shattering it into bits of shadow. More and more shot through, splitting the night into day. The lightning arcing around the door crackled in blues and yellows.

The first figure to step through the door held a sword in his hand and a shield of light in the other. An image of the door was carved into his breastplate – a breastplate that shimmered with an otherworldly glow. The same lightning that arced around the door snaked around the man's chest. He was followed by a second figure, and then a third. Soon their numbers couldn't be counted.

"Go!" Screamed the Malic'Uiel to the Cadavers. "The world is ours. Take it from them!"

The Cadaver army moved as one body. They raised their weapons and streamed forward, shrieking like an army of devils. They converged on the door, a black mass of twisted limbs and grotesque faces, hell-bent on destroying life.

Their advancement didn't stop the army of Lumen that poured through the door and plunged into the raging Cadavers. Lumen weapons shimmered while light danced from the blades, lashing out as whips to cut down the monsters in their path.

But the darkness fought back. The black cloaks of the Cadavers caught the light, holding it until it absorbed into the creatures. Then it oozed from their bodies, a viscous substance, taking the shape of the Malic'Uiel. The Cadaver army grew in size, bolstered by these inky fiends.

The clearing between the city and forest was full of dying soldiers from both armies, while more kept coming. Swords raised and the clash of steel on steel rang in the air. Cadavers screamed as the whips of light raked over their bodies, ripping away first the cloaks and then the flesh. Dark, thick blood oozed from the dead monsters, covering the ground in a sticky mire.

Phantoms vanished from the edge of the forests, reappearing in the middle of the army of Lumen long enough to wrap their arms around soldiers before disappearing again. They reappeared in the sky, dropping the men from hundreds of feet above the city. Kyra watched, sick, as the men of Lumen plummeted to their deaths.

Light soldiers also fell under the onslaught of the Cadavers. As the light and life left their bodies, the eyes glazed over and a cold shadow fell over their still forms, their brilliance fading as surely as the day fades into night. The groans and gasps of the dying and injured created a gruesome backdrop to the screams of the waging battle.

Lightning crashed again and again, and night seemed to wrestle with day; moments of blinding brightness lit up the battle and the forest beyond, but they were followed by shadows so thick none could see past them. Still, the battle waged on.

Kyra watched all this from the protective sphere of light. Caden knelt next to his wife, holding her body close to him, protecting her even in death. It would be mercy for Kyra to stay next to him, allow him the protection of her light while he mourned, but she could not watch the battle and do nothing. This army was here because of her. Their soldiers were dying because of her. She'd trusted Avalyn – she still trusted Avalyn – but she could not leave them to fight for her world alone.

She prayed she'd done the right thing for all of them.

She gripped her dagger in one hand, while a ball of light flared in the other. She would stay close to Caden, protect him from the darkness as much as possible, give him the space to grieve, but she would fight.

Before she threw herself into the fray, a hand gripped her arm. "I'm coming with you," Caden said. He stood hunched beside her, clutching his sword. His face was white, and his hand trembled on her arm, but his mouth was set in determination.

"What about Avalyn?"

"There is a time to mourn, but now is not it; Spero is what matters now."

Kyra nodded and threw her light around him, a protection against the darkness. Together, they plunged into the battle.

The light surrounding them stayed close, protecting them from outside attack, but it couldn't protect them from the onslaught of their own senses. The flashes of light and dark left them disoriented. A Cadaver screamed in front of them, sword raised to kill, but the next moment he was gone, enveloped in the shadows. Kyra threw a ball of light into the onslaught. It caught a Cadaver in the chest, and he stumbled backward, clawing at the hole it left behind. Burning flesh mingled with sweat and the Cadaver's sulfuric blood, creating a stench that left Kyra gagging.

Death raged around them, and the bodies piled up as they plunged deeper. Caden's fire snaked into the battle, engulfing Cadavers in flames while balls of light from Kyra burst into the attacking army, forcing away the darkness and destroying the Cadavers in their path.

"Look out!" Caden screamed.

Kyra whirled to her left where a Malic'Uiel seemed to rise from the darkness. He pulled the shadows to him – thicker and thicker they grew, sucking Kyra's light with them. She willed it to fight against him but opening the door had weakened her. For a moment the light flickered, and then it went out. The shadows were suffocating, pressing in against her body, clawing at her face and down her throat as if they could suck the life from her very being. They overwhelmed her, gripping at her arms and legs, holding her head back and forcing her to her knees.

They writhed around her like living, breathing beings...but she knew that these shadows, these creatures of the Malic'Uiel, whatever they were, did not live. They pressed her knees into the dirt, forcing her chest up before they ripped open her tunic, laying her chest bare.

In the darkness, the Master emerged. Lightning crashed again, and for a moment the world was bathed in light. Next to the Master, exposed by the light, was a formless shape darker than the world around it, shifting in the air like smoke. The Master lashed out and clawed a gash in Kyra's chest, just above her heart. Blood trickled from the wound, reaching toward the shadowy shape.

"This is your master," the Malic'Uiel said. "You did not destroy him, merely took him from this world. And you will now bring him back."

The shadow reached toward Kyra, following the trail of her own blood until it burrowed itself deep in the wound.

She screamed, thrashing against what felt like an ice-cold hand gripping her heart. The organ beat against the constriction, fighting for life. She thrashed harder against the shadows binding her down, and screams tore from her lips unbidden as icy pain pulsed into her body, carried on her own blood. It traveled through her chest, into her arms and abdomen. The shadows traveled with it, suffocating the light in her blood.

Panic gripped her, but somewhere far in the distance of her mind's landscape, she saw a star, a spark. And she remembered.

She remembered how they'd attempted to take her soul, and how her soul had refused to bend. She remembered light erupting from her palm to engulf her master. She remembered Lumen and the world her mother had shown her – a world bathed in light, a world she was borne from. And she found, once again, the power that pulsed deep inside her, the power that would not...could not...succumb to darkness.

"I am a being of light," she hissed through clenched teeth, closing her eyes against the burning cold and reaching inside for the warmth she knew she would find. "I am a being of light. I control the darkness. Darkness cannot consume me." The words were her mantra, her reminder, but as she spoke them, the ice seemed to hesitate, briefly, before reaching out again.

"I am a daughter of light," she said, louder this time. "Darkness cannot consume me. Darkness will never live inside me."

This time, the cold stopped as warmth flooded her veins, pushing back against the ice.

"I am a daughter of light!" she screamed, envisioning the warmth enveloping her body and shoving the cold shadows out. "Darkness cannot consume me!"

As she spoke the words, heat exploded in her veins, obliterating the cold and shadows. The Malic'Uiel roared in anger while the shadows of her master shrieked in fear; heat followed him out of her body, consuming him and setting the shadows ablaze. In the sudden light, Caden's fire lit up the area surrounding the door to Lumen, catching Cadaver and cloak aflame. Bright spots of light littered the darkened battlefield; the army of Lumen gained ground and the light grew. Her power raced far beyond her to bolster theirs; like the sun bursting over the mountains, the mingled light flew over the battlefield. Cadavers screamed in pain as the light ripped the darkness from their bodies. Hundreds collapsed. Many fled.

The Master witnessed the destruction of his twisted pollutants in fury. Realizing that he would not win this battle today, he held his arms open wide and the shadows sucked into his being. The other Malic'Uiel followed his lead. The darkness engulfed the Cadavers, who fled from the battlefield under the protection of their masters. The Phantoms, seeing the retreat, vanished from the scene.

The sudden calm after the chaos of death was unnerving. The Malic'Uiel left behind a battlefield covered in the bodies of the fallen, many of which were trampled into the dirt. Blood leaked into the ground, turning the dirt into mud. Weapons protruded from the earth and body alike.

Above it all, the door to Lumen shone, the entrance into the realm of light unbroken.

The same lightning that arced around the door, arced around Kyra's body – the door and the Countess were connected as one. Kyra pushed to her feet, pulling her torn tunic around her body as she looked toward the doorway. There, she saw her mother, Evia, descending from the opening. Her form was ethereal and ghostly, and she was followed by a long line of women, all of them somewhat translucent. When they reached Spero, their feet didn't quite touch the ground; instead, they hovered just above the surface.

The women waited beneath the door while Evia moved to stand next to Kyra. When she reached her, her gaze softened as she cupped Kyra's cheek in her hand. "My beautiful daughter," she said. "Such courage. Such strength." She moved her hand to rest on the gash above Kyra's heart. "You know the truth now, in your soul."

Kyra dipped her head. "I do." As she spoke, the lightning arced from Kyra to entangle itself in Evia's fingers before jumping down the line of women Evia had brought.

Evia's hand swept out to the women behind them. "These are the women who came before you; each is a Countess of Lumen, and each has been responsible for keeping the door to Lumen unbroken."

"I failed in that," Kyra said. "I brought darkness into Lumen."

Evia turned to gaze at the door, a small smile on her lips. "It is beautiful, isn't it?" she said. "Such a small thing, a door – so simple. And yet once you turn the key, it opens to reveal so much. People are like that, you know," Evia said, tilting her head toward the city. "They're endless streams of potential – so much possibility inside each one! But if the key is never turned, the potential remains locked away." Evia took Kyra's hand in hers, squeezing it lightly. "You hold the key to unlock the light in humanity. The Countess of Lumen does more than guard the entrance to Lumen – she is the harbinger of light. She keeps light alive in Spero. No matter how dark the world becomes, light can and will return because of her. By opening the door to Lumen, you are merely fulfilling your role as Countess."

Evia released Kyra's hand then stepped toward the other women. "Each one of us has carried the spark of Lumen inside. In her time, the Countess does her part in maintaining the balance of light and dark on Spero; she does whatever it takes to bring those forces into harmony, especially when they are at odds. You held the spark inside your soul and now it's expanded beyond you – it seeks balance. Yes, my daughter, you opened the door. You had to. If you had not, humanity would not have had a chance."

JULIANNE KELSCH

Evia paused, gazing across the battlefield. After a moment her eyes glazed over, and her body stopped all motion, as if something else took hold. "This war is not over," she called, her voice ringing across the field, a voice that reverberated as the voices of many. Kyra understood; all of the Countesses were speaking through her. "It has barely begun. Today's battle will be the first of many." Evia's eyes slid across the clearing to rest on the walls of Tutis. "You that remain of humanity will find yourself waging a war unlike any that has ever been. Those who triumph will usher in a new era for humanity. Those of you who succumb will succumb to darkness."

Her voice dropped in pitch, and she turned once more to face Kyra. "You are the harbinger of light. You must keep it alive in Spero. You must nurture it in those around you – you must give it life for humanity to survive."

"And if I can't?"

"When your doubts and fears surround you, seek the stillness. Like a pool undisturbed, so also must you become. You'll remember then that though the forces of darkness rise up against you, you have something far greater than they will ever have. They know that which you are, they lust after that which you hold, and they fear that which you will become – no matter how much they rage against you, they cannot hold you for darkness cannot exist where light chooses to shine."

Evia turned back to the city, a radiant smile on her face while light burst from her and the women who'd joined her. "Today," she called to those in the city, "is a glorious day! Humanity has fought, has stood against evil, and has stepped to the future to take back a world stolen by the Malic'Uiel. War is upon us, and many battles will follow, but you have always known strength and courage, and you will continue to find both!"

She lay a gentle hand on Kyra's shoulder, turning her to face the city. "Today is the day humanity gets up from their knees. Today, Spero rises!"

Thank you for reading!

I'm so glad you took the time to read The Rise of Spero. Please take a second to leave a review as well. Reviews make such a difference for me as an author! On bad days they remind me why I want to keep going. They're also helpful when trying to secure promotional opportunities.

If you'd like to connect with me, you can do so on Instagram, TikTok, or Facebook.

To join The Write Life, my newsletter, simply visit www.juliannekelsch.com. All subscribers receive a free novella for signing up.

Read on for the (unedited) beginning of the third and final installment, The Power of Lumen.

ABOUT THE AUTHOR

Julianne Kelsch spent her life immersed in books.
From a young age she learned to disappear into stories,
emerging periodically with a full heart to reconnect
with a world made richer through the tales. The magic
of the words penned by other authors is what inspired
her to write her own books. She is a firm believer that
words have the power to change the world.

Julianne lives in Utah with the most important people
in her world – her husband and five children. In following her dreams, she hopes that her children will have
the courage to do the same.

The Power of Lumen
The Beginning

Kyra slipped out of Tutis and darted across the plain between the city and the forest beyond. The door of Lumen hung in the sky above her, its light spilling from the frame and illuminating the world at her feet; a path of light led her to the forest's edge.

Daylight sighed as night fell, and for the first time in years, the darkness brought with it sounds of life; small creatures rustled in the trees as she entered the forest, and nocturnal insects filled the air with their song.

Bit by bit, life was returning to Spero.

She let the forest swallow her completely before stopping in a small clearing and igniting her palm with light. From where she stood, she couldn't see the city or the door to Lumen. It was just her, alone in a budding world.

She closed her eyes, letting her hands fall to her sides while her senses reached out to the forest. As she stilled, the world seemed to quiet with her. The buzzing of the insects receded to a low human, and the forest creatures stopped rustling. She brought her focus to the light in her palm, relishing the sensation of its dancing form. The energy caressed her hand, sending delicious tingles up her arm and through her body. Eyes still closed, she envisioned it enveloping her, expanding beyond her, filling the clearing in which she stood.

As if commanded, the light rushed to obey. Vibrant energy coursed through her veins, an intoxicating mix of heat and pleasure before exploding beyond her until the light hovered just above the tree line. She sensed the life of the trees reaching for it. The forest animals crept closer, curious, and she felt their spirits mingle with her own. Smiling, she sent the light plunging into the forest.

It raced beyond her, enveloping all life. Through the light, she experienced the growth, the rebirth happening around her.

The light spread and her smile widened. Perspiration dripped down her forehead, but she ignored it. She'd never pushed her light this far before. Breathing heavy now, she urged it farther, urged it faster. It shot forward – an arrow of light piercing the darkness. But then it stopped, hovering on the edge of something she'd never felt before. A sickness twisted in her stomach, and her light flickered, pulling back from whatever waited beyond. She demanded it move forward. But it froze, unable or unwilling to penetrate the barrier she'd found.

Slowly she brought her light back, holding it close against her now as a shield. The forest still teemed with life, but a sense of dread tugged at her throat. Something was out there, something she'd never felt, never sensed, and humanity had never fought.

She turned on her heel, running back toward Tutis.

The darkness reached for her – branches of the trees ripped at her clothing and vines hung like nooses in their depths.

Whispers seeped from the blackness beyond.

Death is coming.

Death is already here.

She swallowed hard, racing against the fears that chased her.

She's known their safety wouldn't last, known that the Malic'Uiel wouldn't give up after one failed battle. But this, whatever it was, sickened her soul.

Spero had risen, but could it regain its strength fast enough to defeat this new enemy?

Made in the USA
Middletown, DE
30 November 2022